HOME ROAD

Allyson Horner

ISBN 978-1-64670-285-5 (Paperback)
ISBN 978-1-64468-243-2 (Hardcover)
ISBN 978-1-64670-286-2 (Digital)

Copyright © 2020 Allyson Horner
All rights reserved
First Edition

Scripture quotations are from the ESV® Bible (The Holy Bible, English Standard Version®), copyright © 2001 by Crossway, a publishing ministry of Good News Publishers. Used by permission. All rights reserved.

All rights reserved. No part of this publication may be reproduced, distributed, or transmitted in any form or by any means, including photocopying, recording, or other electronic or mechanical methods without the prior written permission of the publisher. For permission requests, solicit the publisher via the address below.

Covenant Books, Inc.
11661 Hwy 707
Murrells Inlet, SC 29576
www.covenantbooks.com

Kyndle Redwood has known nothing but life as an exile, so when an opportunity arises for something different, she less than willingly takes it. She could never have imagined just what that choice would mean. Follow her adventures in this exciting novel about struggle, faith, and love.

To Chloe, for just being there;
And to my own Redwoods,
whose branches give me shelter
and whose roots hold me in.

Part 1

PART I

chapter ONE

"Redwood!"

The members of our family briskly worked our way to the front of the crowd.

"Adar!"

Father stepped up, red beard ablaze in the newly risen sun.

"Calinda!"

My mum stepped up beside her husband, and I imagined her a queen at the side of her warrior-king husband, standing proudly together before the crowd of loyal subjects.

"Flint!"

My brother jostled my arm as he stepped forward. It startled me out of my reverie, back to a place where kings, queens, and peaceful kingdoms couldn't be further from the truth.

Imagination often lives far from reality, as far as one can run from it.

"Kyndle!"

As I filled the space by my brother, I met eyes with the representative. His shone emotionless, reflecting the endless blue of snow and ice while mine held the brown sparks of a people long subdued within the reality I so often strove to flee from in my mind—that of a warrior nation growing bitter and hardened after two centuries of exile beneath the Snow Realm's iron thumb.

He looked down, I looked away, and our silent spar came to an end.

"Ruby!"

My sister stepped in place beside me, head hung low. Heavy eyelashes hid the dark eyes I knew were bent toward the cobblestone. She remained that way while the representative consulted his list.

"Draithen!"

As our family melted back into the crowd, the Draithens gathered to confirm their presence. It had been many years since any name had been missed at roll call, but that made no difference. Still they were held every ten days or whenever the representative might randomly call one.

I squeezed my sister's slender shoulder. Born early, she had spent her formative years struggling to survive. Left fragile by an infant fever, she now ran from any situation that made anyone look at her; constantly she fought to blend in, stay unnoticed, be unseen—an impossible fight when it came to roll call.

"You did better," I whispered into her red ear. "Next time, keep your face up."

Her head moved in a slight nod that warned me not to continue and it remained lowered until roll call was over. The representative stepped off the wooden stage which in days' past was a scaffold.

I rubbed at my wrist, the band of leather that encircled it. We all wore them. It was a sign of our exile. The representative is to look for them at every roll call. We hate them with a dark heavy hate but removing them brings a punishment.

Ruby watched the representative as he strode from sight.

"I'm scared of him," she whispered.

I gave her shoulder a second squeeze as the assembly became a churn, separating the adults from the children, the girls from the boys—and as I watched her go, a worry that was all too familiar welled up in my throat. There was always the chance that her frame would give way and never be the same.

I felt a light nudge on my shoulder blade and turned to face a pair of concerned green-brown eyes, those of my best friend.

"You okay?" she asked.

"Just worried about her as usual."

Auburn and I stood quietly, watching, as a rowdy group of boys jostled one another into some semblance of a line. Among all the tall redheads I saw my brother and his best friend, Tinder, who spotted me at the same moment. Cheery waves were exchanged.

"Those two are always smiling," Auburn noted.

"Because they're always up to something," I returned with a laugh. In my mind's eye, I could see them again as boys having too many arms and legs and too little sense to keep themselves out of the pranking which so frequently got them in trouble. Even now, at nineteen, one could always find a bit of mischief hovering just behind the freckles on their faces, just waiting for the right moment to jump out and scare you.

Again I shook from my thoughts, and it was at this moment I realized, our line was the only one left in the town square. The faces of the girls around me mirrored the same realization. As one, we looked to our dorm leader.

"Why aren't we leaving?" someone asked.

"We're to wait for a special announcement from Master Stave," came Maroon's deep scratchy voice. "Until then, we wait."

And so, in the cool morning air, we waited.

As we did, most of the girls settled down upon the cobblestone to talk among themselves. Auburn remained on her feet, at the edge of the group, near the head of the market street.

"They would stop talking if I sat down with them," she told me with a forced laugh that couldn't hide the pain in her eyes.

So I stood with her and we spectated the going-ons of bartering in the street before us. The village—while screaming to our northern captors that unlike them, we appreciate differences among people—were blatant in their dislike toward Auburn. I found this strange.

True, she was the only brownhead in the entire village and the only one to harbor a green to her dark eyes. But how did that affect her character?

They had never taken the time to even talk with her about any of their concerns. They would find that she wasn't so unusual after all.

I was not one to accept differences. I was not one to readily give trust or even friendship. I'd gotten one too many scars from it. One too many times, I had hoped for many different things and been disappointed. So I had learned to sit back and watch, to let others do the talking; to do only what was needed to get by, to truly love only those I knew would love me in return.

However, the exception to my generally apathetic way of life had been Auburn. Many years back, I had decided not to be deterred by her differences. In her eyes, I seemed to find some sort of camaraderie, a sort of unexplained dissatisfaction, and it had sparked my curiosity.

I had found the risk to be worth it.

Differences aside, she was the best friend I had ever had.

Once as a little girl, during the lunch hour, I had confided to Mum that I wished to look like Auburn. Mum had pushed a strand of hair from my plump ruddy face and shaken her head.

"You don't want to be different," she said.

"Why, Mum?"

"Because then you would stand out from your playmates."

I'm certain that my pudgy forehead wrinkled. "Is that bad?"

"It isn't proper."

"Why?" With the persistence of a child.

"Because then, you wouldn't be a true Fireling. One with true Fireling blood running through their veins have dark-gray eyes and red hair, both of which the heavens have blessed you with." Then she had taken me into her lap which smelled of lavender—a result of being a village gardener. "Looking and acting different isn't looked well upon," she continued. "It makes for a difficult life. Always remember this, Kyndle."

"Okay, Mum," I'd said as she stood up.

And I always had.

But that didn't keep me from being friends with a nonconformist, did it?

After Mum had walked off, I had found Auburn leaning against a wall, crying. I had run as fast as I could to put my arms around her and put my forehead to hers in some sort of formal promise.

"I'll always be your friend," I had told her.

She had looked at me like she wasn't sure whether she could believe me. And right then and there, as a ruddy-faced six-year-old, I had made it my mission to make sure she did.

Thus today, I stood alone with her while the rest sat and talked.

Something brushed against my arm, jerking me from my thoughts for the second time that day; and in surprise, I watched Auburn dart into the market crowd. Out of habit, I followed her and, through the bustle, found her kneeling beside an older woman whose foot had evidently caught a wobbly cobblestone. An herb basket lay on the street beside her, and by it, I recognized her as a fellow gardener of Mum. Remembering my place as Calinda's daughter, I quickly snatched the basket out of the reach of any dangerous feet.

"Are you hurt?" Auburn was asking the woman.

"Noooo," the woman said, shaking her head from side to side, eyeing Auburn warily like everyone did. But as she pushed a graying strand of hair away from her eyes, we both saw the bruise already surfacing under the thin skin at her temple.

Auburn helped her to her feet then gestured toward the load. "Where are you taking this?"

"Brawn Street," the woman said, bending for her load.

"I'll take it," Auburn said, jumping to pull the woven basket over her own shoulder.

I found my voice. "But the meeting—"

"It's just a few lanes up," Auburn called over her shoulder as she and the old woman set off. "I'll be back soon."

I couldn't help noticing the strange looks she received as she pushed through the crowd.

Hurrying back to the group, I avoided the glances of the other girls and hoped against hope that Auburn would return before Master Stave arrived. No sooner had the wish crossed my mind than the instructor strode up to our group.

He was tall, several inches over six feet, with a distinguished scar on his left cheek and a voice gritty as a gravel road.

"Maroon," he said. "A word with you."

They stepped aside from listening ears and I breathed a sigh of relief. I glanced over my shoulder again, but there was still no sign of Auburn. My subtle movements didn't go unnoticed.

"What, did she forget to use the privy this morning?" teased a girl to my left.

"Hush, Ashbel," I urged.

"Good morning, Mss. Firelings." Master Stave's voice grabbed our attention and we turned to find him smiling. "I'm pleased to pass on the message that your group has been granted time off," he said, "in light of your average class grade in recent weeks."

"How much time?" asked an eager girl in the front.

"The remainder of the day, Ms. Fratch."

I shifted excitedly in spite of myself. Something brushed at my wrist, and, turning, I found Auburn. She was a bit out of breath and a strand of hair had fallen over her eyes, but her face wore the contended smile of a job well done. We both turned to Master Stave— and found him looking directly at us.

As his eyes found Auburn's face, his darkened a shade.

"You," he said, directing a thick finger at her. "Madam Hybrid. You're late to the meeting."

Her jaw slackened and she pushed the hair from her eyes.

"I'm sorry, sir," she said honestly but didn't drop her head.

"Out and about doing other things more important, are we?" he asked in a sarcastic voice.

I raised a hand. "If I may—"

"You may not," Maroon interrupted.

I shut my mouth.

Master Stave's face took on a baleful look. "As you don't see fit to be present at our special announcements," he said to Auburn, "I don't see fit to include you in them. Maroon," turning to her, "give the chore list to our young *mav'rick* so she can learn obedience."

"I'll do that, Master Stave," Maroon answered, directing an angry stare in Auburn's direction. Behind the anger, I saw her embarrassment.

I didn't turn, but I knew Auburn's face was red.

"Are we clear?" Stave patronized.

"Yes, sir," came Auburn's voice after a moment. I felt the strain in it.

"Good," Stave said. He held her gaze a moment longer then turned to the rest of us.

"Have a good day off!" he said, pleasant once more.

HOME ROAD

I darted my eyes half-heartedly at Auburn, then filed off with the rest, immediately launching into mental reassurance.

This is nothing new. She's always been the scapegoat. She's used to it and so is everyone else. Nothing you can do about it.

But now, I wasn't so sure. Though I had long thought it unfair for her to be treated so, something else shifted in me today. I alone had witnessed her heroism yet stood by as she had been punished for it. I, her only friend, am too much a coward to even stand up for her.

What a rat she must think I am!

Once out of the square, we scattered in different directions—each girl having something specific they wanted to do for the day. My steps led me toward my dormitory.

Along the way, I passed the dwelling homes of many married couples, and open shutters awarded me a glimpse into the domestic scene—mother preparing food for the lunch hour, father fixing the table, children playing on the floor.

Children remain at home until the dawn of their sixth year when they join classmates in dormitories appropriate to their age. Then every day, for the remainder of our childhood, except family days on Saturdays, we are trained in the ways of our people—systematically formed into the Fire Sprites that our leaders expect us to be. Automatically I ran through the checklist in my mind.

We are to be strong and healthy. We are to know our history well and be proud of the ancestors whose bravery had secured them a place in the annals of time. We should strive in every way to be like them.

But most importantly—and most secretly—we are to be ready for war when it comes. And it will come soon, we are told. Someday very soon.

Actual weapon training is only done secretly; the few freedoms we had would go up in a blaze if the Snow Sprites knew we were training to rebel against their rule. We have secret caches of weapons, though only a select few know where those are. Many of the young men hold meetings in the cellars of their dorms, after the lights in the village have all gone out. The girls' opportunities to train with weapons are much fewer, but we take every chance we get.

The Snow Realm doesn't know it, but underneath the normal bustling everyday life of our villages, we are preparing for the day when we will rise up above this exile and reclaim our place among the realms.

I passed by Vendor Street where retired citizens can set up booths to display their various—and sometimes curious—wares.

"Hoy there, Kyndle!"

A salesman hailed me as I passed his stand of fish.

"What sprung you out of class?"

"Master Stave gave us a day free of training," I told him.

"Good old Stave!" he bellowed toothily. "A fine deal! It makes one see how precious free time is around here. Makes me proud that Stave's my cousin. Eh..." he paused to scratch at the back of his gray head, "I'm proud *now,* y'see. When I was *young,* I weren't so proud." He grinned as though some memory was running through his head. "Why, there was the time when Stave accidentally tripped a council member. Pah! Why, his face turned whiter'n that goat kid yonder. No doubt, he wished the South Sea would come up out of nowhere and swallow him whole."

I smiled. It did sound like a funny scene.

"You know," he talked on in his typical rambling way, "if there was anything my mother wanted me to be diligent at, it was being able to find something good in everything. I gotta say," he scratched his head again, "that the good in living here in the south has been that beautiful sea." He glanced around as if to be sure that no one had overheard his comment which verged on unpatriotic. His hand went to his pocket. "Don't get me wrong," he said, turning back to me, "I would give it all up in a minute to be able to go back to where we all came from."

"So would I," I said, nodding at him.

Glancing left and right, he pulled his balled hand from his pocket and casually put it toward me. Responding instantly, I put my hand out and he transferred something into it. Quick as a wink, I had thrust it back into my pocket.

"Read it, pass it on if you can," he said softly, smiling as if to make it look like he was talking about something different, "but don't do it if it's risky. Many others are spreading it as we speak."

I nodded my understanding.

Suddenly he let out a laugh, flapping at me with his hand. "Carry on then. Y'don't need to waste time listening to my blabber!"

I grinned and hurried from the bustle of the market, knowing not to pull out my hand with people around. I passed the mess hall, the tannery, and the dorm for unmarried women. Our women are not permitted to be unmarried past the age of twenty-five. If needed, the council will pair her with a husband. As I walked down the street, I could hear my instructor's voice ringing in my head. "This is necessary to increase our population. Our casualties at the Battle of Enthon were such that we've yet to recover. But we *will*," he reminded us. Like he always did. Like everyone always did.

Turning on a deserted street, I pulled the wrinkled scrap of paper out of my pocket and hurriedly scanned the contents.

> Cardinal missing. Should you come into contact
> with any information concerning his whereabouts,
> deliver it immediately to the five councilmen.

I blinked. Then I blinked again. The cardinal—missing? My mind swirled with the shock of this new information, and it was a few moments before I realized that I was walking again.

The cardinal, our leader, in many ways the very heartbeat of the village—missing!

His name is Aidan which is pretty much everything most of us know about him. My father was one of five councilmen who formed a support group for the cardinal, and he wasn't allowed to tell us anything he may have learned during his time around the cardinal. I didn't doubt that even he knew very little.

The cardinals are purposefully kept shrouded in mystery. It causes all the villagers to hold him in a certain kind of respect.

Where could he be? I wondered. *Did he leave on his own or against his will?* I found it difficult to imagine anyone overpowering a Fire

Sprite cardinal; but with a group of strong men, I knew it could be done.

But why? Ours was a peaceful age—as peaceful as exile could permit. True, we hate our Snowling overlords with Fireling passion; but as yet, we have no real plan to fight back.

So why would the cardinal go missing?

Were the cardinals of the other three townships missing as well?

Another troubling thought hit me. Did the representative know that the cardinal was missing?

The representative. *Pah.* I kicked a loose rock, just because.

Again I could see his eyes—those blocks of ice, proud and unmoving, set like diamonds in his pale face, framed by white curls cropped a couple inches from his head.

The goal of the Snowling representative is to personally ensure that a township acts within perfect conformity to the rules. This one had been sent here as a boy to be a personal aide to the last representative, though I had rarely ever seen him all these years. After the old representative had died a year or so ago, a fill-in representative came down during the week or so it took for the boy-now-man to officially take on the title. The fill-in, a female, had, afterward, gone to live in the eastern Nature Realm.

The new representative had kept to himself, hiding out in his mansion a few miles out, not coming to town, except to call roll, always kept safe behind his entourage of soldiers with their shiny new rifles and golden-button jackets.

What Flint would *give* to rip one of those shiny things off and throw it into the dirt!

Our town, Frieman, was one of the four remaining towns left after the war, which tore the western realm apart, two hundred years back. When it was over, the north reigned supreme and the warrior tribe was displaced to a southern dwelling to be forever watched and suppressed.

There were no walled borders here in the south; the Snow Sprites had enforced a much tighter way of keeping us in line. Every ten days, the representative calls out the names of every villager; and if one is missing, his family suffers for it. Horses are forbidden and the townships spaced *just* far enough apart that one cannot reach them on foot in less than six days, thus not having enough time to be back before the roll call. None have ever tried to visit another town or run away from Frieman.

Thus in turn, no town had ever conspired with another to overthrow the Snow Sprite soldiers watching over them. There just wasn't time for a message to be sent.

Any instance of major nonconformity in one of the other three towns had resulted in the quick and mysterious disappearance of the offender. In one instance, an entire town had tried but failed to rebel; the end result had been a demonstration in which over thirty Fireling women had been executed and deposited into an unmarked grave. This was how Snowlings best subdued the most manly of men—if they acted out, their women paid for it. Not only did it wrench out the heart of our men, less women meant a stunted growth in population.

After this gruesome event, six brokenhearted—and evidently broken brained—revolutionaries tried to steal the women's bodies to give them a proper burial. Instead they earned a place beside them.

Such was the reality of the life we had been forced to live.

My mind spun amid these heavy thoughts but somehow found their way back to the original question. Was the representative informed of the cardinal's disappearance?

Or was he the cause of it?

I tried not to think of the implications.

chapter TWO

I passed the infirmary, a small building barely used as small illnesses are taken care of at home. The only ones who go to the infirmary go in the cases of something major like death or birth.

Exceptions were situations like those of my sister, Ruby. Even though she pulled through it, the fever left her permanently delicate. It had been nearly seven years since Mum had given birth to me, and though the risk hadn't been unstated, we all considered Ruby worth it.

I hurried past, leaving behind the anxious memories.

Two empty houses stood by the infirmary, ready for special use should a patient require a longer amount of care.

Finally I made it to the dormitory. I opened the door quietly, not sure who would be inside; but to my delight—the house was empty. Evidently all the other girls preferred to be outside.

Scrambling up the stairs, I tossed my jacket onto my bed and sat down at the window desk. From the lowest drawer, I drew the aged leather journal that hid away my aspirations, troubles, random facts and anything else on my mind. A quill from the middle drawer acted as the messenger between my thoughts and the page.

But just as I settled down to write, angry voices coming from outside met my ear. Moving to the window, I peered down into the street. A pair of old men stood arguing below. Tumbling back down the stairs, I opened the front door. They both turned when I approached.

"He stole my hen!" one said for my benefit, hooking a scarred thumb at the other.

"Liar," the other returned, crossing his arms.

I offered no reply, knowing it would only anger one or both of them further. This wasn't the first time that I had seen these two arguing, and the last thing that I wanted was to have one of them angry at *me*.

As they went on arguing, a light step sounded behind me. I turned.

It was the Snow Sprite representative. Three steps behind him were a few of his trusty soldiers who glowered at me.

I broke into a cold sweat, remembering the paper in my pocket, but I almost instantly forgot it as I met eyes with the representative who I had never seen this close before. He was much different than I had expected. I couldn't fancy him being more than twenty years old—just a few years older than me, hardly a man at all.

"Is there a problem?" he asked, his voice calm yet firm.

At the sound of his northern accent, I felt my hackles rise and all my prejudice return. The two men stopped their arguing. I stepped back and looked away. It wasn't my fight and I certainly wouldn't involve myself—which might mean speaking with this hoity-toity Snowling in his tall boots and fancy garb.

"He stole my chicken," said one of the men from behind me.

"Did not," the other snapped back angrily.

I chanced a glance at the representative's face, unable to help myself.

His eyes flickered with intelligence yet a veil of annoyance had come over them. "Perhaps a week in the same cell will mend your differences?" he asked in that same quiet and perfectly calm voice.

The men glared at each other.

"He's a roguish lout," muttered one. "No jail time with him'll fix that."

"Ah," returned the Snowling, his voice infuriatingly cool, "but I think it best." He looked into both of their faces, daring them to protest. When neither did, he flicked his fingers and his soldiers stepped forward. As the two were marched in the direction of the prison, the representative turned to me.

"Why are you here?"

My knees suddenly felt weak—this was the one who could kill with a simple word.

Coward, my mind mocked. I mustered my self-confidence.

"I heard them from inside."

"Why aren't you in your class?"

"I was given the day off."

"By whom?"

"The council."

"For what reason?"

His questions galled me. "Good grades."

"Just you?"

"No. My entire group is off today." *Well, almost.*

"And where are they?"

I shrugged. "We all have different places we spend our free time."

"And you?" Rather than nosy, he actually looked curious.

"I journal," I said simply. What I didn't say was, "About how much I dislike you Snowlings…and your golden buttons…and your tall boots…and your clinking stirrups…and everything you stand for."

"I'll let you get back to it." The representative turned to go, but then he turned back. "Your name. Kyndle, isn't it?"

"Yes," I answered slowly, surprised that he remembered mine among all the rest.

Why was he talking civilly to a Fire Sprite?

Amidst the swirl of confusion, I felt my curiosity become visible.

The muscles in his face eased, and for one moment, I wondered if he would actually *smile*. "I'm Hail Frost," he said, bringing his fancy boots together with a clink and offering me a subtle bow.

I stared at him, having the wild idea of returning the formality with a wild bumbling salute and bellowing, "Hail, Hail!" Frost meant that he was somehow related to the royal Frost family. But more honestly, I was surprised to see a semblance of courtesy underneath the Snow Sprite garb. I hadn't known it possible for a Snowling to be anything but cruel, overbearing, superior, and proud of it. So…

"Hail," I repeated with a nod just as subtle.

A shadow passed across his face. With another slight bow, he turned to go; but a few steps away, he turned to me again. And where before there had been an authoritative Snowling representative, I now looked full into the face of a homesick boy. He said nothing but just stood there.

"Is there anything else?" I asked, more curtly than I meant.

"No," he answered hesitantly, his face a war between composure and whatever he was feeling. "I just—"

"Master representative!"

He whirled to face the soldier running down the street.

"Yes?" he demanded, all the bristle returning to his voice.

"A letter just arrived from Galaheed."

Hail stepped forward and the soldier noticed me. His lower lip curled into a sneer.

"A letter?" Hail repeated sharply.

The soldier snapped his eyes back to his master's face. "Yes, count. It seems to be urgent."

Turning to me, Hail bowed less subtly. "I wish you a good day."

Stiffened by the presence of the soldier's sneer, I only nodded coldly.

He turned and strode away, his boots clinking on the cobblestone. The soldier threw another disdainful look over his shoulder, then he hurried to follow.

I watched after them until they disappeared from view.

When I had seated myself at my desk once more, I picked up the pen. But upon trying to pick up where I had started, I found myself at a loss for words. I normally spewed out angry ones, but the surprise of meeting the representative was still on me.

He wasn't the representative of my childhood—the barking, evil-faced, heartless, cruel order-maker who cared nothing about what anyone meant to anybody.

This representative had remembered my name.

That was dangerous.

Journal under my arm, I tumbled downstairs and dropped onto a chair before the fire. The first paper to be eaten by the flame was the one the vendor had given me, followed by the ones that I began to rip out of my journal. I paused to read the last one. Only several weeks old, it had been written when my anger waxed hot. I read it slowly, trying to re-engage my hate and my anger as a Fire Sprite should.

> Bigots. Frauds. Their pride will be their undoing.
> They exile us behind these invisible walls, making themselves believe that they will contain us. They imagine that our defeat at Enthon means that we are defeated forever.
> But they're wrong. We will show them this.
> They will soon learn that the Fire Sprites are a people to be reckoned with, and they'll never forget it as long as they live.
> Which may not be long.

But try as I might, all I could see was the face of a lonely boy, hidden in a gold-buttoned jacket.

I tossed the paper into the flames and watched it burn.

"I'm sorry about yesterday," I told Auburn as we ate our breakfast.

"It wasn't your fault," she said, shrugging.

"I still hate that it happened."

"I know." She glanced down. "I don't know what I did wrong, but when I finished, he made me do everything all over again."

My brow furrowed. "He what?"

"Kyndle, don't." She read my tone as easily as one read a book. "Let's just not talk about it anymore."

In the following silence, I remembered.

"Auburn—" I instinctively dropped my voice to a whisper. "I met the representative."

She looked up in surprise. "What do you mean *met* him?"

"There was an argument outside the dorm, and I was there. He arrived with his soldiers and sent the two men to jail. Then he started to ask me questions."

"What's he like?" she asked curiously.

My prejudice suddenly returned. "He's a Snow Sprite."

"He's more than that."

Glancing to make sure no one had heard her seditious comment, I stopped her. "I know what you're going to say. *Put yourself in his place.* But what's the point in that? It's not like it's going to change anything."

She paused. "It may change *you*."

I looked away, not wanting to tell her about the sympathy I had already started to feel toward him. Then just as fast, I began to prepare myself for the empathetic speech which was probably coming next.

"Imagine being torn from your people." *Right on cue.* "And sent to a place where you know everyone will hate you." She sighed. "It would be a hard life."

"Sure," I said, turning back to her. "But if anyone has had a hard life, Auburn, it's you. Except for me, you would be alone." Even as I said it, I prepared myself for her rebuttal.

She shook her head. "I'm not alone. Christ is with me."

She always had the same answer. She was so predictable, so *gullible!*

I rubbed my nose, trying to cover a smile.

She saw it.

"You don't believe me—do you?" Though over the years, Auburn had grown better at hiding it, I could find the hurt in her voice.

"It's not *that*," I said, my mind groping. "It's just…"

"You don't believe me," she said again when I trailed off. "That *is* it, isn't it?" Her green eyes bored into mine, but I didn't answer. She turned away, and I hated myself for hurting her.

Though I wouldn't have admitted it, there were areas where I had let the general opinion of Auburn sneak into my own thinking. And while I defended her to others and she really *was* my best friend, I still thought she was odd in some ways—especially these religious ideas she had. Our people didn't encourage religion; we looked to ourselves, and each other, for our answers; we were proud of each other, our nation, our ancestors. Those were the banners we pledged our allegiance to.

But Auburn had always believed in someone called Christ. She said he was her God. She had tried to tell me about him in the past, trying to show me the proof of his existence, but I had never believed her.

I guess she was odd in some ways.

But I still liked her.

Auburn thought of herself as an orphan—for all she knew, it was true. She had been found on a doorstep when she was tiny; a small black book on her lap with the word *Bible* stretched across the cover was all that had been found with her. On the first page was written the words: *Always let her read this book and never take it from her,* followed by her age.

Since written instructions were very important, they had been obeyed. The general opinion was that she was the child of an unmarried girl who was too ashamed to come out with it, but no real evidence of this was ever found.

Tomorrow marked Auburn's twentieth birthday, which meant she was to take the tests today.

All Fireling youths have to take the tests the day before their twentieth birthday. They cover the four areas of learning: warfare, how to maintain our health, the history of our people, and how to survive in the wild.

I often wondered why the Snowlings seemed to care so little about the material that we were taught in classes, yet I knew it was because of their self-confidence. No doubt they believed that they would forever suppress us, but they didn't know how wrong they were.

I finished eating as quickly as I could and then went to stand near a window. Across the room, I met eyes with Flint who'd just escaped from a conversation with a girl from my dorm who had been putting her tray away at the same time. I lifted an eyebrow questioningly as he came near, but he tightened his lips and shook his head firmly.

"You don't think she'll work?" I asked as he reached me.

He grinned in full-freckle glory. "I'd rather marry a buzzard."

I laughed at him.

Secretly I wished he would marry Auburn. I'd never dared to tell him this because of how different she was from the other girls in our village. I knew that would be too embarrassing for him. He treated Auburn better than any other man in the village, but I knew it was only because she was my friend; he certainly wouldn't call her *his* friend.

In light of how rejected she was, I highly doubted the council would make any man marry her. So if Flint didn't marry her, no one would.

But in the end, I decided to stay silent and not mention my wishes.

No one got hurt that way.

Except maybe Auburn.

Flint turned to get a full view of the room, but I watched Auburn. She sat all alone at one end of the table while the rest of the girls giggled and chattered at the other; and as I looked at her, a thought passed through my mind—one that I hadn't thought in fourteen years.

I wish I looked like her.

I struggled between my own feeling and the idea that had been drilled into me since my childhood. Was it possible for a person to be different yet still acceptable? Could differences be anything *but* strange?

I couldn't fully decide. And my indecision bothered me.

Within five minutes, the other girls were ready. We all tramped to our training building in silence. The summer heat made even the breeze warm and unpleasant. When we arrived, Master Stave began to hand out daily duties. I sidled up next to Auburn.

"Nervous?" I whispered as he addressed another girl.

"Sort of, yeah," she whispered back. "You know I don't have the best memory."

"You'll do fine." *Confidence is success,* I thought.

"I hope so."

We waited quietly until it was our turn.

"Auburn," Stave fairly barked her name. "Time for your tests."

A slight murmur moved through the girls. I touched her thumb to let her know I believed in her. Yet as she followed Master Stave out of the room, I noticed that her stride lacked its usual confidence.

Later that evening, as the rest of us were getting ready for bed, Auburn walked wearily into the bedroom. I jumped up to greet her; although the other girls had been chatting for a while, I had been anxiously waiting.

"Well?" I demanded.

The other girls stopped talking to hear her answer.

"I can't say for sure," she said, dropping on a chair beside me. "I think I did all right. We'll see in the morning." She ran a hand over her forehead to rub away the doubt etched there.

"It'll be fine," I said, putting an arm around her shoulder.

She sighed but didn't say anything.

At that moment, Maroon poked her head into the door.

"The bell will toll soon. Everyone should be in bed."

"Get up." Maroon's stern voice jerked me awake as did the lantern she held.

"Ma'am?" I mumbled, sitting up in bed.

But she wasn't talking to me. She went to Auburn's bed and threw the covers back. Auburn looked a bit frightened.

"What's going on?" she asked quietly.

"You've been summoned by the council," Maroon said. "They expect you immediately."

Gasps spread through the room. The council usually only summoned a person when they had done something very wrong. Fear pulsed through me.

"The councilmen expect you at Councilman Redwood's home by the sixth bell."

I gulped. My parents' house.

Maroon left. The instant the door shut behind her, Auburn became the target of verbal abuse for all those in the room.

"What did you do this time?" spat the girl in the bed next to hers.

"What a *fine* Fireling woman you'll make someday," mocked another, "if you ever decide to grow up."

I hurried to her side as the string of name-calling continued.

"I...I need to get ready," she stammered, going to dress. A glance out the window revealed that the sun was just beginning to rise. I got dressed as well, knowing there would be no more sleep for me now that this had happened.

When Auburn was all ready, I walked with her to the door.

"I guess I failed the test," she said, her voice trembling. "I don't think any girl ever did before. It's not surprising that I'm the first."

"Stop that." I put my arms around her sagging shoulders. "But even if you did," I said, releasing her, "I'll still be your friend. Besides maybe it's something else."

She smiled a scared smile. "Maybe so."

I put my hand on her shoulder.

"Kyndle, I have to go." She took a step back, and in the early morning light, I caught the unmistakable glint of fear in her green eyes—something I didn't see there often. Turning, she ran down the street. Her brownish ponytail bounced on her back.

chapter THREE

With a choking breath, I turned inside and slammed the door shut. Maroon was waiting for me.

"What's going on?" I asked, trying not to sound worried.

"I don't know. But I don't think it's good."

With that encouragement, I slowly climbed the stairs. The girls were still in bed when I opened the bedroom door, but they were anything but asleep. They confirmed my fears with their mocking and joking and all but demanded I give up talking to Auburn before I got myself lumped in with whatever she had done.

"I can't," I told them. "She has no other friend!"

"That's her fault for being weird," one girl retorted.

"Ashbel!" I remonstrated. "She can't help her features!"

"She can help reading that book."

I stopped. What was I to say? Even I, her only friend, drew the line at the book which she kept hidden away.

"Her guardian wanted her to read it," I said slowly.

"Her *guardian* isn't *here*," Ashbel retorted. A mischievous look came over her face, and climbing out of her bed, she began to search through the drawers. "Speaking of it…"

"Don't you *dare* mess with it—" I warned, even though it wasn't the first time I had had this conversation.

"And why not? She'd be better off without it." She held a book to the light and put it down when it wasn't the right one. "So would the rest of us."

"Ashbel," I said, regarding her with firm eyes. "Touch that book and you'll regret it."

She turned slowly. "And *what*, may I ask, are *you* going to do about it?"

"I'll keep you from harming someone else's property," I said. "If you do anything, and I do mean *anything*, to damage that book..." I shook a hooked finger. "If I find a torn page or a *fingernail* scratch, I promise I will go to the council and report a breach of the village rules established by the forefathers."

Her face twisting into a pout, she crawled back in her bed, muttering under her breath. I was just about to speak again when I heard her voice from underneath the covers.

"I'd watch my back if I were you."

At that, a lightning-hot bolt of anger tore through me from head to toe. It wasn't something I usually let show through, but enough was enough. Sweeping to her bed, I ripped the covers off her face and glowered down at her fiercely.

"Is that a threat?"

She blinked in surprise, but it was quickly erased. "No," she answered slowly, but in the faint light, I saw a grin playing around her lips. Yanking her blanket out of my hand, she rolled over. "Go back to bed."

I tightened my lips. As if I could go back to sleep!

Holding back my angry words, I left the room—slamming the door for good measure. I had to get out before I did anything I would truly regret. Reaching the bottom stair, I came face-to-face with Coaleen—Maroon's sour-faced intern. I instinctively took a step backward.

"So—" she said, a tormenting smile across her masculine face. "I hear that your friend might not be the brightest pupil?"

I turned away.

Grabbing my shoulder, she jerked me back around. Again I felt anger rising in me. Who was she to treat me like this? I hadn't done anything—and besides, just five years ago, we were dorm mates, equal in everything but age. Yet I voided all emotion from my face. We were no longer equal, and I could get in trouble. Disrespect to superiors was no small thing and had no small punishment.

"Hear this," she hissed, smile gone. "I wouldn't keep hanging around her if I were you. Sitting close to a dog gives one fleas."

You aren't me, I thought. But I said nothing.

Releasing me, Coaleen vanished into her room.

I scowled at her door, rubbing the fingermarks on my shoulder, then went to sit near the fireplace.

For a Frieman woman to fail a test meant terrible humiliation. I was alarmed for Auburn. With this new disgrace added to her reputation, there was no knowing what daily life for her would be like—*if* that's what had happened.

As today was the last day of the week, it meant I could spend the day with family. At the stroke of seven, I set off down the street.

Turning the first corner, I nearly ran into Flint and Tinder.

"Well, good morning!" I said, but then I stopped. The usual mirth was missing from their faces. It made me instantly suspicious.

"What's wrong?"

"Come with us," Flint said as they fell in step on either side of me. "I need to talk to you."

We ended up at our usual spot, just outside of the town—an old stone wall from olden days that time hadn't managed to knock over. I boosted myself to the top of it and plopped down, swinging my legs, watching on as the two of them stood quietly, as if deep in thought.

"So what's wrong?" I prompted.

Flint looked up at me. "It's about your friend, Auburn."

I stopped swinging my legs. "What about her?"

"Tinder and I were supposed to meet Dad at his house and go fishing. But when I went to knock on the front door, I heard voices inside."

"Loud voices," Tinder added.

Flint glanced at him. "They weren't *that* loud."

I looked from one to the other. "I'm going to make a wild guess—you had an itchy ear, so you used the door as a scratching post?"

"That's not important," Flint said, waving impatiently with his hand. "It's what we heard that was strange."

"Go on."

"I don't know if you've heard it or not, but the cardinal is missing."

"I heard—somewhere."

"So," Flint went on, coming to lean against the wall next to me, "the councilmen are sending a scout to the representative's house to try and find out if the cardinal is being held there."

"And if he is?"

"I don't know."

I looked at them both. "Where does Auburn come into this?"

"From what we heard," Tinder said, "she took her test yesterday—"

"Oh, let me make another one of my wild guesses," I butted in, anger flaring up in me for the third time that morning. "She failed, so to punish her, they're assigning her this job and putting her in danger?"

Flint grabbed my ankle which I hadn't realized was swinging again. "Slow down. No, and yes."

"What does that mean?"

"Yes, she's been offered the job. But she didn't fail the test—she aced it."

I blinked. "What?"

"In fact," Tinder said, "she got the highest grade count of any Fireling this season. Because of it, she was given the first chance as a scout and she jumped on it."

I put my head down. Of course she had. She'd want to prove herself to the village so they wouldn't treat her like a dirty object.

"When does she leave?" I finally asked.

"I think she already did."

I jerked my head up. "Really?"

"That's why we left," Tinder said. "They came toward the door."

Flint chuckled at Tinder. "You haven't moved that fast since that mad bull came after us a few years back."

"You were ahead of me!" Tinder retorted.

"All right, all right," I butted in. "So what if she gets caught?"

They looked at each other uncomfortably.

"Well," Tinder said.

"Well, what?"

"My dad and Anvil walked past where we were hiding," Tinder said. "I heard Dad ask the same thing. Anvil said that—"

"Yes?"

"Kyndle." Flint touched my foot. "If worse comes to worse—and she does get caught—the council will know nothing about the mission."

I blinked a couple times. "You're kidding."

Tinder turned away from my glance.

"They'll just abandon her to the Snowlings?" I demanded.

"It's that or put the entire village at risk."

"Besides," Tinder put in, "it's for the cause."

I jumped down from the wall and started walking.

Flint followed. "Where are you going?"

"Dad's."

"Kyndle, wait!" Tinder ran to catch up and grabbed my arm to stop me. "You can't talk to him about it."

"And why not?"

"Because you aren't supposed to know about it. Neither are we. We just accidentally did."

I ignored the lie and resumed walking.

"Seriously, Kyndle," Flint said, still following. "You'd get us all in a ton of trouble."

"And what is Auburn in?"

"She volunteered."

"She didn't know what we know."

"That's not our business."

I dug my heels in and turned angrily to face them. "What exactly did she do to get treated like this by all of you?"

"She's an oddball," Tinder said.

"So are you," I said. "You just look normal on the outside."

"It makes a difference."

I said nothing. His biases would only cover his ears which had grown red despite his confident front.

"Flint!"

We all turned. One of the boys from their dorm ran toward us.

"What is it?" Flint called back.

The boy reached us. "Councilman Char sent me. He wants Kyndle and you to go to his house right away."

Great—a councilman. Just who I wanted to see.

"Flint and *Kyndle?*" Tinder repeated. "Don't you mean Flint and *me?*"

"Nope. Flint and Kyndle."

"Thanks, Kurt," Flint said quickly. "We'll head that way."

The boy took off back toward the village. I turned to Flint questioningly.

He spread his hands. "I have no idea."

"I bet we were seen outside your dad's house," Tinder said, "and they thought I was Kyndle."

"Oh sure." I laughed. "You and I look exactly alike, except that I have a foot more hair and you have a foot more leg."

"And a foot more tongue," Flint muttered.

"I think I'll come along just in case," Tinder said, ignoring our jokes.

Flint looked doubtful. "I guess that's okay."

"Sure it is," Tinder said. "C'mon. Char is waiting."

Yes, Char was waiting—for me and Flint. Tinder was thunderstruck and would leave only after a second assurance. I think he came close to confessing his spying, if only to prove that he was who was supposed to be called in. His shoulders sagged as he walked down the street; I nearly laughed at him. However, all urge to laugh vanished as we turned back to Char. His face was worried as he ushered us into his house.

When we walked into the main room, we found three other councilmen already seated at the big table: Anvil, Coal, and Fraith, who was Tinder's father.

But where was mine?

The fluttering of my gut hinted that something was wrong. It was as if I stood at the edge of a dark cloud, unable to see through it, but knowing all the same that whoever, *whatever* lurked within it didn't have my best intentions in mind.

After all, these were the same men who had just sent Auburn off on a dangerous mission, knowing that they would abandon her should she get caught by the Snow Sprites.

"Please sit down," said Anvil.

"What's the matter, councilmen?" Flint asked when we had.

Coal sat without speaking. He looked angry.

"Something that has never happened before," Fraith said quietly.

"And it *would* happen when the cardinal is missing," Char sighed as he came in and took his seat. I noticed how tired he looked. How old he looked.

How uncertain he looked.

Where *was* the cardinal when we needed him?

Anvil finally answered the question. "A boy from an unknown realm was found wandering inside our border yesterday evening."

There was a stunned silence.

A boy—from an unknown realm? What did that even mean?

"He claims to have no idea how he got here." Anvil went on. "He told us that one moment he was standing in a cave near his home and several seconds later was standing on a mountain cliff in the southern realm."

I glanced at Flint. He looked as shocked as I felt.

"Where is he?" he asked them.

"At your parents' home. Your father is watching over him."

"Where do we come into this?" I asked, suddenly nervous.

"You and Flint are to take this boy back to the cliff he found himself on and try to return him, quick and quiet."

There was a second stunned silence.

My mind whirled. They were sending *us*?

I glanced at Flint before asking. "And if we get caught?"

Anvil returned my steady look. "Don't."

I felt little comfort.

There was a knock at the door. The councilmen exchanged glances.

"That'll be them," Anvil said.

chapter FOUR

Char opened the door. My parents and Ruby walked through it. Flint and I immediately stood.

"Sit down, son," Father said, clapping a hand on his arm.

"You didn't leave the boy alone, did you?" Fraith asked.

"No. Your boy was milling around in the street, so I took the liberty of putting him on guard duty."

"You told him about the boy?"

"No. I simply set a chair on the cellar door and asked him to sit on it until I returned. I told him that it was for the good of the village and that he would learn more with time. Besides the boy isn't aggressive. I doubt he will have moved from his place by the cellar wall."

Fraith nodded. I exchanged small smiles with Mum and Ruby as they and Father took seats at the table across from us. When everyone was settled, Anvil rested his sinewy elbows upon the table.

"The mission involves a great deal of discernment," he said pensively. "Adar, Calinda, do you think your children able to do this?"

"Yes," Father said, his voice confident. "I have seen both caution and prudence in them both. Together they have gotten into some scrapes," he said, arching a playful eyebrow at us both in turn. "But even then, they've taken responsibility."

I felt a wild urge to cackle but kept it in check.

"Calinda?" Char asked gently.

Mum raised her chin. "Of course they can," she said in a voice which wasn't entirely her own.

I vaguely noticed that Flint's grip on the edge of the table had eased.

"Then with your permission," Anvil said, "we'll move forward."

My parents nodded—Mum a bit less confidently, I noticed.

"You're free to go," he said to my parents and Ruby. "We'll give you a moment to say your goodbyes." He nodded at my sister as he concluded his sentence.

She blushed wildly at the sudden attention.

The five of us got up and walked to the door. The councilmen began to talk among themselves to give us some privacy. Ruby hugged me around my slight waist.

"I'm scared," she said in a tiny voice.

"Don't be." The Fireling answer flew out before I could stop it, made null and void by the fact that she could feel me shaking. So I squeezed her tighter. "I'll see you in a week or less."

Hopefully.

She nodded mutely, and I saw that she was fighting tears. She glanced at the councilmen in the room beyond, no doubt fearing a rebuke should they see her struggle.

"Don't worry about them," I whispered. "They won't mind."

A tear slipped down her cheek as she turned to Flint, but she quickly dashed it away.

Mum grabbed my hand and smiled warmly at me. "Be safe, my girl. I know your brother will look out for you, but you've got to do your part for yourself. Neither I nor your father have been out there, so I don't know what lies ahead. Just trust your instincts and practice what you've been taught. Nothing can hurt you if you do." She pulled me into a hug as she finished speaking. Then with a kiss on my ear, she let go.

Taking a deep breath, I said to them all, "I love you."

"I'll see you in a couple of hours," Dad said. He opened the door and swathed us all in sunlight. Mum touched our cheeks, Ruby smiled a little smile, then they all stepped out into the street; the door closed, and they were gone.

Reluctantly Flint and I settled back onto our seats at the table, silence weighing heavily on our shoulders.

"Speed is the theme of this task," Anvil said.

I took a shaky breath. "Please tell me why," I said slowly.

Char looked deep into my scared eyes. "The death penalty is why," he said. "There are two risks involved. First, the representative announces a roll call."

"But we just had one," I protested.

"Yes, but he is allowed to do them whenever he pleases. While you're gone, let's say he randomly calls an assembly. He finds you two missing, is unable to locate your names in the cemetery log, realizes we've failed to obey their rules and orders a demonstration. Many Fire Sprites could be killed as they were in Fridton."

I glanced at Flint, my entire body beginning to shake. This was more serious than I had first imagined. We were putting ourselves—and many others—in danger. And for what?

"Why risk this mission at all?" I almost demanded.

Anvil leaned forward. "Because of the second risk. We don't want this boy to fall into the hands of the Snow Sprites. The less they know about undiscovered lands, the better. Keeping this boy out of their hands means three things: return him to his home, imprison him secretly for the rest of his life, or do away with him altogether."

"Some favor the last option," Coal said, and as I turned to him, I saw that he was still angry.

"Unnecessary violence is not the Fireling way," Char protested. "We don't want to be like the Snow Sprites. We can't put our character at risk over such a trivial matter."

"What about putting our people at risk?" Coal exploded.

"Coal," Anvil rebuked. "The decision has already been made."

The youngest member of the council rubbed his forehead but held his tongue.

I rubbed my forehead too. Of all the people in Frieman, why had Flint and I been chosen? Why hadn't they picked ones more ready, more able, more wise?

Char seemed to read my thoughts. "Kyndle." Very gently. "This choice wasn't thoughtless. You and Flint were among many considered for this task, but we chose you two because of your admirable traits, overall good behavior, and the fact that as siblings, you are comfortable being together. Our decision was confirmed by your parents. Besides," he went on, "two youths are less likely to be missed than two adult men, and many of our women must remain to care for their homes."

I clasped my hands. "There's just one more thing."

"And what is that?" Fraith asked gently.

"The representative—he...he might realize I'm gone."

Five pairs of eyes, including Flint's, blinked hard at me for a couple long seconds.

"I, uh, made his acquaintance this week. He recalled my name without me saying it, so I have good reason to think he may also remember—and possibly miss—my face, should he visit town in my absence."

There was a silence and I felt hope stir in my heart. Maybe I could get out of this.

Anvil cleared his throat. "Where did you *make his acquaintance?*"

"In the street outside my dorm. He was there to break up an argument between two old men."

"How often has he spoken to you?"

"It's—it's never happened, sir."

"Then I find it unlikely that it would happen again so soon. Do any of my fellow councilmen disagree?"

Heads were shaken around the table. Anvil took a deep breath then looked back at me. "Then it's decided."

I blinked a few times but nodded. Their choice was out of my hands. Flint and I had committed ourselves, our parents had affirmed us, and the councilmen believed in us.

All that was left to do was pack.

chapter FIVE

I tossed my full pack onto the bed, and then myself. I had three hours to wait. We were leaving at the stroke of twelve.

I hadn't been allowed to return to the dorm. Maroon had fetched what I would need for the next week. No one could know about this journey. It was too risky. I figured the girls would conclude that I had become mixed up in whatever Auburn had gotten in trouble for.

It was the strangest feeling. Early this morning, Auburn had told me goodbye—and now here I was, gripping a packed bag, twice as afraid and trying not to show it.

I was in one of the two bedrooms Char's home had to offer. Flint was still talking to the councilmen in the main room. Being totally alone, I did what I would never do in front of any other person. I cried. One sitting back-to-back with me would never know I was crying as my tears came silently, but I cried all the same.

Part of me was excited—what luck! To be one out of *two* picked from the entire *village!* To be given this chance to spend days on end with my own brother after an entire childhood of only having Saturdays together. What's more, to be given *five entire days* in the wild—a place where my *parents* hadn't even been. It was more than a girl could ever want.

In fact, it was more than I wanted. Because the larger part of me was terrified.

I wasn't afraid of danger, exactly; I just wasn't one to chase after it.

My thoughts returned to Auburn. *Where was she? Was she safe? Had she learned anything about the cardinal?*

I tried not to think of all the predatory animals lurking in the safety of the night, looking for something to nab. I tried not to think of Snow Sprite soldiers out on a night patrol, stumbling across her in the darkness. I tried not to worry.

But *try* isn't always possible.

I rested my face upon the pillow, forcing every muscle to relax. Silent tears brought on a whale of a headache. *Now, now. There's no use working yourself up into a tizzy.* I should just lay still—and not think.

Don't think, don't think—Was that possible either?

The bell tolled, ten mournful times. Two more hours.

Two more hours. Two—more.

My eyes flew open. I lifted my head from the wet blanket, blinking in sincere surprise.

I fell asleep? Was I crying in my sleep? What woke me?

I glanced at the window and listened, but the house was quiet. Another glance showed that there was no longer light under my door.

Had there been a noise outside or had I imagined it?

After a few moments, a rustling sound met my ears. I listened with my entire body, the hair raising on the back of my neck.

"Kyndle!" came a piercing whisper.

I fled to the window. Dropping to my knees, I pulled the curtain aside a bit. Tinder's face came in view, about a foot above the sill. He glanced in all directions.

"What are you doing here?" I whispered.

He turned his face upward, and I was instantly afraid. He seemed older than when I had last seen him earlier that morning. There was an anxiety in his eyes I had never seen there before. My question changed.

"What's wrong?"

His lips parted, but he seemed at a loss. He raised a hand to brush the hair from his eyes and I grabbed at it frantically.

"Mum, Dad—!"

"Shhh!" he said, pulling from my grasp and glancing around. "Let me up. Sometimes those blasted Snowbrains take night walks."

"Is it Mum or Dad?" I asked again as he hoisted himself through the small window.

"No, they're fine." He looked around the room. "Where's Flint?"

"I don't know. I would think in the room across the hall, but I've been asleep. Is it Ruby?"

"Stay here. I gotta find him."

I sat down on the edge of the bed as he slipped out the door without a sound. Why wouldn't he answer me about Ruby? That meant it had to be her. Had she relapsed? It was three agonizing minutes before he returned with Flint. My brother's face was pale with what looked like worry.

I jumped up. "Tinder, what's wrong with Ruby?"

"Shhh." He took my elbow and sat me back down. "Two Snow Sprites arrived in town an hour ago with a message from the Snow Realm."

"A message?" Flint repeated.

"The Snow Realm thinks our population is too large." His voice sunk heavy in hate. "They've ordered every third child sent north, along with any others younger than them. If there's any resistance, they said they'll just start killing them."

Flint turned away. "We won't stand for this," I heard him say.

My heartbeat, formerly pounding, now shriveled inside of my chest. I grabbed Tinder's arm.

"They took Ruby?" I whispered.

He loosened my fingers. "We *didn't* stand for it," he said to Flint.

My brother turned.

"The messengers—" Tinder cleared his throat. "Got, uh, killed."

"So the order hasn't been carried out?" I whispered jubilantly. "Then she's safe!"

He grabbed my shoulder. "Kyndle, our people speak of war."

My heart began pounding once more.

"Not just talk," he went on. "They mean to actually do it."

"But the representative?" I asked.

"Gone. It seems he left quite suddenly two days ago."

I remembered the urgent letter from Galaheed. "Do we know when he will be back?"

He shook his head.

"And the cardinal?"

"Still no word of him."

"Tinder, why are you telling us all this?"

"Your father sent me. He wants you to take Ruby with you."

"Take her—*with us?*"

Tinder nodded. "He says it would be the safest place for her. We have no assurance that a group of Snowling soldiers won't march in and start to—to massacre the children."

I bowed my head, speechless with fear.

"Don't be scared," Tinder went on. "Your father and I have worked it all out. I'll smuggle her out of her dorm and get her to Melting Creek."

"So you know about our mission?"

"Yes. Your father told me."

I looked up at Flint and he winked at me in reassurance.

"I'm going now to nab Ruby," Tinder went on. "It'll take us longer to get there, and I don't want to keep you waiting."

"How will you do that without waking the entire dormitory?"

"Well," he said.

I wiped my eyes, trying to hide the fear in them, but Tinder saw it.

"So I don't exactly know yet," he said, "but I'll figure something out. Besides you know what they all say—trust yourself, trust your instincts, and you'll be fine."

"Thanks, Tinder," I managed. "I needed to hear that again."

He smiled, and the flickering lantern was reflected in his dark eyes. The simplicity of it filled me with a longing for things to be as they had been before. For me to be asleep in my dorm bed like always, Auburn in the bed next to mine. I would have even chosen to be back with snooty Ashbel rather than sit here, awaiting the next day.

Tinder stood up.

"See you in a bit," he said, offering each of us one of his large hands. I took it between both of mine and held on, not wanting to let it go. Not wanting him to leave. Not wanting everything to change.

But as soon as I did, he slipped across the room, hoisted himself back out the window and disappeared into the darkness of the night. I turned to Flint.

"We've been waiting for war our whole lives, Kyndle," he said. "The Snowlings went too far. They took our freedom, they take our tribute, but they're not going to take our children."

I nodded.

"See you later," he said before quietly leaving.

I stared glumly at the empty room before settling into a chair near the fire.

"See you later," I said to my normal life.

Dong, came the fateful toll and I jerked out of my dozing.

Dong! said the bell eleven more times.

I pulled my worn boots on and fiercely laced them up, determined to be prepared for whatever, picturing in my mind the sleepy bell boy being hoisted up and down, up and down, while the grumpy tower master turned the hourglass and settled back down into his doze.

Yes, I would be prepared. *Or at least pretend to be.* A low knock came at my door. I opened it.

"Ready?" Flint asked.

"I'm scared."

"Scared?"

"About taking Ruby with us," I said a little too loudly.

"Shhh!" he fussed, glancing over his shoulder. "They don't know that *we* know about last night, so *they* can't know about *our* plans. They may try to stop us."

I buttoned my lip.

"It'll be fine," he said. "If Dad is helping with the planning, I know I can trust him wholeheartedly. After all, we're only obeying him. And he *is* on the council."

"Right," I said.

Anvil, Coal, and Char were waiting in the anteroom. The lanterns in the room gave off a dull light which matched how I felt.

"Good morning," Anvil said with a soberness that spread.

I clearly saw the night's events on his mind and braced myself for his account of it. But he didn't bring it up.

"Any other questions?"

"How can I back out?" I almost blurted.

"How is this going to work?" Flint asked.

"You'll head north," Char answered, "without anyone seeing you."

I shut my eyes and pictured the drawings of our town as it would look from above. Diamond-shaped, Frieman was comprised of four quadrants, each containing upward of twenty homes; the vertices pointed roughly north, east, south, and west. My dorm sat in the eastern quadrant, Mum, Dad, and Flint's in the western, Ruby's in the southern. The north quadrant was mostly unfinished. The representative's estate was situated a couple miles northeast of it.

"Flint," Anvil said. "Your charge will be bound and gagged until you reach the forest. His motives are still not certain, and we can't have him causing any trouble for you. Kyndle, you'll be the scout."

We both nodded.

"This is his one chance to live," Coal said. "If he causes trouble, bring him back—dead or alive. Just *don't leave him out there*."

"And remember," Anvil said, "move as quickly as possible. I need not remind you of the risk this mission is putting out entire town into. We've laid a heavy responsibility on your shoulders, but I think we've not done it lightly. Flint and Kyndle, you have our trust."

"Thank you, councilmen," Flint said.

For the first time, Anvil smiled.

We all shook hands. As Anvil spoke in undertones to Flint, Char came to me and put fatherly hands on my arms.

"May much luck be with you," he said.

I smiled. "I hope we have more than that."

"Maybe this will help." Putting his hand in his pocket, he withdrew a small scabbarded dagger which he put onto my palm. I pulled it out and held it up to the candlelight. "The handle is small," he said, "but the blade is true. May it prove itself helpful in a time of danger."

I nodded gratefully as I sheathed the dagger and slipped it in my belt. As I did, there was a soft knock at the door.

Anvil opened it quietly and my father filled the doorway.

Behind him was the boy.

His wrists were tied in front of him but he looked comfortable—which wasn't surprising with my father as a guard. Though he kept his gaze just under our faces as he was led to Flint, his eyes caught my attention. I had never seen any like them. Snow Sprites' were icy blue, Fire Sprites' were dark, dark brown—but these were a striking *green,* almost beacon-like in their appearance.

Whether they shone as a harbor or in warning, I didn't know.

I did know that where I had expected to feel only suspicion toward him, I instead felt sorry for him.

"Flint, Kyndle—meet the cause of all your troubles," Coal said with a bit of harshness to his tone. He stood directly in front of the silent boy. "Listen here, kid—" I mentally noted that the "kid" was nearly as big as every grown man in the room. "These two are risking life and limb for you as is every person in this town. If you so much as make a peep or lift a finger, you could cost us all our lives. Understand?"

He met eyes with Coal, and there was a nod beneath the thick brown waves. But the tense of his jaw worried me.

"Flint has charge of you," Anvil went on. "We've given him a dagger that he is to keep at the ready. Once you all reach the safety of the forest, the restraints will be cut. We do not believe in treating men as beasts."

There was another nod.

"These are for each of you," said Char, stepping up with an armful of dark cloth. From it, he untangled three jet-black hooded capes which he distributed among us. The Unknownling's was draped over his head and shoulders, then buttoned tight across the front.

Dad placed both his large hands on Flint's shoulders.

"Protect your sister," he said firmly.

"I will, Dad," Flint told him. "I promise I will."

"Next," Dad went on, "protect yourself."

Flint chuckled but it lacked its usual luster.

Dad enveloped me in one of his big bear hugs, holding my head to his chest with one huge hand. I heard his heart beating loud against my ear, strong and unhesitating.

A Fire Sprite heartbeat.

"I love you." I heard his voice deep inside his chest. "Stay with Flint, be wary of the boy."

"I will, Dad. Love you, too." I would've said more, but it's somewhat hard to give a lengthy speech when all of the air has been squeezed from your lungs. He released me just before it felt like my eyes would explode. I staggered back a couple steps, laughing weakly in spite of the nagging anxiety in my stomach, looking around and wishing Mum was there so I could feel complete in my leaving.

"Now go," Anvil said, "for the glory of the Fire Sprites."

"For the glory," Flint and I repeated.

Dad smiled proudly at us, then nodded at the backdoor. "Go."

The air was warm as I ducked out into the night. I looked down both of the streets facing us diagonally, and when I saw no sign of movement, I advanced a couple steps forward. A backward glance showed Flint with a firm hand on the boy's arm as he softly closed the door. Then he turned to me and gave a nod. We were ready.

Quiet as a mouse, I slipped along, heart pounding, my ears ringing in the dead silence of the night. Reaching the end of the block, I very slowly eased my head around the corner.

Look left, look right. Look left, look right. Nothing. Just tall shadows. I continued forward.

I turned frequently to confirm that the other two were still behind me, so quiet were their footfalls. In the moonlight, I caught a glimpse of steel held to the boy's ribcage, but it appeared he was giving Flint no trouble.

So far.

We still had two blocks to cover before we reached the undeveloped northern sector.

Heel, toe, heel, toe. We slipped through the shadows, avoiding direct moonlight, just *knowing* at any moment, we would be discovered. I'd just begun to myself calm down when the metallic clink of a boot froze me in my tracks—a clink I knew all too well.

I instantly melted into the shadow of the wall.

Very, *very* slowly, I turned my head to make sure Flint had caught the warning. I saw no sign of them.

I waited in silence, my ears tingling.

The clinking came again, a few more steps taken. He was on the lane intersecting mine, moving west along the street.

Toward me. Toward us.

I began to panic. Just a few more moments and he would be reaching my corner. I would be discovered and the mission would've failed before we even left.

I eased to my left a few feet, then quietly stretched myself across the ground, parallel to the building, hoping the black cape would cover me.

The footsteps rounded the corner, a mere three feet from my head.

It was nerve-racking in the extreme, lying so prone.

Moving my head *very* slowly, I let the cape fall away from one eye—and looked full up into the face of a Snow Sprite soldier.

chapter SIX

Fortunately he wasn't looking at me. His blue eyes traveled up and down the length of the street, left, right, and behind him, then he traveled on westward. A few curls of white hair poked from beneath his blue cap. I waited until he was fully a block down before I attempted to move.

I rose from the ground, like a bat, and very cautiously got to my feet as the soldier turned south, two streets down, and vanished from my sight. I was covered in sweat from head to toe. There was moisture even above my lip.

Such silliness. He hadn't even seen me!

Turning I scanned the darkness for Flint. A couple moments went by before he and his charge materialized from a wall. He shot me a nod and we went on.

Two grueling blocks later, we caught sight of the forest line and, after one last left-right-left glance, bolted for it like scared rabbits. It was with unspeakable relief that we collapsed against an outcropping of boulders several yards in.

"That was scarier than I expected." I gasped to Flint.

"It was," he agreed. After catching our breath, we turned to the silent third member of our spunky trio. Reaching, Flint drew back the hood and turned the face within toward a small streak of moonlight so we could get a good long look at him.

His skin was the shade of ours with hair the color of rich soil and the muscular shoulders of some sort of laborer. He looked older than both of us.

"Alright, lad," Flint said, sounding a bit more like his old self. "Were I to cut you free, would you stay put?"

He nodded.

Flint quickly cut through the ropes. The boy used his own large hands to pull off his gag.

"T'anks," he said, his voice a little hoarse from disuse.

"Thank *you*," Flint said, "for not costing us our necks back there."

The boy's lips stretched in a wan smile then cracked.

"Let's get to the creek," I said to Flint.

"Yeah," he said, looking northwest. "Hopefully Tinder is there when we arrive."

It was a less stressful walk there, taking us about fifteen minutes. We didn't exchange words, but Flint and I kept a constant eye out. We were within two miles of the representative's home. There was no telling if he had guards in this area. Shadows could harbor enemies. Thankfully it was the sound of water and not the clink of boots that soon broke the silence. We stopped at the edge of a broad creek. Flint began looking around best as he could in the darkness, and our companion went to get a drink at the water's edge. I leaned against a tree to close my eyes for a moment.

I want to wake up and all of this be just a dream.

"Boo," came a deep voice.

I opened my eyes and found myself face-to-face with Tinder.

"Acht—!" I scrambled backward and would've fallen had he not put an arm out.

He let out a hissing laugh.

"Thanks for scaring me half to death," I said when I could.

He laughed again and clapped my back. "Can't have you falling asleep in hostile territory."

I glanced around him and saw Ruby already standing with Flint inside a moonbeam.

"I dozed off?" I asked them.

"Just for a few moments," Ruby said, trying to hide a smile.

I smiled too. I had probably looked pretty hilarious falling backward as I had. Suddenly I remembered our charge. A quick glance showed him sitting at the base of a nearby tree. He returned my gaze evenly.

"How'd it go?" Tinder asked me.

I turned back to him and tried not to notice the protective look across Tinder's face. "Fairly well. We had one close encounter, but the shadows and these hoods worked to our advantage."

Tinder glanced beyond me at the stranger. That look passed across his features again. "So that's what was in the cellar the other day."

My brow furrowed. He didn't sound like himself.

After a moment, he walked over to him. I had a thought of intervening but quickly thought better of it. I owed the boy no loyalty, and I knew that Tinder was no bully. I watched as he knelt before the stranger, and began speaking in an undertone.

Ruby came to me. I put my arm around her shoulder.

"You all right?"

She nodded but her large eyes seemed a bit frightened. "It was scary, sneaking through the streets like that."

"Very scary," Flint said, coming to stand with us. "But we made it this far. It should be easier from here on out. The farther we get from town, the safer we are, and the faster, the better."

I glanced again at Tinder's back, and the face before him that was set like stone. It would seem that he didn't quite appreciate what Tinder was saying to him.

"We need to go, Tin," Flint called.

Tinder slowly rose and returned to us. The boy rose also but in a way that seemed purposefully nonthreatening.

"What was that about?" I asked Tinder as he reached us.

He shrugged noncommittally. "Just a few hearty warnings," came his response with a grin whose familiarity irritated me somewhat.

He hugged Flint, then Ruby, and then he came to me.

"You take care of yourself," he said.

I smiled archly. "I think I'm capable of that."

He hesitated, and for the first time ever, I felt an awkwardness between us. I didn't move, not sure how to respond to it, but he solved the issue by setting a friendly hand on my shoulder and then stepping toward the trees. I knew he needed to be back on his own bed before any early risers could confront him. We all watched him go, no doubt feeling a similar emotion—one of dull dread. At the last moment, just before he disappeared into the shadows, we saw him turn and thrust up a hand. Then he was gone. A strange question came to mind as I stared at the last spot I had seen him.

When would I see him again?

Nonsense, came my inner critic. *Where is your Fire Sprite courage?*

Summoning our determination, we turned to the fourth member of our group. At our looks, he slowly came over to us.

"I'm Flint," my brother said bravely, thrusting out his bear paw.

With a slight hesitancy, the boy pulled his hands from his pockets and returned the gesture. "Ian Freemont," he said, bringing his spoken words to a staggering three. Yet how he said them brought a little grin out of me. It was his accent—so strange yet possessing something almost homelike in its essence.

"This is Ruby," Flint went on as these thoughts bounced around in my head.

They exchanged nods that could be called polite.

"And this is Kyndle."

As Ian turned to me, something sparked in his face—something like a familiarity. With a hand that seemed to tremble, he shook mine.

I felt a slight blush and was irritated at myself for it.

"Anyway," Flint said, an odd metallic ring to his voice.

We all looked at him.

"Our goal is the northeast mountains," he said, pointing into the dark. "We should reach the foothills in a few miles. We'll get a good distance into it before the sun rises, so we can rest a bit. I think we've all earned it." Flint smiled at us girls then looked at Ian.

"All right," Ian said very quietly in that strange accent.

He met my eye, and I smiled faintly before I could catch myself.

To my surprise, he smiled back.

In heavy silence, we walked through the forest. No one wanted to be the first to speak, so none did. I thought a lot about Auburn. Where was she? Was she safe? Had she been caught or met with any accidents?

After a few uneventful hours, we crashed in a hollow berry patch to let Ruby sleep for a while. Ian dozed off before long, and Flint and I napped in turn.

I stirred Ruby as the sun rose and our voices woke Ian. With the sun as our guide, we carried on, on our northeasterly path. After thirty minutes or so, we stepped out of the cover of the trees and burst into full sunlight. Here was one of our grain fields, planted a few months before. The plants had grown to a height which now marked straight rows, and Ruby and I chose the same one to walk down. The stalks waved in the summer wind that brushed against our faces. Flint had chosen a row on our right, and Ian was directly left of us.

I decided to break the heavy silence.

"So, Ian. If I, as a girl, was the first to speak, would it offend you?"

He glanced at me with an amused expression. "Of course not."

Good, I thought, *because I was.*

"How old are you anyway?" Flint joined in.

"Twenty. You?"

"Nineteen."

"I'll be eighteen in six days," I volunteered.

I felt him look at me, and, on turning, I saw that look from earlier—but then he quickly looked away. I didn't ask what it meant.

"Ruby is almost thirteen," I said to keep things moving and knowing she wouldn't say it on her own.

"Thirteen," Ian repeated to himself.

Suddenly Ruby erupted in giggles.

I grinned, knowing that once she started this, it could be a while before she would be able to pull herself back together. As a young girl, she had suffered from this giggling habit—getting nervous at the worst moments and laughing for no apparent reason. As we went along, with her giggling so furiously behind us, Flint let out a chuckle and I began convulsing in my own bout of suppressed snickering.

"I'm sorry," she finally hissed, holding her stomach. "It's not that it's funny, I just can't help it sometimes."

I chanced a glance at Ian and was relieved to see him near a laugh.

"I done it myself," he said to her.

I grinned at Ruby over my shoulder. The ice was broken.

We traveled on, stopping for a quiet lunch, with help from the supplies the councilmen had stowed into our packs, then pushed on into the early evening. The sun wouldn't set for about an hour. Beside me, Ruby began to droop.

"You okay?" I asked quietly.

"I'm fine." She spouted the expected answer. "I just—*oomf!*"

Flint had come up from behind and scooped her onto his back. With a grin, she put her arms around his neck. Though at first he supported her, he soon let her hold on by herself. To continue her muscle strengthening, I knew.

As we journeyed, the relative silence made for a lot of thinking, and it wasn't long before I was back to my imagining. I paused and looked out across the plains we were crossing, seeing the wind stir the grasses into an unpredictable but rhythmic dance, feeling the gentle warmth of the dying sun resting upon my cheek, watching birds flirt and dive up above. And for a fleeting moment, I was able to make myself believe that I was free. Free from mental boundaries, free to live the life I wanted to live, as the capable woman I wanted to be, watching as my sister thrived and grew a healthier tone to her skin, more flesh to her frame, envisioning what joy that sight would bring to my parents. I imagined Flint growing larger—a mighty Fire Sprite warrior who would not fear for the safety of his wife should he make a wrong move. I envisioned our villages growing larger, thriving under mutual friendship, where we could take the time to visit and meet one another, strengthening each other with stories and laughter, nourishing each other with olden tales of sorrow and triumph, the shared history in which honor and glory were the chiefest players.

For the glory.

Though I knew walking across this plain with no Snow Sprites in sight wasn't true freedom, it was the closest to it I had ever felt before.

I shut my eyes, breathing in the clear fresh air.

"Kyndle!"

I opened my eyes to see the others fifty yards ahead, safe within the reaching arms of the forest's shadow. Ruby gestured with both her hands, urging me on. Readjusting my pack, I set off toward them at a brisk run. Just before stepping into the shade, I glanced over my left shoulder. The red sun completed its course and, with a blinding flash of farewell, sunk below the horizon. A chilling breath from the forest flashed over me, and regretfully, I turned to enter the dim interior of the trees.

Shadows in one's life make for shadows in one's soul. It's harder to dream in the dark.

We hurried to make camp in a small clearing of large sheltering trees. Their broad bases made for cozy sleeping spots and the plentiful branches promised fairly good cover from a possible rain. Ruby and I helped Flint gather leaves for bedding down. Ian lingered near the edge, looking out of place.

"I, uh, I'm sorry if my friend was a bit, uh, *un*friendly this morning," Flint said in an attempt to make conversation.

Ian waved his hand. "It's fine."

"Do you have a family, Ian?" Ruby asked. Very bravely, I thought.

He kicked at something on the ground. "I did," he said. "Now it's just me and Nanna."

"Oh," Ruby said, matching his sad tone. "I'm sorry."

"T'anks."

Another silence followed.

How to follow *that* up?

Ian helped. "The climate here is very similar t' where I come from."

"And where *do* you come from?" Flint probed. "The councilmen said they had never heard of your realm. What is the name of it?"

"My country is called Scotland."

"*Scotland?*" The word was unfamiliar to me.

"Where do you live?" Ian asked us.

"In a prison," I spit out bitterly.

Ian stared at me, no doubt feeling he had said something out of turn.

"Our people used to live in the western realm—the Fire Realm," Flint explained quietly, "but the Snow Realm, in the north, waged war with us two hundred years ago and banished us here to the southern reaches."

"You're exiles?"

Flint tensed his jaw and glanced at me. "For now, yes."

Maybe I imagined it, but Ian looked a bit green. "What is the name of your country?" he asked with apparent effort.

Flint scratched at his head. "I suppose you mean the Fire Realm. The whole of our lands is called Almia."

Ian swallowed. "So ye've never heard of a place called Scotland?"

We shook our heads.

He swallowed hard, his face most definitely sick. "Then I s'ppose that means—I've somehow come t' be in a whole diff'rent land entirely."

Flint shrugged. "I guess so."

There was a third long silence, finally broken by Ian.

"But why cannae the *Snow Sprites*," I almost laughed at how he said it, "know that I'm here?"

"They're power hungry." I spit again. "They want to rule any piece of land they can get their gloved hands on. If they were to learn of a whole new place to conquer, your home would be in danger of attack."

"I see," he said.

Ruby leaned heavily against me, her weariness showing itself. Flint saw it too.

"That said," he concluded, "it's very important that you stick close to us and not wander off. We don't know the movements of the Snow Sprites' soldiers. For all we know, they could be very close."

"I understand," Ian said.

"Good. Then we should all get some rest. It'll be an early morning."

I made sure Ruby was comfortable before leaning back against a tree of my own. Ian bedded down across from me and Flint in a place where he could keep a close eye on us all.

It was a weird feeling. I hadn't slept in the same house as Flint since I was five years old and never had I slept by Ruby. She hadn't even been born by the time I entered the dormitory for six-year-olds.

I tried to stay awake until I was sure Ian was asleep, but my mind was elsewhere as I thought of his earlier words.

There is life outside of Almia?

I had never even considered the thought. Suddenly I felt very small. And very slightly afraid.

Neither of which constitute Fire Sprite characteristics.

We were to be large—both in mind and body. We were to fear nothing, except weakness. I banged myself back into that mental mind-set and told myself I was safer that way.

An owl hooted, startling me back into my task of keeping awake, and I abandoned the thoughts of other lands for another time. I shut my eyes for just a moment, here and there, but found it increasingly hard to reopen them. During one of these breaks, I felt a hand grip my shoulder. My eyes flew open to find Flint crouching in front of me.

"What's wrong?"

"Nothing," he said. "It's just time to head out."

I sat up and looked around. "What time is it?"

He glanced around. "About an hour to sunrise." He moved off to wake the others.

I sat up, rubbing my sore neck.

So much for staying awake.

We ate a hurried breakfast and then struck out.

During the day, we all tried our best to keep up conversation in effort to learn more about each other. It produced some helpful information.

"Tell me about how you came here," Flint posed later that morning.

Ian took a deep breath. "I'll start by sayin', it's a crazy story, one that I don't even fully understand. I started out with my herd of sheep for the daily grazin'. I fetched my pack lunch from Nanna, kissed her g'bye, and filled my water pouch at the stream flowin' to the Dev'n. It was like any other day in Tillicoultry.

"By the afternoon, the sheep had grazed all they wanted and had lain down for a bit o' shut-eye. I lay nearby for a bit, then got an urge t' do a bit of explorin'. Off I went, not too far, t' nose my way around the rocks and crevices of the hill. One looked very deep and smelled a bit musty. I wanted t' find out how far in it went, there bein' tales of brownies and bogles livin' deep in the hills.

"About fifteen feet in, I realized, all of a sudden, my feet were on fire. At least it felt that way, y'see. At first I thought I'd stepped in an anthill, but when I glanced down, I saw that the floor was covered in a smoky fog. When I looked up again, everything around was covered in smoke. I yelled, but my voice fell right t' the ground. I tried t' get out, but in just a few moments, it felt as if I was fallin' right out of the sky. I had a hard time movin' my arms, like bein' underwater.

"Just when I was startin' t' get used t' it all, my feet hit ground and the mist began t' fade. When I could use my arms and legs again, I made my way back toward the light at the entrance, but when I burst out into the sunlight, it wasn't the same place that I'd left before. It was an entirely new landscape, one I had never seen before. I went down the mountain feeling as lost as a puppy. I wandered for about a day before I came upon your village. One of your lads took me t' the leaders."

"That," I said, stopping to look at him, "is the strangest thing that I've ever heard."

Up ahead, Flint said nothing.

"What year was it when you left Scotland?" I asked.

"1378," he answered. "Seventh year of the reign of Robert II."

"It's 598 here," Ruby said. "We're at end of the sixth period. Right now the king is Antar—"

"Ruby!" I snapped.

She stopped talking and her face turned red. She looked down.

"What's wrong?" Ian asked quietly.

I worked my jaw. "He's not our king. He'll never be our king."

Nothing more was said about it.

By evening, we had reached the foothills. I made a mark in my leather band, with my fingernail, to mark one full day.

"I'm sorry for yelling at you," I told Ruby in the silence before sleep. "I just couldn't stand to hear you say his name, much less hear you say that he's our king."

"But, Kyndle, isn't he?"

"He won't be for much longer."

"How do you know that?"

"Because that's what the leaders tell us."

She sighed, knowing that was the end of the discussion. I lay quietly, wishing I had, had something more to tell her.

We set off again early the next morning, and just as the sun began to peek over the horizon, we were beginning our trek up the mountain.

"It was this side, right?" Flint asked.

Ian glanced at the sun. "Yes, facing the west. I watched the sun set as I came down."

"The sun doesn't set in the west." I jumped in. "It sets in the east."

Ian blinked. "Oh."

"About how far up?" Flint asked him.

He scratched his head. "T' be honest, I was so flummoxed on the way down, I couldn't tell you how far up it was."

"All right then. Up we go until you start recognizing landmarks. Ruby, Kyndle?"

"We're ready."

"Then let's go."

Ian led the way. I brought up the rear. It was an enjoyable walk. All around us, life burst through the soil and began putting out green leaves, sometimes colorful flowers. I watched as Ruby drew in a deep breath of the fresh mountain air, and I hoped that it would do her good.

After some time, we paused for a breath, and I settled down to sit and look northeast at the mountain range in the distance. They stepped along the horizon, like skipping stones, and I was a bit overwhelmed with their grandeur. They had never looked *this* magnificent from home.

"Beautiful." I breathed, more to myself than anyone else.

"The mountains are beautiful back home," came Ian's voice, and I turned to find him standing beside me. After a few moments, he settled down onto the grass. Not so close that I edged away but closer than I had expected.

"Every night," he explained, "I look out my window at the high peaks. I watch the stars too, and *sometimes,* I see one falling. It makes me even more in awe of Christ."

I gawked. "You believe in Christ?"

"Yes!" he said, turning to me in excitement. "D'you?"

"Of course not!" I retorted. "I look inward to find all my answers. My heart and instincts guide me—not your Christ."

"I see," he said.

I stood and walked to Flint, my mind attempting to register the shock.

He believes like Auburn does?

Thinking of her made me sigh. Odd or not, I missed her.

chapter SEVEN

The day was another quiet one.

Mountain hiking was a bit more strenuous; none of us felt like talking. The temperature began to lower the higher up we got. Flint, never one to mind cold weather, offered his cloak to Ruby; though when we broke for lunch at midday, it had become fairly chilly. The food seemed to lift our spirits some.

"Nothing familiar yet?" Flint queried.

"No."

"Is there *nothing* you can tell us to help out?" I asked, trying to mask my irritation. Talk about a wild-goose chase!

"I remember the passage being very narrow…" He rubbed his chin for several moments, then— "Of course! When I stepped from the cave, my foot hit snow. It was the first thing that let me know I wasn't in Scotland anymore."

"Snow?" Flint glanced up. "That means we've gone about halfway."

"At least that gets us somewhere," I commented grumpily, but inside, I felt a spark of excitement. We rarely got snow in the village. It would be fun to walk around in it.

I knelt at the small stream of water nearby which was so cold that the touch of it pricked at my fingers like knives. I quickly filled my pouch of water and then deposited it over the small fire. Flint kicked it around. We were trying our best to not leave behind any tracks.

"So does that group o' five men run your village?" Ian asked.

"Not usually. Our townships are run by a cardinal, and the council is just his support group," I answered. "But as the cardinal is missing, they had to make the decisions."

"Missing, eh?" Ian asked as we struck off.

"For several days now. No one knows what's happened to him."

"Not even his family?"

"He has no family. The Snow Sprites appoint the cardinals, and at any time they fancy, they rotate them around the townships. This cardinal has been with us nine years. He was appointed by the old representative."

"Who is that?"

"He's the Snowling who makes sure we obey the rules. He's who can't know you're here. His soldiers sometimes walk the streets at night."

"Like the one we nearly ran into?"

"Yes. So our goal is to find whatever cave you came from and get you back into it."

"I see," he said.

"Won't your grandmother be worried about you?" Ruby asked. There was a gust of wind and I heard her teeth chattering.

Ian nodded. "That she will. I'm all she has left."

"What happened to the others?" I ventured.

He shrugged as if shrugging off a heavy weight. "Plague."

"A sickness?"

"Aye, a bad one. It took nearly the whole village, includin' me mither and Granda."

"Did you have any siblings?"

He nodded painfully. "There were two, both girls. One was born right before Mither died. Faither took the other with him to fetch clean water."

The way he said it made me ask, "Did they ever return?"

Jaw set hard, he shook his head. "Died themselves along the way."

"So the new baby died too?" Ruby wanted to know.

To our surprise, he broke down and began to weep.

We all stopped, and I tried in vain not to stare. I had never seen a man cry before. He made little sound, but his shoulders shook with emotion. Ruby blushed deeply, ashamed to have caused the outburst.

"I'm sorry," he said a moment later, trying to dry his tears.

"It's fine," Flint said quickly. He too seemed surprised to see a full-grown man reduced to tears.

Ian wiped his face with the back of his sleeve. "She didn't die of the plague. She died in an accident when she was thirteen."

Thirteen.

"I'm sorry," Ruby said.

He brushed back a strand of hair. "We can go on now."

We all did, feeling a bit embarrassed.

By evening, we were within sight of the snow line. It was decided that we would begin again in the morning when visibility was better; so while the sun set, we made camp. I pressed my fingernail again into my band. It had now been two full days since we had left.

"I'm so cold," Ruby chattered.

"Me too." The temperature was getting frigid.

"I'm going to build a tent with your cloaks," Flint said to Ian and me, "if that's all right."

"Good idea. I'll look for firewood," Ian said.

"That's my job," I argued. "Besides we can't have you wandering off and getting lost or hurt."

"D'ye really think I'm just a weak shepherd boy?" he retorted. "I've kept my Granda's flock safe for eight years. I haven't lost a single one. I kin find my way around as easily as you can. You look around there, and I'll look around over here." He gestured.

I glanced at Flint who nodded. "Just stay close," he said as I passed him.

We struck out our separate ways. I felt a bit squished by Ian's speech. Perhaps I had been a bit hard on him. He was, after all, apparently quite used to finding his way around.

I ducked down here and there, but kindling wasn't as easy to find as it was down below. Trees were almost nonexistent up here. Concentrated on my work, I didn't realize how far I had wandered until I saw the snow, several feet up the trail. A small pile but still snow. I scurried toward it, forgetting the firewood, and with a satisfied sigh, gathered some of the freezing stuff into a small ball. I felt myself smiling as I chunked it at the nearest rock face.

Firewood, my mind prompted. I returned to my task.

HOME ROAD

Up ahead, the trail forked, and the right side led to what I realized was a sort of room within the wall. The initial entrance was narrow, though it grew to at least twelve feet wide once I stepped inside. The walls of rock offered shelter from the wind. And lo! Twenty feet away, at the other end of this room-like opening with no ceiling, was a tree. It was no more than twenty feet tall and its branches hung low.

Firewood! my mind said again.

I started toward it, but suddenly, the ground beneath my boot cracked. I froze. After a moment, I knelt. Brushing away the thin layer of snow at my feet, I found ice below it—evidently some sort of water hole that had frozen. A small gust of wind caught the opening and blew away the thin layer of snow to reveal more of it.

A water source, my mind exulted, though at this very moment, it was a hindrance to me reaching the tree. There was nothing for it but to cross. Cautiously I set a foot out on to test it; it was firm. I took a second step, bouncing my weight a bit. When it gave no sign of breaking, I set out. Slow at first, then less so. I was making good distance and was a mere ten feet from the tree when I heard a frantic voice behind me.

"Stop! What're you doing?"

Turning, I saw Ian hurrying toward me with a panic-stricken look on his face. I heard a crack as he reached the ice and he jerked to a stop.

"Gathering wood, of course," I said, turning and taking another step. I didn't want to linger on the ice for a conversation.

"No! Stop!"

Frustrated, I turned again. "What's the matter?"

His face was white, and he held out his hands pleadingly. "Please."

"Please, what?" When he hesitated, I hurriedly took the last two steps to firm ground.

"Nooo!" he cried.

I turned to face him. "What is your problem?"

"Just please, do nae come back over the ice."

"Ian—there are *rock walls* on both sides. There's no *other* way back over." I turned away from him. "I have to get wood."

The branches near the ground were still alive and wouldn't break, so I tried further up. The branches were low, allowing me to easily climb up toward the top. I started snapping off branches toward the top, dropping them below.

"If you want to be helpful, you can come and get an armful," I called down to Ian.

He made no move to do so.

"Suit yourself," I said, more to myself. A few of the thicker branches, apparently also still alive, wouldn't snap. An idea struck me. I whipped my knife from under my belt and began sawing away at them. When I had all that I could carry, I scurried down the tree trunk and began collecting the wood into a bundle. Binding it up with a sturdy strip of bark I had pared from the trunk, I tossed the bundle across my shoulder. Then I set a boot on the edge of the ice. A sound from Ian made me look up. His face was ashen.

"What do you want me to do?" I asked in exasperation.

"Just—" He tousled his hair. "Just please, go slow. You're a bit heavier now."

I humored him.

"See," I said after a few safe steps. "It's safe."

His face looked sick as he waited. As I neared, he held out his hands. I eyed him a bit skeptically. Did he think I would grab his hand? As I took my last step, the ice gave way under my heel and my foot broke through to the freezing water below. It only plunged to my kneecap, but before I could even react, I felt myself bodily lifted up and placed on firm ground again.

"It's all right." Ian panted in my ear. "I got ya."

I staggered back out of his arms, shocked at the suddenness of it all, but more so by how scared he looked. He was breathing heavily as *tears* streamed down his face. It was a couple moments before I recovered my senses.

"Thanks." *I think?*

I mean, if I had been alone, it had only been a short drop. It would've been fine, nothing to even mention. Just a cold foot to set by the fire.

So why had he taken the whole thing so seriously?

"Of course," he said, turning away. He swiped at the tears and seemed embarrassed. I readjusted the sticks on my back and brushed past him out into the fresh air.

Ruby sat where I had left her, but now, all three cloaks were wrapped around her shivering frame. Flint came to take the stick bundle from me. Ian didn't join us. His face was still white, and his eyes were heavy with some sort of anxiety. He hung back by himself.

"I couldn't find anything to prop the cloaks up," Flint explained as I looked over at Ruby.

I dropped my bundle of sticks.

"Some of these might be sturdy enough for the job."

"They just might. I'll work at it. Ian, can you get the fire going?"

He wordlessly moved to do so, and in no time, we had a glorious blaze to warm our hands in as Flint put the finishing touches on the makeshift shelter.

"Come and warm up," Flint called to the quiet boy.

After a moment, he came opposite us and put out his hands above the warming flames.

"T'anks," he said.

Flint glanced at me, but I just shrugged. *I* certainly had no idea why he was acting this way.

We ate a light supper, then all began trying to get comfortable for the night. Inside the tent, protected from the wind, I heard, with gratitude, that Ruby's teeth had finally stopped chattering. She fell asleep with her head in my lap.

"Did we do the right thing, bringing her with us?" I asked Flint who sat just outside the opening.

"I think so, Kyndle. She might be cold, but at least she's safe."

I glanced into the shadows beyond the fire's light. "Is she?"

He tightened his lips. "For now."

There was silence around the fire for a few moments. Then Ian spoke up. "I'm sorry."

"For what?" Flint asked.

"For a lot of things. For getting you mixed up in this, for crying like a bairn yesterday, for acting out like I did to Kyndle."

Flint glanced at me, a quiet alarm in his eye.

"Don't be," I said quietly, shaking my head slightly at Flint.

"Well, I am, and I mean to explain why I cried so." He took in a deep breath. "I was very close to my sister, Fran. She was two years younger, but we did everythin' together. I promised her I would always protect her from harm."

Suddenly the looks he had given me made sense. Fran and I were the same age. Or we would've been. Ian went on.

"She loved to go along with me an' the sheep, so one day, we set out like normal. T'was a cold winter day and almost everythin' was covered with a white snowy blanket. She went off explorin' not far from where I had sat down among the sheep, but then, I heard her scream. I ran fast as I could, but when I reached her, she had just disappeared under the ice of a pond."

He glanced at me, but I looked away in shame. His actions lined up.

And I had made fun of him!

"She was a strong swimmer and managed t' stay above the surface till I arrived. I barely managed t' pull her out. As I did, a blizzard struck up. It took all my strength t' carry her home in it. By the time we did, it was too late. Nanna did everything she could do, but Fran couldn't get warm and worked hard to get a breath. It wasn't long before we knew hope was lost. When she knew she was dyin', Fran cried, and all through the night, I wiped away her tears.

"That next morning, just as sun rose, she turned to me with her sweet little smile and said, 'Ian, don't cry.' I told her I wouldn't, but as she kept on smilin' at me like that, I couldn't help myself. 'I'm sorry, Fran,' I said. 'I'm sorry I didn't protect you. I'm sorry I can't save you this time.'"

Ian's voice broke with emotion.

"As I sat there beside her, cryin' despite my promise, she clumsily put her cold little hands on my face and said in a slurred voice, 'Ye did save me. I'd much rather die here in my own little bed than in the dark water. T'anks for savin' me, Ian.' And with that, her little eyes locked fast onto mine and she was gone."

I closed my eyes. It was all so horrible. When I opened them, Ian was looking at me.

"I always take a bit of flowers or somethin' to set on her grave every morning," he said. "Just t' remember her. Not that I could *forget*. It's just, I didn't want t' just move on with my life and leave her entirely out of it. She was different than Mither and Faither and the others—I actually *knew* her."

"I'm sorry," I said quietly.

We all sat in silence for what felt like a few minutes. Neither Flint nor I knew how to reply—it just wasn't the way of our people to sympathize. We weren't cruel; we just didn't dwell on these kinds of things.

"We should all get some rest." Flint stood and stretched. "It'll be an early morning. I for one want to get home as fast as we can."

Ian smiled, though it was a sad one. "Me too, Flint."

I glanced up. That was the first time he had used my brother's name.

Flint recognized it too. A look passed between them—one of mutual hardship. They seemed to draw strength from each other in that moment, and though I couldn't explain it, I felt like I was watching something truly *real*.

I felt strengthened too, just enough to make a third indention in my wristband.

chapter EIGHT

The next morning was spent trying to find the cave in the snow.

As we searched, I tried not to think about the possibility of any of us being sucked to other lands. Surely you could get away from it before it all set in. Yet to my immense relief, when dusk fell, both my siblings were accounted for.

So was Ian.

It was much harder than any of us had expected. We found that there were a lot of small caves on this side of the mountain. By evening, we all felt discouraged. That only grew when the next day, and the next, proved just as fruitless. The evening of the fifth day found a rather forlorn group huddled by the fire. Ruby shivered in her sleep. Ian sat quiet as usual, his arms wrapped around his knees.

"We're out of water again," I said aloud.

Ruby was sleeping, huddled against my leg, so I couldn't leave her.

Flint lifted a tired head from his arm. "I'll get some." He sighed as he began collecting the flasks for his trek to the broken ice.

I for one was growing frustrated by the whole venture and directed a hard stare at Ian, just *daring* him to raise his head. Everything was going wrong. We were going to fail our mission, and all he could do was sit there with his head on his knees.

All this fuss is about you, you know. You might help.

He didn't look up.

"Can you carry all four?" I asked Flint, darting eyes at Ian, hoping he would catch the hint in my voice.

"Yep, I got it," Flint said, tired and oblivious. "Be back in a jig."

I huffed to myself after he left and rested my chin in my palm. "You know, you might be more helpful."

Ian glanced up. "Sorry?" he said, but he didn't sound angry.

When had he ever sounded angry? His control made *me* grow more upset.

"All this trouble is on your behalf. You might try to help more."

His face clouded. "I've volunteered to help on everythin' that doesn't involve goin' near the ice."

I took on a softer tone. "Ian, it's been five years. Can't you move past your fears? You can't let them tie you down forever, and they will, unless you move past them."

He put his head back down. "You cannae understand."

And just like that, he shut me out. Assumed I couldn't understand. Assumed I was unable to relate to his hardship. Something sparked within me and I scoffed aloud.

"Don't kid yourself. You aren't the only one here to have ever felt the touch of pain."

Still his head stayed down. *"You* certainly haven't, not like that. You still have all of your family. I have none but Nanna, and I don't even have her now."

"You certainly won't if you just lie around and mope about it."

That was low, my mind rebuked.

"Lie around?" He looked up at me in surprise. "For the past five days, I've worked harder than you both. Why are you pickin' a fight?"

"Me, pick a fight?" I tried to look blank. "This isn't a fight."

He blinked a few times. "What would you call it then?"

"Conversation, for the Firelings. We say what we're feeling. We don't tolerate weakness."

"Weak?" Then he *laughed.* Not bitterly but in true amusement. "Is that what I am then?"

His unconcerned reply to what was meant to be a pointed blow irked me. A lot. More than it should have.

So I asked, "Well, *are* you?"

He looked away and brushed a hand across his eyes. "I don't want to fight with you, Kyndle. There's no point in it. Let's just let things go." He put his head back down and wouldn't look at me. I glared at him.

Go ahead, just brush me off. Not so fast.

"Let what go?" I asked. "What've I done to you?"

He lifted his head. "Maybe I should ask you that."

He said it so calmly.

I squared my jaw. "Go right ahead."

"All right then. Kyndle, what've I done to make you angry?"

I stared at him. *Just what is all this about? How can he seem so very unconcerned with his bleak reality? Did he really come from some other realm through a magic portal? Or is he the biggest liar ever? Where did he really come from? Is that charming accent just put on?* I found myself surprised at the possibilities. *Is he a Snowling spy, sent down to draw us all into nonconformity? To give them a reason to punish us even more?* I studied his hairline very closely. *Was it dyed that color or was that a wig with white hair underneath?* But his eyes—their color couldn't be altered, could they? So I just let out a laugh. I was surprised by how much hurt I heard in it.

"A lot. Maybe more."

I watched him closely, but my reply sparked nothing suspicious in his frank face.

"How can I fix it?" he asked.

I leveled him a heavy stare. "You can do everything you can to find the hole you came out of and get back into it so *we* can be home in two days or less."

"Do you not think that's what I want?"

"*Do* you?"

"Of course I do. I want nothing more."

I grasped at straws. I had to win this argument. "Since you've arrived, you've done nothing but mope about and wear a long face. Do you think you could apply that energy to other things?"

He took a deep breath. "Per'aps I could then."

I looked away, unsatisfied.

"I'm sorry, Kyndle."

I felt like patronizing him. I wanted to see him angry. I wanted to see some *fire* in his eyes. "Sorry for what?"

"For bein' the cause of all this. For not meetin' your expectations in my performance and not fully applyin' m'self in every way. For violating your trust."

I blinked. "My trust?"

He blinked twice. "Why, yes. I thought—"

"You thought what?" I demanded as his face blanked.

"I thought that, well, that you trusted me."

I continued to stare. He fumbled on.

"I thought that you cared, even just a little."

I was truly shocked. "You thought we *trusted* you? That we *cared* for you?" I let out another laugh, and my suspicions flew out before I could stop them. "Like we'd trust a Snowling spy."

"What?" He choked. "I am *not* a spy!" He roughly rubbed at his eye with a fist and a tear steamed down his cheek. His eyes were filled with a hurt he didn't try to mask.

I laughed, satisfied to see *something* emotional, but my laugh sounded so *mean*. I ignored my inward warning. He stood up and so did I.

"You don't believe me, do you?" he asked.

"And why should I?"

Ruby stirred awake. "What's wrong?" she asked in a quiet voice.

"Why should I believe you?" I repeated.

He said nothing but looked at me like the answer was something that I should already know.

"Let me tell you," I spat. "I have no reason at all. In fact, I have many more reasons *not* to believe you or trust you, much less *care* for you. All because of you, I was torn from old my life with no warning. Because of you, we're out here in this wind. Ruby hasn't been warm in days, Flint's just about worn himself out worrying, there's no *telling* how my parents are faring. If we don't find this thing by tomorrow, we have to go back as failures. If we don't leave tomorrow, we won't be home on time and our people might be *killed*. It's bad either way."

Ian was silent, and his eyes began to fall from my face.

"And after all we've been through at your hand," I went on, "you think we *cared* for you? That we even *trusted* you? Why?"

"We talked—" he faltered.

"So we ask how old you are, ask a little bit about your homeland, and listen as you tell us about your sister. That made you think that I *cared*? It was a mere *formality*."

"I—"

"You what?"

His mouth clamped shut, and his face went hard. "I was wrong." His voice trembled, whether in anger or sadness, I couldn't tell. "I had thought you were different."

Seeing the look on his face, I began to feel sorry.

He took in a small breath. "I thought you had a heart, Kyndle."

"That's enough." Flint's voice barked from the shadows.

We both turned in surprise.

"We *do* have hearts," Flint said, stepping into the fire's light, his arms cradling the water pouches. "But we just want to go home."

Ian took several steps backward, looking at us in turn with surprised eyes. "And you think I don't?"

We said nothing.

Ian choked out a short breath. "I just thought that you were different. I thought you possessed a bit of kindness for your fellow man, even if I'm not from your village. And yes—I had thought you cared." He turned and disappeared into the shadows.

Stalking to a nearby boulder, I dropped to a seat. All I knew was suspicion. For my entire life, I had been trained to use trust sparingly, especially when it came to outsiders. This boy couldn't be *more* on the outside. So why did I feel bad for doing what I was supposed to do?

Why, when he walked away, did I feel a prick of anger at myself—for destroying any chance of forming future trust? Wasn't trust just another opportunity to get hurt? Footsteps neared, stopping before me. I lifted my gaze to meet rebuke in Flint's eyes.

"Don't look at me like that," I said, hiding my face again.

"What possessed you to rankle him like that? I was there for most of it. You didn't sound yourself."

"I don't know what came over me. I just, I got tired of how—how he almost always keeps it together. Flint, there's no real *spark* to him. Had you ever seen him be anything but mild?"

Flint offered no example.

"It was getting under my skin. Maybe I was wrong to do it, but I just had to know if there was any *anger* in him. I don't know." I lowered my head again.

I looked up at Flint, waiting for him to reprimand me. He just stared into the distance.

I tried to sound positive. "I suppose I should say something to him."

Flint didn't turn.

"But I don't know what," I finished lamely.

Flint turned back, and after a moment, his eyes re-engaged. He shook his head. "No, you two stay here. I'll go and talk to him." He walked off in the direction Ian had gone, then turned back. "Don't wander off."

When he joined us at the fire nearly an hour later, he simply shrugged at my questioning look and sat beside me. His eyes were heavy.

"I've said all I can say," he sighed softly.

We sat quietly, watching shapes form in the flames.

"It's up to him to believe or not believe me," he said.

I turned to him. "What if he doesn't?"

"I wouldn't be surprised. You hurt him deeply, Kyndle. I don't know if we can gain his trust again."

I stared into the fire for several minutes.

"Why should we gain his trust?" I finally asked aloud. I heard a touch of irritation in my own voice. "He isn't even supposed to be here!"

Flint sighed. "I suppose it is useless. It would just make it pleasanter if there wasn't this tension between us."

I fell back onto my back and sighed. By now, Mum and Dad would be locking the door, hoping we were safe as they settled down to a restless evening. I missed them terribly. I missed Frieman. There was a long silence.

"Good night," Flint said.

"Good night."

As I lay there, I felt an unwillingness to humble myself to Ian. What was I to say? He really *wasn't* supposed to be here. He was a foreigner who had stepped into my life and interrupted it. I tried to forget the fact that none of it had been his fault.

Some time had passed before a soft step approached. I lay quiet as Ian came near. From where I lay in the shadows, I knew that he wouldn't see my face; but the firelight illuminated his so that I could see him clearly. His hair was tousled, and in his eyes was a soft sadness that chilled me—a sadness than seemed used to being there. He lay down a few feet from the fire, then all was still.

My guilt pricked at me again. Maybe I should say something now, not let it go on until tomorrow. I had all but decided to do it when something like a whisper met my ear.

"Dear God."

My urge to speak evaporated into thin air, and I lay still in the echoey darkness of the night. I wasn't about to interrupt.

"Dear God," came his soft plea. "Everything within me is asking why you've brought me t' this place, what you want me t' learn here, what you want me to *do* here."

Curiosity tickled my ears and I strained to listen as he went on.

"They think I'm a spy," he continued. "They think I've come here just t' exploit them like so many others have, and I want t' be angry at them, but then I remember how fortunate I am t' have been giv'n this chance at all. They could've just killed me. I'm sure many still want t'. They have been so hurt by those over them, they don't know how t' be anythin' but suspicious. They don't know how to trust anyone not of their own blood." He sighed. "I couldn't be further from that."

There was a silence so long I wondered if he'd fallen asleep, but then I heard him again. His voice shook so I could hardly decipher his words. The pain from earlier was recalled in his voice.

"If there's somethin' I need t' do," he wept, his voice rising in pitch. "If there's something I need t' say…show me." I heard his sobs clearly as he paused. "I just want t' go home. She's *waitin'* for me. 'Tisn't good for her t' be so worried again."

His sobs quieted, and there was another long silence.

Suddenly a falling star streaked across the sky, and Ian's words flashed across my mind, *I watch the stars, and sometimes, I see one fall. It makes me even more in awe of Christ.*

I hoped he had seen it. Maybe I was feeling guilty. Maybe I wasn't. It didn't really matter. I just hoped that despite his pain and hurt, he could see something out of the ordinary.

"Lord," Ian prayed long after I thought he had fallen asleep. "T'anks for all that you've already done that I can't see jist yet, and t'anks for the things I have been able t' see."

It was just a few minutes before I could hear him breathing evenly, in sleep; but for a long time, I sat in quiet reflection, thinking long and hard about this strange boy from a strange country, praying to his strange God. They weren't ridiculing thoughts; rather they brought a realization of the even stranger fact that somehow, during this still quiet time of listening, I had grown to respect him.

Such faith—to believe not only that something *good* was being worked out *through* a trial, but that he hoped to one day *see* the results of all of it. As I lay there, recalling his quiet prayer, something deep in me whispered *t'anks* right along with him.

At first it startled me, but then I wanted to say it again. A fierce desire welled up to thank *someone* for the mountains, for the warmth of the fire, for the shooting stars—for all the bad things that could have happened to us but hadn't yet also the simple good things that *had* happened despite the odds—to acknowledge that though I couldn't yet see the good ending, I fully believed that, one day, it was surely coming.

It felt strangely right.

I watched for another falling star, but it didn't come.

chapter NINE

When I awoke, Flint was waiting for me.

"Morning," he whispered.

A yawn prevented me from answering.

"Time's running out," he said.

"I know."

"Kyndle, we're *going* to be home by tomorrow night. I'm not putting our people at risk. We have till midday. If we don't find the cave by then, we have to head back."

I growled in frustration. "I don't want to fail."

"Neither do I, but I'd rather fail him," nodding in Ian's direction, "than our people."

Ian stirred and we quickly hushed. Flint quietly got up, but I chanced a glance at our companion. The sunlight touched his face and showed the silver trails that I knew to be dried tears. All at once, I recalled his prayer and the strange effect it had had on me. I slipped away quietly to fetch the morning's supply of water. I didn't want to be the first thing he saw when he awoke, and I'm sure the feeling was mutual.

When I returned, everyone was up.

Reviving the glowing embers of the previous night's fire, I set a large flat stone in the fire and laid several slabs of salted bacon over it. In the meantime, Ruby scavenged around and was able to find some berries to accompany our simple breakfast. Then we set to work with a will, all but Ruby who remained at the fire, warming herself and keeping it alive.

The hours passed without us finding anything that Ian recognized. I watched his eyes grow discouraged.

By midmorning, we all had to admit that it was time to give it up. Ian was sorely disappointed. And while we tried our best to sympathize with him, it was hard to mask our happiness at going home. Tossing my pack on over my cloak, I suddenly realized how near Ian was standing to me. He stood at the fire, his back to me. Ruby sat across from him but didn't look up at him.

"Ian," I said.

He didn't turn.

"*Ian*," I said more firmly.

I heard him take a deep breath through his nose, then exhale through his mouth as if to calm himself. He straightened, then I saw him turn his head very slightly to the left. I took it as my cue.

"Ian," I said, looking at the ground. "About last night—"

"Who did I think I was fooling?" He kept his back to me. "You really *don't* want me here, you're glad t' be goin' home and mad at me for takin' you from it."

"Ian—"

"No, it's okay," he said, turning. His eyes were full of disappointment. He looked away for a moment and then looked back. "There's no use in tryna hide the fact that you don't like me. I don't blame you so go ahead. It's normal to miss your family. I know." He shrugged and began to walk away.

Ruby glanced at me, pleading me not to give up.

"Ian," I called to him, "you're wrong in thinking we don't like you."

He stopped and slowly turned back around.

"I know I can speak for both myself and the others when I say that we all *like* you."

He cocked his head and glanced at Ruby. She nodded. He glanced back at me as though unsure.

"Truly," I said.

His face looked halfway curious, so I hurried on.

"What I said last night wasn't fair. I let my words run away and said things that aren't what I feel. Not in my right mind, at least." I laughed, and his face lifted a bit. "Your quiet attitude toward life irritated me, but it wasn't until last night I realized I actually respect you for it. So I want you to know that—I'm sorry."

There. I had said it. And I had really meant it too. His emerald eyes regained a bit of their sparkle, and Ian smiled—the first *real* smile I had ever seen from him.

"T'anks," he said before leaving.

I went looking for Flint and found him sitting among a group of large boulders, deep in his own thoughts. I went up to him.

"I talked to Ian. We're fine now."

He was surprised into a grin. "Just like that?"

I nodded and glanced down at the vista below. "Maybe things will get better when we get home." As I finished speaking, I turned back to Flint's face and was puzzled to see that his smile had faded.

"Kyndle," he said hesitantly. "You know what may happen when we go home."

I thought for a moment. *Surely not.*

I chuckled, but it wasn't real. "They wouldn't."

Flint was in earnest. "We couldn't find this magical cave he swore he came out of. They may conclude that his story is fake and start jumping to their own conclusions."

My conclusions.

"A spy?"

He nodded then looked at the ground. "You saw their faces."

I had. Again I heard the conversation at the table; again I saw Coal's angry face, looking at me from my mind's eye. I felt the blood drain from my face.

"They wouldn't," I said again. "They can't."

He said nothing. Fear began to pound in my ears. I grabbed his shirt.

"Flint, you have to do something!"

"I can't, Kyndle!" He flung my hands off, a fear of his own surfacing in his eyes. "I don't know what else to do!"

I paced in a frenzy, biting my thumbnail. What *could* we do? I missed Mum and Dad; I missed being home, but I couldn't stomach the thought of going back now. We just *had* to keep looking, even if we went over our allowed days. It would be unthinkable to take Ian back. Flint was right—Char had said that some favored the option of "doing away with him." If news of him got out, I didn't doubt that the villagers would follow through with it.

Ian wasn't my friend, but I did have respect for him. The bloody image of him being killed by a mob made me feel sick. Yet if we missed the roll call, there was no telling what consequences it would bring. Other people, people I actually *loved,* and truly *cared for,* could be killed by the Snow Sprite soldiers.

Boots clinking and smiles flashing, the soldiers would enjoy it. I was so torn. More than that, I was suddenly exhausted. Dropping to my knees beside Flint's rock, I cried. Had I really thought this opportunity was a dream come true? It was quickly becoming a nightmare.

"Kyndle, *don't,"* Flint said, his voice pleading. He had never seen me cry.

But I couldn't help it. It was all just so unfair. Why couldn't they have chosen someone else? Why *us?* I knew Ruby would be heartbroken when she heard what lay ahead.

And Ian. How could we tell him? Alone in a faraway land, not even knowing where home is anymore. His grandmother waiting for him, hope beginning to wane as another day passed and another sun set.

Fran's little grave, mossing with age, empty without its daily visitor.

A footstep that wasn't Ruby's met my ear. I swiped at my tears, my embarrassment evident as I looked up at Ian. I watched his face grow sad.

"I wanted to apologize, too," he said, sitting on the rock beside ours.

Flint and I said nothing.

Ian took a deep breath. "I was wrong, Kyndle—you do have a heart. I can see it now."

I couldn't answer. I was surprised. He didn't need to apologize.

He sighed softly. "You cry because they may kill me if we go back."

I nodded, swiping angrily at my nose with my sleeve. "They'll think *you're* a spy because *we* couldn't find the cave."

His brown eyebrows lifted. "And you don't?"

I shook my head. "Not anymore."

This time, it was he who couldn't answer.

"I suspected it," I explained, "but I was wrong. You're like my friend, Auburn—you're different from the rest, in a good way."

He gave a faint smile.

"I've been watching you for the last several days," I stammered. "I've seen how you wanted to give up but didn't. You wanted to be back with your grandmother because you miss her. You're scared of going back to Frieman, but you didn't ever lash out at us about it."

"I did last night," he said, looking down at his lap.

"No, you didn't," I objected. "I did." I dropped my head and one tear traced down my cheek. To my surprise, Ian reached across and brushed it from my cheek with the back of his hand.

Flint leaned forward slightly, chest expanding in a quick breath.

I drew back, embarrassed, and so did Ian.

"I'm sorry," he said after a moment. "I just—I can't bear t' see anyone cry. It so broke my heart when Fran did."

I drew in a shaky breath. "I'm sorry."

He rose. "It's almost time to go."

When he had gone, I looked up at Flint who sat without moving.

"We can't go home."

"Kyndle, we *have* to. We can't just stay out here. Pretty soon, they'll come looking for us. What then?"

"We can't take him home!" I began to cry again. "They'll *kill* him!"

"We can try to talk them out of it."

I was about to protest again when it occurred to me that he was right.

"Listen." He leaned forward. "You know the costs. The representative will notice that we're missing. Firelings could be killed. On top of that, we have Ruby to worry about as well. You know how cold she's been for days on end."

I looked away.

"Kyndle," he said, "I think the councilmen are reasonable, and I know Dad is. Besides the cardinal may be back. Surely he'll understand."

With a sigh, I surrendered. What could I say?

We shared our hopes with Ian, and he shook our hands quietly.

"T'anks," he said with another of his sad smiles.

I went to Ruby and very gently told her the situation. She took it very calmly, but as she pulled the cloak tighter around her, I saw fear beneath her features.

Our few belongings in hand, we began the trek down the mountain. Flint took us a slightly different route down.

"For a different view," he told us, but I knew it was really in hopes of keeping our minds off the difficulty ahead.

He went first, then me. Ruby followed close behind, then Ian came last. We made good progress. The breeze seemed to get warmer with each step, brushing the hair back from our foreheads. Ian and I soon pulled off our cloaks and stuffed them into my pack.

Flint said little. I knew that he was preparing himself for the return to Frieman and all of her invisible walls. As well as the tragedy that might await us there.

The hours passed quickly. It was much easier going down, so in much less time than before, we found ourselves nearing the mountain's sloping foot.

"Whoa now," Flint said, startling me from my thoughts. "This looks a bit unsteady."

He stopped, putting an arm out to stop further progress. I peered over his shoulder.

The grass had been replaced by a long stretch of small dusty pebbles and rock fragments—all that was left of a small landslide. It certainly did look very unstable. I glanced around, realizing quickly that our only other option was to retrace our steps and find another path down—which would take up considerable time. Flint started forward.

I grasped at his arm a bit frantically. "What are you doing?"

His forehead creased. "I have to find a safe route down."

"Flint—" In my mind, I could see my villagers' faces, taunting me for my weakness. Swallowing my words, I forced myself to release his arm. "Just be careful."

"Of course," he said over his shoulder. Gingerly he tested his weight on the loose rocks.

I felt Ruby take hold of my arm. "I hope Flint doesn't slip," she said.

No sooner had the words escaped her lips that he did that very thing. I watched in horror as the entire slope gave way, carrying him down the side of the mountain, leaving behind only his panicked cry. Before I could even let out a scream, the ground underneath my own feet trembled and broke.

Ian snatched Ruby backward to safety as I too was borne away.

My ride was short-lived. The rocks on which I had slid met a slightly flatter plane and halted altogether. I lay panting amid the dust, Flint's cry ringing in my ears. In a moment, my wits returned. Without a thought of my own peril, I vaulted onto my feet and found myself once more being borne downward. Something hard knocked against my head, and I drifted into semiconsciousness.

I'm not sure how long I lay at the mountain's foot. As consciousness gradually returned, I strove to reorient myself. Pulsing adrenaline pushed away the pain of any injury as I struggled to my feet amid the debris. I vaguely noticed that my knee was bleeding through my torn pant leg, but my only thought was for Flint. I scanned the dusty slope fearfully, but he wasn't in sight.

I suddenly became aware of a stealthy step behind me. Before I could turn, a heavy hand clamped over my mouth.

Lashing out angrily with my foot, I made contact with what felt like a leg. There was a hiss of pain; but rather than being released, a strong arm wrapped around my middle, lifting me off the ground, and I felt myself being carried away. I struggled but could feel the adrenaline wearing off. The bruises and cuts I hadn't known were there began to sting fiercely across my entire frame.

Suddenly, with an unexpected gentleness, I was set down in a patch of tall grass. Surprised, I looked up into Ian's face.

"Don't move," he gasped, dropping to his knees beside me.

"But *Flint!*" I argued, starting to my feet.

"Y' can't—!" He pulled me back down.

"Would you stop it?" I demanded, trying to shrug off his grip.

With lightning speed, Ian used both arms to restrain me with a barrel hold, then put his mouth close to my ear.

"Be quiet," he whispered, his voice firm, "and look straight ahead."

Following his instructions, I saw Flint.

chapter TEN

Due north, in a clearing, Flint stood encircled by five or six uniformed soldiers, arms pinioned. All the men had white hair.

I felt myself stiffen.

"What's your business here, boy?" asked one who seemed the leader. His arms were crossed across his narrow chest and an ornate sword hung from a jeweled scabbard at his hip. His voice carried well over the dusty rocks to our hiding place.

Flint coughed but didn't reply.

The leader hauled off and struck him right across his face. I heard it even from where we hid in the grass.

Flint wilted in the guard's grip, head falling wearily onto his chest.

The leader thrust his face inches from Flint's. *"What* is your *business here?"* he repeated cruelly.

Flint lifted his head to look the man in the eye but still said nothing. Panic rose in my throat as the leader took several steps back and crossed his arms again.

"It would appear that he needs some encouragement," he said.

The soldier to Flint's left promptly struck my brother in the stomach. As Flint fell onto his knees in the rocks, a second soldier planted a boot in his ribs. My throat squeaked as blows rained on Flint.

"You have t' be quiet," Ian whispered in my ear, but his voice broke as he said it.

Flint let out a soft cry, followed by another, then another. Tears began to pour from my eyes and I felt the anger pounding in my chest. Ian put his hands over my ears and pressed my head to his shoulder, doing all he could to shield me from the sound of the vicious blows—but I still heard them. I ground my teeth, my mind whirling with thoughts of black anger and hatred.

After an eternity of Flint's cries, they finally stopped. Wiping away my tears, I peered through the tall grass.

Flint lay on the ground, curled into a ball, face hidden from view. The subordinate soldiers stood nearby with fists balled, awaiting further order with apparent readiness. After a moment, their leader spoke.

"What a surprise to find you out here," he said crisply. "We're on our way to Frieman to replace the squadron stationed there. Does your representative know you're so far from the village?"

Flint didn't answer or imply he had heard. I wasn't sure he was even conscious.

"Pull him up."

Flint was jerked to his feet, but if they hadn't held him, he would have fallen. He swayed dangerously as it was.

"What is your business out here?" came the grating question for the third time.

Flint didn't—couldn't—respond. It cost him. The chalky-white hand flapped, and they began to beat him again.

Every fiber of my being screamed at the injustice before my eyes, and I found myself starting to rise from the grass.

"Don't be daft," Ian whispered, yanking me back down.

I tried to shake him off. No longer could I sit and watch on as these northern cowards loosed their hatred on my brother—my own blood. My entire life had prepared me for this one moment. This was what our hate was for. I felt for the dagger still sheathed at my belt.

For the first time in this second beating, Flint loosed a yell. I tossed my head, a rebel war cry rising in my throat.

But it was not to be.

Ian slapped his hand across my mouth and firmly held me down.

"We're outnumbered," he said in my ear. "There's nothing we can do right now."

I watched as Flint's beating ended with a vicious kick.

"What mischief could he be working up on the mountain?" the leader asked out loud.

For a few moments, eerie silence cloaked the mountainside. Then the Snowling leader began to look at his surroundings. His eyes scanned right over right at our hiding spot. I closed mine as if to keep him from seeing us.

"And is he alone?" I heard him ask.

When I opened my eyes again, he had turned back to Flint. "Take him back to camp and tie him up," he said to two of the soldiers. "Tell Stag of our little discovery and let him know to be on the alert. He may want to remain behind and search while we continue on. You other four, come with me. We're going to have a look around."

The two yanked Flint to his feet and dragged him east; the others trudged after their officer in the opposite direction of our hiding place. Letting out a sigh of relief, Ian took his hand off my mouth. Rising to a cautious crouch, he watched until the soldiers went out of sight. Then he leapt to his feet.

"Come on," he said, extending a hand. "We've got t' get out of here."

Now that the immediate danger was past, all of the muscles I had been tensing suddenly went limp. The two-hundred-foot rock ride hadn't been a fun one, and the adrenaline had officially worn off.

"Come on," he said again.

I lifted weary eyes to his, feeling again a hesitation to trust him.

He dropped to his knees in front of me. "I can't demand your trust for my sake. That's something that only comes with time. But I can ask it for Ruby's sake. I can't leave her alone, and I can't leave you alone."

For one moment, I hesitated. Then, almost against my will, I grabbed the hand he offered.

He pulled me onto my own feet and began nearly dragging me up the side of the mountain at breakneck speed.

"But what about Flint?" I demanded when out of earshot.

"There nothing to be done," he said over his shoulder. "We need t' get back t' Ruby and find somewhere t' hide until they finish their search."

A few minutes passed, then we came to a sudden stop before a jagged wall of rock. Pulling aside a net of shrubbery near the bottom, Ian leaned down and called, "Ruby, come!" into the hollow that had been revealed. I tried to catch my breath as my sister crawled out. Her face lit up when she saw me, but when she leapt to hug me, I almost toppled.

"Where's Flint?" came her sudden question.

"Tell you on the way," Ian said, striking off. "Right now, we've got to find a place to lay low for a couple hours."

"Where do we go?" I asked, nearly tripping over a low-hanging vine. Part of me recoiled at his taking charge; the rest of me was glad that he'd done it.

"Back to our campsite. There's no tellin' how many of them there are on the ground. If we make a run for your village, we may run into more of them. But since we know there aren't any more of them on the mountain, it's the safest place t' stay. They probably only came this far up because they saw the avalanche."

"And once we *reach* camp?"

"We'll find a place to hide," he replied. "The most important thing at this point is getting there."

After a grueling two-hour hike, we arrived without any incident. Ruby dropped beside the cold ashes of the previous night's fire, but she was too overheated to shiver. I stood at the cliff's edge.

"Maybe we can spot them from here," I said.

"Kyndle," Ian urged. "We have to find a place to hide. Further up."

"Wait," I snapped, craning my neck. By now, I was tired of his giving orders.

"If you can see them, they can see us. Let's go. Ruby, come."

I turned to see her wearily pull herself to her feet. I pushed down my frustration and we fell in step behind Ian. He was right—I now had Ruby to think about.

We reached the snow line and the sweat on our bodies quickly chilled. We stumbled miserably along, our arms hanging loose. I was about to ask for a rest when a distant voice met my ear.

"Down!" Ian whispered, and we dropped to our faces.

He wriggled forward on his stomach and very slowly looked over the edge of the cliff. He instantly drew back.

"Soldiers," he whispered. "Not far down. They didn't see me."

Ruby and I exchanged fearful looks, then turned back to Ian.

"We have to hide," he said. "Now."

Keeping low and close to the mountain face, we had edged thirty or so more feet up the path when I glanced back over my shoulder. Something caught my eye. "Ian."

"What?"

I pointed. "How about that?"

He hurried to my side and followed the trajectory of my finger. From this angle, standing basically up against the rock, I saw a narrow crevice further down the mountain face—invisible to anyone unless they stood in this very peculiar spot. Even now, it was hardly visible. I turned to Ian and he nodded quickly.

"It'll have t' do. Maybe they won't even come this far up."

We hurried back down and paused at the entrance. It was barely wide enough for Ian to enter straight on but we had no option. He tossed a rock into the cavern and, when nothing stirred, turned to us.

"Ruby first," Ian said. "If something happens I want her farthest from the door."

With a glance that reminded me of her dislike of dark places, she did as she was told. I followed quickly behind her and Ian behind me. About fifteen feet in, Ruby and I came face-to-face with a solid cold rock wall. Thankfully there seemed to be no tenants. None that were home, at least. Ruby shivered in the chilly air.

I slid down to a seat on my haunches, but the others remained on their feet. I noticed that Ian had grown very quiet. Listening for any movement outside, no doubt. It was a quick gasp from Ruby that struck fear into me. I jumped up to look into her face.

"Kyndle," she said in dismay, "my feet are burning."

HOME ROAD

I stared at her, then turned to Ian. All the blood had drained from his face.

"Run!" I cried, slamming up against him, trying to push him toward the entrance but unable with all my might to even budge him or myself, for that matter. We both now seemed to weigh a million pounds.

"I can't go!" I screamed at him, each word coming out painfully slow. A gray mist began to fill the air.

He pushed heavily down on my shoulders, and I sank to my knees in a tormenting slow motion. The mist continued to fill the cave. I vaguely felt Ruby against my back, and I realized dimly that she was on her knees as well. Ian sank down in front of me, a helpless expression on his face. His mouth seemed to form words, but I couldn't understand them.

Before I could think anything more, the ground opened beneath us. We plunged into nothingness.

From behind, I thought I heard Ruby screaming. I attempted to turn but it took all my strength to lift my knee. What was my knee even sitting on? I gritted my teeth, bent on getting to her, but a sudden wave of nausea hit me like a ton of bricks. I gave up. A wind stirred up around me, whipping my hair around my face.

Just as it seemed as though it could get no worse, everything began to return to normal.

As if out of nowhere, I found myself on firm ground. It was as though we had never left it, and I tried to figure out if the falling had just been a dream. I pulled my arms away from my face and glanced around.

Ian and Ruby sat on either side, their faces reflecting the shock I felt. We got to our feet and waited for the mist to fade. When it did, we stood in a cave larger than the one we had just left. We broke out into sunlight across a grassy hillside. Up above, the sky held no clouds. A gentle breeze tickled our faces. A sheep *baa*ed nearby. I turned to Ian.

"Scotland?"

For an answer, he took off running down the hillside.

"He'll be looking for his grandmother," I said, tossing an arm around Ruby's shoulders. "Let's go slow to give them a moment."

We worked our way down the hill, taking in the sights around us with the shock of newcomers. It was similar to our home, but these vistas were much more vast and beautiful. Yet despite the beauty around us, my mind threw all my troubles in my face. The cardinal was missing, Auburn sent to find him, this mission, Flint captured, we were due home by tomorrow or catastrophe could ensue—and now, to top it off, Ruby and I had been sucked through a portal to a place called Scotland, and we had no idea how far away it was from home. Or if we could get back.

In short, everything had gone wrong. All worst-case scenarios had become reality. So much for an adventure.

After several more minutes, a small cottage with a thatched roof came into view below, waiting with the welcoming familiarity of an old friend. There was a door nestled in the closest side; two wooden steps led up to it. A basket with freshly cut flowers spilling over the sides completed the homey scene.

I glanced down at Ruby and smiled in spite of our troubles.

As we approached, the door was pulled open and Ian stepped through it. Following close behind him was a small elderly lady who I knew was Nanna. Her silver hair was pulled into a neat bun and ancient laugh lines framed her thin face. She smiled at us as we approached, her face aflood with both disbelief and delight.

"Nanna," Ian said as we reached them, "this is Kyndle and Ruby."

Her smile brightened. It wasn't till I pulled my arm from Ruby's shoulders that I realized how much I was leaning on her. I dropped to my knees. When I tried to lift my head, my vision spun. I shut my eyes and fell forward on my hands.

"I'm sorry," I heard myself say.

"Don't you worry, m'dearie—" came a sweet aged voice in an accent matching Ian's. A soft hand came to a rest upon my head. "Come inside and rest." Her voice grew more distant with each word, and I felt a strong pair of arms encircling me.

I had just enough brainpower to say, "Wait."

The arms pulled back.

My hands heavy as logs, I fumbled at my belt and somehow managed to pull out my dagger. I didn't resist when it was taken from me or when I felt myself lifted off my knees. It felt *so* good just to give in. Then all at once, I was sinking into a soft bed.

I cracked open my eyes and vaguely saw Ruby take a seat beside the bed. Clouded bits of conversation met my ears, Ian's soft voice foremost among them.

"As you kin imagine," I heard him say, then his voice went so low I couldn't hear it.

"The poor dearie," Nanna said, and I knew they were referring to me.

Despite my nearly-unconscious state, something deep inside rebelled at such a title. *The poor dearie.* This said of a Fire Sprite! Unable to make my mouth form words, I groaned my protest. I felt a blanket tucked under my chin and remembered nothing more.

chapter ELEVEN

Bigots. Frauds. Their pride will be their undoing.
My journal entry, now a distant memory, echoed throughout the dark shadows of my mind.

> *But they're wrong. We will show them this.*
> *They will soon learn that the Fire Sprites are a people to be reckoned with, and they'll never forget it as long as they live.*

Out of the murky blackness, color and depth swirled to form Char's face, then his crackled voice met my ear. *A boy from an unknown realm was found wandering inside our border yesterday evening.*
We've laid a heavy responsibility on your shoulders, but I think we've not done it lightly. Anvil's voice. *Flint and Kyndle, you have our trust.*
I love you. My father's deep voice boomed in the boundless reaches of my mind.
Be safe. Mum's gentle words calmed me.
Auburn's voice overcame me. *I'm not alone. Christ is with me.*
But I was afraid.
As usual I turned to Auburn for the comforting words she was always so willing to give. But she wasn't there. Cloudy fingers groped for where her existence should have been but met only mist.
Auburn is gone!
Panic surged through me, and I screamed again.
She's gone! And I didn't believe her!

Ian Freemont. The gentle introduction soothed my fear for a moment. I wasn't alone after all. Maybe things weren't as bleak as they seemed.

The temporary relief was quickly blanched by Flint's words.

You know what may happen when we go home.

He avoided my gaze.

You saw their faces.

We can't go home. My own voice was firm. *They'll kill him!*

A hand reached to brush my tears away.

Whoa now. This looks a bit unsteady. Flint's voice was wary. In my mind's eye, I saw him stepping lightly over the shifting stones. Then they swept him up, devouring him in one dusty gulp.

I ran for him, but then a wind whistled across my vision and the scene changed. Before my eyes, my brother was being beaten. I tried to go to him, but my arms were pinned.

You have t' be quiet, came Ian's broken whisper in my ear.

What's your business here, boy? The voice dripped with hate.

Eerie silence filled time and space.

It would appear that he needs some encouragement.

Again I heard every blow that had been inflicted on Flint's body. But now, there were no answering cries.

This time, when the memories swirled to form a picture, Flint lay on the ground without moving. I saw myself—weeping across his still body. The echoes of my cries streaked through my mind, piercing the darkness in shafts of burning lightning.

Kyndle. Spoken in a dying whisper, I heard Flint's voice say my name one last time.

Flint, no! Don't leave me!

I thought that, well, that you trusted me. Again the wind whistled, this time bringing me face-to-face with Ian and his emerald eyes—holding so much hurt.

You thought we trusted you? My laugh echoed loudly.

I thought you cared for me. The pain in his voice tore through me like a plow rips through dirt.

You thought that we cared *for you?*

That hateful voice—was it really mine?

Like we'd trust a Snowling spy.

You don't believe me. The voice was mostly Ian, but I heard overtones of Auburn's soft voice as well.

I do! my mind answered, but the memory of my own voice answered in sarcasm and scorn, *Why should I believe you?*

In my mind, Ian stiffened. His eyes went hard.

I was wrong. I thought you had a heart, Kyndle. Yes, I thought you cared.

Gone was any trace of Auburn's voice; I now spoke to Ian alone. On his shoulder was a pack. He was ready to leave me. As he turned to go, I grasped at his arm but my fingers passed through him as if he was a ghost. Finally I managed to smother all the memories with my own voice.

No, I want you to stay!

Again I grasped for his arm. He turned, but his face was changed. His eyes stood out heavily among his other features.

In them, emerald tears swam.

Please, don't leave! I begged, the guilt of all I had said washing over me like a tidal wave.

I guess I was wrong. Again he turned to go. *I thought you had a heart, Kyndle. I thought you cared.*

I do have a heart! I shouted wearily. *I do care for you!*

You care for me? he repeated.

But when he turned, it wasn't Ian—it was Tinder. A smile covered his freckled face. I took a step back, feeling again that awkwardness between us. His smiled faded and hurt came into his eyes. The wind whistled, and in an instant, it was Ian once more. *I thought you cared.*

I do care!

I thought you had a heart, Kyndle.

The wind whistled a fourth time, and Ian blew away like dust.

No! I cried, but he was gone.

You just don't believe me, do you? Auburn suddenly took Ian's barren place, and the sorrow in her question pierced my heart like a poison dart. No shield could protect me from it.

That is it, isn't it? she demanded in her quiet way.

All deflective words caught in my throat. I couldn't reply. It was true—I hadn't believed her.

In my head, I could hear mocking thoughts which I knew to be mine. I felt them written all over my face, like a stain I couldn't scrub away even with my best intentions. The wind began to blow again, and before my eyes she faded, just like Ian.

All Auburn left behind was her heart.

It was empty, carved clean by loneliness.

It was torn, shredded by doubt.

It was wounded, sliced by unbelief.

All the friends I had truly loved were now gone—banished by my own hand. Now I was left in darkness.

Empty, alone, yearning to be filled. That was how I felt.

I stood in silence, my arms reaching, hoping.

Is there no one left to love me? I cried to the stillness.

"M' dearie…"

The soft voice pulled me back to reality. It was the piece of driftwood to which I clung with all my being—lest drowning memories overwhelm me again.

"Kyndle." The voice sounded closer.

Summoning consciousness, I opened my eyes. Nanna was seated by my bed. On her lap was a book.

"Are you all right?" she asked. "Y' seemed restless."

I found my voice. "Just a bad dream."

"Is there anything I can get you?"

"No. I'll just stay here a little bit longer."

"That's fine. You need all the rest you kin get. You've been through a lot, m' dearie." She leaned to pat my hand. "Ian has told me all."

"Thank you, Mrs.—?"

"Just call me Nanna."

"Nanna, where is my sister?"

"She's asleep in the loft. I hope Ian is restin' as well. He refused t' do so till he was sure you were both comfortable."

"I've been glad to have him near since my brother was taken," I said, and to my consternation, I felt tears tickle the back of my eyes.

I refused to let them out. They would disappoint Flint. I knew he would want me to be strong like he had been.

"I'm proud he kept you safe," Nanna said. "He's always been good at doin' that for others."

For a moment, I said nothing. Then I glanced into her face and found in her eyes a welcoming which encouraged me to speak. I drew in a deep breath before doing so.

"He told us about—about Fran."

The brightness slowly left her eyes, forced out by that same sad smile I had seen on Ian's face.

"Fran," she said. "Our little ray o' sunshine."

"He told us how he rescued her from the ice—"

She closed her eyes as if in pain, and I suddenly wished I hadn't said anything.

"Yes," she finally whispered, "he did."

"You don't have to say anything else," I said. "I—I just thought you should know."

"It's been five years now." She opened her eyes to look at me. "All I know is, Christ was her strength. He never left her, even in the wake of death."

Maybe it was the way she said it—so familiarly, so lovingly, as though speaking of a person as real as me. Maybe it was my own weariness—or maybe it was something else entirely. But to my surprise, I didn't cringe at the name of Christ.

Instead I asked my first question.

"Who *is* Christ?"

She smiled, and the strength that wasn't there before now shone in her voice. "Christ is the only true Son of the only true God," she said softly. "He was sent from heav'n t' rescue his own from the punishment for their sin, to become the perfect Lamb that tore apart the dividin' line between God and man. He became the bridge connecting us for good. No longer do we need to offer up lambs and bulls in payment for our wrongdoings. On that day—the dark day of his bodily death—he became the *ultimate* sacrifice."

I said nothing for a few moments. "I'm not sure I understand."

She chuckled quietly. "It's hard t' take in. Even I, believin' over fifty years, still learn more about him as the days go by. Most the time, I feel more a bairn in the ways of God than the seasoned woman I thought that I would be by now. Want me t' continue?"

I nodded eagerly.

She smiled. "Let me read t' you from his Word."

"Is it," I asked as she opened the book in her lap, "called Bible?"

"Yes, the Bible."

"My friend, Auburn, always read from it. I thought it weird, so I never let her read it to me."

She paused in her page-turning. "And now?"

What are you doing? my mind shrilled.

"Please go on," my mouth said.

With a smile, she continued flipping as if searching for just the right thing to read. "Here," she said at last. "I'll read several verses from John, chapter 1."

I nodded and she began.

"In the beginning was the Word, and the Word was with God, and the Word *was* God. He was in the beginning with God. All things were made through Him and without Him was not anything made that was made. In Him was life—and the life was the light o' men. The light shines in the darkness, and the darkness has not overcome it."

I smiled. "That sounds like something my friend would say."

She smiled. "When you love Christ, he permeates your every word— your every thought."

"Auburn must have loved Christ a lot."

She was silent, giving me time to continue if I wanted. I did after a moment.

"Everyone thought she was just weird. I was her only friend, but even I was unkind to her at times." A sudden strange feeling came over me—why was I speaking of her in past tense? Shaking it off, I glanced back at Nanna. Her brow had saddened.

"When we follow Christ," she said slowly, "we can expect persecution. For some, it has meant death. For others, a harsh word or action."

I clasped my hands. "Though I never told her, even *I* thought she was weird in some ways."

"Persecution doesn't always come from just our enemies. Sometimes the deepest wounds are from those we love most." She paused. "My own husband scorned me for many years until Christ drew him t' himself."

"I wouldn't believe her. I still don't. And I know it hurt her."

"But despite the hurtful things you did, is she still your friend?"

"Yes."

She patted my hand firmly. "That's forgiveness. It's what Christ does when we repent of our sin, and that unmerited love—the thing we deserve least of all—makes us strive t' be more and more like him."

I glanced away. Was it all so strange after all? Or was I who was strange for thinking so?

I rubbed slowly at my eyes. "I miss her." A tear fell onto my blanket.

Weakling.

She brushed my cheek with a handkerchief from her apron pocket.

"We can't predict if or when if the portal will take us home." I sniffed. "It might be *years*. Maybe *never!*" More tears came despite my protest.

Nanna gave me the handkerchief for my own, then she left. After a few minutes, I heard the door open again.

"I'm sorry." I sniffed as the distinctive footsteps came near. "We've caused so much trouble for you and your grandmother."

"I've caused you plenty of trouble too."

I took a deep breath. "We have to go home, Ian."

"I'll get you home, Kyndle. Somehow. I promise."

"No, you won't," I said, looking up at him. "You can't go back with us. The whole reason we left to begin with was to get you home. We've done that. Now we need to do the same before…" My voice died in my throat. "Before they kill Flint."

He looked down, a battle clearing playing out across his face. When he lifted his eyes, I inadvertently latched onto his gaze. I needed whatever I saw there, whatever it was that seemed to have calmed him.

He sat on the edge of the bed and set his large hand on mine. Quiet panic jumped up and down my entire frame. Here he was again, looking at me with eyes that seemed to see straight through me; in them, a plain question I now was forced to ask myself.

Just *what* did I think of him?

More importantly, could I trust him?

Could I lower the weapon to which my fingers had nearly conformed, the weapon which seemed to so often protect but which, in the end, I now felt had hurt only me?

I took a deep breath, and I didn't pull my hand away.

He smiled and patted it reassuringly. "I want to help."

I shook my head. "You've done all you can. This is up to me now."

Yet as the words left my mouth, I wished I had accepted his help. He looked unsatisfied.

"Rest," was all he said before leaving.

chapter TWELVE

After a light supper, we all retired early. I learned that the room I had slept in before was Nanna's, so I moved into the loft with Ruby. My head barely hit the pallet before I was asleep again.

Fortunately I had no dreams.

Early the next morning, I crept from my pallet with care so as to not stir Ruby but also for other reasons. Every muscle I owned, including a few I didn't know I had, were now stiff and sore from the previous day's adventure. There was a small window nestled in the end of the garret, and I clumsily knelt in front of it. As I pulled back the coarse curtain, a quick gasp escaped me. Ruby stirred.

"What is it?" she said, a stretch expanding her syllables.

"It's so beautiful," I said, not turning. The huge mountain peaks stood bold and glorious in the sunrise, bolder and more glorious than any that we had back home. Ian's earlier words came to mind and rang true.

Turning, I saw that Ruby had fallen asleep once more.

Very quietly, I slipped into the robe Nanna lent me and climbed down the ladder into the small main room below.

Nanna stood at the far end of it, back to me as she stirred something in a large black pot nestled in a fireplace. She turned at my step. A sweet smile warmed her already-rosy cheeks.

"Come, sit close to the fireplace," she said, pulling a small chair close and patting the back of it. "Did you sleep well?"

"Oh, yes!" I said, smiling as I sat down.

"Pottage," she explained, in answer to my questioning look at the pot. She turned back to her stirring. "How old are you, dear? I think Ian told me, but I've forgotten."

"I'll be eighteen soon. What's today's date?"

"The fifth of April." She set four bowls on the small table behind us but, after a pause, returned one to the shelf. "Little Ruby," I heard her say. "I'll set some aside for her so she can sleep."

"Your months must be different from ours," I said as I stood to place spoons on the table. "My birthday comes on Elindar 12. That should be tomorrow, but I could be wrong."

"Happy early birthday!" she exclaimed, shaking a spice into the pot and stirring it in.

I glanced out the small window near the door, watching Ian approach.

"I hope I'll be home by then."

Nanna said nothing.

The kitchen door opened, and Ian came in. A fresh pair of clothes had greatly brightened his appearance.

"Morning," he said, setting down the bucket he was carrying.

"Morning," Nanna and I said in unison.

"You're just in time for breakfast," she said.

"A man usually is," he said, grinning at her as he pushed her chair in.

I quickly took my seat. I didn't need his help. I was capable. Yet at the same time, part of me regretted my independence. It might feel nice to be cared for.

Ian sat at the head of the little table. He and Nanna closed their eyes and I looked back out the window as he offered up a short prayer. When he had finished with an *amen*, Nanna stood to get the food. Ian buttered his bread thoughtfully, and when she had seated herself again, he spoke.

"Nanna," said very gently, "I've put a lot of thought in t' this, and I've decided that if you're willing, I plan t' try every possible way t' get these girls home—even if it means I go with them."

"Ruby and I will be fine," I said quickly.

"No, you won't be," he said firmly. "There are soldiers scouring that mountain. Even if you made it t' the ground, they might catch you."

"They might not."

"If I'm with you, you have more of a chance."

I said nothing. I knew he was right. Nanna sat down quietly, looking down at her steaming bowl. Clasping her hands, she set them on the table.

"Ian," said in a low trembling tone. "Those men—"

He set his hand on hers but said nothing. What *could* he say?

I leaned forward. "I can't guarantee anything," I said, "but I *can* assure you that Ian's kindness toward us will do much in turning the tide in his favor." What was I saying? Couldn't I handle it on my own? I couldn't seem to stop the words coming from my mouth. "Once Father hears our story, I'm confident that he'll do all he can to get Ian home safely to you again."

"So the men in your town will do as your father suggests?" I heard the agitation in Nanna's voice.

I paused. "It's very likely. We may have a few hotheads in the village, but even they possess a character that upholds honorable behavior. Ian's has been more than that."

He nodded at me, his eyes reflecting gratitude.

Nanna looked at Ian. I saw the struggle plainly on her face. "I just got you back," she said, her voice strained.

"She's right." Rubbing my arm, I leaned back in my chair. "Ruby and I will be fine. You don't have to worry about us." But despite my words, I turned my face to hide the sadness that I so suddenly felt at the thought of leaving without him. Without Ian!

"Kyndle."

I looked at him.

"I *do* have t' worry. It was me who you got in t' this."

"But it wasn't your fault," I said firmly. "The council sent us. Ruby and I aren't your obligation. We're theirs."

"But what if things have gone badly since we left and you walk right in t' a full-on war?"

At first, I didn't answer. That thought had troubled me as well.

"We have to try," I finally said. "I can manage."

To get us in trouble, I thought.

Nanna looked at her hands, and Ian looked at me with troubled eyes. Neither spoke, and we finished the meal in silence. I excused myself and climbed up to the loft to wake Ruby.

"And so you think we'll be able to use the portal again?" she asked when I had told her everything.

I shifted on the edge of her pallet. "We'll have to try."

"Kyndle?" Nanna's voice came from below.

I scooted to the opening and glanced down. She stood, looking up at me. I saw the trace of tears on her face.

"I need t' speak with you," she said softly.

I glanced at Ruby. "Be ready," I said as I went down the ladder.

I followed Nanna to her small room where she motioned me to a seat on the bed. She took the chair from the day before.

"Ian will take you home," she said simply.

I was stunned. "But you said—"

"That doesn't matter now," she interrupted. "Ian will do nothing else because he knows this is the right thing t' do." She drew in a deep breath. "And so do I."

Relief flooded over me in warm waves. I felt so much safer knowing he would be with us. And I wasn't even ashamed of it.

"How can I thank you?"

"Don't," she said with a crinkly laugh. "If my flesh had won, I would nae have allowed him t' do it." Despite her words, I couldn't help but see the heavy sadness lining her smile—like the colors bordering a sunset. In her eyes, I suddenly saw the memories of her loved ones dancing away on an eastward wind.

"I know that this is very hard for you," I said, "but I swear to do all I can to see he returns safe to you. That's a promise."

"I know you will," she said.

I was surprised. It felt *so* good to be trusted. I knew right then that I couldn't let her down. I would do whatever it took to get Ian back to her.

Whatever it took.

Nanna looked away, took a deep breath, then looked back. "You must get ready. Ian is eager t' be off. He says that he owes it t' you."

I lingered just long enough for her to gently touch my cheek.

"Hurry up," I urged Ruby, sticking my head through the loft opening. "We don't have any time to lose."

She tied her hair back with the twine Nanna had lent her. "I'm ready," she sighed, looking mournfully at her worn clothes. "Ready as I can be, I guess."

We paused to give the little room a last loving look. Then we climbed downstairs.

Ian was waiting at the door. He had a pack slung across his shoulder and he held mine out to me. "Nanna packed a few things you girls might need."

"Thank you," we said as she walked in from her room.

"You're welcome, m'dearies," she said, taking my sister into her arms and giving her a firm hug. "I pray you have a safe journey home."

Then she turned to me. I rushed to her embrace, a sudden unknown emotion surging through me. When I released her, I looked hard into her wrinkled eyes.

"I hope I see you again," I whispered.

"I hope so too, Kyndle," she said softly. "Children of God are reunited in heav'n after death." Her gentle grip on my shoulders became firm and her eyes locked hard onto mine. "If not again in this life, I hope t' see you there."

I smiled, and one tear slipped down my cheek.

When Ian stepped forward, Ruby and I hurried outside. Neither of us wanted to see their goodbye. It was a couple minutes before the door opened. Ian made no effort to hide the tears in his eyes, and I could see the difficulty with each forward step.

"Come, girls," he said, his voice strained.

We followed him up the slope. I glanced across my shoulder. Nanna was leaning on the doorframe, her arms crossed on her chest. We worked our way up the slope toward the rocks, but at the very last moment, Ian turned.

"See you soon!" he cried, raising his hand.

She lifted a hand to her lips and blew him a kiss. As she did, a gentle breeze touched our faces. Then we rounded a boulder.

The walk to the cave was governed by an eerie quiet. Neither of us girls ventured to say anything. The expression on Ian's face was too much for small talk. When the cave loomed into view, we timidly stepped into it.

"Well," Ian said, leaning against the stone wall.

"I guess we'll just wait and see what happens," Ruby said.

"Yeah," I said.

We sat down. Ruby leaned against the wall and closed her eyes. I was glad she could rest. Ian stretched out on his back and put his hands across his eyes. I began to dig through my pack.

Thankfully Nanna had replenished it to the hilt. My water flask had been washed and refilled, and there were enough snacks stowed inside to last a few days. My dagger had also been put back in, the blade protected by the leather sheath. The cloaks had been neatly folded. Then at the very bottom of the bag, I found an object wrapped in paper. Unwrapping it, I held in my hands Nanna's small black Bible.

At the noise, Ian pulled his hands from his face. Seeing the Bible, he let slip a little smile. "She knew you were curious," he said, working up to one elbow. "I'm not surprised she gave it up."

"She didn't need to," I breathed, looking up at him. "I know it was so special to her."

"She wouldn't have given it up if she hadn't wanted to," he reassured. "While it certainly was very special t' her and she read it every day, she must've known that you needed it more."

I gently put it back into my pack.

"Ian," I said without looking up, "I don't know how to thank you for making such a big sacrifice for us."

He didn't answer, so I went on.

"I know how hard it was for you to leave after all you two have been through together. I can't begin to—"

"Kyndle."

The strangeness of his tone made me quickly look up. When I did, I could hardly see his face for the mist which had formed around it. A smile played at my lips. I reached through the smoky air to be sure Ruby was awake. I felt her pat my hand very softly.

We sat in silence as all of our surroundings—and the ground beneath us—faded completely.

chapter THIRTEEN

It worked! I thought in triumph as my feet hit solid ground. I trembled with excitement as the mist began to fade. The first thing I saw was Ian's face. He smiled—a sad smile.

From somewhere in the cloud, Ruby took my hand. We waited as the last swirls of the mist blew away on the mountain breeze.

It was very quiet.

"We need to find a place to hide," Ian said, his voice flat. "We can't be sure if those soldiers are still searching the mountain for us."

"Good idea," I said shakily.

"But where?" he asked aloud.

"What about another cave?" Ruby suggested. "There must be others."

"Probably," Ian said.

"It would have to be well-hidden or they would find it too," I said.

He shrugged. "It's worth a try."

We picked our way among a nearby outcropping of boulders, creeping here and there, peeking for an inconspicuous place in which to hang tight until we were certain the soldiers were gone.

I clung to the hope that, just maybe, we could rescue Flint.

"What about this?" I heard Ruby ask some time later.

I could hear her voice but didn't see her anywhere. "Where are you?"

"Here. Follow my voice," she said.

We did, between two large rocks Ian and I were barely able to squeeze through, and found Ruby standing by a crevice in the ground, barely two feet across at the widest point but ten or so feet long and about that deep. We all stood staring down into it.

"It could work," Ruby said.

"It could?" I cringed to think of going down there.

"I think it's our only option," Ian said, and after a moment, he dropped down into the hole. We heard an *oof* as he hit the bottom.

"Are you all right?" I asked, readjusting my pack.

"I'm all right," he called up. "It's a bit bigger down here than I thought it would be. It widens the further down you get. There's a big boulder at the far end that I can step on to get back out."

"Good," I said.

"The first thing we need is leaves," he went on. "This floor would be very uncomfortable t' sit on even with the cloaks."

"I'll get some," Ruby said. "I just saw some around the boulder."

I squatted beside the edge as she scampered off. "You really think this will work?"

He looked around before looking up. "It's our best hope for now."

I swallowed hard but said nothing.

"It'll be dark in a few hours," he said. "That should help too."

"What else do we need?"

"Just leaves."

"I'll get an armful too."

"I'll be right there," he called up.

I hurried to follow Ruby. But as I rounded the boulder, I was met by a brutal blow to the face. I dropped to the ground, speechless with pain. My pack fell from my shoulder.

"Got another one, have we?" came a cruel voice.

In shock, I looked up into the face of a Snow Sprite soldier.

"On your feet," he hissed, jerking me up.

"What did you do with my sister?" I slurred through throbbing lips.

"Shut yer yap," he snapped, "or she'll regret it. Answer my questions and she'll be spared. For now."

I forced angry words down my throat.

"Are there any more of you Firelings hiding around here?" he asked.

"No," I said.

"Liar!" he spat. "Where are they?"

"In your imagination," I said through gritted teeth.

"You think you can spare them," he said with a coarse laugh. "We'll find them. As for you, you'll pay for your lies—" And he struck me across the face a second time.

"I'm not lying!" I protested, shielding my face with my free arm.

Jerking my arm from my face, he twisted it so fiercely I was forced to turn backward in an effort to relieve the pressure. He then shoved it up against my back. I held back a pained cry. Wrapping his other arm around me, he pinned my free wrist to my waist.

"I'll give you one last chance to tell the truth," he hissed into my ear. "Where are the others?"

I didn't respond. There weren't any more Firelings for me to speak of. There was only one Scot, and he hadn't asked about Scots. Yet I knew that answering with denial would only anger him further.

As it turned out, my silence gave much the same result.

He kicked my feet out from under me, and I fell with him still holding my arm twisted. Flaming pain tore through my arm and shoulder as I hit the rocky ground. Then before I knew what was happening, he slammed down hard beside me. I glanced up in shock to see him straddled by the aforesaid Scot.

"Get out of here!" he said as I scrambled to my feet. As Ian spoke, another soldier appeared behind him.

"Kyndle, run!"

I ran like I had never run before. I heard the other soldier close behind, but I didn't look back as my father had always told me. I broke out of the trees into a partial clearing.

Good—I could run faster in the open. Unfortunately so could the soldier chasing me. I felt his fingertips graze my shoulder blades an instant before our feet got fouled up. We went down the slope in a tangle of arms and legs, and I got the bad end of the deal.

Puffing angrily, he got off me and to his feet. I didn't move—every bone in my body ached. He was no lightweight and acting as his sled hadn't been a pleasant experience. Reaching down, he jerked me to my feet by my collar which I heard rip.

Turning me roughly, he began to bind my arms first at the elbow, then the wrist. "Like chasing a bloody rabbit," he muttered.

Steaming under his very touch, I didn't bother to reply.

When we returned to where we had left Ian, I found the tables turned against us. I winced at the sight of his bloodied face as he was bound the same way I had been by a third soldier. The Snowling who had struck me stood to the side, glaring at me as we approached.

"Good catch, Rime," he said to the soldier with me.

Ian's eyes met mine, and I couldn't discern what I saw written there. We were marched away.

They led us to our old campsite, now occupied by at least ten Snowling soldiers. Ruby stood by the dead campfire in the firm clutches of a sour-faced soldier. Relief ran through me when I saw she hadn't been harmed or bound. As we came to a stop near her, our gazes met.

Hers was filled with tears.

"Well, what have we here?" came a voice.

All three of our guards snapped to attention.

A Snowling man, no more than forty, with a fancy jacket and numerous crests pinned to it, sauntered toward us. His bearing told all that he was in charge.

Gold buttons and clinking boots. *Wonderful.*

"Two more, General Stag," answered the soldier who struck me.

"Well done, Canton," Stag said, coming to stand before us. He looked at my face with seeming amusement. "What a fiery young woman!"

I wasn't amused. "Let her go."

For an answer, I received a stinging slap full across my face.

"Prisoners do not speak unless spoken to!" he shouted.

My cheek throbbing, I sagged in Rime's iron grip. In my mind's eye, I had a sudden image of Flint. He had been treated this same way—right before he was beaten. I felt the blood drain from my face. Rime lifted me until my boots hovered several inches off the ground. Then he advanced forward until I was nearly face-to-face with General Stag.

"Now that I have your complete attention," Stag said, "I'll ask my first question. Just *what* are you all doing out here?"

My eyes fluttered shut as lightheadedness came on. I was terrified. If I didn't answer, would they beat me in front of Ruby? I had to think fast.

"We're on our way home," I blurted.

"And where is that?"

When I hesitated, the grip on my arms tightened.

"The Fire Realm," I said as stupidly as I could.

Again my face pulsated with a slap. Ian growled his anger.

"I know *that,* you obstinate donkey," Stag snapped. "*Where* in the Fire Realm?"

I said nothing.

An evil smirk spread across his face. "Have you nothing more to say? If you don't, I can get answers out of the little one." As he spoke, he took a step in Ruby's direction.

"Frieman," I spat.

"Ah," he said, his voice infuriatingly cool like the representative back home. "That's better. *What* are you doing out here, may I ask?"

Don't blow it, I thought.

"Trying to find something," I finally said.

"It seems you found it," he said. "Or something strange. It's not every day that you see three people emerge from a crevice with smoke pouring out around them. What was it?"

"Let me explain," Ian jumped in. "It—"

Suddenly he doubled over from a blow to his stomach. I glanced at Ruby. The anger on her face matched my own.

"I didn't address *you*," Stag spat, scowling at Ian's bowed head before turning back to me. "What were you looking for?"

"I'm not exactly sure."

"Why wasn't the matter reported to Representative Frost?"

Fierce pride welled up. I answered before I could stop my tongue.

"We don't answer to *you*."

His blue eyes flickered dangerously, and my arms were twisted until I cried out. I hung limp in Rime's grasp, not wanting him to hurt me again; not wanting to, again, show my weakness before Ruby.

"Don't you *dare* harm her!" came Ian's dark warning.

I turned and found a changed Ian. His face was white with anger and green fire sparked in his eyes. The muscles in his neck were strained, and he had spread his feet apart as if in defiance.

"And *what*, may I ask," Stag patronized, turning slowly, "are *you* going to do about it?"

In my mind, I heard Ashbel's voice repeating those exact words to me in our dormitory in Frieman. Pain coursed freely through my aching heart, and my anger showed itself in a gasping breath.

"Take him over there, Canton," Stag said to Ian's guard. "I can tell we won't get anything productive out of him."

Ian was pulled away by two men.

Stag turned back to me. "Do you plan to be cooperative?"

I looked down. "It depends on the question."

He grabbed my face, forcing me to look in his steely eyes. "The boy." Nodding across his shoulder at Ian who was being lashed to a tree. "Your brother?"

"No."

"But the one we caught yesterday, is he?"

I hesitated, but it cost me.

He moved like lighting. Snatching Ruby by the arm, he shoved her up against the cliff edge. One push, and she would be gone forever. I didn't dare to even breathe.

"*Is he your brother?*" he repeated, attacking each word.

I nodded, looking at Ruby's face. It didn't have an ounce of color in it; all had gone white.

"This is your sister, isn't it?" Stag asked, shaking her.

"Yes, she is," I said, my voice trembling.

He stared at me for what felt like minutes. Then he very slowly pulled her away from the edge.

I let out a deep breath and waited for him to speak. But when he did, it wasn't directed at me.

"Let's get back to the ground," he said to Rime.

The next few hours were miserable as we prisoners were forced down the crude trail with our arms still bound. We had to depend entirely upon our guards to catch us if we tripped—and they only came through half of the time.

Finally, close to sunset, we reached the bottom of the mountain where a campsite had been set up. Sturdy tents were pitched in a circle around a dead campfire. A soldier leapt from one at our approach and gave a hasty salute. I could tell he had been asleep. I could also tell he hoped that fact would go unnoticed.

Beyond this tent grouping was a larger tent to which Ruby and I were led. Rime jerked open the flap and thrust both of us through the opening where we fell heavily on our faces. Neither of us moved until, after a few moments, his shadow moved away.

Rolling painfully onto my back, I spoke softly to Ruby.

"Are you all right? Did they hurt you?"

"Not yet," she said, rolling partially onto her side, "but I'm scared they will."

"Just do as they say."

We lay quietly, grateful to be alone. I shifted around a few times in an effort get comfortable, but with my arms tied as they were, shifting didn't do much good. Soon the strain on my shoulders grew almost unbearable, and I was grateful that they had merely bound Ruby's wrists. I bit my lip, recalling my Fireling training.

Pain will be over sooner if you just get over it.

chapter FOURTEEN

As the sun broke over the trees, casting dark moving shadows upon the sides of our tent, the flap was pulled open, and Rime stood there.

As I looked up at him, I realized that he wasn't as old as I had thought. In fact, he probably wasn't but a few years older than me.

Reaching down, he picked me up by my collar. I dropped back to the ground, leaving a ripped collar in his fist. Tossing it aside, he hauled me onto my feet by the arm. I tried to glance at Ruby across my shoulder but the flap shut before I could.

Rime nudged me forward. When I didn't perform well enough, I found myself slung over his shoulder like a sack. I didn't even try to resist. In that moment, I realized how exhausted I was and just gave in.

Some Fire Sprite, I thought to myself.

Then quite suddenly, Rime jerked me forward by my belt. I just barely landed on my feet. He turned me—and I stood face-to-face with General Stag. The superior crossed his arms.

"I trust you rested well."

I pursed my lips. "Sorry to disappoint."

"I'm not disappointed," he said without hesitation. "Less rest for you means less trouble for us."

"I guess we'll see."

"Now," he went on, "I have a few questions. It's obvious that this boy is not Fireling and is somehow wrapped up in this entire situation. Why wasn't he executed like the last stranger to your lands?"

I winced at the painful reminder of the blackest blot upon the Fireling history. Over a hundred years back, an alleged spy had been hung at the hands of an angry Frieman mob.

No trial, no justice. Just a hate which had led to murder.

I let my gaze fall slightly from his eyes as I pondered his question. It was one I had asked myself many times since we left home.

Why *had* we been sent? There was no way I could know.

Maybe it was because back then, the idea of betrayal and loss was too much for the Fireling people to take. Maybe now, we had a better control on our anger.

Or maybe not. I certainly didn't.

"I don't know," I finally said.

I waited for him to strike me. Instead when I looked up into his face, I saw, with surprise, that he believed me.

"So where is he from?" came the dreaded question.

I said nothing.

He leaned closer. "Answer my question."

I still said nothing.

He squared his jaw. "Don't make me use harsh means to force you to speak."

I lifted my chin. "Give it your best."

Slap!

I staggered back into Rime's arms—stunned at first, angry at second by the vicious backhanding. When after a few moments I licked my lip, I tasted blood. That impressive ring glittering on his finger had done some damage.

"Now will you speak?"

I looked up at him. Was that *supplication* I heard in his voice? For an answer, I straightened my shoulders, looked into his blue eyes, and waited for the next blow.

To my surprise, it didn't come.

He looked into both of my eyes in turn as if searching for an answer to some question other than the one he had asked. When he finally spoke, his voice was more gentle than before.

"Take her to the boy. I'm finished with her for now."

I limped quietly along beside Rime, halfway glad that he was holding my arm. Ian was bound stoutly to a thick tree some distance through the trees. When he saw me, speechless anger clouded his bruised face. I tried to smile at him but couldn't.

Rime cut the ropes binding my wrists and elbows. I gasped with pain as I tried to stretch out my shoulders. He stood by until I had worked out the initial soreness, then motioned me to the tree beside Ian's. I sat at the base of it, dropping my head back against it and just leaving it there as he bound me to the tree, hoping he wouldn't notice that I had filled my lungs to full capacity with air. I kept my eyes shut until his footsteps had faded and then released all the air I had been holding in. However, he had bound me too tight for a simple trick as that. I felt Ian looking hard at me.

"Oh, Kyndle."

"It isn't your fault," I mumbled through my swollen lip.

"I hate them." His teeth were clenched so that I heard them grinding. "Every last one of them."

I turned to him. Here, at last, was the anger I had craved from him. But as I looked upon it, I found it wasn't as satisfying as I had hoped. Rather it broke my heart.

It made me want to help him. But I didn't know how to begin. I said nothing for several minutes. When I did, it wasn't about him.

"Ruby?"

He drew a shaky breath. "I don't know where she is."

"I'm grateful they haven't hurt her."

"I'm praying they don't," he said, his eyes wandering. "If they do I—I don't know what I'd do. I'd probably get us all killed." He let out a sigh and closed his eyes.

My head dropped wearily on my chest as I let a few tears fall. "We're probably going to be killed as it is."

There was a moment of terrifying silence.

"Kyndle." His voice was tight as a bowstring. "What do you mean?"

"Flint, Ruby, and I are Firelings," I said, looking at him dully, "and we were caught outside our borders. That's a capital crime."

Fear came into his eyes but I knew it wasn't for himself. He shook his head from side to side, and when he looked back at me, the fear had been replaced by anger.

"I got you into this."

"Don't, Ian. It's too late for that now."

ALLYSON HORNER

    Then I turned away, not wanting him to see the tears in my eyes.
I had promised Nanna to get him home, and she had trusted me.
    I had broken my word.

chapter FIFTEEN

An hour or so later, Rime and Canton came and freed Ian from the tree. As they pulled him to his feet, Canton hissed, "You move, she'll regret it."

Ian stood quietly as they each began to cut the ropes around me. I saw that Canton held the knife near my ribs, ready for use if Ian attempted to run.

I wasn't afraid. I knew he would never desert us.

The ropes fell away and Canton yanked me roughly to my feet by the arm he had twisted the day before. It hurt, but I pushed the pain aside. I owed it to Ian and Ruby. And Flint.

And my Fireling name.

Ian and I stood quietly as our hands were tied in front of us. The tents had been pulled down, and it appeared that another group of soldiers—and horses—had recently arrived. This only added to my fear. There were now fourteen soldiers. Any hope of escape vanished.

Ruby was mounted behind a burly soldier, looking tired and sad, and they rode further up the line out of sight. Ian was lifted on his own horse, with his hands tied to the saddle, and I was put up behind Rime a couple horses behind Ian. A rope was looped through my tied wrists then tied to the saddle in front of Rime.

There went any chance to jump off.

General Stag rode up beside us and gave something to Rime. Surprised, I saw that it was my pack.

"Keep your junky things," he said, "but I have the dagger." He patted his waistline, and I saw it hanging beside his sword on his jeweled belt. I nodded my understanding.

I was grateful he let me have the pack at all.

"Let me be crystal clear, Fireling," Stag continued. "If you make one wrong move, your sister will pay for it. And should he," turning to look at Ian, "do anything unwise, you'll feel the consequences."

He rode off toward the front of the line. I sneered at his back. Such was the Snowling way of keeping us obedient. Only the likes of a coward would now dare to misbehave—and cowards were few and far between in the Fire Sprite ranks.

Rime spurred the horse forward, and we took our place in the line. After a few minutes, it began to slowly move; and at a steady walk, we advanced in a northern direction. Every plodding step took me that much further from home.

The ride was wearying.

We went along in a sullen silence. No words were exchanged between the soldiers and us. Ian and I communicated strength in our glances, but I was still afraid. I wished Ruby was with us.

I hated the soldiers. I hated the Snow Realm. More than that, I hated myself.

I had supposed we would have no problem getting back to Frieman. I had fooled myself into thinking that we would be okay, if only the portal would bring us back.

Now look at us; prisoners of the people I hated most, being carried to the place I hated most.

Around dusk, we stopped. Several soldiers stood near Ian and me as they let the horses get a drink. Though I craned my neck up the line of horses, I could still see no sign of Ruby. When the horses finished, the soldiers took us back to our horses.

"Where *exactly* is my sister?" I chanced.

"With the general," Rime said as I mounted.

The general, I thought angrily. *The same general that put this wound on my face. The same general whose orders have beaten Ian. If he lifts a finger towards her, I'll—*

Do what?

Helplessness washed over me. I couldn't do a thing if the need arose. To keep from panicking, I clung to the hope that Ruby would be fine. With her submissive spirit, I found it hard to see her giving out much resistance—unlike me.

HOME ROAD

Ian was now four horses behind me. I was glad he was so close. Even though he was just as helpless as me, it seemed to offer strength to have him there. Maybe it was his faith that gave me courage.

I didn't know.

Dusk came on, and we stopped for the night. Panic washed over me at the idea of Ruby staying with the soldiers, but to my relief, they brought her to the back with Ian and me. She trotted along like a little goat, striving hard to keep pace with the soldier's large stride, thrown a bit off-balance with her hands tied behind her back.

"Ruby!" I cried when I saw her.

"Kyndle! Ian!" she yelled back, equally as happy.

"Quiet, you!" her guard hissed, shaking her.

I strained hard against the ropes which tied me to the tree trunk but quickly realized that his shaking wouldn't hurt her. She was quiet as he roped her to the tree.

The soldiers pitched their tents near us and their fire even closer still. It gave enough light for us to see each other's faces, but it wasn't so close that our conversation could be heard by the soldiers.

"Ruby," I asked her as soon as we were alone, "have they hurt you? At all?"

She shook her head. "They just shook me around a little bit."

"Thank God," I heard Ian breathe in the growing darkness.

There were a few moments of silence.

"They've hurt you though, haven't they?" she asked.

I hesitated. I hated to upset her, but I wasn't about to tell a lie. "Yes," I finally said, though I kept the right side of my face hidden.

"Kyndle, how have they hurt you?"

"Ruby, it's not important."

"It is to me," she insisted. "If I had been hurt, you would demand to hear every detail."

I sighed. She was right. So I turned my bruised, cut face into the light.

Her eyes grew wide. "What happened to your face?"

"She got backhanded by that daft general," Ian snapped.

"Why?" she demanded, joining his anger.

I shrugged. "I didn't answer his question."

Ian looked away.

"I want to go home," Ruby whimpered. "They're going to keep hurting you."

Or kill us, was my private thought, but I thought it best not say aloud.

"God, deliver us from the hands of these men," Ian prayed. "All according to your perfect will."

"Ian," Ruby asked when all was quiet, "who is God?"

"He's the one who made us all," came his reply. By his tone, I knew he was smiling. "Even though we sinned, he loved us enough t' send us a Savior."

"But if he loved us," she persisted, "why has he put us through this?"

Ian hesitated.

"It hasn't been that hard for me," she continued, "but you and Kyndle have been hurt. I know it by the pain in your eyes, even now."

I chided myself for not being more discreet, but the pain in my back, from my tumble with Rime, had grown dreadful. Ian glanced my direction just as a wave of pain hit me, and I was unable to hide my tears from his scrutinizing glance. I turned away.

"Ruby," he said softly. "When God created life, he created everything that would happen to each and every person. He hasn't missed a detail."

"How comforting," I said bitterly.

Ian turned. "What do you mean?"

"What kind of a God would let a person hurt? Why would he let Flint be caught? Maybe killed?" My voice was gritty with emotion.

"Kyndle." His voice was as gentle as a hand on one's shoulder. "Hard as it may be now, it's all a part of his will. Nothing happens for nothing. Everything we go through serves a purpose in the end, whether we see it or not. It's comforting to know that he's always there and that he never looks away."

Sure. He just watches and does nothing.

The soldiers had all retired into their tents, and the fire had burned to almost nothing. The darkness was blanketing, pushed back only when the moon came out from behind the clouds.

"How can he watch everyone at once?" Ruby asked.

"I don't know," Ian said humbly.

"Does it say why in that book?" she asked.

"The Bible? No, it doesn't."

"Wouldn't God want you to know everything about him?" she asked innocently.

"No."

"Why not?"

"Because if we did, he wouldn't be God. If we knew all his mysteries, we might try to *be* him." Ian paused. "Someone did that once."

"Who?" I asked, my curiosity piqued.

"He is called the devil."

"Oh—I've heard of him," Ruby said in a hushed tone. "The men back home talk about him when they're angry."

I smiled in the darkness.

"The devil was once the highest angel," Ian continued, "second only to God himself. But it wasn't enough. He wanted to *be* God, not serve him. He got a large number of others to join him, and they all tried to fight God. But God cannot be defeated, so the devil and all his followers were cast from heaven."

"To where?" I asked.

"To the domain of men."

Despite the darkness, I saw the whites of Ruby's eyes. "You mean, he's here—now?"

Ian nodded. "Yes, but he is seen only through his evil works."

"You mean in the soldier's hate," she pointed out.

He nodded. "But the devil can do no harm unless he is permitted by God."

"Great." I scoffed. "So God is *purposefully* letting this all happen?"

"Yes," Ian said softly. "But it's for a specific purpose."

"You know," I said suddenly. "We should all get some sleep. It'll be a long day tomorrow for all of us."

"You're right," Ian said. "Good night, Ruby."

"Good night, Kyndle and Ian," she said, a big yawn stretching her last syllable.

"Good night," I said, watching her lean her head back against the hard tree and shut her eyes. Before two minutes had passed, she was breathing evenly with sleep.

"You're worried about her." Ian's words weren't a question.

I sighed. "Yes."

"I'm surprised she hasn't been hurt," he confessed.

"I'm relieved," I said. "Maybe your Christ is watching her."

He hesitated. "He's watching over all of us."

That angered me. "You know what, Ian? I'm not sure about that. Ever since this journey started, I've had nothing but pain come my way. Being torn from my family, putting my villagers at risk, losing my only brother after watching him be beaten, and now we're being taken to our deaths." An angry tear steamed down my face, but I was unable to dash it away.

And Ian sits here, acting like everything is okay.

He said nothing. I couldn't see his face. All at once, I remembered that night on the mountain when I had heard his prayer—and had admired him for his faith to believe that good would come out of the bad and make it all worth it. My conscience stung me. After all, he was only trying to make us feel better.

"I'm sorry, Ian," I said after a while.

He didn't answer. I hoped it was because he was asleep. But I knew he probably wasn't. A few more tears trailed down my face in the darkness. I couldn't bear to lose another friend because of my disbelief. I blinked, startled by my own thoughts.

Friend?

Is that what he was? It didn't take me long to know it was true. But that made the ache worse.

chapter SIXTEEN

As we rode along, I tried to distract myself from the ache of my bones by counting the marks in my wristband. There were now six.

Only six?

Nearly two days had passed since Flint's capture, one since ours. Tomorrow our people would begin looking for us. So would the representative, if he had returned.

This only brought faint hope. I didn't underestimate their abilities. We were just too far ahead. By my estimation, we were about halfway up the western edge of the mountains. I chided myself for not studying the maps better, but I knew that the land we were currently traversing was the former territory of our people before we were exiled. It was mostly wilderness since none had lived in it for two hundred years.

I looked lingeringly, *longingly,* at the fields as we passed them.

Here, generations before, the Fireling people, *my people,* had worked and toiled to build a life for themselves, their children, and grandchildren to come. They had poured their hearts into the very spirit of these lands, never dreaming that their hopes were not to be—that their children, their beloved grandchildren, would fight a losing battle and be bereft of every part of what they called their own.

"As pruning is a necessary part of growth, so pain is a necessary part of life."

So the instructors said. So Ian said in his own way. I wasn't so sure. Pain seemed pretty unnecessary right now. I was sure I could grow perfectly fine without it.

More piercingly at the moment was the pain in my back which soon grew so uncomfortable that I ventured a question.

"Can I walk?"

Rime scoffed aloud. "Like I'm going to let you do that."

"It's not like it's my fault." I pointed out. "My back hurts because *you* tripped me."

He hesitated and I jumped on it.

"I'll walk right beside the horse. I promise not to run away."

He scoffed again. "As if the promise of a Fire Sprite means anything." Snowling haughtiness was plain in his voice. I held myself back as anger flared up.

Now is not the time to act out.

I took a deep breath and tried again.

"You have my sister and friend. Running away isn't an option. Not for me."

He was quiet for so long I thought he hadn't heard me, but just before I repeated it, he pulled the horse to the side of the trail.

"Thank you," I said as I dismounted.

When I got down, I stretched a couple times, relieved to hear my back pop. Suddenly something heavy and metallic touched my shoulder blade. As I started to turn, Rime spoke.

"If you run, I will shoot."

I slowly turned to face him, looking at him along the top of his rifle. "All right."

With a nod, he waved me on. I followed behind the horse in front of me, taking care to match my pace to his, slow and deliberate, not wanting to give Rime any reason for accusation. Walking was much easier on my back than the jolting step of the horse. I didn't want to lose the privilege.

Two or three horses ahead, Ian glanced back to check on me. When he saw me walking, a grin lit up his face.

Yes, smile. I'm moving up in this cruel life.

After a few moments, he turned forward again.

From the back, with the sun shining full in his hair, bringing out all of the highlights, I could almost trick myself into thinking that he was Flint. Even as I thought it, a pang hit my heart.

Where was he? Was he safe?

Is he even alive? my mind asked.

HOME ROAD

Of course, my heart decided. *We're talking about Flint. He can't die.*

He can *die,* my mind reminded, *and you know it.*

I took a bristling breath and gritted my teeth. *Not if I can help it.*

But that's just it. My logic was merciless. *You* can't *help it. You can't help Ruby, you can't help Ian—you can't even help yourself. You haven't seen your little sister since morning. Anything could happen to her—and you won't hear about it until tonight.*

I swallowed angry thoughts and stared at the horse in front of us. The thought of Flint, possibly somewhere up in the Snow Realm, spurred me on and gave me new determination.

We *had* to make it. Even if we never left, I had to get my sister to the Snow Realm in safety so we could see him together, one last time.

One last time?

Yes, one last time.

Because in my heart, I knew we were never going back to the place we called home.

Half an hour passed, and I grew tired.

Up ahead, Ian rode with his head bowed low, whether in his prayer or in exhaustion I didn't know.

Suddenly one by one, all the horses began to stop. We looked at each other in confusion. There was silence up ahead for about a minute. Then voices met our ears.

"Get on' 'er feet, lazy lout," came a gruff distant voice. "Now!"

Every muscle in my body tensed. *Ruby is up there.*

"Here, this should help you!" came the voice again. It was followed by a scream that ripped my heart out. I began to run, ignoring Rime's warning yells.

I wasn't running away. My sister was being hurt. I was *going* to do something about it. The scream pealed again, and I ran faster. Soldiers wheeled in their saddles and a few yelled at me, but I didn't stop.

When I came to the front, my heart stopped with horror. Ruby lay on the road, arms pulled over her head in terror. Across her back there were two slits in her shirt. Through them, I saw long bleeding wounds on her skin.

Standing over her, with a horsewhip in his hand, was Canton. A crooked smile on his face, he raised the whip again. Dashing forward, I threw myself on hands and knees across her body, shielding her from the blow and taking it in her place. The pain that sliced across my back was unreal. I steeled my jaw but couldn't keep a muffled cry from escaping me.

"Lookoo's tryna be a hero," came Canton's slurred voice as he let out a drunken laugh. There was a whistling sound, and I writhed as a second stripe was laid across my back and shoulders. Beneath me, Ruby panted with fear and her own pain.

The whip descended again. Tensing my torn muscles, I waited for the next anguishing lash. But the pain didn't come. Using all my will to turn my head, I saw Stag towering over Canton whose lowered face was turning red and pale by turn. The whip lay in the dirt at their feet.

"So." Stag's voice was an angry hiss. "I go ahead to verify the path and this is what happens in my absence."

"The lil one wouldn't gettup, sir," Canton mumbled, looking down.

"Why was she off the horse at all?"

"She wan'ed to walk," he slurred. "Then she fell down and wouldn't get back up."

"So you give her the whip to help her stand? Hmmm?"

Canton fumbled with the button on his glove and didn't answer. The general leaned forward. I heard him sniff. When he stepped back, anger seemed ready to melt the white skin off his face. He spoke through gritted teeth.

"Get a washcloth, you drunken swine. Now!"

"Sir!" Canton gave a crooked salute and stumbled to obey.

I let my head drop on Ruby's shoulder, and a cold feeling ran over my lashed back. I felt her shivering beneath me, her breath coming in small, little pants.

"You must get up."

General Stag's voice was commanding, but the usual barking sound was gone. I felt his hand on my forearm. It chilled me.

"You must get up," he said again.

I tried to get to my feet, but the movement stretched my wounds open even wider. Pain burned into my back and consciousness began to waver. My hearing faded in and out. I felt like I was bobbing in water. My own breaths echoed loudly in my ears, followed by a far-away voice. I thought it sounded familiar but did it? Closer to my head, Stag's voice penetrated the fog of my mind.

"Of course," he said. "Do what you can." Then his boots clinked away in angry strides.

Even in semiconsciousness, I felt my anger stir at the sound. I heard someone kneel on the road beside us, but I lacked the fortitude to raise my head a second time. Ever so gently, a cold hand was laid on a part of my shoulder that wasn't torn up. It made me gasp, and I instantly smelled Ruby's blood.

"Oh, God," came Ian's whisper. His voice was streaked with fear.

I clamped my eyes shut, hoping to wake up and realize that all of this was just a dream. But after a moment, Ian spoke again. He now sounded like his old self again.

"Kyndle, come. You have t' get up. I'll help you." He took hold of my other shoulder.

I drew in a deep breath.

"Good," Ian said, gently pulling me to my feet.

"Thanks." I gasped, wiping away the tears on my face with one hand and holding his arm for support with the other. A tiny part of me recoiled at crying in front of so many Snow Sprites, but it wasn't enough of me to care about.

"Can you stand?" he asked me.

"I'll hold her," came Rime's voice as he came up on the other side of me and gently did so.

Ian blinked in surprise. "T'anks."

Rime shook his head. Ian bent down and lifted Ruby off her face. She groaned but amazed me with her fortitude. Her fists were balled, but her mouth stayed shut.

"Look at that Fireling," I said softly.

She raised her teary face and gave me a little smile.

Ian and Rime helped us to a stream nearby where Ruby went down on her hands and knees. Canton stumbled up beside me. Ian thrust out a paw.

"Give me the rag."

With fear plainly evident in his shifty eyes, Canton gave the rag to Ian. The latter dipped it in the stream, then gave it to me. Squeezing some of the water out, I laid the cloth on Ruby's raw back. Her muscles tightened so much that they quivered.

I quickly washed her two cuts which weren't as deep as I had feared. Canton fumbled around in the saddlebags and found some bandages that we wrapped her up with. Then Ian and Rime helped her to a spot in the shade of a nearby tree. Through all of this, she made no sound.

Next came my turn. I attempted to wash my own back, but the pain of twisting my arm fairly took my breath away. Ian spoke soothingly in his warm accent as he took over and bandaged me up.

"'Tisn't as bad as I'd first thought," he said. "You two will be back t' normal in no time."

"That would be nice." I chuckled with my mouth only.

When it was all over, he helped me to a place beside Ruby.

"Rest now," he said as I dropped into an exhausted sleep.

When my eyes opened, it was dark. The sharpness of the pain across my back had been replaced by a dull burning sensation. I groped into the blackness near me and made contact with Ruby's leg. Steady breathing told me that she was asleep. However, the movement brought back some of the sharp pain. I lay still.

"Kyndle?" Ian's soft voice didn't even startle me. "How do you feel?" Hearing him shifting around in the dark, I realized that he had been there all along.

"I'm okay. Where are the soldiers?"

HOME ROAD

"Up ahead. Stag is still furious with Canton. He said we're waiting as long as necessary before you girls have to ride again. If there's any anger in the Snow Realm when we arrive, it will be Canton's fault."

I was touched by this unexpected sensitivity, so I tried to be positive.

"I'm hoping to be back up by sometime tomorrow, but..." I rested my hand on Ruby's leg again. "She's always been so fragile."

"If we bandage her up good and tight, the ride won't be too difficult." I could tell that Ian was trying his best to be strong, but I heard a quiver in his voice. "We just need to pray that infection doesn't set in."

I closed my eyes, fear streaking through me. There wouldn't be much we could do if infection did come. I suddenly felt very small. Very insignificant. Very unprepared. Very afraid.

I wish Mum was here. I could see her in my mind. She always had such a good laugh. Even in my memory, I heard it ringing through the shadows.

"Trust yourself," she'd told me. "Nothing can hurt you if you do."

I looked up into the black sky. Trust—myself? *Me?* That idea was almost laughable. *I* certainly wouldn't trust me if the need arose. What was wrong with me? Fear raged throughout me again, red and burning. I needed to think of something else. I needed to talk.

"Ian, what was your mother like?"

He chuckled. "She died when I was two, but I have a clear image of her in my mind. She had long brown hair, nearly touching her waist, and the greenest pair of eyes you've ever seen."

"Like yours?"

He shook his head. "More so."

I found it hard to imagine eyes greener than Ian's. "That must've been something."

"Yes." I could tell he was smiling. "She was."

"What was her name?"

"Una Freemont."

"What about your father?"

"Faither was a drifter, an orphan. He did nae even have a last name. He walked int' the village one day and said he was staying. No one knew who he was, but Granda took him on as a field hand. He showed his worth in a very short of time, so Granda decided to keep him.

"Mither was only seventeen when Faither came to the farm, but I'm told that their attraction to each other was immediate. After three years, they were married. Granda and Nanna gave their full blessing, and since Mither was an only child, they all stayed living together. They liked it that way. And since Faither didn't have a last name, he took Mither's as his own."

I said nothing but let him talk on. It was good for both of us.

"My sister, Gillian, and I were born a year after their marriage. Hardly a year later, Fran announced her comin'. But just in time for her t' arrive, plague hit the village."

"I'm sorry, Ian," I said in the long pause that followed.

"The village was nearly destroyed. Those who survived moved away to family members. I think the only reason Nanna, Fran, and I made it at all was because we lived up in the hills, away from the village.

"Granda was the first of ours to go. An hour after Mither came down with it, her pains came upon her and she took to her bed. She lasted just a few hours after Fran was born.

"Faither never even got t' see his new baby. He took Gillian with him t' get water, down by the village. To get there, he had t' crest the ridge and go down the other side. He thought it would be safer for Gillian out in the fresh air than in the sick house. But not long after they had left, it began snowing. Nanna waited as long as she dared, then went to look for them. I remember sitting by Mither's bed, watching Nanna go out the door, all wrapped up in her big shawl. But she never found them." He lowered his head.

I said nothing.

"Like I said, Mither left us not long after the baby was born." His voice was turned away now. "I think losing Faither and Gillian hastened the end for her. But to our surprise, Fran lived. She thrived under Nanna's hand and helped t' fill the huge space left in our home."

I waited a long time before saying, "Then the ice pond."

He sighed. "Yes. A few days after her thirteenth birthday."

"So you were two years apart. Like you and I."

"Yes," he answered slowly. "You are what she would've been—if she were alive. When I first saw you, I knew you had to be around her age. It made you feel special to me." He chuckled softly. "But I think I offended that friend of yours."

I flushed in the darkness, remembering Tinder's "warnings" to Ian.

"He and I grew up together," I explained. "He's just overly protective. More so than Flint."

In an entirely different way from Flint, I thought but didn't say.

He chuckled again. "Don't worry about it. I would've done the same for Fran." To my surprise, his voice broke as he said her name. "If only I could."

The sun began to break over the horizon, and I could see Ian's face for the first time in our conversation. The soft morning rays highlighted the tears on his face, but more than that, the great strength which had settled over it. Deep inside, I wondered if I could ever be as strong as him in the face of such pain. He seemed like someone you could trust in hard times, unlike me.

Which was ridiculous. I was, after all, a Fireling of Firelings; a woman who should be capable of leading others with ease.

Again I wondered, *What was wrong with me?* I looked at Ian's face. I envied his strength, wanting it for my own.

And again I wondered if what he said could be true, if we weren't just alone in this life—aimless, purposeless, and left to make what we could of ourselves, all by ourselves.

chapter SEVENTEEN

"Welcome to the Snow Realm," General Stag announced at my side.

I sat silently, staring ahead at the distant spires. Here was Galaheed, capital city of the Snow Realm, but I withheld all emotion from my face. I couldn't let him see the pain flaming throughout my chest like wildfire through dry fields.

"It's been a long journey," Stag said, rising in his stirrups then settling back into his saddle with a contended sigh. "I'm glad to be home."

I said nothing. My home lay at the other end of our known lands.

"How's that bitty sister of yours?" he asked me.

I turned to glance. She sat quietly in the saddle in front of Ian which had been allowed due to her injuries. None of the other soldiers wanted the responsibility of caring for her, so it had been slotted to him. It was a comfort to us all. However, it meant I had been kept separate from them for the last three days. It had given me a lot of—in fact, too much—time to think.

"She's fine," I finally said.

Stag scoffed and turned an angry eye at Canton. "No thanks to certain others."

I ignored the comment. It wasn't worth my effort to be angry.

"The horses have had sufficient rest." General Stag waved his hand to the watching soldiers. "Let's go." He chirruped and his horse surged on. The whole company began to follow.

Canton watched Stag pass with bitterness in his eyes.

Rime made a soft whirring noise with his mouth and his horse reacted instantly. The reins hung loosely where they were fastened to the saddle. His horse was so well-trained that he didn't need them.

This had made it simple for me to ride in the saddle when I felt I needed it. However, since we would be entering the city today, he had resumed his place in front.

As we joined the line, our horse passed close to Ian and Ruby's. I was grateful to get to be so near to them. We all smiled warmly at each other—trying to encourage one another. I lingered in Ian's gaze, hoping to get some sort of indicator on Ruby and was relieved to receive a nod and a wink. She was doing all right.

Taking a deep breath, I looked forward. Good, Ruby was on the mend. Just in time for our execution. I wondered if Ian would try to speak to Ruby about what was coming or if he would let me. He had such a gentle way with words and I didn't. I hoped he would speak to her.

In time, the city walls neared. I studied them closely. Made from what looked like granite, they rose what had to be fifteen feet into the air. The craftsmanship was impressive, for on reaching them, I saw that there were intricate carvings worked into them. Most were swirls and patterns, but I also saw gold faces. They stared at us with eyes that couldn't see—faces cruel and proud. I shuddered.

These walls weren't made to keep people in. They were made to keep other people out.

Then there were the gates. Huge and ornate, made of what looked like burnished gold, their carvings were even more intricate than those upon the walls—patterns covered the gates from top to bottom. Deep inside, I knew this was the gold our men had labored for in the southern mines as tribute.

"Ahoy, general!" came a call from above.

We all looked up to see a soldier on the wall. He was dressed the same way as our soldiers. It seemed that he knew plenty of them by the way he grinned and waved.

"Evening, Fritz," Stag called up. "We have returned."

"Very good, sir. I'll tell them to open the gates." He disappeared from view. Within a few moments, the golden doors began to open. The horses started forward.

As they did, I turned. I wanted one last look at the countryside.

It was a beautiful sight. A gentle breeze brushed against my face, and a flock of birds flew homeward over my head. As I watched, the last ray of light glimmered over the mountain's peaks, then the sun disappeared. Dusk settled over the land; night was coming on.

"Farewell," I whispered.

"What?" Rime asked, turning his head.

I looked at the side of his youthful face. "I was saying goodbye to the sunset," I said. "We both know I may never see it again."

He looked forward and said nothing. As our horse passed through the gates, I turned again. There was just one more soldier behind us, and before he'd even come fully through the gates, they started to close. My eyes stung with tears that wouldn't come as they slammed together.

Then taking a quivering breath, I turned forward.

Galaheed was a busy city. Hordes of people, light-skinned and white-haired, bustled throughout the streets. We passed many soldiers gathered at the street corners; one with icy eyes looked up at me in a bit of shock, and it was then I realized just how many people were gaping at us. This wasn't surprising since we were likely the first Fire Sprites they had ever seen. Women stopped in the middle of the street then were jolted back to their business by the soldiers who were striving to keep the cobblestoned street clear enough for us to pass through.

"So this is Galaheed," I murmured to myself.

"Sure is," Rime replied, and I was surprised he had heard me. "I was born and raised here. This is home."

"How far is the prison?" I asked dully.

"A few streets down." He shifted in the saddle. "I confess, I'm sorry to take you there."

"Oh."

"It's a rathole," he said in disgust. "No place for one like yourself. Or that tiny sister of yours. It just isn't fair."

I blinked in genuine shock. "What?"

"You're so young. You're at that age when life is beginning to unfold right before your eyes, when every day is an excitement, every dream is possible." As he spoke, I got the feeling that Rime wasn't speaking about me anymore. "You have so many dreams, then suddenly they're snatched right out of your hands. You didn't ask for change, and you don't deserve it." He sighed, heavier than I had expected him to. "It isn't fair," he said again. "For anyone."

I didn't try to offer a response. I was too confused.

Up ahead, a tall stone building I knew was the prison came into sight. Torchlight flickered from isolated windows. A large stone wall encircled the entire perimeter. My heart pounded as we approached it. What terrible things would happen once we went in?

We pulled to a stop at the wall, and the soldiers began to dismount. Rime assisted me down and, out of habit, grabbed my arm as we joined the others by the gate. It hung in the stone wall like a mouth, just waiting to swallow us. Stag didn't turn as I approached but looked straight ahead at nothing in particular. We all waited, expecting him to speak.

"I don't know what your future will hold," he finally said.

"I do," I snapped.

"You know nothing," he said harshly, still not looking at me.

"Really?" I countered. Rime held me back.

Stag wouldn't turn his eyes.

"I do know this," I spat. "If we were treated this badly on the journey, there's nothing here for us but our deaths." I turned to find that Canton's eyes bored darkly into mine. As I looked at him, I noticed that there were dark rings around his eyes and his skin tone wasn't normal. He knew his guilt and, no doubt, feared the consequences.

"You were maltreated by a drunken soldier who will be *dealt with* in time," Stag grated with a poisonous glance at the referred. "I cannot be blamed for his decisions."

"What about this?" I turned so that my cheek was fully revealed in the light.

His left eye twitched in the silence that followed.

"You should have answered my question," he finally said.

I scoffed. "As I said, if it's this bad already—"

"Enough!" he barked.

I wasn't worth his mental effort. So I turned away.

"I confess," Stag went on, turning to Ian, "you're the oddest prisoner I've ever encountered. Your ways puzzle me."

"Ways?" Ian repeated.

"Yes. You were beaten yet you didn't retaliate. When questioned, you usually cooperated. Which can't be said for others here." He glanced at me with superiority full across his face.

I raised my head. *Glare if you want.*

Ian, however, shrugged. "I'm to love even those who hate me."

Stag raised his eyebrow. "Says who?"

"God does." Ruby jumped in.

I stared at her in shock.

"God," Stag repeated with a mocking tone in his voice. "Is this a deity who has spoken directly to you?"

"No," said Ian. "He says it in his book, the Bible."

Stag turned to me. "You believe this too?"

"No." I shot a glance at Ruby. "Neither does my *sister.*"

"Yes, Kyndle," she said firmly. "I do now."

My intimidating stare became one of surprise. Ruby had converted? She believed in Ian's God?

I found my voice. "I can't believe it."

There was an uncomfortable silence which Stag finally broke.

"As far as your trial, I can give no information yet."

I jerked to face him, blinking in shock.

"We're getting a trial?" Ian asked for all of us.

But Stag had already turned. "Tristan, Rime, Canton." The last name spoken in a sterner tone. "Take them to their cell." Then drawing in what seemed like a difficult breath, he mounted his horse and trotted down the street toward the impressive buildings in the far distance. I watched him as long as I could. He didn't turn back.

"Come, then," said Rime, pulling at my arm.

A catch in my throat, I turned and looked over my shoulder at the sky. The colors, so vivid just a short time ago, were quickly fading into a misty darkness.

Like everything I had known.

I turned forward to face where I was going and not to pine for where I had been.

HOME ROAD

The gate was guarded by steely eyed soldiers, one of whom began to bang on the door. We heard a board being slid upward on the other side, and then with a hesitant creak, the wooden gates swung open.

We were ushered through them, and then they shut behind us. Inside we found a dismal courtyard. Dark doorways were guarded by dull soldiers who had muskets resting loosely on their stiff shoulders. We approached one of these and the guard stepped forward. Resting beside the long scabbarded sword at his belt was an iron ring holding a myriad of keys, all of which looked the same to me. He surveyed us with interest through his one eye; the other was sealed shut by an ugly scar.

"What's their crime?" he asked, fumbling for the right key.

"They're Firelings," Canton snapped.

I glanced at Ian. Though the low lighting shadowed his hair and eyes, his height did make him to appear like one of us. I realized that Stag was the only one to have thought otherwise. Probably a good thing.

The soldier finally found the right key. Shoving it loudly into the lock, he twisted it clumsily and then pushed the door open. A dank scent came from the opening.

"There we go," he said, stepping aside for us to enter.

Ian was pulled forward and the dark doorway engulfed them. Canton led Ruby through next, and I heard a tiny whimper escape her lips. Rime guided me forward behind them.

The key-bearing soldier laughed coarsely. "Have a nice stay."

The moment I stepped through the door, the acoustics changed. There was an echo to every noise. Rime stepped in after me, and the sturdy door clattered shut.

The loud noise bounced into the darkness and then came back again. I could hear the others up ahead of us, but my feet refused to move of their own volition.

"Come now," Rime said. "Don't be a fool."

His grip on my arm was more reassuring than domineering. Suddenly I felt him slip something over shoulder. Glancing down, I saw that it was my pack.

"Go," the councilmen had said, "for the glory of the Fire Sprites."

For the glory. I straightened my back. *Don't be a fool,* I told myself. *Be a Fire Sprite.*

I offered no further resistance as Rime led me into the darkness.

chapter EIGHTEEN

Torchlight flickered ahead. Rounding the corner, we came on the others.

"What happened?" Canton snapped.

Rime shrugged. "Nothing, sir."

Canton's eyebrows lowered. "I asked a question."

Rime looked away. "She was only frightened."

"Frightened?" Canton's face stretched into a scary smile. "She should be."

I did my best not to tremble, but it was harder than I expected.

"Onward," Canton said, pulling Ruby forward. "Your accommodations are just around the corner."

We stopped a few cells down, before one that seemed especially dark. Iron bars stretched across an opening at the top. It seemed like this door had been here for centuries by the way it fit so seamlessly into the rock. Pulling a key from his belt, Canton unlocked the door then shoved Ruby through it. Ian followed close behind her.

I was next, but I hesitated again.

"Come, Kyndle," Rime softly said.

Surprised by his use of my name, I turned to look in his eyes. He met my gaze and something stirred in his that I didn't understand. Then it was gone, and he urged me forward.

Fear pounding in my ears, I entered the cell. The door heaved behind me with an ear-shattering *boom*. As I stood there trembling, I heard the soldiers leave. Their footsteps faded with the flickering light of the torch. We were left in total darkness.

I let my pack slip from my shoulder to the floor. "Ruby?"

"I'm here," came her tiny voice.

My eyes unadjusted, I groped with my arms and, after a moment, met a wall. Lowering to a crouch, I found Ruby in a huddle on the floor. I put a hand on her back and listened as her tears finally came.

"I miss them," she cried. "Mum and Dad and Flint."

"Me too," I said, squeezing her fingers. "I bet Flint escaped from the soldiers and they're all out searching for us as we speak."

"But they won't find us," she blurted, her tears coming afresh. "Never in a thousand years. We could die in this dark hole and they would never know."

Mutual hopelessness washed into my heart. I mingled my tears with hers.

"Don't be frightened," Ian said.

I turned toward his voice, and after a moment, his hand found a place on my shoulder.

"Christ is with us wherever we go," he said.

Ruby raised her head. "Oh yeah," she said, the despair fading from her voice. "I forgot."

"He hasn't forgotten you, Ruby," Ian comforted. After a moment, his thumb tapped my shoulder. "Nor you, Kyndle."

There was a moment of silence.

"Ruby, you better get some sleep," I said, shifting from under his hand. "We don't know what tomorrow may bring."

Ian pulled away.

"Here, Ruby," I said, reaching into my pack and pulling out my and Ian's cloaks. "Sleep on these." As I spoke, I shook them out and formed them into a makeshift bed.

"Thank you," Ruby yawned as she stretched across the ground on her stomach. "Good night."

"Good night, Kyndle." Ian's voice hadn't moved.

"Good night, Ian."

The floor was cold as ice on my face, so I crossed my arms and rested my head upon them. The weight of the day suddenly weighed down upon me, squeezing out a tear onto my sleeve. I didn't bother to wipe it away.

What good is it to dry a raindrop when a deluge is coming? And it did come. My tears silent and undetected, I cried myself to sleep.

"Up, you Fireling brats!"

The sound of a key in the lock greeted me as I stirred out of my sleep. As the door grated open, I sat up and turned bleary eyes on the tall soldier who stood there. I had never seen him before. Ian also sat up, but Ruby slept the sleep of one who is exhausted.

Before I could even comprehend what was happening, the big soldier strode into the cell and planted his boot in the small of her back. Instantly awake, she gasped in pain and scrambled out of his reach.

Ian leapt onto his feet, face dark with anger, but before he could make any further move, the soldier struck him up the jaw. He slammed backward into the wall.

"How'd you like that?" the man jeered, brandishing his fists. His back was to me.

Rendered speechless, Ian slid down the wall and into a heap upon the filthy floor, instinctively using one arm to shield his head from the blows he expected. I leapt to my feet.

Something stirred deep down inside within me, something I had never felt before—an *overwhelming* urge to strike a blow for this Scottish boy. With a strength I didn't know I even possessed, I jumped onto the guard's back, both legs swinging, and somehow managed to trip him. He clawed at me, twisting as he fell; and when we hit the floor, I somehow came out on top. Perched on his chest, I pummeled his face with both of my angry fists.

It was only a moment before he recovered his wits, then I was tossed off like a kitten. Before I quite hit the floor, he had me. Blood streaming from his nose, he held me above the floor by the back of my shirt.

"Stay away from her!" Ian barked from the floor, struggling to get to his feet.

"Quiet!" The guard spat over his shoulder.

My shirt ripped and I dropped to my feet with a jarring *thud*. Instantly he had me pinned to the wall, his large hand gripping my neck.

"Think you're brave?" he asked, his voice scornful. "Well, you're not, little Firehead. This should remind you not to try it again."

He raised his hand, and I braced myself. Instead quite suddenly I found myself on the floor again. My senses swirled as someone brushed past, and I raised my head. Rime stood over me.

"You can go now, Clifton," he said levelly.

The other soldier laughed meanly. "Why should I, softie?"

Suddenly there was a revolver in Rime's hand. He leveled it directly at Clifton's chest.

"You can go now, Clifton," Rime repeated. "As you are or with a few new holes in you."

"Okay," the other replied in a voice wholly different. "I'll go."

His wide eyes looked down the barrel of Rime's gun as he smoothly edged toward the door. Rime kept the gun poised until the man's shadow had disappeared down the hallway. When certain that he was gone, Rime lowered the revolver.

"Did he hurt you?" he asked as Ian scrambled to my side.

I felt for where my shirt had burned my neck. "I don't think so."

Rime slipped the gun into his belt. "There's blood on your shirt."

"Daft brute," Ian muttered, fussing over me like an old aunt. The skin at his chin had split from the blow. "All that movement split the wounds in several places."

"Ruby?" I asked, turning.

"I'm okay," came her little voice. She moved into the lantern light, and I saw that she really was. She came to me. I ran my hand down her dirty cheek as a strange feeling came over me. This slight quiet girl surprised me more and more. And I was proud of her.

Rime shuffled near the door and I turned to him. "Who was he?"

"Doesn't matter. He wasn't supposed to be in here."

Stiffly, I got to my feet. "Oh?"

"General Stag's orders," he explained. "None but myself are allowed in this cell."

"What time will we receive trial?" Ian asked him.

There was a silence. Rime leaned all his weight against the stone wall as if he suddenly weighed a thousand pounds. "I don't think you will," he finally said.

I turned to Ian, doubt wringing all the hope from my heavy heart.

"Then when?" Ian asked, stepping forward confusedly. "Stag said—"

"Stag lied," Rime interrupted. "He was unable to tell you the truth."

The truth. It hit me full in the face. It was so quiet I could hear the sound of water dripping somewhere in the dungeon. So quiet that I could hear the anger churning in my throat.

"And what is the truth?" Ian finally asked.

"It's like I said all along, Ian!" I said, angrily hitting the wall with my knuckles, not even seeing how it skinned them. "There's no point to hope but I hoped all the same." I laid my forehead against the cold stone wall. "Look where it got us."

Rime opened the door. "I'll get your breakfast," he said miserably.

After the door closed, there was another silence. I kept my face to the wall. Ian finally came to me and rested an arm across my shoulders.

"God's will be done," he said quietly.

"God's will," I scoffed, pulling away. "What does that even mean?"

"It means his ultimate plan for everything."

"You know what, Ian? I don't care much about everything right now. I care about us."

Sorrow blossomed across his face. "I do too. Believe me, I do. I'm the one who got you into this. If—if anything happens, it will be my fault. I just wish I knew what to say."

I turned away. "Just don't."

The morning passed at a painfully slow rate. I paced the cell, my mind racing and my heart full of anguish. Not for myself, not even for Ian but for Ruby. She was so young, so afraid of everything. When I could pace no more, I sat down beside her. I knew I needed to be a comfort to her. I needed to keep her mind steady. I needed to talk to her about something other than our reality.

"Tell me about your new faith."

She looked at me with a new smile on her face, one that I hadn't seen back at home. "When I realized *just how much* he loved me," she said, "I couldn't do anything *but* love him and believe in him."

I forced a smile. "I'm glad for you."

"It's like—like I've finally found something to fill the emptiness I've always felt inside. Like finding the right answer to something that's been bothering you for a long, long time. It's God, Kyndle, and his love." She leaned on my shoulder.

"But how do you *know* that he loves you?" I asked in exasperation. "How can you be so sure that he truly cares about what all goes on here? What if he doesn't even exist and all that Ian calls 'faith' is just a really optimistic view of life? What if there is no God and we are really just on our own? What if—"

She leaned heavily on me and I stopped. Her eyes flew open.

"I'm sorry, Kyndle. I think I fell asleep."

"Don't talk anymore," I said. "Rest."

She put her head on my leg and did so.

"I'll talk t' you, Kyndle," Ian said, coming closer.

I compressed the irritation that had taken over me and settled down to listen to him. Listening is a skill that Fire Sprites take very seriously. You may not believe a word of what someone is saying, but you are expected to hear him out. Ian licked his dry lips and began.

"We can know that Christ loves us by the life he lived," he explained to me. "He left heaven t' take a mortal body and spread the news of the kingdom of God t' all who would listen. He healed the sick. He touched those who hadn't been touched for years. He taught new ideas—some of which went against all the legalistic laws of the day—but ideas that spoke right t' the heart of every matter. It was a time of miracles. It was a time when men dared to hope.

"But after three years, the jealously of some grew t' the point that they stirred up the multitudes against him, accusing him of crimes he didn't commit, and he was executed like a common criminal. Jesus Christ, only Son of God, member of the Trinity and author of the faith, was nailed t' a wooden cross and died."

I sat quietly, somewhat impressed by the old story.

"But even his death was miraculous," Ian went on. "Down in the city, in the place of worship, the curtain through which man could not pass—the entrance t' the room where God's presence dwelt—split in two. It was the start of a new covenant between God and man, a covenant that didn't require the blood of bulls and goats t' atone for man's sin. Christ ended all that. His death paid for the sins of man. He became—"

"—the ultimate sacrifice," I interrupted softly.

His eyes widened in surprise. "Why...yes."

"Nanna told me a little about it," I said. "She said I would understand better with time."

He nodded. "And with help."

I glanced into his face, surprised by the curiosity stirring deep within, like what I had felt back in the room with Nanna at my bedside. After a moment, I reached for my pack. Pulling out the little black book, I put it into his hands.

"Would you tell me more?"

He glanced down at it for a long moment, tracing the gold letters over the cover. When he lifted his head again, his tired face had broken into a smile.

For the next few hours, Ian tried to tell me some about what he called the myst'ries of God, using Nanna's tiny Bible as his guide. He hardly stopped to eat the measly breakfast Rime brought to us. I found myself listened eagerly to every word he spoke. In fact, I clung tightly to them. I couldn't explain the sudden willingness I found in myself.

"Ian," I asked during a pause, "are you afraid of death?"

"No."

"How?"

"Because God is my strength."

"What do you mean?"

He flipped to the middle of the book and began to read. "The Lord is my light and my salvation, whom shall I fear?" He glanced up. "Because he is my salvation, I know that he loves me. Because of that, I love him in return."

"Do you trust God, Ian?"

"Most o' the time. When I don't, it's not because I shouldn't. It's just because I trust myself more. It never turns out well though."

"What do you mean?"

"Because I can't see what is ahead. God can—he planned it. He puts us right where we need t' be. I don't always know why, but I can rest in knowing that he does. Trust and love go hand in hand."

"But *if* I did want to love him, how do I know he would want me?"

"In John 6," he said, flipping through the worn pages, "Jesus tells those around, 'I am the bread of life; whoever comes t' me will not hunger, and whoever believes in me shall never thirst. But I said t' you that you have seen me and yet do not believe. All that the Father gives t' me will come t' Me, and *whoever comes t' Me, I will never cast out.*'"

I rubbed my forehead. "I'm just so tired, Ian."

He laid a hand on my shoulder and brushed the other across his own eyes. "Get some rest."

"No," I said. "I feel tired *inside.*"

He gave me an encouraging pat and I went on.

"For my entire life, I've been told to trust in myself and my instincts. I've been told that if I do it, I'll be fine. But the truth is, I *wouldn't* trust myself. The whole idea is almost comical. I'm no more trustworthy than a messenger with a broken leg. Why would they tell me that if it isn't true?"

What was this—was I distrusting my leaders?

"Maybe because it's what *their* parents told *them.*"

"But when all is said and done, who *am* I to trust? Who can I turn to? Should I trust at all?"

"Come t' me, all who labor and are heavy-laden, and I will give you rest. Take my yoke upon you and learn from me—"

"Yoke?" I looked away. "I can't bear another weight, Ian."

"For my yoke is easy, and my burden is light," he finished.

I looked back at him. What was that supposed to mean?

"The laws of God are written on the hearts of everyone. It's harder t' go against them and trust yourself than it is t' just rest in the love of God for you. In the end, obedience is much easier than the alternative."

"Auburn's life wasn't easy," I objected. "Because of Christ, she found only scorn and mockery from everyone, including me."

My head dropped onto my chest as did a tear.

"Though she was rejected by men," he said softly, "she found limitless comfort in the assurance of *God's* unceasing love for her. Am I right?"

I said nothing. He went on.

"That same love caused the morning stars t' sing at creation." Passion surfaced in his voice, and he waved his hands in excitement. "That same love flowed from his fingers as he comforted his children in a hardship. It was the same love that made him send Jesus, his only Son, to die for crimes that he didn't commit! The transgression of every man who was, is, and ever *will* be lay upon his sinless shoulders."

An unexpected tear stung in my eye. "But *why?*"

"God made us. He cares for us above all other created things. He loves his children most of all. He looks forward to the time when, after death, all will be restored. On that day, death itself will be defeated." He closed his eyes and smiled.

"Ian," I asked after a minute, "what happens after death?"

"When a child of God dies, their body remains in the grave, but their spirit goes to be with God."

"Yes, but—what about those who don't believe?"

"Well—" His voice had a strange ring to it.

The echo of feet came down the hall. I shook Ruby awake and we all got to our feet. A key grated into the lock, and the door swung open with a rusty creak.

In the doorway stood Canton, accompanied by several soldiers whom I had never seen before.

chapter NINETEEN

"You." Canton pointed at Ian. "Your presence has been requested." His pointing finger changed to a beckoning one.

"It has?" Ian repeated, not moving.

"At once." Canton stepped aside and the others came into the cell. I snatched Ruby out of their way and pressed her to the wall with my own body. Snatching Ian's arms, they began to bind them behind his back. He stood quietly, just a couple steps in front of us. I saw tears at the edges of his eyes as he smiled down at us. It made my chest hurt.

"No fear," he whispered, looking at us in turn.

Canton, overhearing his words, glared at him. "The one you should be fearing right now is the king. Your fate rests with *him*, not some God who doesn't exist."

Jerking Ian's bonds tight, the soldiers shoved him toward the door. He glanced at me over his shoulder, and in it I read a thousand words. All of them said goodbye.

I had to say something.

They jostled him through the doorway and out of sight.

My mind spun, and into my mind flew one of the many verses he had quoted in the past few hours. "He is your light and your salvation!" I called out.

Above all the noise, I caught the muffled sound of Ian's reply, "Whom shall I fear?" His words were followed by a cry of pain. Canton slammed the cell door shut and locked it.

The sounds faded, then we heard nothing more. Ruby slid to the floor. I staggered to the far wall and buried my face in my hands. "Where was God?" I asked amid the tears I tried to contain. "Where was he when we needed him, Ruby?"

"He's right here," she whispered, lifting her head.

I slid down the wall to a sitting position. "So why can't I see him?"

She worked her way beside me. "Maybe you aren't looking."

"I don't know."

She put a hand on my knee. "Ian told me a verse yesterday," she said, "and though I can't tell you where it's found in the Bible, I did memorize the words."

I nodded for her to continue.

"For the moment all discipline seems painful rather than pleasant, but later it yields the peaceful fruit of righteousness to those who have been trained by it."

I nodded numbly at her. *Later* wasn't our reality.

"I hope Ian will be all right," Ruby said with tears in her voice.

"Me too."

"But Canton is wrong."

I looked down at her. "What do you mean?"

She glanced up, righteous anger covering her youthful face. "Ian is in God's hands, not their king's. Right?"

I looked away. "I don't know."

"But—you just quoted Scripture!"

I shrugged it off. "I just wanted to make him think of Nanna."

"I think you made him think of God."

"Ruby, I don't even think I know your God."

"You can start to know him. He won't turn you away."

I patted her hand. "Even if he isn't with me, I know he's with you."

I expected her to smile, but I only got tears. She put her head onto my shoulder and just cried.

"What's wrong?" I asked, rubbing her arm.

"I want you to trust him too." She wept. "I want you to feel this same peace, this same love. Kyndle, you heard about his life. How can you *not* thank him for all he has done?"

My mind flooded back to that night on the mountain when I overhead Ian's prayer. I had wondered if he really was the Creator of the stars. An unexpected desire had stirred in me to believe that God existed.

"Trust your instincts," said everyone around me.

But now I knew how instincts can mislead you. At first, I believed that Ian was a spy. I had even told him so. Now?

He was one of my dearest friends, one that I would never forget, even if he was the first of us to taste death. His words came to mind, *My yoke is easy, and my burden is light.*

Then Ruby's words, *For the moment all discipline seems painful rather than pleasant, but later it yields the peaceful fruit of righteousness to those who have been trained by it.*

I repeated these two passages to myself over and over again that next hour as Ruby slept, committing them to memory without knowing why. I only knew I had a feeling I might need them for the hard times ahead.

The hard times came sooner than I had expected. Only a few hours after Ian was taken, our turn came.

Canton reappeared with two new guards who brusquely tied our hands and shoved us into the hallway. My pack was left behind, to be forgotten forever in the shadows. We went the opposite direction that we had come in from, into deeper darker tunnels. Terror gripped me, but I was thankful they hadn't separated us. If something terrible was to happen, I wanted to be right by Ruby's side. I wanted her by mine, too.

We were led down hallways which were dark and cold, passing many cells holding others as miserable as us. In some of these, I heard weeping; in others, a silence reflecting my heart. Each subsequent doorway seemed lined up like razor-sharp teeth in the mouth of death, ready for their next victims.

Us?

The passage veered hard to the left, then widened into a small room. A doorway stood in the far wall. Going through it, we then began working a maze of passages and doorways which all looked the same to me. But at one of the rooms we came to was different; it held an actual *door*. By it, on the wall, hung a lantern. Canton took a key ring from his belt and the lock in the door succumbed to him.

"Take her," nodding toward me, "to the royal chambers. I'll take the little one with me." As he spoke, he began to drag Ruby down a passage I hadn't noticed before.

"No!" I protested, jumping forward.

I was promptly checked by the hold on my wrists.

"Resist, and it will be to her harm," Canton said as he kept walking.

"It's okay, Kyndle!" she called though her voice broke. "I love you!"

"I love you!"

Canton and Ruby disappeared into the shadows. I didn't resist as the remaining two soldiers dragged me through the door. I had clung to the hope that I wouldn't be separated from Ruby but—like all my other hopes—it had been dashed.

I was taken down several more passageways and doors until we came to a dismal staircase. Though I did what I could, they nearly carried me up the steps. Till then, I hadn't realized how weak I was. Meager rations and mistreatment were starting to wear on me. After the endless stairwell came a door. This opened up into a hallway that showed clean floors and light-colored walls, covered by fancy decorations. The golden chandelier confirmed to me that we must be somewhere in the palace. I hoped Ruby and Ian would be waiting for me in the royal chambers, though I knew it was unlikely.

We padded softly down the hallways, turning this way and that until I had lost my sense of direction. The few servants we passed wouldn't raise their eyes to even glance at me. Finally after another exhausting stairwell, we stopped before an imposing white door. It opened noiselessly to reveal a richly furnished chamber.

A big mahogany table stretched up the center of the room, flanked by a number of comfortable chairs. Windows stretched across the entire left wall. Priceless tapestries and gold-framed mirrors covered the walls in a gaudy fashion. In one of these, I caught a reflection that wasn't my own—and it was only then that I noticed another presence in the room.

Standing quietly in front of a window, watching me very closely, was a white-haired man. He was dressed finely, boasting a boisterous display of gold buttons and pristine white gloves. Around his waist was a jeweled belt. From it hung a lightweight sword upon which he rested his hand. Hanging directly beside it was my dagger—the one Char had given to me just before we left.

"Ah," he said in a haughty voice, coming closer. "So this is the older girl?"

The guards let go of my arms.

"Yes, Your Grace," one replied, bowing. "You asked to see her?"

"Indeed I did." He studied my face. "You may leave us."

"Yes, Your Grace." The men bowed low again then left the room. The door shut softly behind them. In all this time, his eyes never left my face. It nearly unnerved me.

There was a long, heavy silence before he finally spoke. "What is your name?"

I immediately made a decision to not give any more information than what he had asked for.

"Kyndle."

"A simple enough name," he said. "I am Glacier, the brother and chief advisor of King Antares." The hint of a scowl studded his pale brow.

Whoa. Chief advisor. One of the big ones. No doubt one of the masterminds behind our way of life.

"I see," I said calmly.

"Our first order of business is to free your hands. There being no way of escape, they would only serve as an encumbrance to conversation." As he spoke, he put his white hand on my shoulder and turned me around. I heard my knife being pulled from the sheath and fear pricked me. I didn't breathe again until the ropes fell from my hands and I had turned back to face him.

Glacier urged me in the direction of the table. "Take a seat," he said, doing so himself at the head of the table. When I had done so, I put my hands on my lap and turned to my interrogator. I was ready for whatever he had for me.

Probably.

"Our meeting shouldn't take long," he said stiffly. "All that I need to know is why you were out in the mountains, contrary to the explicit orders of the Snow Realm."

"Did your officer not communicate all he knew?"

"That is not your business. Your only present concern is to answer my questions. So I ask again, why were you in the mountains?"

I nearly rolled my eyes. "We were searching for something."

"Did you find it?"

"Yes."

"What were you looking for?"

The dreaded question. *Remember, say as little as possible.* I considered my words carefully. "A...cave."

"What made it worth looking for? And how is the boy involved?"

I stopped breathing. As far as I could tell, no one knew Ian was from the land on the other end of that cave or even that there *was* a land on the other end of that cave. And I was resolved no one should know now. I set my jaw.

"We were looking for it because the council told us to look for it. The boy came because they told him to."

A shadow entered his blue eyes. "I'll give you time to reconsider how to make your answer less vague. However, in the meantime, I should like for you to tell me who the members of your search team were."

"Myself and my brother." I watched his face closely for any signal of understanding about Flint. Confusion filled me when I saw none in those vast blue eyes. Rather there was a spark of anger.

"Who is the little one?" was the next question.

"My sister," I said hesitantly.

"Why didn't you name her before?"

"She was not part of the searching party."

"Why was she there then?"

"It was a—last-minute decision."

"Made by whom?"

"My authority," I said after a moment.

"So who is the girl?" he asked.

I paused. "My sister," I said again.

His face grew another shade darker, and he took a deep breath through his nose. "Don't play games with me, Fireling," he said in a warning tone. "You will regret it."

"I'm not playing any games," I replied, more calmly than I felt. "I am simply striving to be truthful."

"Ah, yes." A subtle smile played around his mouth. This was the trait I so despised in Snow Sprites—an infuriating calculated coolness. It was a smiling mask, covering up the evil thoughts behind it. Finally he spoke his thoughts. "Truth is a highly upheld virtue in your lands, is it not?"

I didn't respond, but my face told him it was so.

"This being a major factor in your conscience," he said. "I'll cut right to the point." He leaned forward menacingly. "*Who is the boy?*"

I felt my heart-rate increase. "Well—"

"You are to answer me directly and truthfully. No games, remember?" Though his tone wasn't as hissing, it was just as intimidating. It told me if I failed to comply, he held the authority to punish me however he chose, whenever he chose.

I looked away, licking my dry lips, but knowing one thing. No matter what they did to me, I wouldn't be the one to disclose Ian's Scottish blood. Calmness settled over me. My heart rate normal again, I turned back to him.

"He is my friend," I told him. "His name is Ian."

His face was unsatisfied, but he said nothing. Leaning back in his seat, he clucked with his tongue, touching his fingertips together a few times. I was a bit unnerved by his expression.

"Is he?" he said, as if to himself, but I knew he hoped I would hear it. Not meeting my gaze, he rose from his seat and went to stand in front of the windows. I couldn't see his face, and something told me that I didn't want to.

After a full minute of strangling silence, he turned back to me. There was a disturbing smile on his face.

"Kyndle," he said. It chilled my blood to hear him say my name. "I'm giving you a choice." He came nearer and I instinctively shrunk further in my seat. "If you answer all of my questions, without hiding anything, you'll be given the freedom to go home to Frieman. Back to your friends. Back to your *family*. That *is* what you want, is it not?"

I nodded, and to my surprise, a tear slipped down my cheek. I think it encouraged him.

"You want freedom, right?"

I nodded again but didn't allow anymore tears to fall.

"If this is all you want," he said, "you'll answer my questions."

"Or what?" I said, my voice low and trembling.

Wildfire exploded in his eyes and voice. "Or you will be subject to the full vengeance of the king's will and court!"

I stilled my tumultuous heart.

"I am the king's second hand," he said, eyes narrowing. "If you fail to comply with my terms, know that I play a large role in the determination of your fate." He stood a mere two steps in front of me.

"I see."

"What we want to hear more of is this green-eyed boy," he said very significantly. "We've never seen any like him. I want to know where he's from and who his parents are."

I looked into his eyes; he thought I would give in. So I thrust out my chin.

"Remember, girl," he said. "You will have *freedom*."

I blinked. Freedom—is that what he called it?

Getting to go back to a village surrounded by invisible hateful walls in a land we couldn't call our own, constantly watched and pounded into submission by cold blocks of ice wearing blue uniforms, gold buttons, and tall clinking boots.

This was freedom? I waited.

"I'll give you a few minutes to make a decision," he said. "I'll be back at," consulting the clock on the wall, "four thirty-eight." Turning on his heel, he strode from the room through a door at the far end.

Rising slowly from my seat, I went to the windows. Stretching before me were the endless buildings and, in the distance, lush forests of the supreme Snow Realm. Birds soared in the sky, and the wind brushed gently over the tops of the trees, bringing in the autumn.

These, and the home road, could be mine. I could run into Mum's arms—feel her laugh and her tears falling on my shoulders. I could disappear in Dad's arms and never want him to let go. Auburn would be waiting, greeting me with her sunny eyes, less of an object because she had completed her mission and brought the cardinal home.

I felt myself smiling. I could roam once again in the streets on off days, listening to the rip-roaring stories of the elderly citizens. I could lift my tray in the mornings and find a hearty Fireling breakfast beneath. I could sit down at my own desk and pour out my troubles to the page. I could step back into my role of an exile as our people plotted and planned for the day when we would break apart our Snowling chains and reclaim our place as a society in the beautiful western realm; again I could sit and watch the sunset, dreaming dreams of the future that was coming to me.

No, it wouldn't be freedom. But it was familiar all the same. All I had to do was answer Glacier's questions. It would all be over. But what of Ruby? What of Flint? I considered what they would do if they were in my place. Deep down in my heart, I knew what their answer would be.

And what of Ian? If I did answer their questions, what would it mean for him? What all would a greedy brood of Snowlings do to this Scottish boy? Could I ever laugh again, not knowing what horrors I may have brought upon him? Or upon Nanna? Or upon his entire *people*?

As my eyes wandered across the beautiful green landscape below, an unbidden tear slipped down my face, followed by a second, and then a third. Letting out a little sigh, I whispered goodbye to the home road—to my parents, to Auburn, to life as I knew it—and turned my back on it.

My place was here. I couldn't betray the others. The clock struck four thirty-eight and the door at the end of the room swung open. Lord Glacier entered, his white-skinned face set like stone. He strode toward me, hands clasped lightly behind his back.

HOME ROAD

"Have you made your choice?"

"I have," I said.

His face fell, for my answer was spoken in those words. But I think he knew it already.

"This is your final answer?" Darkness came into his face and eyes—like the smoke one sees before a fire erupts.

I lifted my head to look him full in the eye. "I'll not say anymore."

His jaw tightened and he looked lingeringly into my face. That quiet calculation came to the surface.

"Your fate isn't the only one determined by your decision," he said.

My heart skipped a beat. He turned. His hands met in a brisk clap, and instantly, a door opened to my right.

"Behold the error of your ways," came Lord Glacier's voice.

But I barely heard it. Ian's bloodied face had my full attention.

chapter TWENTY

His brown head hung low. The soldier behind him shoved him forward, and Ian fell into the room on his hands and knees. Several drops of blood fell from his face and stained the perfect carpet. In an instant, I was at his side.

"I already knew what your answer would be," Glacier said darkly, "so during the few minutes between our meetings, I had him soundly beaten." He came to us and stood before Ian. "I want you to know that this girl has brought death upon you with her defiance. I only wished to ask a couple questions about you, but she refused to comply."

Ian lifted his head, and his bright green eyes bored into my dark ones. Beyond the pain raging inside them, I saw gratitude. He drew in a heavy breath, and his words were for me only.

"Don't regret your choice. What you stood for matters more than me."

I reached and brushed a tear from his cheek. *Did it?*

I heard Glacier move away from us and begin speaking to the guards in an undertone.

"Have you seen Ruby?" I whispered to Ian.

He shook his head from side to side then quickly grabbed my fingers and squeezed them hard. I knew he was in pain. I got to my feet, scanning the wall nearest us. A small tapestry, which depicted what I knew to be the Battle of Enthon, hung proudly within my reach. I snatched it roughly from the wall and knelt again by Ian, ignoring Glacier's disapproving gasp. I placed the fabric gently against the split on his cheek, and his blood smeared across the woven pattern of Fire Sprite men showing bravery in their own time of pain.

"T'anks," he whispered hoarsely.

I heard a step at my side, and turned to find Glacier looking down at me. "Kyndle, my dear," he said, "this raggedy boy isn't the only one who will suffer at your hand."

I stared up at him, waiting, not breathing. He nodded at the guard standing by the door through which Ian had come, and the soldier pulled the door open.

"So will she," Glacier said.

A brutish soldier dragged Ruby into the room by her tied hands. Her face was white with terror.

"No!" I cried, starting to my feet.

A soldier appeared out of nowhere and held me back.

"Take her to her cell," Glacier barked.

They pulled Ruby from the room again. I heard her crying. I dropped to the floor and the soldier didn't bother to catch me. I burst into violent tears. *This is no way for a Fireling to act before a Snowling.* But I didn't care.

"This was your choice," Glacier spat.

"Please!" I sobbed, crawling to his feet. "She's only a *child!*"

"Get away from me!" he snapped, lashing out with his leg. "You have made your choice and you shall pay for it."

I laid my head upon the floor. My hearing numbed. I would never have imagined not getting to tell her goodbye. The entire situation was crashing down around my ears, and I could do nothing about it.

I felt rough hands on my arms which lifted me to my feet.

"Put the two of them in the same cell," I heard Glacier say in a voice that was disgusted. "We'll give him the chance to look at his killer."

I don't remember that journey back down into the darkness, but all of a sudden, I found myself landing, hard, on the floor of the cell, Ian beside me. Our only light was from a torch out in the hallway. The cell door fell shut.

Drawing up my knees, I buried my head. Freedom, home, my family—all were now in the past. And it had been my own choice.

"Kyndle?" Ian whispered.

I wiped my face with my sleeve. "Yes, Ian."

"You may not want t' hear it, but may I recite a passage?"

"Sure," I choked.

"The Lord is good t' those who wait for him, t' the soul who seeks him. It is good that one should wait quietly for the salvation of the Lord. It is good for a man that he bear the yoke in his youth. Let him sit in silence when it is laid on him. Let him put his mouth in the dust, for there may yet be hope."

"Is there more?" I finally asked.

"Yes," he whispered.

I shut my eyes and listened quietly as his voice rose and fell in gentle rhythm, sounding like the recitation of a song too beautiful for music.

> Let him give his cheek t' the one who strikes,
>   And let him be filled with insults,
>   For the Lord will not cast off forever,
>   But, though he cause grief,
>   He will also have compassion
>   According t' the abundance of his steadfast love,
>   For he does not willingly afflict or grieve
>   the children of men.

Yet I groaned as the last line ended. "Then why is he doing it now?"

"I don't know for sure, Kyndle—I wish I did. I just know that it's for the good of those who love him."

I shivered. "I'm so cold. And I'm frightened."

He drew near and put his arms around me. "Me too."

"Ian, what do you do when you're frightened?"

"I go t' Christ for comfort."

I took in a deep breath. "How do I do it?"

He drew back to look in my face. "You want t' pray?"

"Yes," I whispered.

He grabbed my hands. "Let me show you."

Kneeling on the floor of that cold dungeon, we prayed. First Ian, then me. At first I was embarrassed, but that was soon swept away by the very *rightness* of it. My prayer was nothing special; it was nothing like what I sometimes heard Auburn whispering in the dead of night. Hers reminded me of a conversation between a child and its father, full of the love she so often spoke of, while mine had sounded more like a letter requesting furlough. Yet I wasn't ashamed of it; rather in a weird way—one I didn't think I'd ever feel—I was glad I had done it. When we finished, Ian sat back. He said nothing.

"So will God deliver us now that we asked him to?"

"Kyndle," he answered hesitantly. "Just because we've asked God for deliverance doesn't guarantee that we will receive it. He always answers our prayers, but it isn't always a *yes*."

I felt anger prick in my throat. "Then why did we even ask?"

"Because he wants us to talk with him. He doesn't always give us what we think we need—he gives us that which will benefit us the most. The answer isn't always a *yes* but do you know what, Kyndle?"

I took a strained breath. *Listen.* "What, Ian?"

"Receiving a *no* makes the *yes* much sweeter when it does come."

"What kind of a God is that?" I demanded of him. "Doesn't he even care about the pain we feel?"

"He couldn't care more. But he will always do what is best."

"Death is best?" I dashed away a blinding tear.

He was quiet.

"Since when did death become good?"

He sighed, resting an arm across my shoulders. "We don't know what our deaths may spark," he said softly. "This may change someone else's life."

I jerked out from under his arm.

"I don't care about someone else! I want to keep on living! I want you to go back to Nanna! I want Ruby to grow into a strong healthy woman!" I buried my face in my arms.

"I know it's hard to understand," he whispered. "I still struggle with asking for God's will to be done. It's a daily thing."

"I just don't understand you." I raised my head. "For a moment, for a few moments since I met you, I thought I maybe could. I thought maybe I could see how your faith wasn't blind—but now, I've never felt further away from you."

For several moments, Ian was quiet. Then I felt his hand close over mine.

"I'm right here," he whispered.

I felt tears rising as I turned to him. "So why can't I see the light you claim to follow?"

He hesitated. "Maybe you've closed your eyes."

I pulled my hand away but said nothing. I didn't know how to answer.

"Look at me, Kyndle."

Slowly I raised my head.

"Now look *hard*. What do you see?"

I studied the grimy face before me. "Kindness," I finally said.

"Go on."

"Generosity and hope and faith and a love like I've never seen."

He smiled. "All those things you see in me are a mere reflection of the things Christ has taught me t' do. I don't do them perfectly. Sometimes I don't even do them at all. Yet each time I fail, he gives me courage t' try again. It's love like you've never seen because any other love is only an imitation, and until you go to the source, to the very mouth of the river, it won't feel the same—it isn't the same."

"But, Ian." I glanced around the dark cell. "How can this be love?"

He stroked his chin for several quiet moments with his head drooped onto his knee. From this angle, I could see a full catalogue of our journey on his face; a jaw tight from hunger and stress, a split chin from a brutal blow, the beginnings of bruising from his recent beating. However, when he lifted his head, I was surprised to see a soft smile cover his face. The look in his eyes reminded me of the way you feel when you light a match in a pitch-black room.

"I have no doubt that every disciple watching, as Christ died in agony, asked himself the same thing," he said. "Yet I can't help but think, if they could look now and see all the beauty his pain brought, would they see the answer?"

I looked away.

"We're on this side of it, Kyndle." He sighed. "That doesn't make it easier, I know, but maybe it makes it more meaningful. That fellow Rime—if I didn't know better, I'd say he's been changed by this experience. I can't say exactly what that will mean for him, but I can say that seeing an innocent creature suffer, Fireling though you may be, has made him look at life differently. Seeing a criminal pay for his wrongdoing wouldn't have the same effect since he fully deserves it. But ever since the day you took Ruby's lashes, Rime has taken the time t' be kind. Some people see pain, and it brings out the cruelty in them. However, I think your suffering has changed Rime for the better."

I rubbed my forehead. I knew he was right. Our deaths might bring a change. They might bring *the* change which might set in motion the revolution we had so long dreamed of.

"I think you're right," I said at last. "When those back home get word of this, it will only hasten what's coming."

His forehead furrowed. "War?"

I nodded. "Every moment, we plan our revenge."

"So it's revenge that you want," he mused.

"Snow Sprites treat us like animals." My voice darkened with hate as I quoted my journal. "But we'll show them. They will learn that the Fire Sprites are a people to be reckoned with—and they'll never forget it as long as they live." I tensed my jaw. "Which may not be long."

Ian touched my hand again. "I'm sorry for all you've suffered."

"You aren't the one who should be apologizing."

"Yes, I am."

"Ian, don't."

"If it hadn't been for me, you wouldn't be here."

"I don't know what Ruby and I would've done if you *hadn't* been."

"If I had never shown up, you'd be safe and sound."

"Ian, we can't change that. We can only face forward courageously."

He bowed his head and nodded slowly in acceptance.

I soon lay down, weary of waiting, and tried to fall asleep. I had laid there for some time when Ian's voice met my ear.

"Dear God."

I didn't move a muscle.

"Thank you for your mercies. Thank you for your kindness, and thank you for finally showing me why you sent me here. I pray for Ruby, in this time of trial, that you would grant her escape from death, and if not, that you would strengthen her for this great testing. I pray for Nanna, that You comfort her hurting soul in the days and years t' come. Thank you for the great gift she has been t' me. And dear Father, I pray for Kyndle. Her soul is looking so desperately for something more. Please, help her t' see that everything she needs can be found in you."

Ian said no more, apparently falling asleep, yet I lay awake for a long time, thinking about his words—wondering if what he said could really be true.

I woke to blinding light and the sound of voices. I leapt to my feet. Ian was surrounded by soldiers. Rime stood in the doorway, holding a torch. The look on his face was broken.

I petitioned him with my eyes, and he understood what I didn't say. If this was the end, I wanted to say goodbye.

"Halt!" he thundered.

The soldiers hushed instantly and, at a signal from Rime, let me pass through. With a fast-beating heart, I stood before Ian.

"This is it," he said.

My throat ached, and I quickly looked down.

"I didn't want it to end like this," I said hoarsely.

He grabbed my shoulders.

"If you see Ruby," I said, striving vainly to hold in my sobs, "tell her that I love her."

"I'll tell her," he whispered.

"Thank you, Ian. Thank you."

So much was happening, and I couldn't find the right words to say.

"No," he said.

Something in his tone made me look up. His eyes were full of tears.

"Thank *you,* Kyndle." He choked. "For being my friend—for believing me."

Then his dry mouth stretched into a smile that, though bordered by grief, spoke more to me than a speech. I looked up into his face and tried to memorize the beautiful eyes, the freckle above his eyebrow, the lock of hair hanging down on his forehead—everything about this moment that was passing by too fast. And reaching deep into my sorrow, I drew forth a smile of my own.

"What's going on?" came an angry voice.

We turned to find Canton in the doorway.

"What are you waiting around for?" he barked at the soldiers.

Rime stepped from his position by the wall. "I told them to," he said. "I was giving the prisoners a chance to say goodbye."

Canton's eyes narrowed to icy slits. "I'm aware of your *feelings* for the prisoners, Rime," he said, "but they don't give you permission to discard orders. They've had plenty of time to say goodbye."

Rime lowered his head. Canton strode toward us, his eyes full of black hate.

"I don't pity you," he hissed. "You should've agreed to Lord Glacier's terms, but you didn't. So say goodbye."

I looked up at Ian, emotion swelling in my chest. He pulled me into a fierce embrace. The stripes across my entire back cried out for relief, yet the pain in my heart was all that seemed to matter in this moment. I stood numb as he drew back. Then with tears coursing freely down his grimy cheeks, Ian took my face between his large hands and gently kissed my forehead.

"God be with you," he whispered.

"Bind them quickly," Canton ordered. "Their deaths await."

Laughing coarsely, the soldiers tore us apart. Hands quickly bound in front of me, I was slung over a wide shoulder and all breath was rammed from my lungs. Ian's voice called out another farewell, but it was cut short by a cry of pain. My senses swirling into a vortex, I was carried out into the hallway.

I woke in another cell. This time I was alone. I thought I heard the faint sound of a multitude of voices, somewhere above, but the pounding of my heart made it hard to tell.

Pushing off my face, I pulled up my knees and laid my head on them. I wondered how I was to die. I couldn't know. But there was one thing I was sure of: I would be brave. No recanting, no tears, no lowered eyes. I would prove to them that Fire Sprites were made of tougher stuff than they thought.

After what felt like an eternity of silence, the iron door unlocked and someone entered. I sat still and didn't even bother to lift my head. There was a deep sigh.

"I had hoped for something different for you, Kyndle."

I looked up at Rime dully. "You had hoped I would forsake the others and go home alone? There's no glory in that." I put my head back down. "So I choose death."

His footsteps came near. I felt the toes of his boots touch mine. "For all of you?" he asked, quietly.

I didn't answer. Here I sat, trying to sound brave, while inside I was bent like a sapling before the wind. Fear consumed me like a disease. Fear for Ruby—and for myself. Because if I admitted it, deep down inside, I was terrified to die.

"I don't think they've ever executed a female before," he said. "I think they're scared to 'cause I'm to give you a second chance to change your mind. But I don't think you will."

I looked up. "I'm not turning my back on the others."

He reached down and lifted me to my feet by my tied hands. Then he sighed again. "Then this is it."

Ian's words.

"How will I die?" I asked in as brave a voice as I could muster.

He swallowed hard. "They'll shoot you."

I tried to hold his searching gaze but had to look away. My terror was growing more difficult to conceal. When I finally did look back at him, I was surprised to see anger across his face.

"Don't you get what all of this will mean?" he demanded. "Don't you understand?"

I couldn't hide my tears as he shook me roughly by the shoulders.

"It means a bullet *ripping* into your chest!" he spat. "It means that you stop breathing, you stop *existing*. It means you never again see the sun. It means you never see your family again, never marry the man whom you love, never know the joy of bearing him children, never live the long life that you were meant to have. This isn't a game, Kyndle! This is *death!*" A tear coursed down his flushed cheek.

My own face was wet, but I couldn't dry it. "I know."

"But you don't have to die!" he went on. "They've given you an out—take it!"

"Why? So I can go back to Frieman and live like a prisoner?"

His one tear was now followed by others. "At least you get to live."

"That's no way for someone to live, Rime. I can't do it."

For a moment more, he looked hard at me. Then he let me go to wipe away his tears.

"Thank you," I said softly.

His brow furrowed. "For what?"

"For treating me as you have." I looked at my feet. "The other soldiers wouldn't have been so kind."

"I didn't want any of this," he said.

That made me look up. "What do you mean?"

"I'm a conscript," he spat. "I didn't want any cruelty. When I treated you bad at first, it was because I hated my own life."

"Oh, Rime," I breathed.

"My mother hated violence. When my father was killed in a duel, she vowed I would grow up a peaceful man. I can only imagine her grief when I went missing."

"Did you ever see her again?"

His voice was strained. "I met her in the street one day. I saw the pain across her face. But I haven't seen her since."

"I'm sorry," I said softly.

"It's ironic," he said. When he lifted his face, that strange look from the prison hallway flashed across it. "You love your life and can't live. I hate mine and can't die."

I said nothing. He grabbed the rope on my wrists and opened the door. We went out into the damp corridor.

"My nonconformity isn't accepted," he said as we walked. "A soldier is expected to be cruel to his prisoners. I pay for it. But I don't know if it's worth it anymore."

We reached the end of the hallway and came to a large door. Sunlight peeked from underneath it and the voices I had heard before came from the other side of it. I turned to look up into his trouble face.

"Rime, whatever happens, don't stop being different."

Conflict clouded his eyes. "I'll…try."

I looked down at my wrists. So did Rime.

"Let me see those," he said, taking a knife out of from his boot to cut the ropes binding me. Then pushing my sleeves up, he found the leather bands around my wrists. "You don't need these anymore," he said softly, slicing them in two. "You're going to walk out there a free woman." The cut pieces fell to the ground.

Smiling my gratitude, I very deliberately ground them under my heel. Then I turned to face the door.

This is it.

"You ready?" he asked.

"Yes, Rime."

Reaching for the handle, he wrenched open the door. The sunlight was blinding as we walked forward. When my eyes had adjusted, I saw that we stood on the ground floor of some sort of stadium. It wasn't very large; only a dozen or so soldiers were stationed around the perimeter.

Above us sat hundreds of Snow Sprites, laughing and talking among themselves as if they were spectators of a wedding. They didn't seem to notice my entrance until small a group of soldiers from the other side of the arena came toward us. At their head was Canton.

I couldn't help but notice the care with which he was walking, how he kept the upper half of his body very still, his shoulders very straight. His jacket too was unbuttoned.

I turned to Rime questioningly.

"He got the flogging he gave you," he said in a low voice.

I was surprised to find pity, not satisfaction, arising in myself.

"Looking lovely," Canton taunted when he came near.

I didn't respond. I wasn't going to show anything. Especially my fear. By now, the crowd had begun to hush; hundreds of eyes watched my every move. So I stood straight and proud in Rime's gentle grip, ready for whatever was next.

Ready, my mind mocked. *You couldn't be more unready.*

From the other side of the arena, a door opened. A soldier, bringing a prisoner, came out of it. I saw long red female hair, but the distance kept me from recognizing the face. My heart beat fast.

A double execution? I turned to Canton.

"Double the fun," he mocked.

I closed my eyes. *Dear God, if you can hear me, don't let it be Ruby. I can't do this.*

But I had no reason to believe the request would be answered. Seconds turned to hours as we waited for their approach. I broke into a cold sweat as fear overwhelmed me—and my heart stopped as I finally saw who it was. A startled tear leaked down my face.

Opposite me, the other prisoner met my eye.

chapter TWENTY-ONE

Questions that I couldn't answer filled me. My voice lodged in my throat which had tightened like a bowstring. She didn't say anything. She only smiled. But I also saw tears reflected in the sunlight.

I felt Rime watching me. "You know her…" he breathed.

I had no words. I had no *thoughts*. But his question was answered by my silence.

The soldier jerked Auburn to a stop, fifteen feet before us. Her hands, always so gentle, were tightly tied behind her back. Sunlight shimmered in highlights across her hair.

Canton leveled a steely glare at Auburn and then turned to face me. Behind him, the soldiers stood rigid at attention.

"Step forward, Rime." His voice was taunting.

Letting go of my arm, Rime obeyed reluctantly.

"You've been selected for dispatching this Fire Spritess," Canton said brusquely, nodding at Auburn. When Rime hesitated, Canton yanked him forward by the collar. I knew the movement hurt him, but Canton showed no sign of pain. Condescension crowded all else out.

"Do it at once," he snapped, shoving a musket into Rime's hands.

After a second, Rime turned his eyes Auburn's way and, with a broken stride, slowly followed Canton toward her. Another soldier stepped up to grip my arm, and I heard laughter ripple through the soldiers. They were laughing at Rime.

Canton roughly yanked Auburn a few steps forward, closer to Rime. Anger flared up in me. She didn't resist, but she didn't falter. I saw her look right in Canton's eyes. I was proud of her.

Here was the one person our village had been so ashamed of, making the Fire Sprite name prouder than it had ever seemed for the entire Snow Realm to see.

Canton flicked out a knife and with it cut her bonds.

"I have one last request," she said when he stepped back.

It was the first time I had heard her voice since the morning she had gone away. As it met my ear, it brought with it the myriad of memories we had made together.

They hurt.

"Yes?" Canton asked in a piqued voice.

"I wish to address the crowd," she said firmly.

After staring her down, Canton about-faced north. Lifting his chin, he called loudly, "Prisoner wishes to address the crowd."

I followed his gaze to the far end of the stadium. From the high platform, a man rose from his seat. I couldn't make out his features, but his garb conveyed royalty. So this was Antares, the Snowling king.

Suddenly a second man rose. I recognized him as Glacier, even from my distance. Hate churned in my heart. There was a silence as Glacier whispered something in the king's ear. Then the king faced the crowd. His posture revealed cowardice, a lack of the leadership needed for a ruler. He nodded at Glacier and then returned to his seat. Glacier remained at the rail.

"Permission granted," he called to us. He didn't sit down.

Clearing her throat, Auburn turned her eyes upon the crowd.

"I must die for a crime that I did not commit."

Canton scoffed.

"They call me a spy. But I was nothing more than a good citizen."

Oh, the pain that coursed through my heart.

Oh, the regret that ripped apart all past good intentions.

"You are a spy!" Canton interrupted. "And even if you weren't, being a Fireling is a crime in itself!"

Auburn looked him steadily in the eye for several moments. Then she deliberately turned away. A chorus of applause rang in my mind. His face red, Canton spun on his heel and returned to his men. Rime stood alone, the rifle drooping in his hands.

Auburn scanned the crowd. "I," she said, "an orphan without a family to miss me, stand blameless before these gathered and my God. Motives have been ascribed to me that I haven't been able to shake. Truth doesn't matter to some, and that is something I cannot change. It would seem that honor and love are no longer very important in this place but they are to someone else, and this I hold to. I only hope my death will play a part in setting us Fire Sprites free."

There it was; a thought I had never even thought. Auburn, different as she was, was a Fire Sprite. She carried within her the same set of feelings about our exile and the same burning desire to see us a free people once again.

Complete silence reigned in the stadium. Complete silence reigned in my heart.

This is not how things are supposed to be.

Letting out deep breath, Auburn turned to me. Tears trailed down my face. After waiting so long to talk to her again, I never expected our words to be a *goodbye*.

"Auburn, I'm sorry!" I blurted out, my voice high and strained.

I saw her take in a deep cleansing breath, then she smiled again.

"For the glory!" she called, and I knew whose glory she was referring to. In her voice I could find no trace of fear.

My heart quailed, and it took all my strength to smile back. Her hand rose in a final greeting, then she looked away. Her nod told Rime she was ready. Trembling so that he could hardly stand, he raised the rifle.

Not removing her eyes from his face, Auburn spread her legs slightly, squared her shoulders, and raised her head high. Her chest rose in her last breath as Rime's shaking finger latched onto the trigger.

And as Auburn looked into the face of her executioner, peace entered her eyes.

She was ready, but I never would be.

My senses were numbed by the blast of the rifle. Rime staggered back as though struck, face white as death. When the smoke cleared, I saw my friend stretched motionless across the sandy floor.

I broke free from my guard's grip and ran, falling to my knees at her side. She lay very still with her eyes closed. A groan burst from my lips, and I bowed my head in sorrow.

She was gone.

Noiseless sobs shook me. As if losing Ruby and Ian wouldn't be enough, I had lost her too. My dearest friend.

"Kyndle," came a soft whisper.

I opened my eyes and found her looking up into my face. She was still alive, but by the trembling of her chin, I knew she was in great pain. Her hand clutched her chest and I glimpsed blood through her fingers. I leaned close.

"I'll save you," I said, trying to sound strong.

"It's too late, Kyndle." She gasped, laboring for every breath she took. "Death is precious—in God's sight." She choked for air. "Now—I know why."

"There is no hope?" I attempted to smooth the creasing pain from her brow.

"I hope...in Christ." Her gaze strayed past my face, seeming to search for something. As I looked on, the anguish in her eyes was replaced by a soft smile. It shone forth like a long-awaited sunrise. Her breathing grew more steady and more thin.

"The light," she whispered. "All is light."

She looked more beautiful in that moment than ever before. Her eyes slowly wandered back to my face. She opened her mouth to speak, but no further words would come out.

Tears falling fast, I gathered her broken body in my arms and pressed my forehead to hers. Years ago, I had promised to always be her friend, to help her through the hard times; now here, at the end of it all, I realized it was I who had been helped. I drew back to smile into her face one last time.

"Auburn," I whispered. "Thank you. For everything."

She looked at my left eye, then my right. From her parched lips came a long shuddering sigh. Then all was still. Gently I lowered her to the ground.

Her green eyes, viewers of lifelong scorn, looked sightless up into the sky. Her gentle spirit, so abused by the hardships of this life, had finally flown to its long-awaited rest. And as I looked down at her face, forever clad in a gentle smile, countless memories of all the different emotions I had seen in those eyes rushed across my mind: joy, patience, forgiveness, determination, the sting of rejection, even anger.

Yet most of the time, they had been filled with a yearning. Now they were at peace. Leaning forward, I looked down into them one last time. Then, my hand steady, I brushed them closed.

"All right, get her up!" Canton called.

Footsteps approached, a hand took a hold of my shoulder and I was yanked to my feet. I saw a second soldier lift Auburn's body and carry it away. The soldier jerked me to face Canton.

"Have *you* any words to say to the crowd?" he taunted.

My thoughts swirled, but my eyes finally landed on his face. A smug smile had spread across it. When I couldn't manage a reply, no patience was shown. The soldier pulled me in front of Rime.

This is it. The time had come. *I will be brave*, I told myself.

"Rime," came Canton's command. "Do your duty."

But what was this? What was wrong with me? I strove hard to make myself look right in Rime's eyes but found myself unable to do so. I was terrified to die, and managed only a passing glance at Rime's face.

Where had Auburn's strength come from?

Rime wasn't able to even raise the rifle. A look of anger and terror had combined on his face to create paralyzing sorrow.

Remembering your training! Remember your ancestors!

Canton strode up to him. Ripping the rifle from his hands, he shoved Rime forward. Then turning to me, Canton raised the gun. My knees nearly buckled. My heart pounded. And I realized in that moment that I wasn't truly strong.

There was a soft *click* as the hammer fell into place, then there was a blasting shot.

But instead of pain, I felt myself propelled backward onto the ground. All breath was knocked from my lungs as I landed flat on my back.

Bewildered, I looked up to find that Rime had taken my bullet. I crawled to his side. Eyes rolling in agony and fear, he clutched frantically at his stomach. I reached to draw his hand away, but with his other, he clutched at mine. With huge effort, he raised his head from the ground. All the veins in his neck bulged from the strain.

"Rime, why?" I whispered. My eyes began to fill as I put my fingers to his neck.

"Got my wish," he gasped with a tiny smile, letting his head fall back. His eyes shut. "No more violence. I'm free." His pulse beat feebly under my fingers and his lifeblood flowed freely from his chest.

Just then a *click* sounded in my ear. I looked up into the barrel of Canton's gun. His upper lip curled in a grin as the hammer clicked into place a second time.

Fffft!

There was a strange whistling sound immediately followed by one of impact. Canton staggered back, his face a mixture of pain and confusion as he clutched the thick-shafted arrow embedded in his chest. My heart thrilled wildly as my eye settled on it. The feather pattern was strangely familiar.

It had been made by a Fireling.

Canton hit the ground, lifeless.

Pandemonium broke loose. Soldiers began running all over, gesturing wildly with their white hands, shouting unheeded commands. The crowd was dispersing rapidly. Screams echoed all around the stadium. Footsteps sounded behind me, and someone dropped to their knees at my side. I was shocked to look into a familiar face.

"Flint!" I gasped.

A good-natured smile spreading over his face, he pulled me to my feet. Gripping hands, we ran for the safety of the nearest wall. Shots pounded in our ears and thick arrows whistled past as Fireling war cries rang out all around. We reached the wall, and I dropped to my knees.

Swiveling around, I got my first good look at what was going on.

Fire Sprite warriors were everywhere—clad in leather armor, carrying swords and axes. Snowling soldiers, offering faint resistance, fell before them. A few of my countrymen formed a line to protect Flint and me as we leaned against the wall.

"Are you hurt?" he demanded, grabbing my shoulders.

I shook my head, absolutely dazed. How was he free? The last I had seen of him, he was being beaten by Snow Sprite soldiers. Yes, I had urged Ruby to hope, but I would never have truly imagined he was alive. Yet here he was—free and rescuing me from death.

But how?

"What about Ruby?" came his next anxious question. "Have you seen her?"

I shook my head. Were she and Ian still alive?

He turned back to the fighting. "We've got to find her."

As he spoke, I caught sight of another familiar face. With the speed of a petrified squirrel, Tinder Draithen sped across the arena and dropped to his knees beside us. A sturdy bow was slung over his shoulder, a quiver hung from a strap on his back. There were nine arrows in it. I gestured at the missing tenth, a question in my eyes.

He nodded. "I was almost too late." His eyes bounced from my face to the fierce fighting beyond us. "If not for that soldier jumping in front of you, you would've been killed before I could grab my arrow."

An image of Rime's pain-racked face flashed across my mind, and I leaned against Flint for support. Near us, a Snow Sprite soldier fell to the ground and lay still. An arrow *plinked* off of the wall just past our heads and Tinder ducked.

"This is a bad meeting place," he said.

They both jumped to their feet then pulled me to mine. Flint pointed across the arena, at the door through which Rime and I had come.

"That's our target."

To my horror, one of the Firelings defending us fell dead. His sword, stained with carnage, fell to the sand.

"It'll be dangerous," Tinder went on, "but we'll make it."

Flint drew his sword and it shone brightly in the sun. Tinder pressed a small dagger in my hand, then pulled the bow from his shoulder. He set an arrow to the string.

"Don't be afraid," Flint said. "Tinder and I will protect you."

They both nodded at me, and I felt safer than I had in a long time.

"I know," I said.

We all smiled. Then, we plunged out into the fray.

chapter TWENTY-TWO

"Kyndle, duck!" Tinder cried.

Without a moment's hesitation, I dropped to my hands and knees. An arrow whistled over me—where my head had just been—and embedded itself in the chest of a Snow Sprite to my left. He shuddered and fell over dead. I crawled across his body with my breath held.

"Kyndle!" came Flint's panicked voice over the din of the fighting. Up ahead, I glimpsed him frantically looking for me while simultaneously dodging and ducking swinging swords and maces. But before I could get to my feet, a random heavy boot sunk into my ribs. I toppled on my back with a cry, but it was cut short as a heavy body fell across my torso. One of my hands was pinned to my chest. The other, still gripping the dagger, I held across my face. The fighting grew fierce all around me.

"Help!" I shrieked to any who might hear, trying to get out from under the soldier. His oppressive weight, plus his armor, told me this was one of my countrymen. I tried not to guess who it could be.

"Where are you?" came Tinder's voice from nearby.

"Down!" I heaved.

"Keep talking!" he yelled.

I tried but could hardly draw air into my lungs. A glimpse of Tinder's face through the fighting renewed me, and I fought to get out from under the crushing weight.

A movement to my right caught my eye, and I looked up into the face of a Snow Sprite. He grinned and began to raise his sword. Summoning all my courage, I plunged my dagger into the top of his foot and felt the blade hit sand. He roared in pain and toppled backward, but I snatched the dagger out before he fell out of reach.

Just then, I met eyes with Tinder. At that, he strove even harder to get to my side. As I looked on, he took a terrific blow to the cheek with a sword butt and fell. Rolling left to avoid a second, he swept his leg out to topple his foe who then became occupied with a new Fireling warrior. He crawled toward me.

"Are you hurt?" he panted, swiping at the blood on his face.

I shook my head no. Just then, his eyes fell on the person lying on top of me. His face lost all color.

"Tinder!" I wheezed desperately.

My voice pulled him from his stupor and he dragged the person off me. I scrambled up to my feet. With huge effort, he heaved the man across his broad shoulder. We turned toward our destination.

Suddenly Flint was at my side. Grabbing my hand, he began pulling me in the direction of the door. I stumbled along as fast as I could. Tinder followed behind, bearing his load, his face pale and sick. We reached the door.

Flint slammed into it in his haste, fumbling with the handle.

"C'mon!" Tinder urged, shielding me with his body. I now saw clearly the large gash in his cheek.

"Got it!" Flint gasped, heaving the door open.

We tumbled through it, and I managed to shove it shut using my foot. Sounds of battle were suddenly muted as we collapsed against the wall in a sweaty heap, panting for breath but thankful to be alive. Tinder slid his burden to the hard floor, and for the first time, I caught sight of the lifeless face of his father.

"Tinder," I whispered, putting a hand on his trembling shoulders. "I'm so sorry."

I felt his back heave with suppressed emotion. We were silent for a moment, but then a shout from somewhere in the depths of the prison brought us to our wits. Flint got to his feet and then assisted me to mine. Tinder remained on the floor, unwilling to leave his father's body yet knowing he had to.

"We can put it down this hallway," I suggested softly. "Once we find Ruby, we can come back for it."

"Good idea." There was a tremble in Tinder's voice.

Without a word, Flint reached down and grabbed the shoulders and I jumped to grab the ankles. I'm sure I wasn't much help, but I couldn't let Tinder do it either. We retreated down the hallway for several yards and then ever so gently lowered the body to the stone floor. Flint dropped to one knee beside the fallen warrior.

"Farewell, Fraith." His soft voice echoed in the stone passage. "You have brought your people great honor." Reaching down, he gently closed the dark still eyes. The move brought Flint's chin to a resting place upon his own kneecap, and I saw the effort it took to raise it again. Here was a giant among his heroes, the father of his best friend—his own father in many ways—pale, cold, and dead, his body to be left in a prison corridor, perhaps never found again, killed in a struggle for the freedom that every man deserves.

Reaching, I folded the large hands upon the broad chest and arranged my dirty dagger between the fingers. We both stood.

"May your blood not have been shed in vain," Flint said.

We returned to where Tinder still sat on the stone floor.

"We don't have much time," I said.

Flint stepped before Tinder and put out a hand. It took a few moments for Tinder to return the grasp and be pulled to his feet. A long look passed between them, then Flint returned to my side.

"Let's go," he said.

We hurried down the hallway, using the occasional shout as a guide to the action. I had absolutely no information as to where Ruby or Ian were being held or if they were even alive still.

"Shhh!" Flint said, stopping midstride.

It was all I could do not to run into him. "What is it?" I whispered.

"I thought I heard a scream."

We all listened intently. Sure enough, a scream pealed out somewhere ahead of us.

"Run!" Tinder urged from behind. "Someone's behind us!"

We plunged forward, turning this corner and that until we completely lost our bearings. Still we heard the sound of pursuit close behind—never stopping, ever nearing. The more we ran, the less light there was.

Suddenly I tripped on an uneven stone and lost my footing. But when I fell, I didn't hit Flint. I groped with my hand but he wasn't in front of me.

"Flint!" I whispered piercingly.

When there was no reply, I strove to remain calm. "When did you last hear him?" I asked over my shoulder.

Silence.

I felt the hair raise on the back of my neck. "Tinder?"

There was no reply. I was completely alone and lost as could be. Any effort to stay calm disappeared. I ran up the passage as a gripping feeling of panic rose in my throat.

"Tinder!" I called as loud as I dared. "Flint!"

After several terrifying minutes, I made myself stop running. Leaning against the stone wall, gasping for breath, I tried my best to remember the last time I had spoken to either of them. To my distress, I realized it had been quite for some time. There was no way to tell how long we had been apart. All sense of time vanished in this echoey dark space beneath the ground.

Just how long could these passages run? As I stood there, trembling, trying to figure out what I should do next, a heavy foot wiped my feet backward from under me. I hit the stone floor with a thud, all the air knocked from my lungs. I struggled to get free, but someone dropped onto my back.

"Stop!" I finally managed to scream as my hands were pulled behind me. I felt a rope being wound around my wrists.

"Quite the fighter," came a gravelly voice.

"Let me go!" I shrieked, squirming under his weight.

"Button your lip." A cloth was pulled over my mouth and tied tightly behind my head, then I was yanked back onto my feet and made to walk down the dark hallway. I tried to turn my head but was instantly shoved further forward. Wanting to create as many delays as I could, I began to drag my feet.

"Stop it," came his growl. "Walk or you'll regret it."

Instead of complying, I went completely limp and tripped him on my way down. As we both hit the floor, I struggled to escape, but in a moment felt my ankles being cinched together with another rope. I was jerked to my feet. Muttering curses under his breath, he pressed me to the wall and backhanded me. Then he slung me over his shoulder and we went on.

My entire head ached from the blow, and I quickly realized that I had no hearing in my right ear. I hung limp, too worn out to offer any further resistance. Right then, a second voice materialized from the shadows.

"Is this the Fireling girl?" it asked.

"Sure is."

"Where are you taking her?"

"Glacier," was the response. "The city is overrun with rebels. He and the king are making their escape. They want to bring her with them."

"He thinks she's worth something?"

The other scoffed. "When was a Fireling ever worth anything?"

My mind whirled. I had seen no sign of either Ian or Ruby, so I clung to a hope that they had escaped or, at worst, been shipped to some other prison. At least in a cell, they would be safe from all the violence. Yet as I thought of Ian, I felt a sick feeling stirring in my stomach. I didn't know why and I didn't like it.

Consciousness wavered.

I was brought back to life by the gag being ripped from my face. As I opened my eyes, the soldier slid me off his shoulder. I was turned around and looked directly into Glacier's icy eyes. Heat ignited in my chest, and I dropped my gaze. I couldn't bring myself to look him in the eye—this murderer of those whom I had loved. I felt him lean close.

"Are you so certain of your decision now?" he asked.

I didn't show him my face, but my anger was betrayed by my voice. "I regret nothing."

He took my chin firmly and raised my head, forcing me to look right into his steely eyes. The burning ignited into a full fury in my chest. The ring on his finger pressed hard against my jaw which I was clenching so tightly that my teeth felt ready to crack.

"The boy," he said, studying my face. "He was your friend?"

Was?

Though restricted by his hold, I nodded. He laughed a cruel laugh—one that struck fear into my heart. Then he released my face.

"This turned out better than I had expected," he said. "It was you who was so cocky in the face of the death that you chose. Yet here, in the end, you are the one to have escaped it."

My mouth went dry and I felt all strength leaving my body.

"Oh yes," he crooned on. "He begged and pleaded with his guard that he be allowed to go first, in hope that I would change my mind and spare you girls. Of course, I had no intention of doing that, but I did honor his request. Then I had his miserable body dragged from the arena before you and that other Fireling girl were brought out."

He smiled wickedly.

I staggered back, the burning in my chest replaced by shooting pain. I felt the guards grab my arms and hold me on my feet.

Glacier leaned close, almost into my very ear. "And they told me you were so strong," he mocked. "It seems to me that you're not very strong after all."

A tear steamed down my face. I knew he was right.

"Go," I heard Glacier tell the guards. "Load her up."

Nearly insensible, I was carried from the room. As the door fell closed, both on the room and on my consciousness, Glacier's words rang loudly in my ears, reviling me for my weakness.

First Epilogue

I don't remember much of the journey that came afterward.

Heartsick with grief, I drifted in and out of consciousness for most of that jarring trip in the back of a luggage wagon. All I knew was darkness, heartache, and the faraway sound of horses.

Dad, Mum, Flint, and Ruby marched boldly across my mind's eye like unattainable dreams—ever present, ever just out of reach. I clung to hope that they were still alive, but as the rest of my hopes, it hung by a frayed thread.

And I thought of Ian. It wasn't until he was gone that I realized what a large part of my heart had been his.

Ian's love had been real.

And now?

That love was no more than a memory.

Part 2

chapter 1

Footsteps echoed down the passage, and I stirred from my position on the stone floor with a shiver. It was only midautumn, but it didn't matter. This wasn't the chill you feel as a breeze floats by; this was a *wet* kind of cold that drifts through clothing to permeate your very bones.

In a dungeon, being cold becomes a part of who you are.

As does the pain of physical maltreatment—the chronic fatigue left by nonnourishing rations—the ache of inactivity. But most of all, the pain of being away from those you love.

At times, not knowing whether your family is alive can feel worse than actually losing them.

A key grated in the lock, then the heavy door of my cell swung open with a groan. A gust of air brushed my face as the only Snow Sprite that I didn't despise was shoved into the cell. He landed hard on his hands and knees but said nothing till the door had been slammed to and locked once more.

"How'd it go?" I asked as he picked himself off the ground.

"Same as always," he spat, swiping blood from his chin. "They think they can force me to talk by beating me, but it just makes me stronger. I'll never give the others away."

"Good man."

He nodded at my untouched supper. "Why haven't you eaten?" There was a wolfish gleam in his weary eyes.

I nudged the tray toward him. "I wasn't hungry."

He pulled it toward himself. "Wish I could say the same." He chuckled but winced. His hands went to his ribs, and I knew he was hurting.

Seeing me notice, he scowled. "I don't want your pity, Kyndle."

"I'm sorry, Hail."

I didn't have to ask to know the beatings were becoming more severe. I wondered how long it could go on before the pain brought names to his lips. How long would he last?

Finding Hail after all this time had come as both a surprise and relief. Though I hardly knew him, there was something about him that made me feel safe. His quiet companionship lifted me from the darkness which had become my constant companion. I think I only liked Hail because he reminded me of home.

After being summoned back to the Cold Realm to give a report, strife had stirred up and he had quit his position as representative to become a leader of an underground rebellion—*against* the aristocracy. All had been going well, but then he had been betrayed by a fellow rebel and arrested. All his efforts for the cause hadn't been enough to protect him from inner treachery. Strangely enough the whistle-blower refused to give any information about the rest of the rebels. It had cost him. From what we had been told, he inhabited the cell down the hall.

The only reason Hail and I shared a cell was due to the huge number of war prisoners. I longed to speak with any Firelings who may be kept in the cells nearby, but all communication had been expressly forbidden and guards patrolled regularly.

"Can you call me Jack?" Hail's voice interrupted my thoughts.

I turned to him. "Jack?"

He nodded. "It—it was what my mother wanted to name me. Or so the nurse told me when I was young."

I was surprised. He had never spoken of his family before.

"Of course I will, Jack."

"Thanks."

"Any news from the front?" I asked after a moment. There were times when he caught snatches of conversation to and from interrogation.

"It sounds like your people are putting up quite a fight."

"Of course we are," I retorted, but my anger wasn't for him. "Nothing was expected from the Firelings but submission. But they're wrong. One defeat doesn't mean an eternal one." I pushed down the passion that had risen in my throat.

"I expected more," he said softly. "Victory wouldn't surprise me."

"You don't know how *hard* it is to sit here idle, hour after hour, while my countrymen are out there *dying.*" I let out an exasperated sigh. "Not a single time has Glacier called for me in the month since my arrival, so I know he doesn't need immediate information. What he *does* need me for, I can't imagine."

"I can't pretend to know," Jack said. I vaguely noticed the hurt in his voice. "We never got along very well."

I scoffed. "You aren't the only one."

"It's different." He rose and began pacing. "You're a hostage, Kyndle. He's *supposed* to scorn you. But me…"

I hugged my knees and rocked for whatever reason.

"I didn't think a count was so special. No offense," I added quickly.

He stopped midstride and slowly pivoted. "You don't know?"

"Know…what?"

He sat down by me.

"Jack, what's wrong? Tell me."

He swallowed hard. "Glacier is—my father."

My eyes grew wide.

"I suppose I should tell you more about myself," he said.

"Yeah," I said. "I think you should."

He drew in a deep breath. "My adopted paternal grandfather, Leander Frost, married the last Ice Lady, Lily. A widow, she had a child from her first marriage, Glacier. Leander and Lily sired a daughter, Icelyn, then a son, Antares. This son was proclaimed the heir to the throne because, as an Iceling, my father could never be king.

"Time passed. Each child grew up, married, and had children of their own. The same day I was born, Antares's wife also delivered a daughter, Allabelle. My mother and aunt both died within a few days. My cousin, Princess Allabelle, died in infancy. After her funeral, Antares declared he would never marry a second time. My father said the same.

"I never really fit in with the other noble children. My only friend was a girl named Winterose, eldest daughter of a high-ranking nobleman. She always stood up for what was right." He smiled at the memory, but then his face fell dark once more as he continued. "When I turned nine, Father sent me to a lonely school on the border, and after a few years there, I was appointed junior aide to the Fire Realm representative."

"I only saw you a few times in all those years," I commented.

"I only went out when I had to," he said. "After ten lonely years there, the representative finally died and I was appointed as his replacement. An ambassadress filled in while I was being instated. Then she went to live somewhere in the Nature Realm."

"I remember her," I broke in. "Why did she go to the Nature Realm?"

He shrugged. "That entire ordeal was a bit private."

"Oh."

"After just a week in Frieman, I received the summons to return to the Snow Realm for their annual report. I left the same day I first met you in the street."

"Hail—I mean, *Jack*," I said after a long silence. "What did you tell them about us?"

"I told them your people were obedient if not bitter." He let out a sigh. "I couldn't predict what the future would hold."

"You didn't know all this was coming?"

"Of course not!" he retorted, a slight anger sparking in his voice. "Did you think that I would foresee it and *not* warn them? That I'd *knowingly* allow my countrymen to die by the hundreds?"

"I'm sorry," I blurted. "I spoke without thinking."

"You misjudge me, Kyndle." He got to his feet. "You take my kindness toward you to mean that I hate my own people and love yours." He shook his head, and I heard the anger surface in his voice again. "The Snowlings have a host of faults, I'll give you that—but I'll always be more loyal to them than Firelings who swoop in and murder innocents."

I leapt to face him. "You accuse *us* of murdering innocents? We who have been kept under your realm's thumb for two hundred years for no just reason? We whose women have been brutally killed at the least sign of resistance? *We're* to be called murderers?"

He didn't answer.

"And another thing." I barreled on. "Explain to me, Sir *Count*, how the executions of two of my friends, and maybe my sister, wasn't a murder of innocents."

"I know nothing of that," he said, backing up defensively. "You would hold me accountable for their deaths?"

"I don't hold you accountable, Hail, but I do hold you to speak truth."

He held up his hands. "Didn't your soldiers swoop in and kill?"

I leveled a hard stare. "They killed *soldiers* who were armed—hardly what I would call 'innocents.' In war, that can't be called murder."

"What is then? Our men had no warning."

I laughed. "You don't really expect a warning before each and every engagement, do you? Is that a rule your men follow?"

"Our realm respects war. We also respect innocents."

Something snapped deep in me and the hair stood up on the back of my neck. "You respect *innocents*?" I repeated.

"Of course."

"What would you call me then? Guilty?"

He turned away.

"Maybe in an ideal sense, your people respect all peoples," I said in a trembling voice, "but not the real one. I am *wholly* innocent yet I've suffered more heartache since leaving home than I had expected to suffer in my entire life. And for what? I didn't do anything wrong."

"You should have consulted *me* when such an important matter as the unknown boy came up," he snapped, turning. "Making that decision was *my* job, not yours."

"You think *I* made the decisions?" I asked in exasperation. "You think I *wanted* all of this? I didn't ask to be dragged into *any* of this. I only wanted to stay in Frieman. The council made the decisions. I had no choice but to obey. And now—" I turned to the one window, high in the wall. "Now both my best friends are dead, I have no idea if my sister is still alive, my brother may be a hostage, and I haven't heard anything from my parents." A tear slipped off the end of my nose.

"I'm sorry," he said in a much softer voice. "I'm just anxious."

I slid to the floor. He came and sat beside me. I didn't want him there. Just when I was convinced I was beyond the point of tears, he had raked at my emotions and made them bleed. My eyes stung, and my throat grew raw.

"I'm sorry," Jack said again.

"Did you ever see Winterose again?" I asked after a few minutes.

He shook his head. "I've never gotten the chance. But I have friends who tell me how she is doing."

"How is she?"

"A few months ago, a group of rebels bombed a theater her family was in. She was uninjured but the event put her life in danger. She's currently in hiding."

"And—her family?" I ventured gently. Somehow I sensed his answer would be difficult to hear. His words came out painfully.

"All of her family was killed."

chapter 2

The dying sun cast long reaching shadows across the chilled cell as I waited for Jack's return the next day.

I drew my knees up to my chest, straining to catch the faint sound of a bird singing somewhere outside my window. As the shadows lengthened, the song notes grew less frequent until they were gone altogether. I waited in silence, hoping there was more, but all was quiet.

My heart ached with the harsh bitter reminder that the freedom of the songbird wasn't mine. The ever-constant sting of loneliness pricked at my heart again, chilling me even more. Fond memories washed over me like an evening tide, etching familiar faces into the sands of my mind.

If I listened hard enough, I could almost hear their voices.

My strong father, tender mother, fearless brother, gentle sister. My family. My very heart.

Were we never meet again?

Auburn, the dearest friend I had ever known. So different yet still so beautiful—and brave to the bitter end of a rifle.

Tinder, my childhood friend. So plucky, so protective.

Nanna, that ancient well from which I had drawn precious wisdom, a strong support to which I had clung when the floodwaters rose.

And there was Ian, the only boy I had ever dared to love.

The boy I had lost.

I sat long into the night, anxiety gnawing inside my stomach. Jack still hadn't returned. What could have happened? Had two weeks of beatings finally broken his will? Had he finally given in? Or worse?

Surely not, I thought. Jack was stronger than that.

I paced the cell, trying to push back the dread that had come over me, trying to calm the clamoring of my soul. All would be fine.

But what if it wasn't? What if Jack never returned? Such things did happen. And what if I never found out *what* had happened?

The suspense was not to last long. Around dawn, the key grated in the lock. I cowered in the corner as the door opened. A dark silhouette filled the doorway then stepped *through* it. My throat tightened in terror in the silence that followed.

Then—"Kyndle?"

I rose slowly, the panic draining away. "Jack?"

He turned toward my voice, the faint light revealing his face. "Yes." He sighed. "It's me. Sorry it's so dark. I tripped on a stone and shattered my lantern. I'll have to ask for another one tomorrow."

I stared in shock at his new clothes, the ring of keys in his hand.

"Jack, what has happened?"

"They said since my will wouldn't be broken by beatings, they would make me a prison guard instead."

"A *prison guard*?" I laughed. "Jack, you're free!"

But he just scoffed. "A prison warden is a prisoner himself. It's eternal silence and shadow. No end to the sentence." He looked into the cell and sighed dramatically. "I, Jack Frost, doomed to eternal imprisonment in a black hole."

I couldn't hide my amused smile. I was just glad he was alive.

Time passed much slower, now that Jack was no longer with me at all times of the day, but he did his best to make life easier for me.

"Jack," I said, glancing up as he brought my supper one day. "Is there any way that you can get me some paper, a pen, and a jar of ink?"

His eyebrows lifted. "Why?"

"I journal, remember?"

He smiled blandly. "How could I forget?"

HOME ROAD

He returned that evening with a generous stack of paper and a pen in his hands. I fell to writing with fervor, barely having the presence of mind to thank him. He left me alone with my thoughts. I filled the pages with my heartache and griefs.

> Twelfth of Philor, 598
> How long it's been since I held a pen! I hope that there is enough time in this day to write of all that has happened to me.
> It all began on the thirtieth of Jenth, 598.
> I was a normal, Fireling girl who was friends with the town's scapegoat, Auburn. When she got high marks on her Tests of Transition, she was sent on a special mission to find our missing cardinal.
> Later that morning, my brother and I were called to a meeting with the councilmen. There we were told that a young man had been found in our borders and the place he claimed to live in was one we'd never heard of. To our surprise, Flint and I were then told that we were to escort this young man back to the mountain and try to send him home. We were told the most important tools we could use on this mission were speed and secrecy. If a portal to a whole new land lay within our border, we didn't want the Snow Sprites to know about it.
> That night, two Snowlings arrived in town with a decree from the Snow Realm. The order was that all families could have only two children. All others were to be sent north or else be executed.
> That was when we knew—war was coming.
> That same night, our men killed the two Snowlings.

We began our journey early in the morning of Elindar 1. Due to the decree, our friend Tinder got my sister Ruby to us, then we set off. We all tried to be warm to the Unknownling boy who called himself Ian Freemont.

For days we searched but could find no trace of the portal he described.

On Elindar 6, having no success, we started back for home. During the descent, Flint and I were carried down the side of the mountain in a small avalanche. When I awoke, I began to search for Flint but was kept from doing so by Ian. It angered me until I saw that he had saved me from being captured. We watched from the tall grass as Flint was beaten by Snowling soldiers. Then he was taken away. A second group of soldiers began to search the mountain for any other Firelings.

With all haste, Ian, Ruby, and I went back to our campsite to find a place to hide. We did so in a niche in the rock face which, as it turns out, was the portal we had been looking for. In a matter of seconds, we were transported to Ian's home where Ruby and I made the acquaintance of Ian's Nanna. She took us in, fed us, and comforted our sad hearts.

The next morning, Ian told Nanna he intended to see us home safely through the danger which awaited us and she agreed to let him go.

Ian, Ruby, and I bid farewell to Nanna and then successfully traveled back through the portal to the mountain where, almost immediately, we were caught by a group of Snowling soldiers.

Then we were brought on a long difficult journey to the northern land of the Snow Sprites. Along the journey, Ruby and I had the unfortunate opportunity to learn a fuller meaning of the word *flogging*.

Upon our arrival, we were all separately offered freedom if we agreed to answer all questions concerning our mission. When I refused to do so, I was given a sentence of death. I soon found out that my sister and Ian had both received the same fate. I got to say goodbye to Ian before we were separated but wasn't allowed to speak to Ruby.

My guard, Rime, came to get me, giving me one last chance to recant. I didn't. He then revealed his desire to take my place, being a soldier only due to conscription.

In the arena, I came face-to-face with the last person that I ever expected to see—Auburn.

To this day, I don't know why she was there. I probably never will.

Before my eyes, she was shot.

Rime, who had been chosen for the job, trembled so that his aim was inaccurate and Auburn wasn't killed immediately. Thus I was given a moment to speak to her, to say goodbye, and then to close those eyes into which I had so often looked with secret admiration.

They took Auburn's body away, then I was jerked to my feet. My turn had come.

When the shot rang out, I felt no pain but only the impact of my body hitting the ground. Sitting up, I realized that Rime had stepped in front of the gun and taken my bullet. I crawled to his side, and, as he died, he told me he was glad to go.

An upward glance showed that the gun was aimed at me once more. I drew in what I thought was my last breath. Imagine my shock when—a mere moment later—I beheld my executioner stretched dead upon the sand. Embedded in deep his chest was a thick arrow, which I instantly knew was of Fire Sprite make. Chaos broke out in the stadium as Fireling warriors broke upon the scene.

I was rescued by my brother, Flint, who I hadn't expected to ever see alive again. Tinder Draithen joined us, and together, the three of us made our way to the dungeon to find Ruby. In silence, we wove our way through the dark and confusing passages.

Then all of a sudden I was very lost and all alone. To this hour, I don't know what became of my brother and friend. While I stood there alone, fear pulsing in my heart, I was knocked down by a silent opponent and quickly subdued. Slung over a shoulder, I soon found myself in the presence of the regent of the Snow Realm. He laughed in my face and then informed me of the death of Ian Freemont. He said Ian had begged to be allowed to be executed first, in the hopes that us girls would be let go. After he mocked me for my weakness, Glacier ordered that I be taken away.

I was brought to this desolate place as a war hostage.

Jack informed me we're in the dungeon of Straven Tree, a fortress on the western edge of the Snow Realm. Straven Tree has become the home of the royal family since the evacuation of Galaheed.

I set the pen down, stretching each of my fingers in turn to banish the cramps that had seized them. When they dissipated, I didn't pick the pen up again. I gathered the pages into a stack and set it by the wall.

In a way, I felt less heavy. Journaling had always been how I unloaded my thoughts then decided how to go on.

Except now, there was no going on. It was just sit, eat, sleep, wake up, sit some more. In that way, I felt more heavy than before. How many days had I spent in his timeless stone cell? How much longer could I sit? Seizing the pen, I grabbed my last paper and added a few more words to the lines written there.

> I do not know what will become of me or if I'll ever be free again. All I know is that I feel alone in this dark place.
> > Very terribly alone.

chapter 3

Twelfth of Philor, 599

It's been exactly one year since I wrote those forlorn words.

I'm still a hostage, in the same cell, writing in the same shaft of light shining from the same window. I still haven't had a single audience with the regent after all of this time. So why does he keep me?

There have been very few changes in all this time, except that my hair has grown further down my back, so I can nearly sit on it, and my stack of paper grows a little more each time I journal, even though each new entry turns out about the same as the last.

My age too has grown. I am now nineteen years old.

A few weeks ago, when Jack told me the date was Elindar 12, 599, I realized that my birthday the year before had slipped by without me remembering it. After a long hard train of thought, I found that my eighteenth birthday had been the day on which Auburn and Ian died.

Oh, saddest of days.

I wonder whether my people know I'm a hostage. Wouldn't they send a ransom if they knew?

I looked up from my paper in shame. *Of course they would,* I forced myself to admit. *They wouldn't abandon me.*

Rolling my neck from left to right, I tried to ease some of the familiar ache. I laid my pen aside and put the new page on the stack by the wall. Just then, Jack's footsteps sounded outside my door.

I glanced toward the door, confused. He only came to bring meals. I glanced at the shadows on the floor, cast by the bars on the window high above. It wasn't mealtime yet—my stomach would have complained if it had been.

"What is it?" I asked as Jack walked in. He was the same gentle-eyed Snow Sprite from the year before.

"You've been summoned." This said in his usual vague way.

"Really?" I stood up in my wonder. "But why?" I took a halting step toward him, fear knifing my heart. "Has anything happened?"

At his shrug, my fears disappeared. He opened the door. "Nothing has happened as far as I know," he said as we walked out, "except that they want you immediately."

"Maybe someone has offered ransom," I said excitedly as we went along. "Maybe I'll be free!"

Jack shrugged again. Suddenly nervous, I raked my long fingers through my thick orangey red hair. "I've never met the king before," I murmured.

"It's not the king you'll be speaking to," he said. "It's Lord Glacier."

The lid of my memory jar flew open and I was instantly angry. "Your father?"

"Yes," he said in a sighing voice.

"Why don't you call him 'father'?"

"His rank demands a proper title. Even when I was a count, I wasn't allowed any form of familiarity. Since I'm just a prison warden now, it's even more forbidden."

"You seem very different from your father, Jack."

He chuckled. "Whenever I do something unsatisfactory, I'm reminded how much I'm like my mother."

"She must have been kind then," I said, softly.

He glanced sideways at me and a slight smile came across his face. Then he looked ahead once more.

I inhaled deeply, we emerged out into the courtyard where small piles of snow gathered in the corners. The winter wind, knowing that it's time was short, cut into us with a vengeance. I sighed and my breath came out as mist.

"I have a feeling this won't be pleasant."

"Probably not," he replied softly. "But don't give up hope yet. It may turn out to be more productive than either of us could have imagined."

I shrugged, uncertain. *Productivity seems impossible with these bigoted Snow Sprites.*

Glacier was waiting for us when we arrived. At a flick of his jeweled fingers, the soldiers at his side slipped from the room.

"Ms. Fireling, is it?" he asked in that same haughty voice.

"Yes, Your Grace," Jack said as we came to a stop before him. "This is Kyndle."

"I know her name, Hail," Glacier snapped. "We've met before."

Jack bowed his head submissively.

Glacier turned back to me. "I trust your time here has been pleasant?" he asked sarcastically.

Jack's hold on my arm tightened in a plea.

I bit my lips shut to keep back an angry reply and stared at the floor.

"Now onto business," Glacier said briskly. "I'll be brief. I've brought you here to discuss your role as middleman—er, *woman*, when I debate a peace treaty with your countrymen."

I jerked my eyes from the rug. "Peace treaty?"

He nodded slowly. "The Snow Realm has spent too much money and blood on this silly war. I'm ready for it to be over."

I checked my eagerness. "What are the terms of the treaty?"

"Those aren't for you to know just yet," he replied cooly. "I simply wish to know if you plan to cooperate and do as I say."

I squared my shoulders. "I will not say or do anything to bring shame on myself or my countrymen, if that's what you mean," I replied evenly. "I'll only discuss terms that are *fair*."

His face, so calm before, twisted with mockery, and he took a step in my direction. "You will do exactly as I bid."

I instinctively drew closer to Jack who remained motionless.

"You haven't changed," Glacier said angrily. "You're just as defiant and stubborn as when we spoke last. A year in an isolated cell has done little to sober you. But no matter," he growled. "I'll hammer it out of you yet." His eyes flashed.

I smiled boldly. "You may try if you like. Until now, no one has been able to do it."

"Until *now*," he repeated harshly, "you have not felt *my* hand. You'll soon realize I'm a man who gets what he wants—exactly *when* he wants it."

I shrugged defiantly. "I'll do all that you ask as long as your orders do not violate my conscience."

"You'll do all I ask whether or *not* it violates your pretty conscience!" he roared, sticking his face within inches of mine. Unable to back up any further, I steeled my jaw.

"Is that understood?" he whispered through gritted teeth.

I offered no response. I wouldn't compromise in any way yet I didn't want to anger him further. Taking a step back, he studied my face through narrowed eyes. After a tense moment, he looked away.

"Return her to her cell, Hail. I'll call for her when I need her."

"Yes, Your Grace." Jack bowed slightly.

Glacier turned to me as if waiting for me to bow as well. I did no such thing. He waved us away.

Jack was silent as we walked down the luxurious halls of the castle. I chanced a sideways glance and wasn't surprised when he stared ahead.

"What did you want me to say?" I said, shrugging helplessly.

"I wanted you to say what you felt like you needed to say," he replied somewhat indifferently.

I stared ahead as the guards opened the door which led outside.

"You might have been a bit less metallic toward me."

"Well, what did you want me to do?" he blurted as the door closed.

I turned in surprise. He rarely raised his voice.

"He's my *father*," he said.

I couldn't decipher what emotion I heard in his voice. Was it loyalty—or bitterness?

"I'm not permitted to say anything, except 'Yes, Your Grace,'" he went on, and my uncertainty was extinguished. He raked his hand through his snowy white hair. "Otherwise it's sedition."

We began to cross the courtyard. On the opposite side of it, a few soldiers came toward us, bringing a white-haired prisoner. Tall for a Snow Sprite, he walked with head lowered and a lurching, awkward gait that made me wonder his age. Was he an old man or young and injured man? As we neared each other, I studied his face.

His gaze, lowered until this point, lifted to meet mine for a fraction of a second.

Dark circles encompassed his eyes which, I noticed, weren't blue like other Snow Sprites, but brown. In them, I saw a weariness which seemed to match mine. His face was careworn and defeated as the soldiers pushed and shoved him along.

Then in a moment, we had passed each other and I couldn't turn for a second look. The dark doorway yawned open and engulfed us and I was surrounded by the familiar darkness.

Jack deposited me in my cell, leaving without a word.

I paced back and forth restlessly. What in the face of that prisoner had tickled at something, deep down inside my memory? It bothered me more than I had thought possible.

Nearly an hour had passed before I heard voices outside my window. Jumping, I grabbed ahold of the window ledge and raised myself to get a full view of the courtyard. As I had hoped, the voices I heard were those of the soldiers escorting the prisoner I passed earlier. His head was still lowered and his shoulders drooped with weariness. Was that blood on his cheek? I searched the wall with my feet for some sort of support between bricks. Before I knew what was happening, my mouth opened.

"You there!"

The soldiers hushed their guffawing and stopped walking, searching for the source of the random voice. And, to my triumph, the white-haired prisoner also raised his head. At last, his dark eyes met mine.

My fingers slipped from the ledge and I landed hard on my feet, stunned. Painful questions whirled through my mind—questions I couldn't answer. I felt anger slipping into my peripherals. Sliding down the wall, I put my fingers to my throbbing aching temples.

At last, I had placed the memory.

Tightening my knees up against my chest, I struggled to hold back the convulsing gasping breaths that were coming from deep inside me.

Grief tugged at my heart like a heavy anchor, dragging me back down into the darkness.

When Jack came in, sometime later, to bring my evening meal, I didn't raise my head to greet him. There was a long silence.

"Kyndle?" came his voice.

I pulled my knees closer, turning away from his searching eyes. What could I say?

I heard the clatter of the metal tray as he clumsily set it down on the stone floor and then his footsteps as he came to my side.

"Kyndle," he said again. "Are you ill?"

I shook my head weakly.

"Then what's the matter?" he persisted, lowering to a squat.

I turned dull eyes to his but no words would come out of my mouth. He seemed alarmed at the sudden change.

"Kyndle," he said firmly. "I'll get a physician if you don't talk."

"Don't—"

"Then speak." He gripped my shoulder.

I swallowed hard, forcing the grief down my throat. Taking in a deep breath, I slowly and painfully drew the words forth.

"I just saw my brother."

chapter 4

Jack's mouth hung open in surprise. "Your brother?"

I nodded numbly. "We passed him in the courtyard."

For a few moments, he looked confused, but then his face went blank as the realization dawned on him.

I turned away. "His hair is white."

"Kyndle—" His hand fell away as did his voice.

I swiped feebly at my cheek. What had Flint endured to produce such a drastic change? I felt myself trembling. Anger and sorrow mixed to result in one miserable me.

"Jack," I said, turning suddenly. "Can I see him?"

He looked startled.

"The dungeon is jam-packed." I hurried on. "You and I had to share a cell, so why couldn't he and I?"

"Kyndle, I can't—"

"Please." I felt my lips trembling.

His mouth opened then shut. Looking away, he sighed. "I'll do what I can," he said, shaking his head. "But I can't make you any promises." He started to rise, but I clutched his arm.

He looked at me in surprise.

"I saw his face…"

My voice died away. How could I say this? I swallowed hard.

"Jack, if something doesn't change soon, he's going to die."

Jack nodded slowly, his jaw set with determination. "I'll do my best." Hesitating a moment more, he got to his feet. The door closed behind him with an ominous *clank*.

He came back a few hours later, his face flushed with anger. Though he didn't say anything, I knew the answer. I hid my face, my emotion. Why had I even hoped? When had hope ever helped anything? Hope was cruel.

Jack huffed. "There are days I wish I was back in the Fire Realm."

My tears, unable to be further contained, burst forth. The sound of his pacing instantly hushed.

"Kyndle, I'm sorry," Jack said at my side. "I spoke without thinking. It was careless of me."

I waved him off, wiping at my nose with my sleeve. He stood up and walked a few steps away.

"What did he say when you asked him?"

"He said that I was much too fond of the prisoner." His voice was full of heavy bitterness. "That I'm treating her much too well—that I need to stop pampering her." He turned around. "He said you're stubborn, so he wants to use any means possible to—"

"Crush my spirit," I interrupted hoarsely. "I know."

He nodded, his face tight with anger. I looked up at the faint light coming through the window.

"I already knew what the answer would be, but I had to know for certain. I couldn't have gone on knowing that I hadn't asked." A shiver ran down the entire length of my spine, and I hid my face. "We tried."

Jack squatted by my side. Pulling my cold hands away from my face, he chafed them gently until the warmth returned.

"I won't let your brother die," he vowed.

I didn't answer. I wouldn't allow myself to suffer yet another disappointment. Seeing my unbelief, Jack left without another word. Both of his hands were curled into fists at his sides.

That blow took more life from me than I thought possible. At last I knew he was alive, but now I knew his misery and suffering. Now I knew his time was limited.

I had been wrong—this feeling of helplessness was far worse than not knowing if he was alive.

I had no desire to eat the food Jack brought and could hardly get to my feet. By the next afternoon, I had hardly the strength to lift my pen to the page.

I struggled desperately with each word, each letter.

Is this what dying feels like?

The pen fell from my trembling hand. I reached for it, but then a thick darkness overcame me, choking out the light like a hand over my vision. The last thing I heard was the faint song of a bird outside my window.

I opened my eyes. Jack's face, framed by shadows, looked down at me.

"Kyndle," he said, but his voice sounded far away.

I struggled to form a word, but my tongue felt dead inside my mouth.

"Kyndle!" he said frantically. "Can you hear me?" I felt arms around me, lifting me from the ground.

Wind whirred in my ears.

When I woke, I lay in a bed. A tiny white-haired man held a spoon to my lips. A strange odor filled my nostrils.

"Drink this," came the order. "It will make you feel better."

Somehow I managed to do what he said, and a warm bitter draught of liquid went down my parched throat. It took all of my nerve to keep it down.

"What will that do?" asked a familiar voice, and for the first time, I noticed Jack sitting on a chair by the bed.

"It should help to restore her strength," replied the shriveled old man, adjusting his spectacles on his prominent nose. Seeing that I was staring at him, his wrinkled face lifted into a smile.

"You'll be back up and about in no time, young lady," he said with a laugh that sounded like the wrinkling of crisp paper. "You had a classic case of plain exhaustion, physical and mental."

"Where am I?" I finally managed to ask.

"We're in the home of Doctor Verglas," Jack told me. "He's the only doctor who will care for prisoners. Since you're valuable, I was allowed to bring you here."

A sudden cramp in my neck made me let my head drop back. I hadn't even realized I had raised it. A heavy sigh expanded my chest underneath the sheets.

"That's so," said Verglas and my eyes fell shut under his gentle aged voice. "You just rest. We'll leave you now." It was the last thing I heard before I drifted to sleep.

"She *will* obey me!" The booming voice ungraciously jerked me from my rest.

"But, Your Grace—"

"Silence, Hail! I'll not have you undermining my authority." I heard danger in Glacier's tone. "There are two options. Either she does as I say or she is executed. I'll *not* be wrangled with!"

"But, sir—"

"I said *silence*!" I opened my eyes in time to see Jack receive a vicious slap to his face. Stunned, his hand went to his cheek and he was silent.

"Get out of my sight!" Glacier snapped.

Glancing at me, Jack left the room. It was several moments before his footsteps moved away from the other side of the door. Glacier turned to me.

"Listen here, Fireling," he said, gripping the bedposts. "You have two choices. Will you yield to my orders or will you die?"

"My convictions haven't changed," I said, my voice poised. "I'll not violate my conscience to pacify your purse."

His eyes narrowed threateningly.

"We are not as weak as you supposed," I said with a smile.

He strode from the room. The door slammed shut with such force that the floor quivered beneath me. After a moment I heard another lusty slam as he went out the front door.

When all was quiet, I looked out the window over which a thin curtain had been pulled. There were no clouds in the dusky sky.

Again I was faced with execution. Trouble seemed to follow me like a shadow. *How does someone shake a shadow?* I wondered. After a moment, the answer sadly surfaced. The only way to lose a shadow is for the sun to set.

Through the thin curtain, I watched as the dying sun swaddled the sky in warming colors. In it, I saw the approach of own sunset. I closed my eyelids which had grown heavy. Jack came in a few minutes later.

"I won't let him," he said, his voice soft but determined.

"Now, Jack—" I began.

He turned away and put his hand on the doorknob.

"Jack!" I said again as he began to open the door. "Don't do anything to arouse his wrath. It's not worth it. You have Winterose to live for."

Releasing the knob, he turned slowly. "How did you know?"

I smiled. "I could tell by the way you said her name."

His face lifted, but he didn't smile. "And who do *you* have to live for, Kyndle?"

"My family. If they're still alive."

"Yes, but—" Jack hesitated. "There's no one else?"

My head dropped brokenly as green eyes sparkled in my memory.

"Kyndle?" he persisted.

I lifted dull eyes to his. "Not anymore."

After a moment my meaning dawned upon him. His face hard, he left the room.

chapter 5

After two more days, the doctor declared me well enough to get out of bed. All this time, Jack didn't visit me. Had he said or done something to get himself into disfavor? I began to grow more and more worried as the minutes ticked away.

On the afternoon of the third day, I was sitting at the window, soaking in the sunshine, when suddenly, a very flustered and breathless Jack burst into my quiet room. Doctor Verglas appeared behind him in the door, his wrinkled face drawn tight with worry.

"Come! Quickly!" Jack said, crossing the room in two strides to grab both of my hands. I noticed quickly he was back in his formal clothing.

"What is it?" I gasped as he pulled me to my feet.

"We have to leave as fast as possible," he said, dragging me toward the door.

"Take the path along the river," Doctor Verglas breathed in a worried voice as he closed the bedroom door and led us down the dim hallway. "Cross the river. That will throw the hounds off your scent."

My blood ran cold. I glanced at Jack. He looked straight ahead, avoiding my gaze.

"Make your way through the woods," Verglas continued, unlocking a door that opened into a narrow alleyway. "Climb the trees if you must."

Jack swept me outside, then turned to the doctor.

"Many thanks," he said earnestly. "I hope that I've not put you in any danger."

"Don't think of it, lad," Verglas said, stepping further into his house and partially closing the door. "I wish you success."

"Thank you, doctor," Jack said.

Grabbing hold of my arm, he hurried me down the alleyway.

We jerked to a stop at the street edge. Glancing both ways, we darted across the street to the alleyway on the opposite side. We continued on in this pattern—sneak, look, dart—for several blocks without encountering anyone face-to-face. A couple people milled around on a street here and there, but Jack had chosen the right time of day to sneak around. Finally we came to a seemingly abandoned street. All the houses were in almost complete disrepair; bushes and shrubs grew in an untended way in front of each house. At the farthest end of the lane, I caught glimpse of trees.

Jack nodded in response to my questioning glance, then we quietly made our way toward them. The cobblestones fell away to grass and then a small creek. Jack glanced in all directions as we reached it, and then we quietly began to cross. I gasped at the coldness of the water. The creek was only about ten feet across and barely reached my knees. We achieved the other side and slipped into the shelter of the trees. I began to swipe excess water off my pants and shoes.

"You made it," came a voice to my right, and I jumped a few inches. A man with black hair and dark eyes emerged from out of the shadows.

"Alfonse!" Jack replied, shaking his hand fervently. "Did all go well?"

"Smooth as hen eggs, my lord," came the answer.

"Perfect!" Jack released the man's hand and turned to me. "Kyndle," he said, "this is my servant, Alfonse."

"A pleasure," Alfonse said, bowing slightly. Then he turned and held out a hand to a shadowy figure I hadn't noticed before. The man stepped into the light, and with a smothered cry, I leapt into my brother's arms.

"You were not seen by anyone?" I heard Jack ask his servant.

"Not a soul."

"Look at you, cryin' like I'm dead," Flint teased in my ear.

I drew back to look into his face. It was as worn as it had been when I had seen him in the courtyard, but this time, a tinge of joy colored his wan cheeks.

HOME ROAD

"We have to go," Alfonse said behind me. "We don't have much time to make our escape."

"Right," said Jack. "Once my father realizes we've escaped, he'll spare no means to find us." I saw a streak of fear across his shadowed face.

Flint took a double take at Jack. "Representative?" he said slowly.

Jack nodded. "Come. We have to hurry."

The four of us set off into the aged forest, and Flint and I fell in step a few feet behind Jack and Alfonse.

"Our *representative?*" Flint asked me. "What, how—"

I gave him a condensed answer. He shook his head.

"Maybe there is still some good in this life," he commented.

"I think there may be," I said just as quietly.

"Where are you taking us?" Flint asked Jack a moment later.

"To the Nature Realm," Jack replied. "I know someone there who will hide us until the storm is over."

As dusk fell, Jack seemed to grow more anxious. He and Alfonse spoke in hushed whispers. Trying not to notice the tension, I talked with Flint of the happenings since we were separated.

"What happened in the dungeon at Galaheed?"

"I still don't know," he said, shaking his head. "One moment, we were running along, and the next moment, I was alone. I searched for you and Tinder both, but within a few moments, I was attacked."

"It was the same with me," I said. "What then?"

"I struggled but was knocked unconscious. There was more than one, so I had no chance. When I woke up, I was tied in the back of a wagon. When the wagon stopped, I was thrown deep into the dungeon of Straven Tree."

"Flint," I said after he finished. "They hurt you, didn't they?"

It was a full minute before he quietly said, "Yes."

I looked sideways at his white hair, and a burning surfaced inside my chest. I gritted my teeth tightly. "There are times when I feel so angry at them that I feel ready to strangle something."

His shoulders rose in a shrug. I knew that the memories made it hard to speak, beaching him like an anchor to his pain.

"I'm sorry to interrupt," Jack said, stopping and turning to us, "but we need to find shelter. Imperial soldiers are probably already on our trail."

"Do you have a plan?" I asked him.

"I've always been told that a hermit lives in this part of the forest," was his hushed response. "Alfonse knows the way."

"Is he acquainted with the hermit?"

"No. But servants learn a lot through each other."

"How far is it?" came Flint's question. Here under the trees, the wind was actually chilly.

"Not more than three miles southeast," Alfonse told us.

"Night is falling fast," Jack said, glancing at the sky. "We must hurry. Alfonse," turning to him, "take us the fastest way."

Flint took my elbow, and we all hurried after the quiet dark-haired man who slipped among the trees like a fox.

"Who is he?" I asked Jack in an undertone.

"He's a Nature Sprite," came the equally soft response. "He's been in my service for fifteen years."

"Why was he brought here?"

"He accidentally killed the son of his village's chief. To rescue him from execution, his parents sold him to passing slave train on its way to Galaheed. They believed a life as a slave would be better than no life at all."

"What a hard decision," I commented.

"My father bought him for me just before I went away to school. The only time Alfonse and I have been apart was during my time in the Fire Realm."

Talk faded away, and we fell to walking with all our energy. The trees thinned somewhat; for no real reason, the tension increased and we broke into a dead run. The thought of recapture plagued me, causing my legs to move faster than I thought possible. We ran for a full ten minutes before Alfonse jerked to a stop.

"There." He pointed, panting.

Following his finger, I spotted a glimmer of light through the trees.

"It's not too far," he said, seeing how out of breath I was.

"Good." I gasped, doubling over and sucking drafts of air into my parched lungs. My throat burned from the cold air I had been drawing in during the run, and I felt a bit nauseous.

"Come," Flint said, taking hold of my elbow again. Jack and Alfonse took the lead, Flint and I followed close behind. Within a moment, the shadowed form of a house loomed through the trees ahead. A lantern hung in the window.

"We'll stay here for the night," Alfonse told us. "The hermit will take us in. Come."

We moved stealthily through the trees and into the clearing. Through the window, I glimpsed a stooped figure working over the stone fireplace. A thin shaft of smoke rose from out of the chimney. Confidently Alfonse went to the primitive door, knocking twice, then thrice. I huddled between Jack and Flint who were trying to shelter me from the cold wind.

The door opened a crack and eyes set deeply within wrinkles looked out at us. "Can I help you?" came a croaking voice.

"We desire shelter for the night," Alfonse said politely.

"How many?" The door opened a little more.

"Four. Three men and a woman."

The door flew open, revealing the aged host within. "Come in, come in!" he urged, stepping aside to let us enter.

We stepped gratefully into the warm cottage and cold became a thing of the past. Bidding us to take a seat on several wooden stools nearby, the hermit bustled around the cottage, pouring hot soup into stone bowls and placing them in our chilled hands. His face darkened by a loose hood, he wore a long tunic that reached the floor. All I could see of him was his careworn face and hands.

"I haven't had any guests for ten years," he said, his throat so full of phlegm that I inadvertently cleared mine.

He turned, his face full of pity.

"Poor dear," he said, studying my face.

Embarrassed, I raked at my windblown hair, though it did no good.

He turned his back to us as he stirred the ashes in the fireplaces. "And what brings you to these parts?" came his question.

I froze. Jack glanced at each of us in turn and was silent for so long that our host turned. Before he could repeat himself, Jack said, "We're fugitives." Then we all held our breath.

The white eyebrows shot up, covering his forehead with new wrinkles. "Fugitives, eh?" he repeated, studying each of us for a terrifying moment before turning around and beginning his work once again.

"You're in good company," he said, his voice chipper once more.

I breathed a sigh of relief. I'd dreaded being thrust out into that wind again.

"Where are you heading?" was the next question as the man took our bowls and put them into a large basin at the far end of the tiny cottage.

"The Nature Realm," Jack answered, glancing at Flint and me.

We nodded in response. We would have to trust this hermit.

"You've a good several days' journey ahead," he commented. "I hope you don't run into any bad weather on the way."

"So do we," I said, speaking for the first time.

The old hermit turned and looked at me again as though noticing my features for the first time. "Fireling?" he asked.

I nodded slowly.

"And you," the man said to Alfonse. "You're a Nature Child, aren't you?"

"Yes," Alfonse replied, and as he spoke, I looked closely at him for the first time. Jagged scars reached out of his collar, across his neck and up the left side of his face. He smiled at Jack. "This is my master."

The hermit followed Alfonse's gaze. "From your clothing," he said to Jack, "I'd wager that you're a count or something."

"I'm just that," said Jack. He glanced at me and his eyes said, *Well, I used to be that.*

At last, the hermit's eyes rested upon Flint. After a moment, sympathy came into his face. "You have suffered much, son of the fire," he softly said.

Flint gave a stony nod. It wasn't the Fireling way to acknowledge pain. The hermit sighed and began to sweep the dirt floor. No one spoke for several long minutes.

"Understand this," he said suddenly, scowling fiercely at each of us in turn. "They'll be coming for you. Soon. And when they get here, you need to be far away."

"And if we aren't?" Flint posed.

He barreled past the question. "If they come before morning, there's a warren, a burrow, twenty southern paces from my backdoor. If I give you the word, you must get there as fast as possible. Am I understood?"

We all nodded. My heart pounded for some strange reason.

The hermit sighed. "You'd better get some rest," he said, and we got to our feet. Striking a match, he lit a small lantern and gave it to me.

"How can we thank you?" I asked.

He smiled, and I thought it a sad one. "You can't."

I was about to ask what he meant when a sound in the distance made my blood run cold. The howl of a hound met our ears, answered by another, then more. Terror leapt rapidly across the hermit's wrinkled face.

"Go!" he cried, stepping back. "Get to the burrow as fast as you can!"

The three boys sprinted for the backdoor, but I stood transfixed by the profound sorrow on the hermit's face.

"What about you?" I demanded. "You're just an old man! They'll—"

He pulled the hood away from his face. I staggered back as I realized it was an old *woman*.

"Go," she said again, and there was such authority in her voice that I had no choice but to let Flint to pull me toward the door. Turning at the last, I realized with surprise she was at my side as we hurried out into the night.

With a surprising speed, she led us to a patch of berry brambles at the forest's edge. There we found Jack and Alfonse, frantically brushing aside the vines. I thrust my lantern up, and a small trapdoor was revealed.

The baying of the hounds grew closer. Jack heaved the trapdoor up. Snatching the lantern from me, Alfonse hurried down the wooden steps. Jack held out his hands, eyes wide with fear.

"Come!" he prompted.

I hesitated, unable to tear my gaze from the misery spreading across the hermit woman's face. What was wrong? What was I missing?

"Kyndle!" Jack said.

Lifting me off my feet, Flint carried me down into the burrow. Above us, Jack said something to the woman. I couldn't hear her answer. When we reached the bottom, Flint, stooping under the lower ceiling, deposited me on the dirt floor. As I glanced around, the lantern revealed fear across Alfonse's face. Turning, I expected to see the hermit coming down behind us. Instead I found Jack. Above his head, the dim moonlight disappeared as the trapdoor creaked shut.

"No!" I cried, lunging forward.

Flint snatched my arm, holding me back. "Sit," he said in my ear.

I obeyed mechanically. Jack stood to the side, a blank expression across his face. The howling grew closer.

Above us, I could hear the hermit frantically brushing the vinery back over the trapdoor. The dirt ceiling vibrated with footsteps, then I heard her cry out. After several moments, pained yelps became intermixed with the barking which seemed to be directly above us. A shot rang out, followed by a cry that froze the blood in my veins. It was followed by a second shot which silenced it.

No!

Words were exchanged above us, but we couldn't make any of it out. The hounds whimpered but didn't bay again. All around was the sound of feet.

chapter 6

"The hounds have lost their scent entirely, general," rang out a voice from directly above. "We can find no trace of them."

"Blasted—" the angry response trailed off.

General Stag.

A chill ran the length of my spine. Jack squeezed in closer beside me.

"Why didn't you save this creature for questioning?" Stag went on.

"She took a stick to the dogs, sir. She would've gone for us if we had gotten with reach."

"Cowards! Could you not take an old woman? Keep searching."

Nearly an hour passed by, and the air in the burrow grew stale. Every moment we were sure they would find the trapdoor and all would be over. As such, we were surprised when we heard the footsteps retreating. Along with it went the defeated whimper of the hounds. Either from tension or a lack of air, we hardly breathed. After a full minute had passed, deathly silence numbed our ears. They were gone.

Alfonse very softly pushed up the trapdoor, and after scanning for any danger, pushed the door up further to let fresh air in for a few minutes.

I leaned against Flint as the emotion of the night's experience washed over me. I now understood the sorrow on the hermit's face. She welcomed us in as guests and wouldn't betray us as enemies. She knew someone had to cover up the trapdoor. From the moment she told us about the burrow, she knew it would have to be her.

After a couple tears had fallen, a calm came over my soul. The others seemed to feel it as well. Peace settled over the burrow and we slept.

When I awoke, it was dark but warm. I heard Jack and Flint speaking in an undertone nearby. I looked around. The lantern the hermit had given me had evidently burned out.

"Where's Alfonse?" I asked.

"He wanted to see how far the burrow went back," Flint said.

I glanced to my left in surprise. It hadn't occurred to me that it *could* go further. As I stared into the black, a light appeared and Alfonse came rushing with it.

"The shaft continues!" he exclaimed eagerly.

"Shaft?" I repeated, glancing for the first time at the walls and ceiling of the narrow burrow. These were reinforced stoutly with roughly hewn slats of wood which, though hazardous to brush up against, seemed to be doing their job.

"Yes, it follows the direction we need to go. Come see!" Beckoning, he disappeared again, and his movement extinguished the dying lantern. Hopefully we all got to our feet and felt our way down the shaft. Alfonse was waiting several yards down.

"I followed it for nearly eighty feet," he said, voice full of excitement. "It may be a passage between borders."

I took a step forward and tripped on something, landing on my hands and knees.

"Root," I grumbled.

Further investigation revealed that this was no small tuber. It seemed to my exploring fingers at least twenty inches in diameter, underground evidence of a tree somewhere above us. I explained what I had found to the others.

"This tunnel must be very old," Flint said. "It could have been dug by smugglers."

"Or Snowling soldiers back during Whittington's War," Jack suggested. "If I remember correctly, this area was a sort of no-man's-land between opposing lines. Well done, Alfonse!"

Having nothing to carry but ourselves, we struck off, groping our way down the shaft. The picture of expertise, Alfonse took the lead.

After a while, Alfonse announced that the ceiling was sloping lower, slowing our progress even more. While the others navigated the center of the shaft, I hugged my way along the right side to avoid the mishap that I was often prone to. Imagine my chagrin when, again, an unknown object took me to my knees on the dirt floor. The others halted.

"Kyndle," Flint said.

I found that I had tripped on nothing other than a lantern. Eagerly my fingers found plenteous oil inside. A slight hollow in the wall revealed a bundle of crude matches, tied together with what felt like twine.

"I found a lantern and matches!" I said excitedly.

"Well done!" Jack said again.

Someone crouched by me, and expert fingers lit the lantern in several seconds, revealing Alfonse's pleased face.

"Many thanks, my Fireling friend," he said as he got to his feet.

After another thirty minutes, the tunnel came to a dead end. Broken pieces of wood littered the ground at our feet.

For one terrible moment, I thought that we had come all this way for nothing. Then Jack, who now carried the lantern, discovered the trapdoor over our bent heads. We realized that the splintered boards were formerly a step-up. Reaching up, Alfonse cracked it open just a little bit.

Soft light poured into the burrow. We watched Alfonse closely as his eyes scanned the quiet stretch above. To my great relief, he looked down at us and nodded that all was safe. Heaving the door open, he shinnied up through the opening with the agility of a squirrel. We waited for a second affirmative which came after a moment. He extended a hand to Jack and helped him climb up. Jack turned and reached down a hand.

"Kyndle," he said.

Flint gave me a knee, then I was lifted out of the darkness. I squinted in the light while Flint scrambled out after me. When my eyes adjusted, I looked around. We were stood in an open meadow, flanked on both sides by thick woods. The wild grasses swayed in the wind. I found that I was smiling as I stretched my back which ached after being hunched for such a prolonged period of time. Flint came to my side.

"These look like the fields back home," he said. "But I bet the ones at home are different now. Probably filled with blood and—"

"Flint, don't." I rested my hand on his arm. "They're doing it for our freedom."

"But how many are still left?" He paced a few steps then came back, and I was surprised to see a tear on his cheek. "How many have died for naught?"

"For naught?" Sadness filled me. "There is no chance of victory?"

"Of course there is." He sniffed and swiped roughly at his wet cheek. "I'm sorry. There's always hope. I just got angry."

I rested the right side of my face upon his shoulder.

"I know Mum and Dad are well-taken-care of," I murmured, "but it's hard not knowing anything about Tinder or Ruby."

He put his hand on my left shoulder and squeezed it.

"I almost wish they hadn't been born," I remarked bitterly.

"Hush," he said. "Don't talk like that."

"It would be better than facing the torture they might be under," I said, looking at his white hair. "Like you did."

"They might have escaped."

I drew in a deep breath. *Just maybe.*

Then my secret fear surfaced again—Auburn and I were brought out together. Wouldn't they have brought Ruby out with Ian?

There was a creak, and we turned as Jack and Alfonse gently lowered the trapdoor closed. It felt like the close of a chapter for me. I was leaving the Northern Realm behind, hopefully forever, and had begun my journey on the road toward home. We covered the door with what brush we could find.

After a moment of silence, we looked around at each other. Then we smiled. It had been one grueling night, but with the help of the hermit, we had made it through alive.

Several days passed. We walked during every moment of daylight then dropped to sleep for a few hours until the sun rose, shooing us along our way.

HOME ROAD

During this time, we all were awed by the level of Alfonse's wisdom. He kept us on a steady southeastward path, constantly checking to make sure we weren't getting off course. He seemed to know exactly where to find all the game animals, how to catch them without weapons, where all the springs lay hidden in the mangled brush. If not for him, I don't know if we would have ever arrived in the Nature Realm.

There was only one thing that Alfonse seemed afraid of and that was returning to his homeland. Jack repeatedly reassured him that, as Alfonse was his personal property, no harm would be done to him without Jack's permission. Despite this, Alfonse was anxious. With each passing hour, he grew more pensive.

I wondered if he was haunted by his memories. Jack told us his story that afternoon when Alfonse was out of earshot.

"He and the chief's son, best friends, were hunting together as young men when a bear ambushed them," he explained. "As it caught the prince across the chest, Alfonse set a poisoned arrow to his bow, but he trembled so his aim was off. Instead of the bear, he struck his wounded friend."

"How awful," I commented.

"The bear then turned on Alfonse and nearly killed him as well," Jack continued, "but Alfonse at last managed to put a dagger through its brain. He rushed to his friend's side, but the prince was already dead. Despite his own terrible wounds, Alfonse carried his friend back to his village, but when he arrived, the chief was so angry to hear of his son's death that he set Alfonse's execution for the next morning." Jack sighed. "Had not his parents smuggled him out during the night, he would've most certainly been killed."

The story gave me a new appreciation for quiet Alfonse. His courage spread to me as well and gave me strength to put one foot in front of the other when the worries grew heavy.

"The border of the Nature Realm lies a mile hence."

Alfonse's throat seemed to tighten with each word. As he spoke, I saw his eyes flit nervously into the woods around us. We stood at the bed of a small creek from which we had just quenched our thirst and eaten a late supper. My hands still felt pricked by the chilly water.

"No harm will come to you," Jack said, laying a hand on his servant's slender shoulder. "Do you trust me?"

Alfonse turned piercing eyes to Jack's determined face. "I trust your word," he said, "but you don't yet understand the ways of my people. Old hurts run more deeply in their veins than the roots of a great tree run into the ground. They will not quickly forget what I have done."

"I am Count Frost of the royal Frost family," Jack said. "They will not quickly forget me either nor will they quickly ignore what I have to say. If they know what's good for them. My father may be angry with me for the moment, but when he hears of mistreatment to any of his bloodline, he will not stand for it."

"We will see," Alfonse said. "Were I you, my master, I wouldn't reveal my lineage unless it were absolutely necessary."

Looking a bit squished, Jack nodded.

Alfonse turned to Flint and me. "I suggest that you keep close," he said. "Nature Sprites can be very suspicious of outsiders." He cast a nervous glance at Jack. "I hope your friends show up quickly."

Jack looked as though he was attempting to reassure himself. "And if they don't?"

Alfonse's face darkened. "It has been nearly twenty years—"

"Alfonse," Jack cut in firmly. "What will happen?"

I glanced at Jack. His shoulders drooped underneath his ragged jacket. His golden buttons were dull with the grime and dust of our journey and his shoes were muddy and scuffed.

"I think they will leave *you* alone, master," Alfonse said, tiredness in his voice. "But as for me and the Firelings…" A worried expression stole across his slender face. His straight black hair, having long fallen from a ponytail, hung limp on his shoulders in the windless afternoon air.

Jack paced along the creek, turned, and came back. Flint and I sat at the base of a huge tree while Alfonse stayed on his feet.

"I wonder," came Jack's voice and we all turned to look at him. He rubbed his chin on which white stubble had begun to grow.

"What, master?" Alfonse inquired, his voice still nervous.

"Flint, Kyndle," Jack said, turning excited eyes on us. "You're to be my prisoners."

I opened my mouth but no words came out. I was beginning to get an idea of what he was thinking.

"I'm still working all this out," Jack said as we began walking again, "but I think if you're under my authority, they shouldn't harm you."

I smiled wearily.

"Well, we're prisoners again," I said, poking Flint in the ribs.

He shrunk away with a pained chuckle.

"I would rather be Jack's prisoner than the Nature Sprites'," was Alfonse's dry comment. I looked up at him and saw that his face was distant. Pity stirred in my heart. But as I watched on, his head snapped rigid, his eyes re-engaged, and his hand went to the dagger hanging at his side. All of the color drained from his face.

I leapt to my feet. Jack and Flint also saw the change in Alfonse and pressed in closer to me. I felt dread churn in my stomach. Before I could even *think*, we were surrounded by a group of heavily armed men. They looked just like Alfonse with their dark hair and slender forms. They kept their bows trained upon our chests, eyes flashing dangerously.

"No one moves," came a voice.

A tall slender man stepped forward from the group. His arms held no weapon but they were massive enough to be a weapon in themselves. He crossed them across his chest. "And who is the leader of this group?" he asked. When none of us answered, he thrust two huge fingers into the air. Bowstrings instantly tightened.

"I am," Jack blurted.

"Who are you?"

"I'm a count from the Snow Realm."

"How dare you enter the Nature Realm during lockdown?" the man demanded.

"Lockdown?" Jack repeated. Moving subtly, he put his hand on mine.

Only then did I realize how violently I was trembling.

"The Nature Realm has closed their borders due to the war. Outsiders aren't allowed to enter. It's my job to make sure this law is obeyed."

"And who are you?" Jack asked.

"My name is Orrick," he replied gruffly. "I'm captain of the Guard for Brimshore, capital city of the Nature Realm."

"I see," Jack said coldly.

"Who are your companions?" Orrick asked, glancing at me.

"Prisoners from the Fire Realm," Jack said.

"Their crime?" When Orrick still stared, Flint shifted closer to me, a protective scowl on his face.

"Crossing their boundaries without leave," Jack said.

"Rebels?" Orrick nodded grimly and looked at Flint. "Been through some terrible times to cause that," he said, nodding at his white hair.

My brother's only response was a steely glare.

Then Orrick's eyes fell upon Alfonse. Something stirred in them as if he was striving to remember something but couldn't.

"And who might you be?" he asked.

"This is my servant." Jack jumped in.

His dark eyes locked on Alfonse's face, Orrick ignored Jack entirely. "I know you," he grated.

I couldn't see Alfonse's face. He offered no response.

Something dawned in Orrick's eyes, and an evil smile spread over his face. He had remembered. Taking a step back, he turned to Jack.

"Did you know that your servant is a murderer?"

Jack's face went hard, and he didn't answer.

"I see you do," came the sardonic reply. "Why have you not inflicted the penalty due him?"

"I did not think it necessary," Jack answered, his voice trembling with anger. "He's *my* servant. I am responsible for his treatment. If I had seen fit, I would've most certainly punished him. But as it is, I don't believe in punishing innocent men."

"Innocent?" Orrick repeated. "*Innocent?*"

"What I said, I meant." There was no mistaking the firmness in Jack's voice.

Orrick leveled a glare at Jack for a long tense moment, then snatched a bow from a man beside him. Glancing at Alfonse, I saw sorrow written across his face in broad strokes. Flint pressed in closer, striving to shield me from any coming harm.

"As I see that you're incapable of sound judgement," Orrick growled to Jack, "I'll take matters into my own hands."

Then, faster than I could blink—Orrick set an arrow to the string and let fly. Whistling through the air, it planted itself deep in Alfonse's collarbone.

Alfonse staggered then fell heavily to the ground.

chapter 7

A scream issuing from my throat, I tore forward out of Flint's grip and threw myself across Alfonse's fallen form. Another arrow hissed through the air and sunk into the crisp leaves, narrowly missing my ribs.

"Don't shoot!" Jack cried frantically. "Hold your fire!"

Dropping his bow, Orrick strode toward me. Flint did also, but he was intercepted by a couple of the Naturelings. Thrusting out one of his huge hands, Orrick jerked me to my feet.

I thrust my chin out at him in defiance, but with a terrifying speed, he twisted my arm behind my back and pressed the flat of his knife to my throat.

"That arrow didn't miss by mere chance," he grated. "Make any more sudden moves, and we won't miss again." To reinforce his words, his men held up their bows, waiting for his command.

I could see Flint's face clearly now; there wasn't a trace of color in it. I swallowed hard and the blade nicked my tight skin.

"Don't harm her." Jack's voice was less cocky. "We'll do as you say."

"I'm delighted to suddenly find you so cooperative," Orrick crooned. "Keep it up, and she will be spared. For now. Unless you have a love for cold steel," he warned me, "don't try anything funny."

I felt cold blood trickling down the side of my neck where the dagger had cut me.

"I'll take her to Brimshore," Orrick announced to the group. "Maybe it will give the rest of you an incentive to behave when you follow us in thirty minutes. As we don't wish to manhandle you, count," to Jack, "we do hope you'll cooperate. However, if you don't, my men will ensure that you do. Macklin," to the man near his side, "you and Gresham bring the killer with the rest of them."

As he spoke, Orrick pulled the knife away from my throat and clinked it into a sheath on his belt.

I could faintly hear Alfonse's ragged breathing. Blood ran freely from his chest, pooling on the leaves beside him. Both his eyes were shut, but his hand gripped the arrow shaft in his shoulder.

"A rope," Orrick said.

Macklin whipped a strand from his belt.

"For some odd reason," Orrick said as he wound the rope around my wrists, "I have a feeling you're going to give me some trouble." Jerking it painfully tight, he turned me to face him. "If you do," he said, staring hard into my face, "just know that I'll give it right back."

A shiver crawled up my spine and I felt no urge to be cocky.

Grabbing my shoulder, Orrick directed me toward a dark trail leading further into the woods. Fighting to keep down panic, I turned for another look at the others. Two of Orrick's men walked toward Alfonse. A couple steps away, Jack and Flint stood watching me, unbound. Jack's face was filled with fear as I walked further and further away.

The anger in Flint's eyes made my heart flutter with worry.

The walk through the woods was miserable. Birds and squirrels chattered incessantly in the limbs over our heads. Orrick said nothing, and I was glad for the time to think. My last hope was that Jack's friend would be there when we arrived, and perhaps, they would be able to talk some sense into these stubborn Nature Sprites.

A knot of dread churned in my stomach. I worried about Flint. One of his strongest characteristics was to protect his own. There was no telling what would happen if he did something rash. Our freedom could be gone for good. Or worse.

And always lingering at the back of my mind was Ruby, my sister. I hadn't seen her for a year now. Flint had heard nothing about her before his own capture. And though I sometimes was tempted to fear the worst, I always ultimately refused to give up hope that she, like me, had been rescued during the first Fireling onslaught. However, I hoped that she had *stayed* rescued.

After a miserable quarter of an hour, we emerged from the woods into a clearing. It was flanked by sturdy but plain houses. A fire smoldered in the middle of the clearing. Through the trees to my left, I caught glimpse of a second grouping of houses, then another, then another. This was no small cluster of natives but a well-populated village.

However, there was only one person in sight. A grizzled man squatted by the fire, sharpening an ancient knife with a gnarled handle. As we got nearer, he scowled fiercely and I thought I heard a throaty growl emerge from his parted lips. He slowly rose to his feet.

"Peace, Darion," Orrick said, raising his free hand. "She isn't going to give us any trouble. Are you?" he added, shaking me.

Darion hesitantly went back to his crouching position, but he didn't go back to whetting his knife. I felt his eyes follow us even after we had walked past him.

Silence hung over the village like lingering campfire smoke, but in the windows of a few houses we passed, I caught quick glimpses of activity. After a moment, I snatched the sound of low voices and a door slam. My best guess was that, upon hearing of the approach of outsiders, everyone had fled indoors.

At the far end of the clearing, opposite of where we stood, was a larger house. Animals skins, decorated with beads and feathers, were pinned all across the front of it. I thought it a grotesque touch.

"This is the home of our chieftain," Orrick said as we neared. "He will want to meet you." When we reached the house, Orrick hesitated before the door.

"Hail, Chief Launfel!" he called.

"Who is calling?" came a brisk young voice from within.

"Orrick. I bring an outsider."

The door swung open, revealing a young man. He moved aside to let us enter.

"Lenard," Orrick said, clapping him on the shoulder.

I glanced around the room which was surprisingly narrow. At the far end of the long room sat a man that I knew was the chief. On either side of him stood a stoic-faced Natureling warrior, armed with thick-shafted sticks I knew would wreak much damage. Long white hair flowed down over the chieftain's shoulders, and he studied me through sharp piercing eyes. His throne was nothing more than a chair upholstered with another grotesque selection of animal skins. My heart beat fast as Orrick pulled me toward him.

"Who have you brought, captain?" the chief asked in a voice that was slow, calculated, and full of suspicion.

"A Fireling prisoner, mighty chief," Orrick replied. As we came to the foot of the throne and its aged occupant, he dropped quickly to one knee and waited there.

The chief gave me a lofty look over. "Where did you get her?"

"From a sojourning Snow Sprite, powerful one," Orrick said, head still bowed. He hesitated, then added, "The Snowling also possessed a Fireling boy and—" A pause. "And a...a *servant*."

The jolted report seemed to annoy Launfel. "And?"

"The servant was a fugitive Natureling." Orrick slowly lifted his head. "One that my lord would recognize all too well."

One of the chief's bushy white eyebrows shot high up on his wrinkled forehead.

"Oh?" he grated.

"Yes, my lord. It was—"

Launfel jumped onto his feet. "His name is not to be mentioned in my presence," he snapped, his face dark with anger. I blinked in surprise. In just a moment, he had transformed from an old man to a mighty warrior.

Orrick bowed his head again.

"What have you done with him?" Launfel demanded.

"I put an arrow in his shoulder, my chief. It won't kill him, but it will prevent him from any attempt to escape."

I breathed a sigh of relief.

The chief sat down, once more an old man. "Good. I'm glad you had not the mercy to kill him." He worked his jaw until I thought it would disconnect from his skull. "As soon as he awakes, bring him to me."

"Yes, mighty chief," Orrick said, getting to his feet. "It will be done."

Launfel pressed his fingertips to his brows and waved his other hand at Orrick. "Leave me," he said, waving at us with his other hand. "I need time to consider his punishment."

Orrick hesitated. After a moment, the chief glanced up, an irritated look on his face.

"Why do you cower, O captain?" he asked mockingly.

"My lord has not yet said what you want done with this Fireling," was Orrick's cautious comment.

The chief threw a disinterested glance my way. "Put her in the shack for now," he said dryly. "The rats are in need of company."

I felt a tremor rise from my toes up the base of my neck.

"Yes, my lord." With a second bow, Orrick stood. Grabbing my bound hands, he pulled me away.

The sunlight was blinding as we stepped from the dim house. Orrick's face wore a satisfied smile, one I found creepy.

"That murderer will get what he deserves," he said casually.

I swallowed hard. "Execution?"

He turned dark eyes my way. "Oh no," he said quietly. "Much worse than that."

I shuddered.

Orrick took me to the back of the house where a crude lean-to sat like a worn-out peddler. The front of it was hardly twice as wide as the door, across which a wooden bar was set. Shoving the bar upward, he opened the door and ungraciously shoved me through it. Unable to catch myself, I landed hard on my stomach and all the air was knocked from my lungs. I winced at the pain in my ribs.

"Don't attempt anything funny," I heard him warn as the door closed. "Remember what I promised—about giving out trouble."

Then the door slammed closed and the light was extinguished. I heard the bar drop into place, sealing my prison shut. When all was quiet, I glanced around me. Despite its gloomy outward appearance, the lean-to was remarkably airtight and light blocking. The only sunlight that made it through the stout exterior was that which came through the small crack between the door and doorframe.

About fifteen minutes later, after trying in vain to find a comfortable position on the dirt floor, I heard the door being unlocked.

Expectantly, I rolled onto my side. Was I to be rescued? The door opened to reveal the man called Darion.

"Having a nap, are we?" he asked, stepping inside.

I wriggled to a sitting position and scooted into a far corner. Instinct told me that this man was not to be trusted. He threw his head back and laughed raucously, then turned to the door.

"Bring him, Macklin."

My heart pounding, I watched as Macklin and the man Gresham came through the door, swinging Alfonse by his ankles and wrists. The arrow was still deep in his shoulder. They deposited him on the floor beside me, and Alfonse groaned, causing them to laugh coarsely.

"Sleep tight, criminals," Macklin sang out as the door shut.

When I was certain that they were gone, I scooted toward Alfonse. His breathing was more regular than before, but his eyes were still closed.

"Alfonse?" I whispered.

His eyelids fluttered slightly, and after a moment, cracked open halfway. "Who's there?" he asked hoarsely.

"It's me, Kyndle." I breathed. With such little light, I wasn't surprised that his hawk eyes didn't recognize me.

"Where are we?" he asked, opening his eyes all the way.

"Locked in a shack at the back of the chief's house."

He groaned again.

"Alfonse," I said anxiously, "the arrow."

"You will have to remove it," he said after a moment. "I don't have the strength to."

I gulped. "Me? But I've never done—"

"It's like—pulling a splinter," he said, his voice growing more weary with each word, desperation lining each syllable.

"All right," I said hesitantly. "I just hope I don't hurt you much."

"You'll hurt me more if you don't do it soon," he groaned. "The skin will try to heal and grow up around it."

Hands still tied, I turned my back to him and, after groping, found the arrow. I gripped as tightly as my bound wrists allowed, nervous because I couldn't even see what I was doing. "Ready?" I asked him.

"Yes," I heard him say.

Taking in a filling breath, I yanked with all my might. I heard the distinct sound of ripping muscle and skin—but the sturdy arrow hardly budged. Though Alfonse made no noise, I felt him writhing in pain.

"I'm sorry!" I turned to him, tears in my eyes. "I can't do it!"

"You have to," he gasped, when he could speak. "You have no choice. Try again."

I again laid hold of the arrow. Tightening my fingers around it, I drew in a determined breath then hoisted upward with all my strength. When it dislodged, I fell forward and lay flat on my face. Alfonse drew in several gasping breaths.

"It's out," I finally said, rolling onto my side and dropping the arrow.

Alfonse made no reply. I wormed onto my knees and wobbled toward him. Sweat glistened on his brow and around his mouth. If he was conscious, he made no effort to speak.

Hunting around in the shadows, I discovered a worn shirt in a corner. With slow, deliberate progression, thanks to my tied hands, I tore it into strips then used it to blindly wrap his bleeding shoulder.

Alfonse remained silent during the entire ordeal, and I marveled at his endurance. When I had finished, he insisted I get some rest. After making sure he was as comfortable as I could make him, I fell into a light sleep.

I didn't rest long but started up at the sound of the door being opened. I couldn't make out any faces in the darkness and realized that dusk had fallen. I lay still on my side.

"If you've hurt her…" came Jack's voice.

Relief came over me, but I was too exhausted to get off of my stomach.

"What's she to you?" Macklin snapped back. "Get in there."

I heard the jingle of Jack's coat buttons as he came into the hut and waited in anxiety for some signal of Flint's presence. There was only the sound of movement.

"Orrick will come for you tomorrow morning, Sir *Count*," came the sarcastic comment as Macklin closed the door. Again the wooden bar fell into place.

"Kyndle?" came a voice.

"Flint!"

Instantly he was at my side. "Have they hurt you?" he asked, grabbing my shoulder. "At all?"

"No," I said, awkwardly struggling to a sitting position.

There was a moment of silence, then he let out a growl which sounded just like Father's. "Your hands are still tied?"

"Well—" I began.

"Jack," he whispered, turning. "Your knife."

"They didn't take it?" I asked in surprise.

There was a jingle of bootstraps, then I felt Jack take hold of my tied hands. I heard a knife clink open.

"Being a Snowling," Jack said with satisfaction, "they haven't laid a finger on me." I heard him sawing away at the ropes, but my hands were so numb I never felt when they fell away. Flint began chafing circulation back into them.

"Here, Flint." Jack tossed him the little knife. "You keep this."

"My master?" came Alfonse's cautious voice.

"Alfonse?" Jack returned in shock.

"I'm here, my lord."

Jack scooted to his servant's side. "At least those rogues removed that arrow," came his remark as he fussed over Alfonse. "I would've thought it above their character."

"They didn't remove it," came Alfonse's reply. I heard his voice turn my way. "Kyndle did."

"Kyndle?" Jack repeated. "But how?"

"I fear I hurt him very much," I said mournfully, "since I had to do it twisted around backward."

"*Ach*," Alfonse retorted. "Even a doctor would have hurt me."

"They'll pay for this," Jack muttered.

"I have a feeling we will too," I said bleakly. "I'm afraid that we've been harboring an outlaw."

"Of the worst kind," Flint added with a smile in his tone.

Alfonse chuckled from the floor.

"I'd rather spend a lifetime with this murderous criminal than one day with their righteous chief," Jack said in scorn.

"You probably won't be able to," came Alfonse's low reply.

"What?" I asked after the silence that followed.

"Alfonse," Jack said almost sharply. "*I* am your master, your owner. By rights, you are my property. They—"

"Did you give permission to put that arrow in me?" Alfonse laughed bitterly. "These are *Nature Sprites*. They do as they please."

"Do you fear execution?" I asked tremulously.

"No," Alfonse replied. "They'll most likely scar or deform me, then banish me from the Nature Realm. If I ever try to return, I'll be forfeiting my life. Anyone is allowed to kill one who bears the mark of a fugitive."

"Why don't they kill you now?" Flint ventured.

"The chief's wrath runs deep," Alfonse replied, hard bitterness returning to his voice. "He would view execution as a mercy. He would rather inflict physical pain and then follow it up with a lifetime of mental pain. This is the manner in which they usually punish their lawbreakers."

"All against his own countryman," Flint muttered. "How can he live with himself?"

"He has more than one reason to be angry at me," Alfonse said after a moment. "Craiken was his only child, but Launfel also raised his niece whose parents died of illness when she was a child. When we had grown, I asked him for her hand in marriage. When Launfel refused, I kept away from her in respect of his wishes. And even though Laylia never objected to his choice, she slowly wasted away. She had never been strong." He let out a soft sad sigh—the most emotion I had glimpsed in him. "A couple of months after her death came the bear attack."

"Oh," I said softly.

"So you see," he concluded, "I did more than kill his son. I ultimately caused of the death of his niece as well."

"Alfonse," I murmured. "I'm sorry."

HOME ROAD

"My life with you has been wonderful, Jack," Alfonse said, and in his voice, I heard a smile. "I'm only sorry I've caused you so much trouble. To you Firelings as well. You might have been home by now."

Yes, we might have. But I held no anger toward Alfonse.

"Our troubles may soon be over," Jack whispered. "Don't forget that I know a person who lives in this area."

"Where does this person live, my master?" Alfonse asked.

"In the northern sector," Jack told him.

"So you think they will help us?" I asked hopefully.

"If they don't, I know a certain refugee in their home who may." A faint smile softened Jack's grimy face.

chapter 8

Early the next morning, the door of the shack opened. Orrick stood there, Macklin and Gresham at his side.

"Chief Launfel wants to speak with the Snowling," he said. "At once."

Jack rose to his feet. "What does he want to speak about?"

"How would I know?" Orrick snapped.

"You wouldn't," Jack said cooly. "How foolish of me to forget you're a mere captain."

Orrick's chest visibly swelled with anger and a couple moments passed before he spoke again. "The chief also wants the presence of the Fireling girl."

My heart in my throat, I got to my feet. Flint followed suit.

"I'd like to go along," he said bravely.

Orrick spat a laugh. "Since when has a prisoner's request counted for anything?" he asked sarcastically.

"It matters to me," Jack said, his words almost like a threat.

Orrick locked eyes with Jack. "Well, that's too bad," he said. "Chief asked for the count and the female prisoner. No one else."

"Why Kyndle?" Flint asked anxiously.

"He wouldn't know," Jack answered.

"Maybe I do," Orrick snapped, glaring at Jack but speaking to Flint. "Either way, I wouldn't tell you."

That same anger from yesterday flared up in Flint's eyes, and he took a dangerous step forward. Both fists were tightened at his sides.

"I'm her brother," Flint said, voice low. "I have a right to know."

Orrick stepped up too until he stood almost nose to nose with Flint. I noticed, with pride, that my brother stood nearly as tall as his antagonist.

"Get this," Orrick said sardonically. "You're just a prisoner. You have no rights. Just because Sir *Count* here treats you like you're special does not mean you really are. You're scarred war trash that nobody wants."

"Hist!" I snapped, striding forward angrily.

Flint put an arm out to stop me.

Orrick looked down at me with amusement in his eyes. "Hist, eh?"

I swallowed further angry words.

He held my gaze for a full ten seconds. "I'll show you how special he is." In one swift move, he struck Flint brutally up the face; but before my brother had even hit the ground, Orrick had me by my shirt. He held me a few inches above the ground.

"I'm about ready to deal out trouble," he hissed, his eyes narrowing to angry slits. His grip tightened, cutting off my air.

I gripped frantically at his forearm to relieve the burning pressure on my neck, hearing myself choking for air, feeling my senses starting to fade. In my peripheral, I could see Macklin and Gresham restraining Jack.

"How tough are you now, *Fireling*?" Orrick spat at me.

My anger fully stirred, I lashed out my leg and made contact. Without warning, Orrick let me go. I dropped onto my hands and knees, sucking in as much air as I could. Jack stopped his struggling. Just when I could breathe, Orrick gripped both my arms and yanked me to my feet.

"Come along, count," he said, half-dragging, half-carrying me toward the chief's house. "Chief Launfel is waiting."

Jack came toward us, looking at my face. Orrick stared him down.

"You have yet to learn respect, Snowling," he said, "and it might cost you." He shook me roughly. "Or it just might cost someone else."

My fire gone, I drooped in his grip. Several feet away, Flint lay still, just inside the shack door. He appeared unconscious, but I saw him breathing.

"Lock him up," Orrick barked.

Gresham stepped forward, shoved Flint further in with his boot, then dropped the bolt in place.

Without further incident, Jack and I were led to Launfel.

Letting go of my arm, Orrick dropped to one knee before his chief and waited there until he had permission to rise. He swiped a strand of black hair away from his eyes.

"It was exciting getting them here," he huffed.

"Exciting?" Launfel repeated in surprise. He looked as he had the day before, a proud arch to his back as he surveyed us harshly. "They resisted orders? *My* orders?" He leaned down, glaring at Jack. "And just *who* do you think you are, Snow Sprite?"

"A more just man than you," Jack spat.

Orrick hauled off and struck Jack hard across the cheek. A gasp shot from my throat. To strike a *Snowling*! After a second, Jack lifted his head and stared Orrick in the face—so severely that the big Nature Sprite actually looked away.

"It would seem defiance runs freely in your blood," Launfel taunted.

Jack turned to him next.

"But," the Natureling chief went on, "you've yet to tell me what brings you to the Nature Realm."

Jack raised his chin, assuming the proud posture of an aristocrat. The blood on his split cheek was a sharp contrast to his fair complexion. "I've come to see someone living in the northern sector," he said.

"Oh?" Launfel's eyebrow lifted. "And his name?"

"*Her* name," Jack replied, "is Primrose."

"Ms. Primrose?" the chief repeated. "Just who do you think you are to be allowed a meeting with such a secluded personage?"

"You are obviously unaware or you would behave differently toward me," was Jack's cool reply.

Orrick seized Jack's arm in a threatening way, but Jack ignored him as he would a fly. Launfel was unimpressed.

"Enlighten me then. It takes a lot to make me change my ways."

HOME ROAD

Jack swiped at his chin with the back of his ragged sleeve. "Not only am I a person who deserves to be treated with dignity, I am the firstborn son of the Snowling regent and nephew to King Antares II."

I nearly laughed at the fear that leapt into Launfel's eyes. "It's a lie," he said unconfidently. "You're bluffing."

"You only hope I'm lying," Jack said with a short laugh. "'Cause if I'm not, you'll wish you had never laid a finger on me." His eyes flashed. "Or those I'm responsible for."

Launfel looked frightened, though not entirely convinced. "And how can you prove this?" he questioned, a bit of his composure returning.

For an answer, Jack rolled up his right sleeve to the elbow, revealing a small tattoo on the underside of his forearm. I saw it was a swan.

"The emblem of Frost!" Launfel said, covering a mouth which now hung open in dismay. Frantically his eyes flew at Orrick. "Unhand him!" he stammered. Orrick did so instantly.

"I do apologize," Launfel began. "Had we been aware sooner—"

Jack waved off the formalities which meant nothing. Smiling now, he glanced at me out of the corner of his eye, then looked up expectantly at Launfel as though waiting for the command to unhand me as well. When it didn't come, Jack's smiled faded.

Turning to Macklin, he said authoritatively, "Release her."

Macklin looked at Launfel, as did the rest of us. The chief's face was not as proud as before, but it was just as confident. He adjusted the vine-woven crown sitting on his head.

"You may be of Frost blood," he told Jack, "but your privilege doesn't spread to your property."

Jack's face went blank.

"From now on," Launfel continued, "you are free to do as you choose with yourself. But the prisoners and your *servant*," his eyes darkened in anger, "are confiscated immediately due to entering our realm during a border lockdown."

"But—" Jack began.

"Please," Launfel interrupted and I couldn't bear to look at his face. "I must ask that you not interfere with my wishes. You're to be permitted to go where you like, but without my permission, the prisoners stay here." He clenched his teeth almost to the breaking point. "As for the murderer, he will be duly punished."

Jack's face was a mixture of anger and shock.

"Macklin," Launfel said to him. "Take the girl back to the shack. Take the murderer to Orrick's hut."

Macklin pulled me to the door, but Jack stepped forward and blocked our way. Macklin's grip tightened, and I felt my heart pounding violently. Jack's lack of cooperation would only serve to make life harder for Flint and me.

"Jack," I blurted, pleading with my eyes.

The anger didn't leave his face, but Jack knew what I needed. With an understanding nod, he slowly backed out of our way. He didn't follow.

Flint jumped up when Macklin threw the shack door open, and in the light, I could see that an ugly bruise was forming on his cheek. Laughing coarsely, Macklin slung me into the shack and I landed hard on my hands and knees.

Flint was at my side in a moment. His labored breathing told me that he was trying to contain his anger. Macklin slammed the door closed and locked it.

A glance showed that Alfonse lay on the far side of the hut. We hadn't received any food since our arrival, and I could see that it was wearing on him. His face was sallow, his breathing thin. He'd declined even further since I'd left him earlier.

"Where's Jack?" Flint asked, brushing a strand of white hair from his eyes.

"Still with the chief," I responded wearily.

"Did they harm you?" was his anxious question. His fingers closed on my arm. I knew the thought had been on his mind for a while.

"No," I said quickly, happy to settle his mind.

I couldn't imagine how he felt, unable to keep any harm from coming to me.

Actually scratch that. I knew exactly what it felt like.

"Did they harm Jack?" Alfonse asked presently.

I shrugged. "A little, but when he told them he was the king's nephew, they basically snapped to attention. Launfel told him he could go where he wanted and do as he wished, but he also made it clear that we're now Natureling prisoners." I sighed and felt my shoulders droop. "Because of the lockdown, Jack can't free us."

"Did they mention me?" Alfonse asked softly.

"Yes," I blurted, trying in vain to steady my voice. Panic tightened my throat. "They'll be coming for you soon."

"I knew the risk," was his quiet response. "I was counting the costs."

"What will they do?" Flint asked.

"I'll probably lose a hand or part of my foot," he replied, and I could hear the fear in his voice. "Then they'll banish me."

"Listen," I said suddenly.

Footsteps approached and Flint and I leapt to our feet as the door was unlocked and pulled open. Two hooded men came in and stepped toward Alfonse. Before I could think, I threw myself in front of them.

I found myself on the floor again, a blow pounding on the side of my head. Flint knelt beside me, and I could hear a growl rising in his throat. Though I felt my consciousness fading, I gripped frantically at his arm. I knew that if Flint rose, bad things would happen.

The last I heard before darkness overcame me was Alfonse's groaning.

"Kyndle."

Flint's voice broke through the black and summoned me to the light. I opened my eyes and vaguely saw his anxious face hovering over me.

"Is she awake?" came Jack's question from somewhere nearby. It got closer with each word.

"Jack?" I murmured. The ground beneath me was hard.

"I'm here," he said and his face came into my view.

"How's your head?" Flint asked. I felt his hand under my neck.

"Sore."

Tender as a mother, Flint raised me to a sitting position and my eyes struggled to adjust to the dim setting. When they did, I saw that we were still in the shack. Nausea churned in the very pit of my stomach.

"What happened?" I asked when it went away.

"Not much after you left. Launfel apologized again for the way I had been treated but restated that you were all under his authority now. Then he told me I was free to go. I told him that I wanted to come back here."

"What will happen now?" I asked after a long silence.

"Since I'm free," Jack replied, "I plan to visit Primrose to see if she can help me."

"It's a girl?" Flint asked in shock.

"Yes, she was the ambassador to the Fire Realm for a mere two weeks before she came here."

"Oh." Flint nodded. "I remember her."

"I'll do my best to get permission for you two to come with me."

I put my fingertips to my throbbing temples. I felt a severe headache forming.

Flint noticed my strained expression. "What's wrong?"

The pounding was growing. "What hit me?"

"I think he used the hilt of his dagger," Flint said.

Feeling around, I discovered a bump on the side of my head above my left ear. My fingers came away sticky and red. The boys saw this.

"It's bleeding again," Jack said, ripping off his jacket. He began to tear it into long strips. The gold buttons, formerly so shiny, fell to the dirt and rolled away into shadows. Jack handed the strips to Flint and he wrapped them around my head.

"I've never worn velvet before," I said, wincing at the growing pain.

Flint lowered me back down to the ground, and I fell into an uneasy sleep.

chapter 9

"They're letting Kyndle come," I heard Jack say.

"They are?" I murmured, stirring.

"Yes," Jack said. "They think if they keep one of you here, the other won't try to escape. I'm sorry you can't go, Flint, but I have to admit, I'm glad Kyndle will be out of their reach."

"Me too," Flint agreed.

Getting up, Jack went to the door and knocked on it. There was the sound of the board sliding on the other side, then the door opened. Darion stood there. Seeing it was Jack, he stepped aside.

Jack turned before leaving. "I'll be back to get Kyndle."

"I'll see that she's ready," Flint said as the door shut upon the Snow Sprite. He put a cool hand on my burning forehead and the pain began to lessen.

I smiled up at him, thinking how glad I was to have him with me. When he smiled back, a pang shot through my heart.

"What is it?" he asked, seeing tears shining in my eyes.

A tear slid down my face, and I sniffed. "You and Ruby have the same smile."

He smiled, though it was a sad one. "You have Mum's," he murmured. "For your sake, I've tried to keep my emotion down, but with each of your smiles, I miss her more and more."

I turned so that he didn't see the tear leaking down the other side of my face.

"So you never saw Ruby that day?" I asked for the millionth time.

Getting to his feet, Flint walked to the far side of the hut and put his shoulder against the wall. "I only ever saw you," came his answer. "We were all hoping you would be together." There was a tremble to his voice, and he ran both hands through his white hair.

"So was I," I said, striving to keep my voice steady. "I thought they'd let us stay together. When they separated us, that last day, I could hardly bear it. All that kept me going was the hope of seeing her one more time before it was all over."

"But you never did." Flint's voice was hollow.

I wiped my nose with my sleeve. "They probably executed her with Ian."

"*No!*" Hitting the wall with his fist, Flint whirled to face me. "I won't believe you! I *won't!* They wouldn't have done that to a little girl!" With his last word, he slipped down the wall, collapsing in a heap.

Though he strove to smother his sobs in his arms, I heard them.

"I didn't want to believe it either, Flint," I said quietly. "But at times like this, when the pain is so real—" I swallowed hard, striving to finish. It took several moments. "I almost wish she was dead, Flint. I really do. I can't imagine her being hurt."

His sobs continued.

"Whether or not you believe Christ is real," I continued, "Ruby did—and it's a comfort at times like these, knowing that if she is dead, she's at peace."

"You speak as though you believe Christ is real," he said in a strange voice, raising his head. I couldn't see his face in the dim light.

I took a deep breath. "I do."

Flint didn't move. He didn't speak. It seemed he didn't even breathe.

"For a while, I resisted it," I hurried on. "But then one day, I just found myself believing it was all true. Flint, it felt so, so *right*." I smiled at the absurdity of my own words.

"I know," he said.

My heart fluttered wildly and I didn't speak, hardly daring to even believe what I thought I had heard him say.

"I reached that place a couple months ago," came his soft voice. "On a day when all my hope had fled. Yet in that moment of crumbling, Christ became my hope, my strength."

"What?" I gasped.

"I still struggle with my old anger," he went on, "but I've never again struggled with the old fear once Christ became mine, once I became his. It's extraordinary, Kyndle."

"But how did you learn about Christ?"

"Ian and I walked together a lot during that trip to the mountain. He talked about him quite a bit. Even though I brushed him off, it all really impressed me."

"I can't believe it!" I sat up and the dizziness wasn't nearly as severe. "All this time, we both believed—yet the other never knew it!"

Flint said nothing. He just smiled and came to sit beside me.

When Jack returned thirty minutes later, so much joy was in the room you would've thought we'd received our freedom. He smiled obligingly as we explained our reason for rejoicing.

"I've never heard of Christ," he said politely, "but I'll be glad to hear about him sometime soon." As he spoke, he pulled a tight-fitting hat from his pocket. "This is to cover your bandages," he explained, gently pulling it onto my head. "We're off to Primrose's."

"Thanks," I said, straightening it. They helped me to my feet, and then Flint and I bid each other goodbye.

"I'll pray for your safety," he said with a wink.

"And I for yours," I returned. I had thought it many times to myself, but it felt strange to actually be saying it out loud.

Darion unlocked the door, and Jack and I stepped through it. I turned, but Darion had slammed the door closed and bolted it again.

"Stay close," Jack said as we entered the marketplace.

"Okay," I agreed, leaning on his arm and trying to ignore the stares we received from those we walked past. Since our arrival was fully under the chief's jurisdiction, the villagers had returned to their normal way of life. However, their glares made it clear that they didn't want us here. The red hair streaming out from under my hat probably didn't help; however, I did notice that their angry stares seemed directed at Jack while their glances at me were merely those of idle curiosity.

Jack seemed unaffected by the stares, humming cheerily as we passed the numerous market booths. I looked closely at all of the different plants and foods that they were selling, most of which I had never seen before. I knew the soil must be very different here to produce such exotic-looking crops. It was a bit thrilling.

We were almost through the market area when two Natureling men stepped into our path, forcing us to stop. Two *burly* Natureling men.

"Who are you?" one of them asked Jack brusquely.

"Count Hail of the Snow Realm," my companion answered in a voice that was confident.

The man looked at me next. "And who are you, Fireling?"

"I'm his prisoner," I said, not flinching underneath his heavy glare as my father had taught me.

He took a step forward. "Prisoner? Then why are you out here?"

Jack gently nudged me backward. "I got permission from your chief to bring her with me."

"Prove it."

I felt my heart beating fast as Jack stuttered, "I'm not sure what you mean—"

"I mean a piece of paper *showing* that you got permission."

"I don't have a paper," Jack said bravely. "Just my word. And since I'm an honest man, that should be enough."

"Well, it's not." The guard shot a glance at his companion. "Unless you can prove that this prisoner isn't fugitive, we'll have to take her with us." As he spoke, he took another step in my direction.

"Don't lay a finger on her," Jack warned, shifting his eyes at me. The glance conveyed he didn't want me in their hands for a moment.

The guard stopped just before his hand touched my arm.

"What would you do about it if I did?" he asked Jack.

I made no move to escape, knowing it would only make things worse. Jack stared hard at him. The man deliberately put his finger upon my arm, then turned to his companion to laugh. When he finished his mocking, he glanced to see if Jack would challenge him.

I looked too and watched in horror as Jack's fist swung, making solid contact with the man's face. He staggered back, stunned.

Without hesitation, his companion stepped forward and used his fist to brutally club Jack on the top of the head. As Jack collapsed,

I opened my mouth to back talk; but at his look, I repented of the idea.

Jack lay unconscious on the ground, and I saw blood in his white hair. Several Nature Sprites had stopped their shopping to watch us.

By now, the first man had recovered. Snatching a rope from his belt, he bound Jack's arms tightly behind his back. The second guard did the same to me. My mind whirled. Did they not know that Jack was of Snowling royalty? Or did they just not care?

Looking down, I saw that Jack was regaining consciousness. His eyes rolled open, and he groaned as the first man yanked him onto his knees. Jack swayed slightly, and his head fell wearily onto his chest.

Just then, I heard a small scream. That of a woman. Jack's head snapped up.

I watched in surprise as a young woman, a *Snow Sprite* woman, pushed through the onlookers. With tears running down her face, she fell onto her knees in front of Jack and threw both of her arms around his neck. They exchanged words I couldn't hear, and Jack strained against his bonds.

"What's going on here?" came another female voice.

I glanced up to see a second Snowling woman standing at the front of the crowd. Her blue eyes were filled with anger.

"Loose this man—immediately!" she said to our attackers.

"Yes, Ms. Primrose," said the first guard, moving to obey.

His hands free, Jack held the young Snowling woman close.

"But, Ms. Primrose." My guard addressed the second woman through clenched teeth. "He is illegally escorting a Fire Sprite."

The young woman by Jack looked up and her eyes lit on me. A loose strand of white hair blew over her face as she got to her feet. Unsteadily Jack rose as well.

"Who's this?" she demanded, gesturing toward me.

"This is Kyndle," Jack said, smiling kindly.

His companion took a step toward me, studying my face very closely. I realized then that she had become very angry.

"So that's it?" she said, whirling on him.

"What?"

"You've replaced me? After all I've been through?"

He put a hand on her arm. "Winterose—"

She slapped it away. "Don't touch me! I can see what happened. Why else would you be illegally escorting her?"

"Look," I said, stepping in their direction. "I think—"

Her cold glare shut my mouth.

"Winterose," Jack said again. "You're wrong."

"No, Hail." Her voice, though soft, shook with anger. "You're the one who's wrong. You have wronged me." Before he could say anything else, Winterose worked her way through the crowd and was gone.

Primrose was disturbed. "Let him go," she said to the guards. When the guard started to pull me away, she added, "Let her go as well."

"But—" my guard protested.

"If you wish," Primrose interrupted, "I can speak with Launfel and see what he thinks about your behavior."

He shoved me up against Jack and then turned away, muttering under his breath. Primrose watched them both until they finally left. Then she turned to Jack.

"I'm sorry about that," she said as the crowd dispersed quietly.

Jack didn't answer her. He was looking back in the direction Winterose had gone.

"Thanks for your help," I offered for both of us. "I don't know what would've happened if you hadn't interfered."

She glanced at me and nodded, but her face was far from warm.

At the silence, Jack turned to her. "I'm Count Hail Frost," he said.

Understanding sparked in her eyes. "I remember you now," she said before casting a skeptical look at me. Jack saw it.

"Winterose can be very emotional," Jack said. "There was no need to jump to conclusions. She should have just asked who Kyndle was."

Primrose lifted her chin. "Then she was mistaken?"

Jack glanced at me and we both blushed. "Well, yes," he said.

"Who is she?" Primrose asked.

I felt irked. She was talking about me as if I wasn't standing there.

Typical Snowling. And a Snowling woman *at that.*

"She's my prisoner. I have her with me so no additional harm comes to her."

"Additional?"

Jack pulled back the edge of my hat to show the bandage. Primrose looked satisfied with the validity of the story. She pulled her shawl closer around her as a chilly breeze floated by.

"You'd better get to wherever you were going," she urged, glancing around. "I can't guarantee that those men won't try to find you after I leave."

Jack smiled faintly. "In fact," he said, "I was looking for you."

"Oh?" Her white eyebrow lifted.

He took a deep breath. "I'm in need of some help."

They stepped out of the main thoroughfare, and she listened quietly as Jack told our story. I watched her face grow worried.

"May I help you with that?" came a voice beside me.

I turned quickly to find a Natureling man. He gestured at my still-tied hands.

"Oh, yes, please."

A knife from his boot made quick work of the ropes, and as I began to rub my wrists, Jack and Primrose returned to us.

"I'll do what I can," she said at my questioning look, "but I can't make any promises yet. Bolivar," turning to the man who had cut my bonds, "will take you to where you're staying to ensure that you arrive safely."

"Thank you, Lady Primrose," Jack said, bowing in gratitude.

"Yes!" I echoed, grabbing her hand impulsively. "How can we thank you?"

She looked at me in what appeared to be shock, but I watched it melt away as she let out a silvery laugh. "I love your realm more than my own in many ways," she said. "I'm ready to aid their cause in whatever way I can." She took a few steps back, looking over her shoulder. "Now go."

Flint jumped up as we entered the shack. As I turned to wish Bolivar a good evening, he was already gone. Darion jostled me in the shack and waited as Jack took his time. Then he slammed the door shut.

Huddled in a corner, Jack and I told Flint about our conversation with Primrose. He seemed somewhat encouraged.

"Maybe she'll be able to do something." He sighed.

"Hopefully," I added.

Flint sighed again. "I admit that I'm getting frustrated with all of this sitting around."

"Typical Fireling," Jack said with a twinkle in his eye.

chapter 10

Nearly a week later, we awoke to find Darion heaving the door open. He crossed both arms across his chest, that familiar scowl over his aging face.

"Launfel wants to speak with you," he said, not addressing anyone in particular.

"All of us?" Jack ventured.

Darion nodded. We got to our feet, Flint more excitedly. He slipped Jack's hat over his head, tucking in a stray white strand. I knew how ashamed he was of this marked new feature. He would want Launfel's first impression of him to be unmistakably Fire Sprite. Besides my head had improved, and I didn't need bandages anymore.

As he put his arms up to his head, dark brown scars came into view, reaching out of his sleeves. I strode to him. Snatching his wrist, I pushed his sleeve up to his elbow. The scars continued up.

"Flint." I choked. "*What did they do to you?*"

He pushed the sleeve back down and put his arms around me. "It's all in the past," he said softly. "Don't think about it. I never meant for you to see it."

I clenched my teeth. "Was that by Glacier's order?"

He nodded.

My head lowered. "I hate him," I whispered.

"That's not your job," he whispered back.

"Good morning," Launfel said as we entered, and he actually smiled.

Well, somewhat.

None of us had the heart to answer.

"A visitor arrived early this morning," Launfel explained. "He wanted to see you." As he finished speaking, he turned toward a doorway to his right.

We followed his gaze to see a large mantled figure step into the light. His clothes were covered with the dust of swift travel, and his boots were spattered with mud. He drew back his hood.

"Cardinal!" Flint exclaimed with a boyish exuberance.

He smiled, nodding at each of us each in turn. "Representative Frost, Flint, Kyndle." The sound of his voice brought back rushing memories of home.

We shifted excitedly, waiting for Aidan to go on.

"A few days ago," he said, "I received a letter from Representative Primrose. She informed me Chief Launfel had come into possession of a few Fireling prisoners whom she figured I might have an acquaintance with."

"Primrose wrote *you*?" Jack repeated as if unbelieving.

Aidan nodded. "I've discussed it with Chief Launfel," he said, the old chief nodding affirmatively, "and he's agreed to free you at once. You're both welcome to return with me."

I felt a broad smile stretching across my face.

"Thank you, cardinal," Flint said with a low bow of gratitude. But as he straightened, a strand of white hair came loose from under his cap and fell across his eyes. Flint quickly swiped it back under the hat, but heavy silence descended upon the room. Flint stared at his own feet.

Aidan advanced forward until he stood almost toe-to-toe with Flint, then he reached and pulled the hat from my brother's head. White locks dropped down around Flint's ears which had grown red. He didn't lift his head.

Aidan said nothing for a few moments. He swallowed hard and looked down. But when at last he raised his head, I saw that his eyes had filled with tears.

A never-before-seen sight.

He took my brother by the shoulders, and for several moments, he was silent, just staring at that bowed white head.

"I'm proud of you." He spoke very softly.

Flint said nothing. Aidan lifted Flint's chin and held his gaze. More was communicated in that look than I could have ever hoped to say on paper.

"I am *proud* of you," he said again.

Flint swallowed hard. "Thank you, cardinal."

Aidan came to me next and—to my surprise—I found myself gathered into a Fireling bear hug.

"That's from your father," he said, releasing me. "He regretted that he couldn't come get you himself."

I stared at him in wonder. "Then he's safe?"

He let out a laugh so booming that Launfel jumped in his upholstered seat. "Adar is one of the most protected warriors I know," he assured me. "The way his men guard him, the man who would attempt to pull a hair off Adar's *leg* would be lucky to get off with all four limbs." He winked. "I don't worry about your father any more than I do the outcome of this war."

I felt my heart beat fast. "What do you mean?"

Aidan crossed his huge arms. "You and Flint weren't the only reason I came to Brimshore," he said. "As of a few minutes ago, the Fire and the Nature Realms have entered into an alliance against the Snow Realm."

My eyes widened.

"What?" Jack breathed.

"The Fire Realm will protect the Nature Realm," Aidan went on, "and in return, the Naturelings will provide us with all the supplies necessary for duration of the war."

There was a stunned silence. I glanced up at Launfel who beamed his ugly smile. I wasn't exactly thrilled at the thought of having him on our side. Jack stepped toward Aidan.

"The Snow Sprite ranks will put forth a dangerous fight," he said. His words weren't a threat but a loyal fact. "I can personally testify to their thorough training."

"As can I," Aidan agreed with the respect one man owes to another. "I have seen many fellow warriors fall before them. They're a mighty foe which is why we need an alliance." He turned to Launfel. "We're grateful for your support."

"Why of course, cardinal," Launfel said, his voice more gracious than I had ever heard it. "I too have recognized the threat that Snow Realm is to our lands. They can hardly sleep for always wanting more."

I glanced sideways at Jack. His face grew a shade darker.

"The Snow Realm has always been a threat to the well-being of our way of life," Launfel continued, now looking directly at Jack. "The royal line is nothing more than a bunch of blithering idiots who know nothing beyond than their own—"

"Launfel," Aidan cut in with a firm look. "While Count Frost is aware of the errors of his people—and I'm certain he doesn't condone them—you surely cannot expect him to speak ill of his own people or remain silent when another does."

"If he is one of us," Launfel snapped, looking at Jack, "then I do."

Jack lifted his chin. "I am *not* one of you," he said, returning Launfel's stare. "I am a Snow Sprite of the royal line. And while it's true that I have come to a place where I *don't* condone their enslavement of the Firelings, I cannot agree with your other accusations. Not now, not ever."

Launfel rose from his throne. "Then you aren't welcome in my house," he spat, pointing to the door. "Get out!"

"Launfel," the cardinal began.

"No, he's right," Jack interrupted, not removing his eyes from Launfel's face. "I'm no longer welcome."

Launfel laughed. "You were never welcome."

Jack turned to me. "I take my leave."

"Wait," I said.

"You'll find me at Primrose's." With that, the offended Snowling swept out of the room.

"We Firelings need to speak alone," the cardinal said in the awkward silence following Jack's departure. "Is there a house where we can rest a few hours?"

"Of course," Launfel said, recovering his feigned graciousness. "I'll have Lenard take you there." He nodded toward the young man standing near the door.

"Thank you," the cardinal said as we left.

"Can you tell me any more news about my family?" I asked when the door of our temporary house had closed upon Lenard.

Flint leaned forward in his seat, twirling Jack's hat in his hands.

"Your mother also is alive and well." The cardinal smiled. "She and your father have contributed much toward the Fire Sprite cause. Last I heard, she was tending to the wounded at Dunmark."

"Praise God!" I whispered, running a hand across my eyes.

Flint swallowed. "No news of Ruby?"

"I'm afraid not," Aidan replied, matching his soft tone.

We hung our heads.

"When did you last see her?" he asked us.

"In a dungeon at Galaheed," I said when I could answer, "over a year ago. We've been able to learn nothing of her since then, but in a way, I'm almost certain she's alive. If she had been executed, I think Glacier would have been all too glad to let me know."

"I promise to keep both my ears open for any news of her," he vowed to us. "Perhaps when we return to Frieman, we'll learn more. Your parents should be waiting for you when we arrive."

I turned to Flint in joy. The home road was nearly ours!

But Flint didn't share my excitement. "Cardinal," he said, looking as if beyond my face, "is it too late to join the others in the battle?"

Aidan's face softened, and he rested his hand on Flint's shoulder. "It's never too late," he said. "I just thought you may want to visit your family first to get some rest." A sadness flickered across his face, one I had seen there many times before.

"They're dying out there," Flint said passionately. "I could never rest until I'm out there helping them."

"I understand," Aidan said, nodding. "I'm returning to the field in the morning. You can go with me. Kyndle," turning to me, "do you still want to go home?"

I looked at Flint, then back at Aidan. "Yes," I said, emotion rising in my chest. "There's nowhere else I would rather go."

Armed with documents certifying our release, Flint and I made our way to Primrose's home to tell Jack goodbye. We were met at the gate by Bolivar who bowed politely.

"Lady Primrose is expecting you," he said. "She and the count both." He led us to the door and ushered us in.

We stepped into the foyer. To our left, a wide door opened into a parlor in which both Primrose and Jack sat. They rose as we entered the room, and Jack came to us.

"I've been told you're going home," he said, voice warm as he took my hands in greeting. "For your sake, I'm glad."

I smiled. I was glad as well.

He turned to Flint. "You're returning home too?"

Flint shook his head grimly. "I'm leaving in the morning to join my countrymen in the fight."

"I wish you well," Jack said, after a moment, as all confidence drained from his features. He glanced at me, and in his eyes, I saw my own fears reflected. Then he swallowed hard and dropped his head.

"Thank you," Flint said.

After several moments, I turned to Jack. "What will you do?"

"I don't know." He sighed. "I hardly think I'll be welcome back home, and part of me wants to stay here."

"There's no rush," Primrose interjected. "I'll provide your lodging in the meantime."

Jack smiled sadly at her. I thanked Primrose again for her help without which we would still be in the lean-to.

"Like I told you before," she said actually reaching for *my* hand, "I'll always be there to aid the cause of freedom for the Firelings."

Flint glanced outside, and then at me. I knew it was time to go. I reached for Jack's hand again and squeezed it tightly.

"I never met Winterose properly," I told him. "Please tell her that I'm very sorry for what happened and that I didn't mean to paint the picture she perceived."

"I'll tell her, Kyndle," he said gratefully.

I put a hand on his arm. "Alfonse?" I asked softly.

He smiled sadly. "I'll take care of him."

I took a deep breath. "I hope to see you again."

Flint stepped forward and put his hand on Jack's shoulder. "We both do."

Happiness rose in Jack's eyes, and he drew both us into an embrace. We had no way of knowing if the three of us would be reunited. When the embrace ended, each looked into the other's face. There was no need for further words. We were all ready for our separate paths—and at the same time, we had never been more unready.

Bolivar accompanied us to the gate. I glanced back and saw Jack in the window. He lifted his hand in farewell. I would miss that moody Snowling. Flint and I stepped out into the street.

"I wish you both a good journey," Bolivar said, bowing politely.

chapter 11

It was a quiet walk back to Launfel's dwelling. Flint dragged his feet, thrust his hands in his pockets, kicked at random stones. More than once, words rose up my throat but I held them back. I didn't want to say anything I would later regret.

Flint's patriotism was, to him, a badge which he wore proudly upon his chest; but to me, it was a belt pulled tightly around my waist, constricting my joy. At last, we reached Launfel's house.

"I'm ready," Orrick was saying as we entered.

"Ready for what?" Flint asked as Aidan shut the door behind us.

Orrick turned. "To begin our journey to the Fire Realm," he said, his voice less of a growl than in days past.

I shot an anxious glance both Aidan and Flint. My brother's jaw was slack.

"*You're* escorting her home?" he asked.

Orrick nodded. "Myself and three other Nature Sprites."

"I've arranged it this way to prove trust in this alliance," Launfel said. "No harm will come to her. And if it does," he said to Orrick, "you shall regret it."

"No harm will come to her," Orrick repeated, looking first at Launfel and then at me.

"When will you leave?" Flint asked in a tight voice.

"Immediately," Orrick replied. "As soon as she's ready."

I met eyes with Aidan. He tightened his lips in a sad smile.

Flint steered me back outside. As the door shut behind us, I felt tears rising in my eyes and looked away.

"I'm supposed to be ready?"

He grabbed my shoulder. "It's for the best. We've always known war was coming, but I see now that neither of us were ready for the separation that would come with it. Call upon your inner courage, Kyndle. In just a few days, you'll be home. Mum will help you through it."

"Frieman won't be home be home without you, Flint." I lifted my eyes to look into his face. "Won't you come back for just a *few* days?"

"That would mean another week or so before I could enlist," he said, shaking his head. "Frieman is just too far south."

I drew in a deep breath, dried my face with the back of my sleeve, and squared both my shoulders. Tears would only make the separation harder. I looked up into his friendly freckle-framed eyes.

"How do I know I'll see you again?" I finally said.

He took my shoulders gently. "You don't."

I hung my head.

"Neither of us can know exactly what our futures will hold," he went on. "Christ must be your strength and your courage when you can't find it in yourself." He set one of his heavy hands upon my head, tousling my hair playfully. "And who knows? Maybe all those years of secret training meetings will pay off."

The door opened and Orrick thrust his head out. "Ready?" he asked with a touch of the old gruffness in his voice.

"I was until you showed up," I snapped.

Flint touched my shoulder. "Down, girl," he whispered.

"The horses are at the door," Orrick went on, ignoring me completely. "We leave immediately." He closed the door again.

I turned back to Flint, smiling through tears that wouldn't be quelled, and put both my arms around him. He patted my back encouragingly as I pulled back.

"Goodbye, Kyndle," he said, smiling quietly down at me. "Tell Mum I love her. So much."

I nodded, swallowing hard. "I will, Flint."

"Here," he said, yanking the hat from his head. "Take this, to keep all that hair off your neck. And to remind you of Jack. And me."

I pulled it over my head and tucked my braid into it. As if I needed a reminder! But I also realized he was no longer ashamed to show his hair to his mates, now that the cardinal was proud of him. He pulled a small knife from his boot and handed it to me.

"Jack's knife may come in handy too."

Together we approached the group of Nature Sprites sitting upon their mounts at the front door. From atop his draft horse, Orrick gestured at the last horse. Flint offered his knee, and I mounted without much difficulty. Physically at least.

Flint squeezed my hand. "He'll be your strength," he told me again. "He'll be your courage."

"No fear," I said.

Ian's voice filled my mind. Strength filled my heart. Tears filled my eyes.

"H'ya!" Orrick bellowed, urging his horse forward.

"Flint." I faltered.

"Go on, Kyndle," he said, but his voice broke. He slapped my horse's rump and it surged after the others.

I looked over my shoulder as we rode away. Flint stood, unmoving, hand raised in a farewell. Aidan stood next to him and put his hand on my brother's shoulder. A sudden breeze brushed Flint's white hair across his forehead.

And so, my journey on the home road began.

For hours, Orrick maintained a fast pace, not slacking in the least bit. Before long, the horses' sleek sides glistened with sweat and a thick foam gathered under their bits. I could feel a rattle in my horse's breathing from where my legs gripped her barrel.

By midday, we achieved the southeastern border of the Nature Realm, marked by a wooden wall. Three sentries stood near the gate. They called us to a halt as we approached.

"Faelan!" Orrick called to the soldier that strode towards us. "I have orders from Chief Launfel."

"I'm sorry, captain, but I'll need to see them." The young man bowed respectfully. "Since lockdown, all the rules have become much stricter. I couldn't let my own mother out without permission."

"Understood," Orrick grunted, fishing around in his saddlebag. After a moment, he withdrew a wrinkled paper and gave it to Faelan.

The young solider glanced briefly at it and then gave it back.

"Very good, sir," he said. "Open the gates!"

The other two soldiers jumped to obey.

"Have a good journey, captain," Faelan said, turning back and waving us on. He smiled up at each rider as they passed but dropped his eyes as I trotted by. I hardly noticed his rudeness.

My horse surged through the gate, and as we emerged out the other side, she pressed to follow the others. Allowing her to set her own pace, I breathed in the cool air with a sigh as each step left the Nature Realm that much further behind.

The home road was finally mine!

With each hour, the trees in the forest through which we rode began to grow farther apart. I knew we were slowly getting closer to the farmlands and fields of the southern Realm. When we came to the occasional meadow, I was able to learn my horse—leaning into her, lifting myself in the saddle on every other of her long strides, merging myself to the rhythmic ripple of her muscles, matching her breathing pattern with my own.

Orrick glanced back periodically to confirm I was still there, but there was no further communication. The hard pace left no room for it. Not that I *wanted* to talk to any of them. Yet as the shadows lengthened, I began to wonder if he ever planned to stop.

Finally he barked out a halt. He and the other Naturelings slid easily from their mounts without any apparent sign of soreness. I dismounted a couple moments later, trying to hide just how stiff I was. They started to gather wood for a fire. I leaned against my mount, glad to close my eyes for a moment. Where my ear pressed against her steamy flank, I heard a thudding heartbeat.

There is nothing quite as connecting as hearing another heartbeat, be it a horse or not. I cared only that it was a comfort as exhaustion washed over me—mingled with my sorrow at leaving Flint and my joy at going home.

Suddenly I was scared out of my wits by an ear-splitting sound. My horse jumped, and I dropped to a squat, covering my head with my arms. After a few seconds, the droning sound suddenly stopped.

Cautiously I raised my head. The other Naturelings were still making preparations for the campfire, but Orrick was hustling something into his saddlebag. Rising to my feet, I strode toward him just as he dropped the flap shut.

"What in the realm was that?" I demanded.

He glared at me for two seconds, then reached back into his saddlebag and withdrew a sizable horn.

"This," he said before stuffing it back inside the bag.

"But what was it for?" I persisted as he walked away.

"Just a precaution," he said over his shoulder. "It will startle all large predators from the area."

"Thanks for the warning."

"Don't mention it."

"Troll," I muttered turning my back to them all.

Dinner was another quiet event. Salted venison and some sort of leafy vegetable left me with a longing for familiar food. Washing the last of it down with some of the water that Flint had packed for me, I went to sit at the base of a large tree. Nearby my mount had found a palatable patch of vegetation and was chomping away happily.

I let my head drop back against the smooth bark, swallowing hard and closing my weary eyes. I vaguely heard low murmurs of conversation but couldn't make out any words. I didn't care about them anymore. My horse snorted contentedly, and the other mounts answered back with noises of their own. My heart beat loudly in my ears as the darkness in front of my eyes swirled, forming elusive shapes that seemed familiar.

I was startled awake, not by a noise but by a silence. Night had fallen, but now the moon was out, sending slivers of white light through the branches overhead. Eerie shadows made my skin crawl as I begrudgingly got to my feet.

The Naturelings sat exactly where I had left them. The fire was now a pile of embers, pulsing with contained heat. As I neared, a dramatic hush came over the men. Orrick glared at up me as usual.

"What do you want?" he barked after a moment.

"Nothing," I said cooly.

They maintained a stony silence. I didn't speak. In fact, I felt afraid. Something wasn't right. Instinct told me to get away. I went back to my tree.

Sitting down again, I sat without moving until I heard the murmur of their voices. When I felt certain I wasn't being watched, I eased around to the far side of the sizable tree and very quietly began to make my escape. But I hadn't got very far before my horse whinnied nervously.

I froze and felt I was trembling. But why?

It took me a few moments for me to realize that it wasn't me shaking. Dropping, I laid my ear to the ground and my mind registered the reality that a group of horses was fast approaching. Why did this terrify me? I glanced back.

The Naturelings had gotten to their feet and were milling about a bit nervously. My heart raced with a fear I couldn't explain. Guttural instinct overruled all reason, and without knowing why, I began to shinny up the closest tree. After climbing as high as I dared, I sat quietly, hardly daring to breathe. Twenty feet down and sixty to my left, the Naturelings stood and waited.

Within a few moments, the expected horsemen appeared in the clearing below. The riders dismounted, and I saw that each wore a billed hat. The Naturelings walked forward to meet them, carrying their bows.

One of the newcomers strode forward confidently. I heard the jingle of his boots.

"Which of you is called Orrick?" he said briskly. Though his voice was unfamiliar, his manner of speech was not.

My stomach churned with dull dread.

"Here," said the guilty one, and the burly Natureling stepped forward. The jaunty inquirer removed his hat, revealing a shock of white hair.

"You must be Hadrian," I heard Orrick say.

Suddenly everything began to piece together into a grotesque puzzle. The horn, the awkward silence, Orrick's persistent glare. My chest ignited in a sudden savage anger that made my throat burn as my mind began to race. I needed to get far away. They would find me up here. They would take me back.

Not taking my eyes from the scene unfolding below, I began my silent descent.

"Where is the Fireling?" came Hadrian's question.

I reached the foot of the tree and dropped to a defensive squat. Sixty feet away, Orrick chuckled in satisfaction as he turned to one of the other Naturelings.

"Go fetch it, Gunter," he said.

I picked my way through the dark trees with as much speed as stealth allowed, my anger swelling at being referred to as an *it*. I knew my time was down to seconds. Behind me, I heard a startled cry.

"The Fireling is gone!"

I broke into a dead run as chaos broke out behind me.

"Split up!" Orrick bellowed.

I felt my courage slipping away. Flint's words came across my heart and mind, *Christ must be your strength and courage when you can't find it within yourself.*

I heard someone moving around not far behind me.

"Oh, God!" I prayed hoarsely. "*Help!*"

My feet moved with more coordination than I thought I had. I should have tripped more than once but didn't. I had almost begun to think that I might actually get away when the shout came—

"I see him!"

I tossed aside all attempts at stealth and exerted myself to the fullest extent, confused at now being called a *him*. Speed was my only chance at freedom. The noises behind me grew closer.

"Stop!" came a voice.

Gathering myself, I leapt across a small brook, landing neatly on the other side and continuing my desperate run. I felt a stabbing pain in my ankle, but it was the least of my concerns. I heard a dull *thud* as my pursuer also cleared the brook.

"Stop!" he called again, and I recognized the voice of the man called Hadrian.

I ignored the command and plunged forward, my breath now coming in quick spurts. I sensed him getting closer and the hair rose on the back of my neck, then a heavy hand came down hard on my shoulder, throwing me off-balance. I pitched forward, landing violently on my stomach, and everything went black for a few moments.

As my senses returned, I fought to draw breath into my shocked lungs. I felt myself being pulled to my feet. My ankles wobbled, but I was kept from falling. My vision cleared, and I looked into a pair of blue eyes.

"Steady now," he said, gripping my arm so tightly that the pain broke through the fogginess of my mind.

Crashing footsteps approached from my right, and I turned. A lantern swayed in the darkness, and as it neared, I recognized Orrick's face. I saw an ugly scowl stretching across it. His jaw tightened as he reached us, and for a moment, he said nothing. Then he hauled off and struck me across the side of the face.

I staggered back, my senses fading in and out.

"Enough!" the Snow Sprite barked.

Ignoring him, Orrick caught me by the shirt just as my knees buckled and held me just above the ground.

"You," he hissed, his eyes narrowing. Mixed with the anger in his face, I saw mortification.

chapter 12

"Unhand him immediately," Hadrian ordered.

Orrick turned to face him, still holding me a couple inches above the ground.

"Him?" he repeated.

Hadrian blinked, not understanding. A few Naturelings ran up, quickly followed by a few Snowlings.

Without warning, Orrick dropped me like a sack of potatoes and I hit the ground hard on my knees. My neck burned like fire. Reaching down, Orrick snatched the hat from my head. I felt my thick braid flop onto my back.

"This brat is a girl," Orrick snapped. "A fiery one."

Hadrian's face registered complete shock. "I—I wasn't informed that I was collecting a female prisoner," he stammered.

"Surprise," Orrick growled, tossing my hat in my face.

I snatched it and then glared up at him.

Recovering his former composure, Hadrian cleared his throat. "What is her name?"

Go ahead—talk about me like I'm not here.

Orrick yanked me to my feet so roughly that my shoulder hurt. "Answer for yourself," he snapped.

I thrust out my chin. "Kyndle Redwood," I said, speaking deliberately in an effort to hide how much my face hurt from that backhanding. I was surprised when recognition sparked in Hadrian's face.

"Redwood?" he repeated. "Are you by chance kin to Red Adar?"

I smiled in spite of the pain it brought. "I am his daughter."

His eyebrows lifted, and he turned to Orrick. "This raises the bounty price," he told him.

Orrick thrust out a huge hand. "Out with it," he said. "We need to be our way."

Pulling back his handsome jacket, Hadrian took a purse from his belt and, from it, a small money pouch. He let it drop, and it was immediately swallowed up by Orrick's huge hand. Quick as a wink, I heard it jingle in the Naturelings' pocket. Then Orrick turned to me.

"So long, trouble," he said with his ugly smile.

I squared my chin. "Always a pleasure."

He let out a laugh, turned, and walked away. I watched as the darkness swallowed him up and all his Natureling companions. Hadrian stared after him for a few seconds, and when he turned, he was wagging his head. I turned away from him.

"It's obvious that your gender didn't matter to that Natureling rogue," he said, "but I assure you that from here on out, your treatment will be with the civility due a female."

I said nothing, but the weight of his gaze finally compelled me to look up at him.

"On my honor," he said formally, "I am not lying to you."

I leveled a hard stare up into his pristine face. "Is this the same honor that prompted you to hunt me down like convicted criminal and drag me the other side of the realm as a prisoner of war?"

He took a deep breath, his face slightly less gracious than before. "I reference the honor which also bids me to obey orders."

I scoffed. "That's what I thought."

I was hoisted up to a seat behind Hadrian's saddle, and then he mounted in front of me. He clucked to his mount, and we all moved off in a northerly direction.

The opposite direction of home.

Within several minutes, we reached their campsite and I was lowered to the ground once more.

"I have to obey my orders," Hadrian said, "but I promise you that neither I nor *any* of my men," he leveled a significant glance at the eight soldiers, "are going to mistreat you."

Each bowed his head in submission. Clenching my jaw, I looked away. I refused to be reassured by another lie.

The campsite consisted of five small tents huddled round a smoldering campfire. At a silent order from Hadrian, the men paired off and ducked into four of the tents.

Hadrian strode to the fire and, using a saber, stirred the ashes back to life. I waited for him to tie me to a tree, but rather, he took me by my arm and nudged me toward the last tent. I dug my heels into the ground. He glanced at me as if in surprise.

"I'm not sharing a tent," I spat angrily.

"I don't expect you to," he said with a proper laugh. "You can have the tent all to yourself. I'll sleep by the fire."

I hesitated.

"As I said before," he went on, "no harm will come to you."

I allowed him to lead me into the tent. He stepped inside, after me, to light the lantern and grab his bedroll. Then the flap fell shut behind him, and I was left alone. Spreading out the bedroll he had left, I sat down on it and put my head on my knees. My mind was heavy with my reality, and there seemed to be no escape from my thoughts.

Yet again I was a prisoner. Just as I thought my troubles were over, they multiplied. Just as I thought freedom was mine, it had become nothing more than a concept which wasn't mine to realize, a reality that I couldn't grasp any easier than I could the wind.

Regret bruised me as I recalled how ready I'd been to leave Flint and the cardinal in my haste to go home. I hadn't known then what my decision would mean.

Here I was: alone yet again, a prisoner yet again, en route to the Snow Realm—yet again. The homeward journey had been thwarted yet again. Suddenly a thought hit me. I raised my head and listened.

Maybe not.

When I heard nothing, I very quietly crawled to the tent flap. Pulling it back, I peered out into the night. The fire had dwindled to ashes and I saw Hadrian's dark form stretched beside it. Straining into the shadows, I watched his sides rise and fall in rhythmic breathing until I was certain he was asleep. Then I made my plan.

Going to the far end of the tent, I used Jack's knife to noiselessly slice upward until there was a large enough hole for me to slide through. When I was safely outside, I began to creep through the trees.

There was a stir behind me. I dropped onto my stomach and waited. After a few moments of quiet, I glanced backward. Hadrian had turned over but was still asleep. When I had waited as long as I dared, I got to my feet and continued on.

I traveled for several hours, the moon giving just enough light to move around and just enough to make me feel venerable. Constantly I glanced to see if I was being followed, but I was alone. Only once did I stumble on a hidden vine, but I managed a quiet fall on my knees. As dawn began to break, I came to a sudden stop, dropping on all fours in the tall fern.

Through the trees, a hundred yards ahead, I saw a group of horsemen, standing at a halt, talking among themselves. Panic welled up in me.

Had I gone in a huge circle? Were they the Snowlings or the Naturelings? How do I get away from them in broad daylight?

As these thoughts stampeded through my head like a herd of cattle, a voice met my ear. A sturdy male voice.

A voice I *recognized*.

I crawled forward until I could see them clearly then peered through the underbrush. A tall, broad man with red hair and beard, astride a huge draft horse, turned so that his face became visible. He spoke to another man nearby, then turned his back to me. I stared in disbelief as tears rose.

I had escaped from my captors and walked right into my own father's detachment.

"Move out!" he bellowed to the group.

The rest trotted forward in a northwesterly direction, but he held his mount still, waiting to bring up the rear. I smiled through my tears and started to get to my feet.

I didn't get that far. A hand suddenly clamped across my mouth and a strong arm looped through both mine, hauling me backward. I watched helplessly as the last of the troops passed before my father.

I saw him lean forward in his saddle, urging his horse on.

Fire exploded in my chest.

I bucked forward savagely, tossing my captor clear over my head into the brush. His hat flew from his white head. I took a flying leap over his body, but as I sailed over him, I caught the gleam of metal. A rattling gasp escaped me as the knife sliced through my shoe and across the sole of my foot. Landing hard upon my other ankle, I tripped and landed among the fern.

"Dad!" I screamed so loud my throat burned. I scrambled to a sitting position and looked around. "Dad, wait!"

But my father and his detachment were gone.

Fierce determination flamed through me, and I leapt onto my feet. Two and a half steps later, I was back on my face in the underbrush, sharp pain coursing through both of my feet. Hadrian rolled over and slowly crawled to my side.

"You are fiery," he gasped.

Looking down, I saw blood through my shoe. My other foot throbbed from how hard I had landed on it. Hadrian said nothing but took a large kerchief from his jacket. Slipping my shoe off, he began to tightly bind my foot. As I watched him, I felt a silent satisfaction, remembering how he had flown through the air.

"You'd make a good bird," I said.

Tying the handkerchief, he glanced up at me. Did he look amused?

"Now what," I said, lacking energy to even make it a question. I felt mad enough to bite if he got close enough. I think he knew it because he didn't get within short-range distance.

"Can you walk?" he asked me.

"Probably not, thanks to you."

"Sorry." He rubbed the back of his neck. "Guess I'll have to carry you back to camp then."

"Not going to happen."

He blinked.

"Since you've so fully immobilized me," I said, "you'll just have to go back to camp by your tough self and come back with a horse. I've never been carried by a Snowling, and I'll certainly not be carried by you."

HOME ROAD

He stared at me, thinking for several seconds, then said, "All right."

I hid my astonishment just in time. *Wow. That was easy.*

He stood up, searching for the sun, trying to get his bearings. When he had done so, he found his cap, pulled it onto his head, tipped it at me, then set off northward. When he was out of sight, I lugged myself to a nearby tree and leaned against it. Resting my eyes for a moment, I formulated a plan.

Getting to my hands and knees, I crawled around, looking around for a sturdy walking staff. It took a full ten minutes to do so, but by leaning on it, I was able to get to my feet. My cut foot was entirely unusable, but since my other ankle wasn't broken, I could brush aside the pain and make it work.

Glancing to make sure I was alone, I set off in the direction my father had ridden, hoping against hope that he had met a delay and I would find him up ahead.

It came as no surprise that my venture failed. Within a couple hours, I was overtaken by Hadrian and his men. The former said nothing as he rode up beside me and vaulted off his dappled horse. He said nothing as I dropped to the ground in exhaustion, wiping away the sweat and tears across my face. He said nothing as he took me in his arms and handed me up to a seat behind one of the other soldiers.

I said nothing either.

The days passed in a blur. Most of the time, Hadrian watched over me and saw that I received meals and rest. I had no fight left, my foot being as it was. I did as I was told and said nothing unless spoken to.

So it went on for nearly a week.

The silence of life gave me time to think about what was ahead. Since I was a fugitive, since I had purposely run away from the Snow Realm, I would likely have only one sentence.

This was now the third time I was faced with execution; but this time, I wasn't afraid. The peace in my soul stilled all my worries and anger. Let the regent roar—let the dark dungeon come—bring out the rifle. None of it mattered anymore.

With time, the forests fell away to the open plains of land that filled the space in between the Nature and Snow Realms. I was reminded of my own home so far away and all of its fields—all of the things I wanted so much but was unable to have.

I tried not to think about Flint, but on some days, a picture of his face crowded out all other thoughts. I tried not to imagine how he had reacted when he'd heard about my "disappearance," for I knew Orrick would've described it that way. He and his men probably arrived, out of breath, with an outrageous tale of how they were ambushed by Snow Sprites, of how the Fire Sprite girl was wrested from their grip and spirited away.

Never in my life had I harbored such anger against a person as I did with Orrick. From the moment I first saw him, I saw the evil in his eyes and knew that it ran to his core.

Launfel too. Even when he behaved politely, I could tell that it was a ruse. I had wondered what was scheming behind that fake smile. Now I knew.

I wondered how Aidan had responded. I sensed he wouldn't be fooled by Launfel's lies about my disappearance. The intelligence I saw in those Fireling eyes made me think otherwise. Aidan would know the truth and it wouldn't make the relationship between the Firelings and Naturelings any better than it ever had been. I wondered if it would make it worse.

Or would it destroy it altogether?

It felt as if during my adventures, I had discovered the only reasonable Snowlings the northern Realm had to offer—Jack, Rime, and this Hadrian fellow, for, true to his promise, the latter saw to it that I received no rude treatment. Each night, he gave me his tent and slept outside. He even gave me my own horse to ride.

But I was beyond trust. When had trusting a stranger turned out good?

Ian, my mind whispered. This was true. Time and adventure had changed Ian from a stranger to a friend.

The thought of his name brought memories rushing over me, and in my heart, I knew he had become so much more than a friend. Oh how I missed that Scottish boy with his green eyes and his strong heart! I knew that no amount of time would ever heal the gaping hole his death had left in my heart.

Then there was Ruby, my sister. The uncertainty of her whereabouts was a burden that had weighed heavily on my shoulders for over a year now. I wished there was a way I could know for sure what had become of my little sister. I pressed my nails so firmly into the back of the saddle that it left ten little marks in the leather. If the saddle survived the war, I knew that many years from now, some onlooker might see those indentations and wonder how they had gotten there.

But they would never understand the pain.

chapter 13

For the second time in my short life, the border of the Snow Realm stretched before my feet—vast and unsatisfied.

I shifted in the saddle, causing my horse to snort in irritation. I twisted her thick mane around my finger, a sigh escaping me. The last time I had been in this position, Ruby and Ian had been by my side.

Now I was alone.

But I sat up tall in my saddle, ready for the stare of the first Snowling we met. I knew that some would have never seen a Fire Sprite before; I wanted their first impression to be one of strength. Knowing the strength wasn't my own and that I hadn't done anything to deserve it made the ache of my throat less severe—and I held my head high as gratitude and unworthiness swept across my heart.

The Galaheed that met my eyes was very different from the beautiful elegant city of a year ago. Filthy rubble lay in heaps at the head of every street. The buildings had an abused look to their ravaged fronts. Where before not one house had lacked a chip of paint, many were now covered with the dirt and mire of war.

We passed a young mother sitting by a pile of rubble, staring straight ahead while softly stroking her sleeping baby's forehead. Her young face was thin, her eyes sunk deep into their sockets.

I shut my eyes in horror as I realized the child wasn't sleeping.

Strange as it sounds, I was eager to reach the prison. I felt suffocated out there in the dark and hurt which wartime had brought upon this once-glorious capital of the Snow Realm. The horses pulled up at the familiar prison gate where two listless sentries opened the gates. As we passed by, they stared, unseeing, into the distance.

We dismounted in the dismal courtyard, and the horses were led away. I reached to stroke my mount's velvety nose as they pulled her away. As I stepped into the prison, I couldn't help but feel it was darker than it had been before, if that was possible.

Shadows in one's life make for shadows in one's soul. It's harder to dream in the dark.

Taking the set of keys from the jailer, Hadrian escorted me to a damp stone cell. I walked into the cell of my own accord and instantly shivered in the damp air.

"Is there anything you need?" Hadrian asked stiffly.

What a question.

I traced a finger down the cold stone wall but didn't answer. A million things ran through my head, but none were needs that he could or would ever be able to meet. When the silence continued, I turned to look at him and we stared at each other for several hard seconds. Then he left.

When he retreated down the hall, he took the last snatch of light with him.

Leaning against the stone wall, I stared at the ceiling for a few quiet minutes before sliding to a sitting position upon the floor. The silence echoed loudly in my waiting ears.

I didn't have to wait long. The next morning, Hadrian entered my cell.

"Your presence has been requested by the regent."

As we began the twisting turning trek to the royal chamber, I tried to not think about how angry Glacier would be now that I had twice evaded his death sentences. I knew he would do all in his power to ensure that I didn't escape again.

But I wasn't afraid. *Now I can be as brave as Auburn,* I thought with a smile.

Finally we came to the royal chamber. I stood outside the same door from over a year ago. Taking in a deep breath, I nodded that

I was ready and Hadrian knocked on the door. I noticed that his knuckles were tense as he waited for an answer.

The door was opened by a middle-aged footman who looked at us and then stepped aside to let us enter. As the door closed behind us, I got my first glance at my old enemy.

"Thank you, Hadrian," he said.

Hadrian bowed and stepped aside.

Glacier slunk toward me like an alley cat, accompanied by two brawny bodyguards. "Kyndle, isn't it?" he crowed, stopping in front of me. "Why, I believe we've met before."

"A few times, in fact," I said testily.

Without a warning, he grabbed my shirt and jerked me toward him. I averted my face.

"This is our last meeting," he hissed in my ear. I felt his hot breath on my cheek, and it sent a shiver down my spine. His fingers curled around my arm. "And you were so close to home," he said in a soft cruel voice.

I chuckled which I think surprised him. I thought of the *home* I was soon going to—the home where others awaited me. Others with shining green eyes.

He shoved me sideways into the arms of his henchmen. Hadrian stood to the side with a shocked expression on his whitening face.

"Take her away!" Glacier barked, waving a hand. "She dies at dawn."

"No!" Hadrian cried, starting forward.

"Hadrian—" Glacier whirled in surprise. "What do you mean by this objection to my authority?"

"You're going to kill her?"

"Yes!" Glacier snapped back. "She—is—an outlaw! Outlaws are to be executed!"

"Don't execute her," Hadrian begged. "Let me marry her!"

"What?" I hissed.

"Preposterous!" Glacier scoffed.

But Hadrian was in earnest. "As my uncle," he said, standing in front of Glacier, "you're obligated to keep your word."

Uncle?

"What do you mean?'" Glacier demanded.

"When I was a boy," Hadrian said, "I saved your leg from frostbite. In return, you promised to grant any wish of mine. All this time, I've saved it for something special." I watched as his jawline grew determined. "This is it."

I hung in the guards' grip—my mind whirling, my voice lodged in my throat.

"You call this Fireling rubbish *special*?" Glacier asked loudly.

"Yes." Hadrian was firm. "Don't ask me why, but I care for her."

I waited for Glacier's objection, but it didn't come. Instead he slowly pivoted to face me.

"This could work," he mused with a finger to his lips.

Hadrian's face lit up. "Then you'll allow it?"

"But of *course!*" Glacier crowed. "What could be better?" He turned to a servant near the door. "Simon, fetch Master Provost and tell him to bring a marriage license with him."

With a bow, Simon disappeared from the room.

"Thank you, uncle!" Hadrian said jubilantly.

"No!" I cried, finding my voice at last. "I won't marry him!"

Hadrian's face fell.

"You will!" Glacier snapped angrily. "You have no choice."

"A marriage license will require *my* signature," I said angrily. "I'm not planning to give it."

Glacier took a step in my direction.

"I suggest you make a new plan," he said threateningly.

"No, uncle," Hadrian spoke up. "I won't force her. She has to sign it of her own accord."

After a few seconds, the fierceness in Glacier's face melted away. It was replaced by that calculating look which frightened me more than his anger. "Perhaps I can persuade you by other means," he said, stroking his clean-shaven chin and turning to Hadrian. "The choice is ultimately hers, of course."

I waited.

Glacier gestured toward the carpet. "Below your feet sits a prisoner whom I believe you know. Though by now, they may not be recognizable."

All sounds except his voice faded.

"I have kept this prisoner for a year or so in hopes that they would be of some use to me," he said, "but as turns out, they can't be. I haven't yet decided their fate, so I'll let *you* do it." The ominous look returned to his face. "Sign that paper or the prisoner dies immediately."

"Tell me who the prisoner is," I ventured.

"No!" he spat. "You'll have to decide if they're worth saving."

An image of Ruby's face entered my mind. A year—it fit. Was she the one he was alluding to? What could she have suffered down there in the darkness?

He's lying, my mind interjected. *It's just a ruse to get you to sign.*

But my heart screamed for compliance. Of course it could be a lie. Of course he was a scoundrel. But how would I know for sure? How could I go on living, knowing that I might have taken the very breath from my sister's lungs?

Remember what they did to Flint.

I lowered my head. I had no choice.

A few minutes later, Simon brought in an arrogant-faced Snow Sprite who, bowing low before Glacier, spread a paper upon the table.

"Your Grace," he gushed. "A marriage license as requested."

"Very good, Provost," Glacier crooned.

"Also," the man went on, "I've brought two marriage bands." He took two jointed metal bracelets from his pocket and set them on the table by the license.

"Hadrian," Glacier prompted, nodding at the items.

Stepping up to the table, Hadrian began to sign the license.

I looked at the carpet below his feet. Faintly visible between his boots were stains of Ian's blood.

Tired tears filled my eyes.

When Hadrian straightened, he didn't look at me.

At Glacier's nod, the guards jostled me to the table's edge.

"Sign here," Provost ordered, putting a long skinny finger to a blank line at the bottom of the page. A quill was thrust into my hand.

Uncertainty surged through me, and I held my pen above the page for so long that a blot of ink fell on it. Then an image of Ruby's face came back into my mind—those large scared eyes of hers—and it was the last blow upon my doubt.

Taking a deep breath, I signed my name. When I straightened, one thing was clear to me. I had given up.

"And now, for the bracelets," Provost said, stepping up. Pulling a set of keys from his pocket, he inserted one of them into the joint of the larger bracelet; it clicked open. Hadrian thrust out his right wrist. Provost closed the bracelet around it and locked it, checking to make sure it wouldn't slide past his palm.

"Just the right size," he said in satisfaction.

Now came my turn. As the bracelet locked shut on my wrist, it felt, to me, no different than the leather wristband I had worn back in the Fire Realm. Both bound me to live in a place that wasn't my home. But this time, I wasn't going to fight it anymore.

"Congratulations to the happy couple," Glacier said with a laugh.

Winter shrieked across the Snow Realm. We lived in a large house outside the city, which was where the well-to-do Snowlings lived; and for two months, I refused to speak. Each day was a tangible struggle with wanting to live. Part of me wished that I had just doomed both myself and Ruby to death instead of dooming us to staying alive to endure these dark days.

The rest of me wondered if my silence was helping anything.

Finally, one morning, I woke up and decided it wasn't.

And so, Hadrian and I began the slow and tedious process of breaking down the walls that divided us, building bridges over dangerous chasms across which hasty passage meant certain death. And though I caught the occasional glimpse of Snowling pride, I found Hadrian different from the others as Jack and Rime had been. In his clear blue eyes that told no lies, I could see he truly, strangely—as best as he knew how—loved me. They seemed to search constantly to find whether I felt the same.

One evening he even asked me. I answered frankly. I didn't hate him. Surprisingly, I was growing fond of his company. But I didn't think I could ever love him.

He looked a bit hurt, but I saw no anger on his face. "Why?" he asked quietly. "Is there nothing more I can do to earn your affection?"

I shook my head. "I have everything I need—it isn't that. I like you a lot, and I'm grateful to you for saving my life and sacrificing so much to be a good—a good—" I couldn't bring myself to say it. "It's just that my love is asleep, somewhere in an unmarked grave."

He lowered his head but nodded. "I understand."

I set my teacup aside. There, I had finally said it. Hadrian stood up, then turned to glance fondly down at me. "I'm just hoping that someday, you can love me, just a little."

I only smiled up at him. I didn't think so.

But I refused to freeze him out. This lot had been handed to me. What else could I do but shoulder it and trudge along best as I could? My lack of cooperation would only mean misery for both of us.

When it all came down to it, he had saved my life.

Time revealed that he was unhappy in the aristocracy. His father died before he was born, and his mother, Icelyn, a few years past. He loved his extended family; he just didn't prefer to be around them. It was tricky, he said, but he didn't mind spending most of his time with me.

"And no matter the outcome of the war," he promised, "I'll take you for a visit to the Southern Realm when this is all over."

I clung to that promise.

Whenever he was gone, I would sit in a chair by the bedroom window and stare out at the blizzard-like weather. Small drifts would form on the windowsill. If I put my candle close enough, I could melt them through the glass.

I saw, in everything, a struggle between fire and snow. Yet how long could one candle last against a winter storm?

I didn't know.

chapter 14

It could be worse, I often reminded myself; because as time went on, I began to realize how blessed I was to have someone who really cared for me. I imagined if I had been forced to marry a harsh selfish man; I didn't like to think how much harder that would be.

We didn't have visitors; it was just us and the small team of servants who kept the house. I did not at all like having servants—it went against every bone in my body—so I tried to be kind to them whenever a chance presented itself.

As it turns out, they didn't much like me; so it was strictly a business relationship.

Meals in the Snow Realm were a fancy affair with several courses and a dessert. I tried my best, but often, it was just too much for me. I missed the simple fare of the Fire Realm.

Hadrian bought me a journal to try to bring some normalcy, and also, through a string of palace officials, managed to locate the stack of papers I had left in my cell at Straven Tree. I felt a slight panic when I thought what could have happened had Glacier had found them.

All in all, the year passed slowly. The seasons took turns playing their games on the lands—some handing their toys over less quickly, others far too fast for my liking. Then one morning, in late Philor, we awoke to find the first snow of my third Snow Realm winter flinging itself against the window pane.

As the season came on, I discovered a real reason to keep myself warm and well-fed. Hadrian suggested a maid to help me through rough days, but knowing that would be a disaster, I buckled down and struggled through them by myself like a beetle striving to get right-side up again.

After three hard months, I began to see the promise of renewed health, like the first-reaching light of dawn after a stormy night, and the first day of spring arrived with the warm embrace of a loved one. I worked up the will to venture out to the garden where Hadrian had arranged a place in the sunshine. I sat with my face upturned, basking in its warmth after so many months of cold. It reminded me of home.

"Well, you've survived another Snow Realm winter," Hadrian said as he took the chair beside me.

I smiled wanly. "Barely."

"I admit," he continued, "you keep me guessing. That Natureling spoke truth when he called you fiery."

I turned away. Any reference to Orrick spoiled my mood.

"Anyway," Hadrian hurried on, "I came to inform you of the outcome of Glacier's speech to the assembly."

I turned back in curiosity. I had followed this story with much interest since it had begun a few weeks back. Since his wife's death in childbirth, over twenty years ago, King Antares had become a wraith, hiding among shadows; and Glacier had clearly become more than just an advisor. His influence over his half-brother had led to decisions which had promoted unrest among the nobles. When it had reached the boiling point, several leading politicians put forth a petition that clamored for an heir to be put on the throne in Antares's place. Glacier then set up a private meeting with the chiefest leaders of the assembly to address the petition.

"And?" I prompted Hadrian.

He rubbed his face in exasperation. "He talked more with the jingling of his purse than with words. When the meeting was over, the politicians had all resworn their loyalty to Antares."

"Who would have been the heir?" I asked after a silence.

He turned as if a bit startled. "Why, me."

I blinked. I had never even thought of the possibility. Of course he was heir; Antares's only child died in infancy, and Hadrian was the oldest son of his mother, Icelyn. Since Jack was half-Snow blood, he was banned from the line of ascension.

I suddenly found myself grateful that Hadrian wasn't going to become king. Because then, I would become queen of the Snow Realm. I felt my nausea returning.

The sound of an approaching horse interrupted us. We both turned as a messenger galloped across the wintery lawn. He pulled up his horse a few feet from us and vaulted lightly from the saddle which bore the royal insignia of a swan.

"I come from the regent, sir," he said with a bow.

"Yes, what does he want?" Hadrian asked a bit curtly.

"Your presence, my lord."

Hadrian cut his eyes at me in annoyance. "I see. Tell him I'll be along shortly."

After the messenger galloped off, Hadrian stood and smoothed out the front of his jacket. "I'll be back soon," he said, leaning to kiss the top of my head.

"Have fun," was my dry comment as he walked away.

He laughed a fake laugh. "I'm sure I will."

The afternoon was soon put to flight, and dusk brought with it a marching band. As the thunder rumbled, I paced the room, anxious about something I couldn't exactly pinpoint. I made myself eat before retiring to my room; but even there, I found no solace.

What if Glacier put his slithering tongue to work on Hadrian to bribe him into some underhanded agreement? What if it had something to do with the war being waged upon my countrymen? Would his loyalty to me be enough? Or was his loyalty to me only that to a helpless wife and not a Fire Sprite?

Of course not—he was the heir to the Snow throne. Why would he hesitate to make a move against the Firelings? All of my worrying put me in a sour mood, and I settled down to my whittling with a vengeance. It was a hobby that I had kept up throughout the year. It was a full hour or so before I heard the bedroom door open. Gentle footsteps approached my chair.

"Sorry it took so long," came Hadrian's voice.

"What did he want?" I made myself ask, though I didn't lift my eyes from my whittling.

"I've been called back into military service."

I stopped midpare and turned before I could catch myself. "What?"

"He gave me a fourteen-month furlough to settle things here, but that time is up. He needs me back in the field."

"He?" I repeated.

"Glacier." He wearily brushed a hand over his brow. "He said I'm one of his most competent officers and he needs me to—to finish things."

My fingers began to shake, and my knife fell into the pile of shavings that had accumulated in my lap. Hadrian was leaving—without me? Here I was, in a hostile place, nearly four months pregnant, viewed on all sides as an outsider—one to be hated. I was terrified of being left behind.

I turned my face up to his. "I'm coming with you."

His mouth nearly fell open in shock. "Into the field?"

I nodded, setting my chin resolutely.

"But I can't just take you with me," he said.

"Why not?" I got to my feet. The pile of shavings fell onto the carpet, along with the paring knife. I nervously fingered the small remnant of the stick I had been working at for several days.

"I'd have to get permission," he said, his voice rougher than usual.

I took a step forward. "Everyone hates me here." My hand strayed to my slowly distending stomach.

He strode to the far side of the room, then back again. I knew he hated asking permission. It seemed as if anything that pertained to me required special leave which is why I stayed at the house most of the time. It was easier, and I preferred to be alone anyway. But not now.

He was just starting another turn around the room when I took a firm grasp on his arm. He turned. I saw that his face was hard.

"You can't leave me here," I said.

He looked at my hand, but I didn't loosen my grip.

"It's not just me that you have to be concerned about," I said after a silence.

When he finally looked up, the old Hadrian had returned. He looked me right in the face with those clear eyes of his.

"I'll ask him," he promised.

He returned an hour later, his eyes dancing.

"He said yes!" he said, grabbing my hands excitedly.

"He did?" I smiled truly for the first time in months.

He lowered his voice. "Glacier wasn't in, so I spoke to a few officials who were keeping watch in his absence." He chuckled. "I guess dear old Unc didn't expect anyone to show up."

"When do we leave?" I returned, matching his soft tone.

"A couple hours," he said, glancing over his shoulder. "I want to be as far away as possible before my uncle realizes you're gone. Communication lines in the field are so sporadic that if he sends a message after us, we might never get it." As he spoke, he pulled a leather satchel from under the bed and began to throw clothes into it.

"Where do you have to go?" I asked as I folded a shirt and wished for my old pack from Char.

"We," he corrected with an arch grin, "will join my brother, Romanus, at a southeastern village by the name of Fallistown." He bent to adjust his boot. "It's a couple miles from the border of the Nature Realm."

I stopped and stared at the floor. The old anger at Orrick and Launfel was still there. Even though I had told myself I was past it all, it always came back. Hadrian's voice pulled me from my thoughts.

"Kyndle, is something wrong?"

I threw a folded shirt into my pack. "Nothing."

In a moment, he was at my side, taking me by the shoulders, forcing me to look up at him. "I ask because I want to know," he said, searching my face. "Don't shut me out."

"Okay, so I hate the Nature Realm." I looked away. "Everything that happened there was horrible." I shifted under his grip.

He knew nothing of my time as a hostage there because I had never told him. I never told him because I might say things I would regret. Like I just had.

"You're safe now," he said, squeezing my shoulders again. "You'll be with me, and I can guarantee that you're kept from all harm."

"Hail said that too." It felt weird to call Jack that, but Hadrian didn't know his cousin's nickname.

Hadrian winked. "Hail didn't have a detachment of soldiers."

By the next afternoon, we were well upon our way. In the beginning, I had ridden on a horse beside Hadrian, but when the ache in my back grew uncomfortable, a place was made for me in one of the luggage wagons. The bedrolls on which I lay helped ease the jostling of the rough roads.

My mind was a mess of thoughts. Why had I begged to come? It was as if I had forgotten what Hadrian would be doing out here—he was here to continue the effort of forcing my people back into exile. No doubt, in the days and weeks to come, he would kill some of them; I might have to watch helplessly.

So why in the realm was I here?

Deep down inside, I knew it was in the hopes of finding either Father or Flint. I knew Hadrian wouldn't kill them if he knew who they were. It was in an effort to spare them that I had come.

As I lay there, idle, I realized in my eagerness to be off, I had forgotten my whittling knife. I could picture exactly where I had dropped it: on the rug in front of my bedroom chair. I chided myself for such forgetfulness. The long ride would have been made easier if I had been able to keep my hands busy.

A light spring breeze drifted through the flap at the end of the wagon, cooling my face before passing through the opening at the front end. The occasional voices and unceasing *plod* of the horses' hooves relaxed me, and before I knew, it I slept.

I awoke to Hadrian gently shaking my arm.

"We've arrived at our campsite for the night," he said. "The men need their bedrolls and other supplies."

"Oh," I said, sitting up. A catch in my side checked me, so I rose with the assistance of his arm. When I was safely out of the wagon, he pointed to a tent nearby.

"That's ours," he said. "You go on ahead. I need to distribute supplies among the men."

Reaching the tent, I pulled aside the flap. Inside I found two bedrolls, situated on either side of the tent. An empty luggage crate was set on its side between them, holding a lighted lantern and—my whittling knife! A smile worked its way over my face as I picked it up, running my fingers along the smooth handle. Where my thumb rested the dark polish had now worn away to reveal the light-colored wood beneath.

The knife had been a gift from Hadrian a couple months back. Even before he told me, I knew it was of Fireling make.

"It came all the way from Smithson," he had told me. One of the four assigned Fireling villages, Smithson was in the southwest corner of the South Realm. At that time, I hadn't realized how much the knife would come to mean to me. Now surrounded by all the ways and traditions of the Snowlings, I clung to that little knife as the last little piece of the life I had once led.

Setting the little knife back onto the crate, I eased into my bedroll.

I sat up suddenly; it was nighttime. Listening, I heard Hadrian's even breathing close by and knew he was asleep. I could hear no noise outside the tent.

Softly I climbed from my bedroll and crept to the tent flap. Hadrian didn't stir, so I slipped outside.

The fire was smoldering, and in the near distance, I saw a light among the trees. The sentry, I knew. Pausing again to listen and hearing nothing, my feet led me to where the horses had been picketed. Moonlight found a break in the thick branches above and lit softly on where all of the tack had been laid over a nearby log.

I found my horse among the others and eased up beside her. Familiar with me, she didn't stop grazing when I laid my hand upon her withers. I rested the side of my face against her shoulder, listening to her heartbeat and feeling comforted by it.

You could go, came a little voice in my mind. *You might get away.*

Again I turned and looked at the saddles, the bridles; voicelessly they seemed to beckon me. I took a feeble step toward them and then stopped. It felt as the battle in my mind now transferred to my chest. It grew tighter with each passing second.

My horse made a noise, and I turned to look at her. She had halted her grazing and was looking expectantly at me—almost as if she were asking to be saddled.

I knew how to do it, Hadrian had taught me last autumn.

"It may come in handy someday," he had said.

That someday was here. All the pieces fit together.

So what was holding me back?

I looked up into the sky. The stars twinkled and winked, not hidden by a single cloud. It was a beautiful night. I shut my eyes, breathing deeply the clear evening air.

Do you trust God, Ian?

I was startled at the vividness of the memory that flooded my mind.

Most o' the time.

I smiled. His voice was still so present in my mind.

When I don't, it's not because I shouldn't. It's because I trust myself more. I can't see what's ahead, but God can. He planned it.

Unexpected tears rose in my eyes. I leaned up against my horse, savoring every lilted word—wishing that I could hear them again in person.

He puts us right where we need t' be. I don't always know why, but I can rest in knowing that he does.

I closed my eyes, waiting for the final truth.

Trust and love go hand in hand.

I ran my fingers gently along my horse's flank, and she returned to her grazing. A peace I had felt before, but never quite understood, came over me. I had my answer.

God had put me here; only he knew why.

I was content with that.

Patting the horse once more, I quietly turned back to the campsite. Hadrian was right where I had left him; without a noise, I slipped back into my bedroll. Only one tear wet my cheek.

Sunlight warmed my face, and I opened my eyes.

A glance at the other bedroll showed that it was gone. Probably packed in the wagon already. Getting to my feet, I rolled up my own. Slipping my knife into a hidden pocket of my pants, I righted the crate, put the lantern inside it, and then carried it all with me outside, the bedroll under my other arm.

The campsite was nearly packed up already. Soldiers bustled around, wiping away all signs of our presence while gathering and packing their belongings into either of the luggage wagons. I made my way to one of these. Rounding the corner, I nearly ran into Hadrian.

"Morning," he said briskly, taking both the crate and bedroll from my hand and bestowing a kiss on my cheek.

"Hi."

"We should reach Fallistown in two days," he said, climbing into the wagon to set the luggage inside.

"Oh," I said. "It's farther than I thought."

"Our realm is very large," came his voice.

In it, I caught a hint of that occasional but all-too-familiar pride.

Out of left field, that same old burning ignited in my chest and I spoke without thinking. "I don't have a realm."

"Sorry?" came his voice from within the wagon.

I felt myself bristle. "I said, I don't have a realm."

The only answer from within the wagon was silence.

"And by the way things are looking," I went on, "maybe I never will."

"Your realm is the Snow Realm," he said at last.

"No, it isn't."

He clambered down from the wagon. As I caught sight of his face, I began to regret my words.

"What's that supposed to mean?" he asked, his tone a bit rougher than I had ever heard it.

One part of me felt sorry, but the rest of me was angry, and my answer reflected it. "I'm married to you, yes. But the Snow Realm will never be my realm."

Shock leapt into his face. I knew I had hurt him.

"You talk as though we're a people to be hated," he said, the surprise across his face quickly followed by slight anger. "As if your life among us is one of misery."

I shrugged. "I am miserable most days."

"Am I to blame for that? Did you not tell me you had everything you could need?"

I didn't answer. I knew I wasn't making much sense.

"I'm the only reason you're still breathing, Kyndle," he said, anger now marching full form across his face. "Had I not begged

Glacier for quarter, you would've been dead, buried, and turning to dust by now. I've done my best to shield you from outside spite and outrage. I've taken more than my share of wheedling from relatives upset over my choice over a wife. I've given you a warm home, a listening ear, and every comfort I could think of. And out of nowhere, you're mad at me?"

A soldier came around the side of the wagon. Upon seeing our faces, he quickly retreated.

"What am I not seeing?" Hadrian asked, raising his voice.

"I'm not mad at you, Hadrian. I'm mad at your people. If they would just be content with what they have, there might be peace for everyone. Instead," I gestured from myself to him, "there's all of this."

"If I may I remind you," he said, "your people are the ones who started this. They're the ones who weren't content with the way things are."

"We just wanted freedom!" I said. Tears tried to fill my eyes but were extinguished by the fire already there. "We shouldn't be denied the liberty of making our own choices. We shouldn't have to grovel under another's man feet."

"Some men are born to lead," Hadrian said and his voice had become cold. In his eyes I beheld all the pride of the Snow Realm. "Others are born to be subject. It all comes down to which men get to be on the fortunate side."

I stepped close to him. "You don't get to decide that."

"I haven't decided these things, m'dear," he said lightly. "I just benefit from them. You were born in subjection, but lucky for you, I rescued you and brought you up to the aristocracy." He rested a hand on my stomach, and I thought his eyes less clear than ever before.

"This child will be a privileged one among Firelings," he said.

Staring hard into his eyes, I opened my mouth to tell him about how I nearly ran away the night before.

Just then, a soldier rushed around the wagon, breathless and wide-eyed with fear.

"Sir!" he gasped. "A group of Fire Sprite rebels is approaching, nearly double our size." Then he disappeared.

chapter 15

"Into the wagon!" Hadrian snapped, helping me up. "Stay low, don't make any noise. This could get ugly." As he spoke, he lifted the back of the wagon in place and yanked the flap shut. I listened as his footsteps moved away, my heart pounding in my ears.

Presently there came a shout, followed by several others. I recognized them as the Snowling soldiers, but I couldn't tell what was happening. After a moment the familiar Fire Sprite yell met my ears.

I lay as flat as I could among the bedrolls, hardly daring to breathe. A moment of chaos passed as each cry blended into one, soon joined by the sparking voice of musket fire. After what felt like a short engagement, it all petered into quiet.

I forced myself to take in a breath, but it was extinguished as a pair of footsteps approached the wagon. I nestled further into the bedrolls.

"They're probably full of handkerchiefs and ladies-in-waiting," came a guffawing voice. The wagon flap was yanked aside, then I looked right into the swarthy face of one of my countrymen.

"Hoy!" he exclaimed loudly, starting back in surprise. After a moment, he stepped forward again. "Up on your feet."

Reluctantly I lifted myself from among the bedrolls.

He squinted, trying to see my shadowed face. "Come here."

I obeyed. He held out his hand and helped me down from the wagon. I looked up to find shock across his face.

"A—*Fire Spritess?*" he asked in a softened tone.

I nodded, unconsciously folding my hands below my stomach. As he saw my condition, I felt myself starting to blush. Anger flared across his face like wildfire.

"How did you come to be among these Snowling ruffians?"

I swallowed hard. "It's a long story."

He exhaled through this nose as if to regain composure, then took my arm in a fatherly way. "Name's Griffon," he said. "Come with me. Maybe you'll know one of our lads." He led me around the corner of the wagon, and I got my first look at what was happening.

All the Snow Sprites, including Hadrian, sat on the ground with hands clasped atop their heads. A large group of Fire Sprite soldiers surrounded them, their assortment of weapons ready for instant use. A few Snowling soldiers lay facedown on the leaves nearby, motionless. I forced myself to not look closely.

"Any o' you lads know this girl?" Griffon asked the Firelings.

Anxiously I scanned their faces, my heart beating fast in anticipation of a familiar face. The young soldier at the end caught my attention. As our eyes met his forehead furrowed. He quickly closed the large space between us. I forced myself to smile as his name, now rusty from disuse, dropped clumsily from my tongue.

"Tinder."

I saw my reflection in his dark eyes, blurred at the edges by the shock I knew he must feel at finding me after all this time. His mouth opened, then closed, as though he had the desire to speak but not the words. I was too impatient to wait for his reply.

"Have you heard from Father or Flint? Are they still alive?"

He seemed to shake himself from his stupor.

"Yes—of course," he said in an agitated voice. "But, Kyndle—!" He took ahold of my elbows, glanced down, and when he looked back up, I saw in his eyes all he wished to say but couldn't.

I looked away. I felt Hadrian's eyes on my face, but I didn't return his gaze. Tinder might see a history communicated in our eyes and conclude wrongly.

"Don't ask," I whispered, turning back to his face. "Not yet."

He searched my face for something that would tell him all was well. When he didn't find it, he let go of my arms and took a step back. I tried to push down the anxiety in my stomach.

"Tinder, please. I need to find Flint or Father."

He composed himself. "Your father isn't far from here. Our group is a detachment from his."

Griffon stepped forward. "Red is your father?"

I nodded numbly.

Seeing exhaustion in my face, all his fatherliness returned. "Take heart, my lass," he said. "We're under orders to deliver these prisoners to him by nightfall."

I grasped his hand, my gratitude understood. He turned to the rest of the Fire Sprites.

"Bind the prisoners," he said briskly, "and load them in the wagons." As the soldiers moved to obey, he turned back to me. "You'll be provided a horse, if that's okay."

I was about to nod when someone said, "Hold it."

We all turned at Hadrian's firm angry voice.

"She can ride in the wagon with *me,*" he said, squaring his jaw. "*I* am in charge of her." He seemed ready to take his hands off his head.

Griffon wasn't fazed. "I'm sorry, sir, but your authority is at an end for now. This young lady is in Tinder's care and will be returned to her father this evening. Say anymore and I'll gag you."

Hadrian glared at him, then me, but offered no response.

"Good," Griffon said in satisfaction, then turned to Tinder. "I'll leave the lady in your hands."

Tinder snapped to attention and saluted. I saw in his face the love he bore for this kind man, whoever he was, and how it compelled him to an obedience that was instant. Griffon turned to leave, but I grasped again at his tarnished hand.

"Thank you," I told him.

"Don't mention it, lass. It's time someone took care of you."

Tinder took me to where the horses grazed on picket lines.

"I'll ride this chap," he said, taking the halter of Hadrian's horse. "He looks friendly enough. Which do you want?"

I chose my own gentle-eyed mare. Next we each chose our saddles. Tinder deftly tightened all the straps while I watched. I knew he wanted to show me his skills.

"Learned how to do this only recently," he commented.

"Good thing," I said, turning as the Snowling prisoners were ushered into the luggage wagons, Hadrian last of all. But before he was assisted to his place, he cast a sweeping glance that came to rest upon me. I saw the whispers of blue fire in his eyes.

"Kyndle," came Tinder's voice.

Turning, I found him on one knee. I stared in confusion.

"Step here," he explained. "Mounting will be easier."

I did as I was told, hiding my smile. When I was in my saddle, he vaulted into his—then we waited as the other soldiers readied their horses. When all was in order, we fell into line, two by two, and trotted off into the lazy afternoon.

"We should reach camp by sunset," Tinder told me.

After that, nothing much was said between us. Where was I to start? Over two years had gone by since I had last seen him at Galaheed. Since then, I had spent a year in prison, escaped to the Nature Realm under the guise of being a prisoner, been released, betrayed, taken back to Galaheed, forced to marry a Snow Sprite, and been his wife for an entire year now. I couldn't bring myself to speak a single word to Tinder.

He sensed my troubles and didn't speak either. Every now and then, I ventured a quick glance at him. His jaw was set tightly, and he stared straight ahead.

"Just another mile or so," he commented half an hour later.

I was glad. A cramp had seized my back, and I longed to walk it off. In addition, the dusky light was making me sleepy.

"We'll probably be encountering a few sentries soon," he explained as the line slowed to a walk. "We'll go slowly to not draw their fire."

Just as he predicted, a voice soon barked out of the shadows. "Halt!"

The line reigned up instantly.

"Who approaches?" came the question.

"Griffon," he said, "and I bring thirty-two Snowling prisoners."

"Any casualties?" The voice was closer now. I thought I could make out a silhouette in the darkness.

"None. They lost three."

"Very good," came the response. "Move along. Gorge will run ahead to let them know you're coming."

"Much obliged. For the glory."

"For the glory."

Griffon clicked to his horse and the line started forward. Within a few minutes, torchlight appeared through the trees, and soon, a group of tents. Dark figures moved about, their features hidden by the darkness. The wagons were directed to one side of the trail, riders to the other. I slowly swung my leg over the saddle, feeling with my foot for the ground. Fingers touched my shoulder blades, steadying me.

"Careful now," came Tinder's voice.

I brought my other foot down. "T'anks," I said, brushing my shirt off, smiling sadly to myself.

Griffon's imposing figure suddenly loomed out of the darkness.

"Come along, lass," he said, taking my arm. "I'm anticipating the look on your pap's face when he sees yours."

I smiled. As was I.

Griffon led Tinder and me to a group of Fireling men who stood around a campfire with their arms crossed. They turned at our approach, and my legs started to tremble. Tinder quickly stepped in front of me, shielding me from their sight.

"Visitor to see Red," Griffon announced.

My heart leapt as my father stepped into view.

"Tinder?" he said, slight confusion across his face as he put a hand on his shoulder. "How are you, my lad?"

"I'm fine, Adar," Tinder said, his tone very serious, "but I'm not your visitor."

I saw over his shoulder that my father's brow creased.

Tinder turned and drew me forward. A blank look came across my father's face as, for the first time in over two years, our eyes met. Silence held for a few moments before I timidly stepped toward him.

"Daddy," I said.

He took a halting step forward, then I disappeared in his arms.

"I've thought about you every day since you left," he whispered.

"And I've missed you every single one of them," I whispered back.

He released me, then held me out to see my face. "When Aidan wrote me about you and Flint being found in the Nature Realm, your mum and I went straight to Frieman to meet you. We waited and waited, but when you didn't come, we feared the worst."

I smiled. "I finally made it."

He looked fondly down at me for a few seconds. "I can hardly see you in this darkness," he said, and, grabbing a torch from a nearby soldier, he thrust it upward to see me clearly.

"No, wait—!"

But it was too late. Blank horror spread across his face.

"Daddy," I whispered again.

At my plea, his face softened, and he once more folded me to his chest. I felt the tremor inside it as he strove to contain a growl. Just then, a step met my ear and Father released me.

Turning, I looked right into Hadrian's face.

"This man is the leader of the prisoner group," his escort told us. "He demanded to see you in person."

I began to tremble so harshly that Father noticed. Holding me at arms' length, he searched my face with concern. "Are you ill?"

Once again, I met Hadrian's eye and the blood drained from my face. How would Father react when he heard I was married to a Snow Sprite? I felt him follow my gaze, felt his grip tighten unconsciously on my arms. After several long moments, he turned back to me and the fire cast harsh shadows over his face.

"Is this him?" he asked as his eyes flashed dangerous heat.

My heartbeat pounded in my ears as I looked up into his dark face. I couldn't manage to reply, but a response wasn't needed. He knew by the look on my face.

"Is this who?" Hadrian asked a bit too boldly.

The shadows danced crazily upon Father's face as he slowly turned to the man who was my husband.

"I wasn't talking to you."

A challenging smile came into Hadrian's face. "You are now."

I heard a sharp exhale, and turned to watch as Tinder strode away, both fists balled tightly. I felt his anger.

Father released my arms. Flexing both his hands at his sides, he went to stand before Hadrian, and I couldn't help seeing just how much larger Father was.

"So I am," he said. He squared his shoulders which made them even larger. "And since I am," he continued, "I would like to hear some about your association with my daughter."

Hadrian tossed his head in disdain, not at all cowed by the many angry faces looking down at him. "In the Snow Realm," he said, "an exchange of names always comes first in an introductory conversation."

"Very well!" The ground basically trembled with Father's voice. "My name is Adar Redwood. Kyndle Redwood is my daughter."

Hadrian laughed shortly. "That isn't her name."

My father's hands clenched into fists. "What?"

"I said, that isn't her name."

"As I recall," came Father's growl, "you have yet to tell me yours."

There was no hesitation. "My name is Hadrian Frost."

Father stiffened as did every other man within earshot. "Did you say—*Frost*?"

"Yes. My uncle is king. And she," Hadrian nodded toward me, "is my wife. Her name is Kyndle Frost."

"Liar!" My father spat.

Hadrian shrugged. "Ask her yourself."

My father turned disbelieving eyes upon me. "Is this true?"

The tension was so thick that it could have been sliced with a dagger. I stared at Hadrian for a few moments before turning to confront Father's anxious eyes.

"It's true," I said.

For a moment, his face showed his unbelief, but I watched as the truth settled into his eyes.

"Look at our wrists," Hadrian said.

Everyone did and everyone saw the evidence locked upon them. Father tensed his jaw under his beard. I saw his temples tighten.

"Take this man to his tent," he said to the escort while not taking his eyes from my face.

Hadrian was led away.

My father walked to me, his feet dragging beneath the weight he now carried. He slipped a heavy arm over my shoulders and word-

lessly took me to his tent. When we had seated ourselves on the pallets inside, he let out a sigh and looked deep into my eyes.
"Tell me everything."

chapter 16

When I woke the next morning, my father's pallet was empty.

I talked far into the night, telling him every detail I could remember since the day I left home. He didn't speak once, listening intently to every word that came from my mouth.

When I finished my story, his mouth opened, then closed. Something lurked in his eyes, like a chained beast that wanted to get out but couldn't. He let out a sigh, bestowed a kiss on my forehead, gone to the flap of the tent, and had started to pull it aside.

"Daddy?" His actions confused me.

He had turned. "Get some sleep, Kyndle." Then he was gone. It was the last thing I remembered before I woke.

The morning air was still as I slipped outside. The camp wasn't astir. Father stood several feet away by the dead fire, his hands clasped behind his back. He was so deep in his thoughts that he failed to notice me until I stood close at his side. I touched his hand, and he turned.

"Kyndle." He spoke my name so fondly.

I looked up into his red-rimmed eyes. "Did you get any sleep?"

He shook his head and put an arm around me. "None at all."

A deep sigh escaped me. "I wanted so badly to be with you, but at the same time, I couldn't bear the thought of putting this weight on you."

"I'm glad you came to me," he said, putting his other arm around me and pulling me close. "I'm glad to have you here, even though the burden be heavy."

"Daddy—" I hesitated.

"Speak, Kyndle."

"When I finished last night, you seemed as though you wanted to say something but couldn't."

He was silent for so long that I wondered if he'd heard me.

"You saw rightly," he finally said. "There is something I need to say."

I felt my heart flutter with fear. Why such strange behavior? "You're scaring me."

"Don't be scared. I just need time to consider a few things. I'll be back in a few minutes." With a kiss upon my forehead, he strode away toward the grouping of other tents. My throat constricted as I watched him go.

Just what did he know? What hid behind his eyes? I stared hard at the ground for several moments before deciding to lie back down. I had just pulled the tent flap back when an approaching step met my ear.

"Morning," came a familiar voice. I turned to find Hadrian.

"What are you doing here?" I hissed, instinctively looking around for an accompanying guard but finding none.

"Greeting my wife," he said cheerily. "Did you sleep well?"

"You're not supposed to be unguarded."

He looked down at me in annoyance. "I'm growing fed up with this separation."

"I think you should get used to it," I said, more to myself.

"Sorry?"

I looked him in the face. "I said, I think you should get used to it for now and try not to be difficult."

Slight anger came into his cheeks. "Since when does a father have any right to take his daughter back? Have I missed something?"

"Yes, you have," I snapped, starting to grow irritated myself. "You've missed the fact that your very *life* has been spared. Don't you understand the mercy that's been given to you? Do you not see the self-restraint that these men have exercised in not laying fatal hands on you? You're a part of the *royal family*! If it wasn't for Father, you would be hanging from a tree right now."

His face went hard. "Your father's very presence has created a marked difference in the way you act toward me. Never before have you spoken so contemptibly!"

"These are challenging circumstances, Hadrian—"

"Maybe if you were away from his influence, you would be different," he said, putting his arm about my waist and firmly guiding me toward the trees. "I'll give you a fair opportunity to talk."

"Hadrian, stop!" I said, putting forth some resistance but not wanting to injure myself. "Let me go!"

"I just need to talk to you," he said.

"It's not allowed," I said. "You could get into trouble."

"And you can get me out of it."

He only released me after we were well into the woods when I pulled from his grasp. He looked at me with arms crossed.

"Well?" he asked. "What do you have to say for yourself?"

"Just that I think you're right." I huffed. "I *have* changed. I've finally seen who you are."

"And who am I?"

"You're as much a Snow Sprite as the rest of them."

He let out a short laugh. "You would have me forsake my heritage?"

"Of course not! I would have you forsake your *prejudice.*"

"I think *you* would forsake *me*," he said, "should your father bid you to."

I shook my head. "He would never do that. Neither would I."

"Then prove that you love me."

I hesitated. I didn't love him. I never had.

"Hadrian," I said gently. "Please."

Slowly the anger in his face melted away, and I saw him as he always used to be. He blinked and regret filled his clear blue eyes.

"Kyndle—I don't know what came over me." He stepped forward and put his arms around me. "I'm sorry for being such a f—"

"Unhand her immediately!"

Hadrian jerked back, startled. I turned to find Father striding toward us, a particularly large Fireling soldier at his side. Hadrian turned to face them as they neared. When they reached us, the soldier brought down a heavy fist and Hadrian dropped in a heap.

"Dad!" I gasped.

"He'll be all right," he said as the solider knelt to tie Hadrian's hands, "but he should know better than to leave his tent without an escort, much less the campsite. Are you all right?"

"Of course," I said quickly. "He's never hurt me."

Hadrian began to regain consciousness just as the soldier lifted him to his feet and began to half-walk, half-drag him back toward camp.

"What happened?" Father asked when they had gone.

"He felt that your influence changed how I acted toward him, so he was giving me a chance to speak away from you."

Father put his hand on my head. "I'm taking you home."

"I can't just leave him!" I protested. "I'm *married* to him!"

"Kyndle, we're going home."

I looked up into his face. "I did it for Ruby, Daddy."

His lips and brows grew sad.

"I gave my word that I would be his wife," I went on. "Glacier said he had a prisoner—"

"Kyndle," he interrupted. "You didn't save Ruby."

Panic crept in. "What?"

He took me by the shoulders. "She was rescued over two years ago at Galaheed. That's what I hated to tell you earlier."

My heart began to beat wildly as a mixture of emotions flooded over me.

Ruby was alive. My sister was *alive!* For so long, I had wondered, and now I knew for sure!

Ruby was alive!

Yet in the same breath, I wanted to curl into a ball and just die. I was doomed to live the rest of my life married to a Snow Sprite. And for no reason! So Glacier had lied after all. I should never have believed him. I should have believed what my mind had tried to convince me of all along: that he was a treacherous rogue who wouldn't care if all my loved ones were killed.

Why had I thought he would care?

The only reason he had let me live at all was because he knew my life would be miserable. He had thought it would be the best of punishments for me. And it was.

I looked up.

"Where is she?"

"Back home." He patted my arm. "Let's get back to camp."

We went slowly, arm in arm, and my thoughts returned to Hadrian.

"Where was his guard?"

"My men found him unconscious beside Hadrian's tent. He must have hit him."

"He's a highly valued soldier. I don't doubt his abilities."

"Neither do I. Which is why he'll have two guards from now on."

"What will they do with him?"

His face was weary. "I don't know. He left camp without permission which could be labeled an attempted escape." He brushed his hand across his eyes. "Most escape prisoners are shot."

I felt all the blood drain from my face. "Who decides whether or not he actually tried to escape?"

"He'll be here at sunset."

"Who, Daddy?"

He stroked the top of my head as if I were a child. I felt like one. His answer came in a soft voice.

"Aidan."

The cardinal arrived at dusk, his face weary and his clothes covered with the dust of swift travel. As he strode into camp, each soldier bowed his head in respect. He went straight to my father—and in his hurry, didn't see me standing nearby.

"You said it was urgent," he said, grasping Father's hand.

"It is. Thank you for sparing your time."

Aidan crossed his huge arms. "I'm listening."

Father held out a hand, beckoning me to him. "You remember my girl, Kyndle?"

"Kyndle!" Aidan's eyes registered confusion and anger.

I held out a hand. As he took it, I lowered my head.

"I'm glad they found you," I heard him say.

I looked up at him. "Much has happened since I saw you last, sir."

"I agree."

"Her husband is the reason I called for you," Father said.

Shock banished all else on Aidan's face. "You're married?"

I nodded. "For over a year."

"Someone from our town?"

I glanced at Father. "No."

"A different township?"

"He's not a Fireling," I said slowly. "He's a Snow Sprite. His name is Hadrian—Hadrian Frost."

Aidan's eyebrows lifted to his hairline or so it seemed.

"As I said, much has happened, sir."

"You're married to a *Snow Sprite*? Of *Frost* blood?" I was hurt by the disappointment I saw in his eyes.

"I had no choice but to marry him. They told me they had a prisoner I knew, and if I didn't agree, they would kill both of us. But if I signed, we would both be spared."

"And you believed them?"

Tears filled my eyes as I battled feeling stupid. "How was I to refuse? How could I know my choice wouldn't bring about not only my death but the death of yet another person I loved?"

Sadness came into his face. "Yet another?"

I looked away.

"Who do you think you saved?" he asked in a soft voice.

"No one!" I snapped, my anger at Glacier pouring forth. "It was all a lie, just as I thought. The only person it could've been was Ruby and she is already safe."

Aidan glanced at my father, eyebrow lifted.

Father nodded. "She was sent home."

"I'm glad of that," Aidan said. "But I'm not yet sure why you sent for me."

"It's concerning…Hadrian," I said. "He and his troops were captured yesterday. Then this morning…"

"He escaped?"

I shook my head.

"No." Father picked up. "He ambushed his guard and forcibly escorted Kyndle from camp."

"Trying to escape?"

"No," I said firmly. "He just wanted to speak to me in private."

"About what, if I may ask?"

"Whether I would forsake him if Father bid me to."

Aidan stroked his beard.

"I knew I couldn't let the matter pass," Father continued. "It wasn't a call I could make—whether or not he attempted escape and was deserving of an escapee's punishment."

As Father finished, I felt my heart start to flutter. We waited as Aidan continued stroking his beard. After several tense seconds, he looked at us both in turn.

"I need to speak with him," he said.

chapter 17

I swung into the saddle.

"May your journey be safe and blessed," Aidan said, laying a hand on my horse's muscular flank. "Tinder should be near Frieman by now to get everything prepared."

I offered him a hand. "I can't thank you enough, cardinal."

He squeezed it. "Your sacrifices for our cause should suffice."

I smiled. "I hope you and your men are kept safe."

He returned the smile. "You can rest well, knowing that at least one of your men are safe and sound," he said, with a wink at Father, who sat on a horse beside me.

"I'm sure she will," Father said, shaking his friend's hand.

Aidan glanced at the wagon behind us. "Two is enough?"

"Two is plenty," Father assured him.

"Well, then." Aidan smiled again. "Goodbye, dear friends.'"

"Won't be long now," Father commented at the end of two days. "If my guess is right, we should reach home before supper tomorrow." He set another log on the campfire.

"Good," I said, hugging my knees as best as I could. I was soothed by the warmth upon my face. With each mile, the temperature grew warmer, yet another confirmation of the reality that I was almost home.

"How is he?" I asked, nodding at the wagon.

Father shrugged. "As well as can be expected. With every step, he is taken further away from his homeland."

I sighed. "It's better than being executed."

But at the same time, I knew that wasn't entirely true.

"I think that's the only reason he's cooperating," Dad said.

"What will happen once we get home?"

"Aidan has given me signed papers, granting me permission to house Hadrian in one of the spare homes. As his personal guard, I'll oversee his daily schedule."

"Where will I live?"

"Aidan is allowing you and Ruby to live next-door. So I'll be able to keep an eye on you both." He winked.

I forced a chuckle, knowing it was what he was hoping to hear, but I couldn't fake full enthusiasm. While going home would be wonderful, it would also hold memories that I knew would hurt.

When Father said nothing more, I fell to gazing at the sky, at the lights that winked at me from their lofty height, but the hoped-for shooting star never made its appearance. I sighed softly.

Even the reminders were gone.

Emotions flooded over me as the familiar fields of Frieman came into sight. As we rode past them, I felt tears rising in my eyes.

I was truly, finally, home.

The wagon rumbled along behind us. One soldier held the reins while the other sat in the back with Hadrian. I was grateful Aidan had sent them with us. It would've been hard for me to ride with him.

"Do you know what the worst part of losing Auburn is?" I said aloud, throwing all the doors of my mind open to let Father's light in.

"And what is that?"

"Not knowing why she was there. Not having the answers that would clear up the questions that cloud my mind."

"Keep hope, Kyndle. Perhaps her tale will yet be told."

The way he said it made me turn. I wondered if he felt guilt for being among those who had sent her in the first place. He turned and looked at me, and I smiled brightly at him. I felt no anger.

He smiled back.

When town came into view, Father called us to a halt.

"Stay on your horse," he said as he dismounted. "I need to talk to the soldiers and Hadrian. I want him to be prepared for what will happen."

"What *will* happen?"

"We'll stop the wagon in the square. The guards will walk us home."

"Why not go directly to the houses?" I questioned.

"There's no need for secrecy. The cardinal's direction was to meet the questions head-on. The townspeople will be angry, but after I show them the cardinal's order, they'll have no choice but to comply."

He came back several minutes later and remounted. Chirruping to his horse, we again started forward.

"We're a go," he said.

My heart leapt as we entered the village. Firelings milled about, doing normal daily tasks that, to anyone else, might seem completely ordinary and mundane.

For me, it was the entire idea of *ordinary* that made my heart soar.

Heads turned. Many went back to their business with an uninterested shrug. Others persisted in their gawking and, upon recognizing me, grew wide-eyed.

According to plan, we dismounted in the town square. When I turned, I saw that we had attracted a small crowd. The majority of those gathered were aged, but there were a couple young citizens as well, their faces and bodies now adorned with bandages, crutches, slings—more reminders of the war, even now, raging inside and outside our borders.

"Adar," came a man's voice.

A middle-aged sprite stepped out of the crowd. I knew his name was Droy. As he approached Father, I saw that his arm was missing from the shoulder.

"You've returned," he said, his lips pursed in what I think was meant to be a smile.

"So I have," was the return, as Father clapped a hand onto the man's good shoulder. "I'm glad to be back with another daughter in tow. Where is Ruby?"

"I'm right here!" came a voice as a young woman pushed through the crowd and leapt into Father's arms. Tears and laughter mingled to form a beautiful song as they held each other close. As she drew back from his arms, her gaze chanced upon mine.

Oh, Ruby Redwood.

But this wasn't the little Ruby from my memories. In her face, I saw the ripening beauty of womanhood. What was she, fifteen?

Fifteen?

She came toward me with her mouth hanging open, eyes wide, hands outstretched, and then all of a sudden the distance between us was gone. I found myself weeping, laughing, both my arms tight around her neck.

"I thought we had lost you," I sobbed into her long hair.

"And I thought I had lost *you*," she answered, her voice quaking with emotion. "I thought I was alone. They told me you were both dead."

Father's arms wrapped around us both, holding us close.

"Flint and I both felt hopeless during our separation," I told her. Then I drew back to look into her face.

"But then, we were each given a beautiful wellspring of hope."

Her eyes twinkled with curiosity—and then she squeezed me tighter. She understood what I meant. My head still on her shoulder, I looked out into the crowd.

"Kyndle!" called a voice.

My heart about stopped beating. I drew back from the group hug and watched as another familiar face pushed through the crowd. We ran into each other's arms.

"You're safe!" was all Nanna kept saying as she stroked my hair.

My mind whirled with joy, questions, and dread. Why was she here? For how long had she been here?

However, my pregnancy was made known to her through the embrace, and when she stepped back, a bit of the joy had left her eyes. She took my hand. She didn't know what to say or ask. Then suddenly, she drew back and began looking around. Knowing for whom she was searching, I put a hand on her arm. It made my entire chest hurt to see the fear that jumped across her face.

Why me? I thought. *Why do I have to tell her that the last of her loved ones is gone?*

She gripped my hand. "Ian?"

I opened my mouth to answer, but our conversation was suddenly cut off by Droy. He stepped forward, nodding over his shoulder at the wagon from which the two soldiers had emerged.

"Supplies?" he suggested.

Father glanced at me. "No, Droy. It's a man. A soldier."

"Ah, one of ours. Is he wounded?"

"No, Droy," Father said again. "He isn't wounded, and he isn't one of ours."

Nanna gripped my hand fiercely.

Droy's eyebrows lifted and murmur rippled through the small crowd. "You've brought a Snowling to Frieman?"

"Yes," Father answered, "and he's here to stay until the war ends."

Her grip eased with disappointment, but I tightened mine.

Droy's face darkened a few shades. "What sort of fool's play is this?" he demanded loudly. "Don't you remember that they stole our freedoms? Or have you forgotten why our town is called what it is? *Free*-men? We can't call ourselves that, thanks to them!"

"But we will!" yelled a young man, shaking his crutch fiercely in the direction of the wagon.

A few other voices joined in.

"Firelings!" Father lifted his hands before they could become unruly. "We *will* give this man sanctuary."

"They didn't give *my* wife sanctuary," Droy snapped. "They gave her a group grave."

Father lowered his head in respect. "I'm sorry," he said.

Droy swiped his nose angrily. "If you're really sorry, Adar," he said, "you'll turn that wagon around and take *him* back to wherever he came from."

"I can't," Father said. "This soldier was brought here by order of the cardinal." He drew a couple papers from his saddlebag and handed them to Droy. He scanned the papers with a scowl on his brow and glanced up when he finished reading.

"Why wasn't he just shot?"

I spoke up. "Because this man is my husband."

Complete silence reigned in the square, and I felt eyes boring into my face.

"Your husband?" Droy repeated, shock crossing his face.

I nodded. His surprise was shoved aside by dark anger.

"You married a Snow Sprite?" He glanced down at my wrist and the bracelet confirmed his question. His voice lifted angrily. "You've betrayed us. You're a disgrace to your people. You don't deserve the title Fire Sprite! While our men are out there bleeding, *dying* for our stolen freedom, you have the audacity to go and *marry* one of the enemy. How *dare* you?"

"There was a reason—"

"There is *never* a good reason to marry a Snowling! If you possessed any allegiance at all, you would have chosen *death.*"

"Yes, I would've!" I cried.

He paused. "What is that supposed to mean?"

"My choice of death would have meant it for someone else as well." I felt tears rise and instantly was ashamed of them. "I married him to save my sister."

"What?" Ruby hissed.

I turned to her. Her eyes were wild with many different emotions. She still hadn't recovered from seeing me alive, only to learn that I'd married one of the enemy—to save her? Her questions would have to wait. I turned back to Droy.

"I thought she was still a hostage."

"But she wasn't." He laughed mockingly and shook his head. "You've thrown your life away for no reason."

"That's enough." Father took a step forward, anger lining his face. "If you speak another harsh word to her, you'll have me to answer to." For emphasis, he tightened his fists.

The desired effect was instant and Droy backed away. Yet after Father had turned, something lingered in Droy's eyes that frightened me.

Father addressed those gathered. "The cardinal has ordered two spare houses be given to my care. One will house me and the Snowling, the other will house my daughters."

The crowd nodded their assent.

"I understand your anger," Father went on. "However, if you're unable to control yourselves, don't speak a word to the Snow Sprite. He isn't here by his own volition, so the very least we can do is to leave him in peace. Much has happened, but since he is my daughter's husband, I'm obligated to ensure his safety." When there were no objections, he dismissed them with a wave.

They didn't go far, however, and I knew they wanted to see Hadrian's face.

I turned to Ruby, who stood by in a stunned silence, but I didn't have to say anything. I knew she would love me despite all that had happened. Nanna too carried eyes of understanding, though she seemed to have a hard time holding back her many questions. I turned to Father, and he nodded.

We walked to the wagon. Nanna and Ruby followed at a distance, arm in arm. We found the soldiers standing at the end of the wagon, their rifles at the ready. I pulled aside the wagon flap and Father boosted me up inside. Hadrian looked up at me with a dull light in his eyes.

"We're going to take you to your new home," I said gently as I knelt beside him.

"Will I make it that far?" he asked glumly.

"Of course you will," I said confidently. "I'll be by your side as will my father and the two soldiers with muskets. Please," I pleaded when he put his head back down. "It's your last chance. Maybe when all of this is over, we can work things out and you can go home."

He raised his head. "Aren't you going home with me?"

I looked in his clear blue eyes, fingering the bracelet on my wrist, and forced my tongue into action. "Of course."

Light came into his face.

Grabbing his hat, he pulled it on over his white hair.

"But listen," I said, "you're going to get ugly looks."

"I know."

"And Hadrian—" I made sure I had his full attention. "You can't walk anywhere without an escort. You barely missed the label of escapee back at the Fireling camp. They could've shot you."

"I know," he said again. "I won't do that again."

"Good." I stood. "Then let's go."

I pulled back the flap and jumped down, then stepped aside as he slid from the wagon with the gracefulness of royalty. I chanced a look at Nanna and Ruby. Neither faces bore malice. Rather I saw pity.

Nanna returned my glance. And though she held a smile on her face, I clearly saw a secret disappointment stir in her eyes. It pained me, for it reflected my own.

Yet God had put me where he wanted me.

I walked on one side of him and Father on the other. The two guards, followed by Nanna and Ruby, brought up the rear of our procession. I felt everyone looking at us and threw a quick glance at the bystanders. Their faces were dark, but they made no move toward Hadrian.

We hurried from the square.

When we were away from the curious eyes, I looped my arm through his, and felt how it trembled. The little love I did bear for him compelled me to comfort him.

"Hey," I said softly. "The tables have turned—you took good care of me, now it's my turn to take good care of you."

He kept his eyes forward.

"It's going to be all right," I told him.

His fingers touched my arm. I knew he trusted me.

chapter 18

Our houses stood at the end of the street. Both were two stories high, tall, and narrow; windows covered the front. An old brick pathway led to each door. Standing in one of the doorways was a familiar friend.

"Tinder," Father said, warmly shaking his hand.

"Welcome home, sir," Tinder said, smiling at him, then us girls. "The houses are all in order."

Ruby ran to greet him, but I approached him slowly. Part of me wanted to remove my arm from Hadrian's, the rest of me didn't. I had promised to take care of him. Acting ashamed of him wouldn't be keeping my word.

Besides Tinder was my friend. He would understand, even if he didn't understand. So I kept my arm looped through Hadrian's and looked right in Tinder's eyes.

His right eyebrow twitched and his chin tensed as that old protective look peeked out from his dark eyes.

"Tinder," I said as we reached him, "this is Hadrian."

They exchanged polite glances.

"Tinder and I grew up together," I said to Hadrian, then I looked up at Tinder. "And Hadrian is my husband."

Tinder lowered his head as if in a bow, but I caught the startled look in his eyes before he did so. However, it was gone when he raised it and the polite Tinder had stepped into place. "You're a blessed man," he said. "But in case you haven't figured it out yet, you got a wildcat for a wife." He winked at me with some difficulty and I grinned at him.

HOME ROAD

The soft-eyed Snowling holding my arm laughed a hesitant laugh and glanced down at me, some of the old fondness returning to his face. Father came to us, and he looked relieved to see our smiles.

"Officer Frost," he said. "Come and I'll show you to your new place."

Hadrian touched my hand again, then left me to follow Father into the right house. The two escorts walked close behind him. When they had gone, Tinder turned to Ruby, Nanna, and me.

"I'll show you yours," he said, turning to lead us into the left house.

"You'll live with us, of course," Ruby said to Nanna and that matter was settled.

Nanna stepped between Ruby and me and put her arms around both our waists as we strolled up the cobblestone walk. "M'dearie," she said to me. "I can't say jist how very glad I am t' see you safe and sound."

"Me too," I agreed, leaning my head toward hers and trying to ignore the fact that my sister was nearly as tall as me.

Tinder held open the front door, and we walked inside. As he'd promised, the house was comfortably furnished. A welcoming sofa stood in the front room, along with a couple other cushioned chairs. The familiar simplicity of the furnishings was a sweet sight for sore eyes after the lavish lifestyle of the Snowlings.

"I feared trouble from that Droy," I confessed.

Ruby touched one of the curtains. "So did I."

"Droy gave you trouble?" Tinder asked.

I shrugged. "He fell in line when Father raised his fist."

"Not surprisingly." Ruby grinned wryly.

Tinder shook from his thoughts but didn't join in our mirth. "I'll show you around."

After we explored the house, which was now our home, I sank into the sofa with a tired sigh. Nanna and Ruby were still poking around upstairs, but Tinder sat down opposite me.

"Do you think it'll work?" he asked.

I smiled at him. "It's wonderful."

Then a heavy silence fell over us. I was the first to break it.

"Tinder, what happened—at Galaheed?"

He shrugged. "I went in circles for what felt like hours. Finally I found the way out and met up with a group of Firelings. No one knew what had happened to you or Flint."

He glanced down at his feet and I braced myself for what I knew was next.

"Kyndle." He lifted his eyes. "Flint told me his side of things, but now, I want to know what happened. To you, I mean." I saw his cheeks flush as he spoke.

Flint. At the sound of his name, I saw an image of his face, his arms—both so scarred—and felt all peace leaving me. Tinder must have read my thoughts because he leaned forward.

"Don't dwell on it anymore, Kyndle," he said firmly. "Flint's a tough one—he made it. He told me about what happened and then told me to leave it behind. He would expect you to do the same. Now," he said after a silence, "he also told me what happened in the Nature Realm—"

"Good."

"But where have you been since you left there?"

I couldn't keep the anger from my voice as I told him of my betrayal, my time in the Snow Realm, and the choice laid before me.

"And you thought it was Ruby," he concluded softly.

I nodded. "I had no choice but to sign. That was all a year ago. When he was called back into the field, I went with him." I sighed. "You know the rest."

He glanced out the window. I followed his gaze, and we both watched as Father showed Hadrian the garden behind the house.

Tinder looked back at me. "So that's him."

I nodded again. "They figured it was the best punishment they could give me." I looked down at my lap. "And it was."

He shook his head as though angry.

"What is it?" I asked quietly.

"Everything's wrong, that's what." He looked at me with his piercing dark eyes. "I had such high hopes for you and me. We've known each other since birth. I thought it was only natural for us to one day marry."

There it was. My secret fears had been confirmed. Nothing to do but meet it head-on. So I forced myself to hold my gaze, and it couldn't hide what I felt.

Hurt came into his eyes. "You didn't?"

After a moment, I shook my head. "We were always just friends."

"Yes, but—" he leaned forward, "I thought that you, well, liked me."

"I did," I said, "and I still do. You never gave me a reason *not* to like you."

"But you never—wanted anything more."

"No, Tinder," I said after several moments. "I never did."

He looked away, biting his lip.

"You've always been a dear friend," I hurried on, striving to comfort him, "and you always can be, if that's what you want."

He turned back to me, but there was no light in his eyes.

"But I never could've been anything more?"

My heart quaked, but I forced it still, and with all my resolve, I slowly shook my head. Tinder rose to go.

"I'm sorry," I said, and I really meant it.

He rubbed his eye with the back of his hand, and it came away wet. "I understand, Kyndle," he said in his honest way. "I am surprised, but I'm not going to cause any trouble for you." His lips turned up, but there was no Tinder in the smile. "Promise."

He left the room. At the door, however, I heard his footsteps halt. Low voices drifted to meet my ear. After a couple moments, his footsteps continued then faded away as he left. Father came in the door, his eyes concerned, and I knew he knew.

"Did Tinder speak with you?" he asked slowly.

"Yes," I said softly.

He came and sat beside me. "And what did you tell him?"

"I told him how I felt and how I never felt."

His eyes sparked a sadness, and I knew then it wasn't just Tinder who had been disappointed.

Tears rose in my eyes. "I stood by and watched him grow into a young man but never once did I want to marry him. Even when I saw him again in Galaheed, after he saved my life, I just—" I hid my face in my hands.

"Loved someone else," he finished.

I raised my head in a bit of surprise. I hadn't told anyone I had loved Ian. "How did you know?"

"I have eyes and ears, don't I?"

Again I hid my face. He rested his hand on my back.

"I was hoping you would say no," he whispered.

"I wish I could," I said sincerely. "It would've made this all so much easier—"

He patted my back encouragingly.

"But I can't," I whispered.

He said nothing, allowing silence to do its work of soothing a grief so long hidden. My thoughts came out fast as words.

"It's all upside down. Tinder loved me, but I didn't love him. Hadrian married me, but I can't love him because I still love Ian. And he's dead." As I spoke, all the tears I had been holding back for a year finally came. I hid my face on his shoulder as he pulled me close. "Why love at all if it ends like this?" I asked through my sobs.

For a moment, he was quiet, then he lifted my chin and made me look at him. "Love is a risk," he said firmly, lifting his red eyebrows. "It could break your heart or it may heal it. You have to decide if it's a risk worth taking." When I said nothing, he asked, "Was it?"

A wind whistled over my mind, and instantly, I was soaring up through the clouds of memory.

Again I was in Char's house, seeing Ian for the first time; again I was hearing his voice, thrilling at the strange accent. Again I was learning his name. Next I was secretly admiring him for his profound strength. Then I was gripping his hand as he pulled me up the mountain, then we were huddled in the cave. Again I felt his strength as he pushed down on my shoulders on one side of the portal, felt his tenderness as he lifted my limp body from the ground on the other. Again I saw his resolve as he walked away from Nanna. Then he was defending me from Canton, telling me to run; and again we stood at the border of the Snow Realm. Once again, we were being laughed down by Glacier; again we faced the coming morning as he guided me in my first prayer.

And then, we were saying goodbye. I felt his hands on my face as the soldiers tore him from my grasp. And again, as I cried on my Daddy's shoulder, I knew. I knew that which I had known all along. I had loved him.

The wind whistled, the clouds faded, and I looked into Father's face.

"It was worth it," I whispered.

He smiled; a good smile, if a sad one. "And what made you love him, Kyndle?"

I didn't even have to consider my answer. "His heart. Even though we were rude to him, he wasn't rude to us. When Flint was captured, he leapt in to keep Ruby and me safe—even if it meant leaving Nanna and coming back to Almia. He never tried to change my convictions, and he didn't let others push theirs upon me. He was always ready to listen, and when he did speak, it was with patience. He never acted like he had it all together. He never pretended to have all the right answers. He never hid the truth from me, even if it was hard to hear." I smiled. "Sure, he was handsome, but I loved what was on the inside most of all—because it was so real. It didn't change when things got hard. The hard times made him even more trustworthy. That's why I loved him."

"Kyndle," he said after a pause. "What about his God?"

That was the one part of my story left untold. I looked at my hands.

"He isn't just *his* God, Daddy. He's *mine*."

I heard him take in a quick breath. "You've taken his religion as your own?"

"Yes. Flint and Ruby have also."

For a moment, he was quiet. "That's your decision. I'm not going to force you to change."

I looked up at him and smiled. "Thank you, Daddy."

Nothing more was said as he stroked my long, wild hair. He was just there, and it was enough.

chapter 19

Life went on, and as the days passed, Ruby and I began the process of getting to know each other again. So much had changed yet so much hadn't. Nanna was often a companion along the path of our adventures.

Ruby's story was simple. She was being held in one of the cells near the arena and was freed by a group of Firelings. They took her to Father; he took her home.

That was almost two years ago.

Mine was much less simple—much harder for their listening hearts to hear, and I mingled my tears with theirs as we wept for Ian's death. Nanna soon left for the privacy of her own room, but Ruby laid her head in my lap and protested all the evil in this life.

"I'm just a silly girl," she wept. "He should've been saved, not me."

"Ruby, don't talk like that," I said, stroking her hair. "You and I both know he would've wanted it this way."

She became quiet as she tried to take in the heaviness I had given her, to accept the death of one she had so cared for. For me, Ian had been dead two years; for Ruby, it was like it had just happened. She had prayed for him often, no doubt, always watching, ever hoping—as he had taught her to do—just to find in the end that her prayers had received a *no*.

"Kyndle," she said after a couple minutes. "I think you miss him in a different way than me."

I took a deep breath which shifted her head from its place on my lap.

"Yes, Ruby," I said. "I believe I do."

She didn't look up at me. She just touched my hand. It was all that was needed.

I glided softly down the hallway to Nanna's room, pausing outside her cracked door. I wanted to be there if she needed me. Fear shoved courtesy aside when I could hear no noise from inside; but upon opening it, I found her sitting by the eastern window. She turned her head as I came in.

I said nothing, knowing that my face spoke our mutual sorrow.

"Come," she said, holding out her arms.

I knelt before her chair, resting my head in her lap as she stroked my hair, suddenly realizing that *I* was who needed comfort—a comfort only his own relative could give.

"I haven't yet congratulated you on your marriage," she said quietly. "He seems to be a very kind young man."

"Thank you," I said, but my sigh whispered many secrets. My solution for pain had been suppression; but as I reflected on the way I had told her of Ian's death, my words sounded harsh and unemotional in my ears—and I hated myself for it.

But how was I to make her feel my own grief when I had suppressed it for so long?

"I'm sorry, Nanna," I said, matching her soft tone.

"He was such a good boy," she finally said, her voice hoarse. "I loved him so much."

Tears filled my eyes, and I raised my head to look at her aged face.

"I loved him too."

She searched my face, and seeing the truth of my words written there, her eyes softened. Not in joy but in a quiet peace.

I looked away, biting my lip.

"I know," she said softly.

I turned quickly, looking back into her understanding eyes, my throat aching. I suddenly needed to hear everything she could possibly tell me. I knew that I had loved him but admitting it out loud had brought a deep ache to my entire being, spirit, and body, and I wasn't ready for it. It felt like I was being pressed under an invisible counterweight.

Nanna reached to touch my fingertips, which had grown cold, and in return, I grasped her hand. She ran a hand down the side of my cheek.

"Ian loved you too," she said. "He told me before he left."

I stared at her in wonder, the tears trembling in my eyes now streaming down my face. "He loved *me*?"

She smiled. "So much so that he could hardly put it into words."

I didn't wipe my tears; they were a souvenir I didn't want to erase as my mind and heart tried to understand that the love I felt for him was the same he felt for me. The hurt I had felt just a moment before was washed away in an instant as I looked back up into her face. "I wish I could have a minute with him," I told her. "Just *one*—so I could try to thank him for, for *everything*."

She put her hand on my head. "I wish it too."

"He didn't just save my body from harm," I went on. "Ian shared the light he carried and pointed me to a path that could save my soul."

"He was a gift," she said. "I thank God every day for him."

"Yes, he—"

Suddenly a strange sound met my ears. I held up my hand for silence.

"What is it?" she whispered.

I got to my feet, and we both peered out the window.

My mouth went dry with terror. In the street below was a small mob of Firelings—brandishing clubs, gathering stones, all the while moving toward Hadrian's house. I gripped the windowsill for support. Turning, I found Nanna beside me, wide-eyed with fear.

"I have to go to him," I said, frantically moving to the door.

"But Kyndle—!"

"*Stay here!*"

I made my way down three flights of stairs, the noises growing louder with each step, and somehow achieved the ground floor without falling. Ruby was waiting for me at the bottom, her slender face white with fear, but she didn't speak. I hurried past her, and she didn't follow.

My heart in my throat, I wrenched the front door open.

HOME ROAD

The noise instantly multiplied—boxing my ears, whipping me up into a confusing, constant whirlwind. I watched in horror as they broke down the door of Hadrian's house.

No! my heart screamed.

When the door gave way, Droy was the first inside.

You have to do something! my mind urged.

I took one halting step into the mob and was instantly swept into it—not able to move forward or turn back of my own volition. Angry faces hemmed in tightly all around me, screaming their hate and holding me on my feet.

I clamped my eyes shut as the front door engulfed me.

Forcing them open, I saw that we were now in the parlor. The rioters pressed on down the passageway. My heart pounding, I realized it led to Hadrian's chamber. I fought even harder than before to free myself from the clutches of the mob but without much progress. As we reached the doorway, someone came hurtling through it to be shoved to the floor.

Daddy.

I tried to reach him but was carried on past into Hadrian's quarters.

There was now but one door between the mobsters and the room that led to where I knew Hadrian would be, but before we could get that far, a young man threw himself in our path and blocked the door with his own body.

"This madness ends here!" he shouted, and the crowd quieted.

"Outta the way, Tinder." Droy swaggered up to him, holding a club in his only hand. "We got a job to do here."

"You'll go no further," Tinder said firmly. "I won't allow it."

Droy's eyes narrowed. "So that's how it's gonna be?"

Tinder squared his jaw and planted his feet. There was a long quiet moment, then Droy turned to face the room. For a moment, I wondered if he would call everything off. Then I saw his grip upon the club tighten. Before I could scream, he whirled, swinging the club over his head and bringing it down on Tinder's with a sickening *thunk.*

My childhood friend crumpled to the floor.

"No!" I screamed.

Droy wrenched the door open and strode through it.

The mob surged forward, reviving their yells. Going completely limp, I dropped hard onto my knees and hugged my stomach as the mob passed over me. When they had all shoved their way into the rooms beyond, I slowly lifted my head which pulsed with pain.

Tinder lay still at the doorway.

As I crawled to him, I saw blood running down the side of his cheek. Snatching a nearby blanket, I gently lifted his battered head, working the blanket up under it. He came to with a gasp and his groping hand found mine. He squeezed it tight.

"I'm sorry," he whispered, his breathing constricted. "I tried—to stop them. I tried—to save him—for you—"

"You were brave, Tinder," I said as my scalding tears fell fast on his colorless face. "They're all cowards. That isn't your fault."

"I wish—"

"For what?" I whispered, leaning in close.

"That—" His grip on my hand grew fierce. "That I could tell you—how much—"

I gently stroked the side of his face. "Tell me."

"Tell you—" He struggled to lift his head but couldn't. "How much—I—loved you—Kyndle—!"

I brushed a piece of red hair from his dark eyes and smiled.

"You just did," I whispered.

Peace entered his eyes, followed by the dull glaze of death.

Very slowly, his grip on my hand eased.

I bowed my head in a grief too great for tears. Everything had gone so wrong.

A dragging step met my ears, and I turned to find my father painfully limping toward me.

His face went white as he fell to his knees beside me. As the scene told its own tale, he leaned forward until his face rested on his knees and drew in several gasping breaths that made his entire frame shudder.

"He tried to stop them," I whispered.

After a few moments, Father straightened and rose to his feet. I saw a bloodstain covering his shirt across his ribcage. He was hurt. But duty was forefront.

Reaching down, he gathered Tinder's body in his arms with a growl of pain and then set it upon the sofa. I awkwardly struggled to my own feet. Snatching a blanket from the armchair, he gently spread it across the body of the boy who had, in so many ways, been his son.

At this moment, I realized just how quiet the house had grown and we turned as Hadrian's bedroom door was pulled open. The rioters staggered through it, faces white as the death they had just seen, arms hanging limp at their sides, weapons dulled with murder. Droy came out last of all, and one by one, they stumbled out into the hallway. Father grabbed me by the arm, and we followed in silence as the mob went back into the street. But at the door, he placed a hand onto my shoulder.

"Stay," he said. "I'll talk to them."

I dropped in a chair by the window, covering my face with my hands as he stepped outside the front door. There was a prolonged silence.

"What are you standing around for?" he finally asked in a voice which was terrible in its wrath. "You've done what you came to do. Are you not satisfied?"

I heard no answer but mournful howling of the wind.

Father's voice took on an authoritative tone. "Your crime will not go unnoticed," he snapped. "At your hand, two less hearts are beating in this town, one of which thrived in the body of a brave soldier raised on these very streets. A soldier who offered undying loyalty to the cause. A soldier who—" His voice broke and it was a few moments before he went on. "A soldier that I loved like my own son."

I pulled my hands from my face and looked out the window. The mob made no reply, but their faces held a different shock. To see a Fireling man cry—what an anomaly.

Father angrily swiped his face on his sleeve. "Get out of my sight," he barked. "*Now!*"

I watched the crowd disperse.

When he came inside, Father dropped onto a chair. An eerie strangling silence filled the house. My entire body began to tremble as a shuddering breath flamed from my throat. Father was instantly at my side, resting his hand on my head.

"I never thought this would happen," I breathed, my voice sounding as a leaf blown by a cutting wind. "I knew they didn't want him here, but I never—" A paroxysm of tears cut my words short and I hid my face.

Father tried but couldn't make a reply. Striving in vain to hide his own tears, he dropped to his knees and took me in his arms as the sobs swept over us both. I dug my fingers into his tense shoulders. I felt how they trembled. I *felt* his grief.

When our tears passed, we rose with the grim determination of those who have lost unjustly. But when we reached the front door, I felt myself drawn to Hadrian's chamber as by an invisible irresistible force. Father held me back.

"No, Kyndle," he said firmly yet tenderly.

I looked into his face, my tears brimming. "I can't leave him."

"I will tend to him," he said, drawing me away. "That is a sight I don't want you to be haunted by."

chapter 20

Today hate won the victory against mercy and stole so much more than just the heartbeat of a Snow Sprite.

It stole a son from his home. It took the rightful heir from his throne.

It stole a father from the child he will never know.

His lifeblood, so unjustly shed, stained the purity of a village, a country, and a people— all of them mine.

I will not record the date, for it is one I want to forget forever, but I will write his name, one last time.

Hadrian Frost

Another face that now only lives in memory is Tinder Draithen who fell beneath a club and so sacrificed his unfolding future for the cause of a justice by which all men should live.

Yet again, the hand of death has marred the smooth surface of what life used to be—a surface which has known love only to lose it. A surface that is now gashed, rent, broken.

Will things never be as they were?

I slapped the journal shut and threw it from me just as Ruby walked in the room. Without a word, she picked it up, set it gently upon the shelf, then dropped to a seat by me. Her slender arms stole around my neck.

"I didn't know the hate here ran so deep," I said quietly but angrily.

"Their hate doesn't have to be a reflection of ours, Kyndle."

I hid my face on her shoulder. Now that I had her back, I realized just how much I had missed her.

Footsteps approached, and we both looked up as Father came in. His face wore a weariness beyond his years and a black bruise had surfaced on his cheek, another reminder of the morning's tragedy. He now wore a different shirt and walked with care.

"Do you hurt, Daddy?" Ruby asked as he sat down on the ground in front of the sofa.

"Yes," he said. "In many ways."

"Has the cardinal been notified?" I asked.

"I've dispatched a messenger." He paused. "I expect to hear from him soon."

The cardinal arrived three nights later, an unexpected but welcome presence among our heavy hearts. Since Ruby and Nanna had both gone to bed, it was just Father and me in the den when he arrived.

"I can't believe this happened," he said after offering his condolences. "Murdering a man to whom we had promised asylum."

"He wasn't the only casualty," Father said from deep within his chair.

Aidan glanced up quickly. I looked down at my lap.

"Tinder tried to stop them. He didn't."

There was a long silence, and when I finally raised my head, I found a darkness spreading across Aidan's face.

"Who led the mob?" he growled.

I glanced at Father, hesitant. "I can't say for *sure*—"

"Kyndle." Aidan was firm. "As an enforcer of justice, I need to know. I *have* to know."

Father spoke up. "When we announced Officer Frost's arrival in the square, Droy Fallow was the first to offer any hostility."

"And with the riot," I said, "he was the first inside the door."

Aidan settled into a pensive silence.

"What happens now?" I finally asked.

There was no hesitation. "Droy will be executed."

I blinked several times in shock. "You can't be serious."

He nodded grimly. "Droy instigated Frost's murder and was the direct cause of Tinder's. By this, he brought death upon his own head."

I put my head down but I nodded.

He rose. Reaching in his bag, he pulled out a parchment and handed it to me. Looking down, I numbly read the words *Certificate of Death* across the top.

"I filled out what information I knew," he said, "and I've signed it. If you wish, you can fill out what's left."

I looked up dully. "Thank you, cardinal."

He nodded and stepped back. "I should go. I want to set aside some time to talk to Frieda before I give her Tinder's."

He looked tenderly at us both before turning to go.

Just before he reached the door, I pushed down the lump in my throat enough to ask, "Did you ever make one for Fraith?"

He turned slowly. "So he is gone?"

I lowered my eyes. "We put his body in one of the dungeon passages in Galaheed. We planned to go back for it but never got the chance."

He and Father shared a sad look. Fraith had been more to them than a fellow council member—he had been their close friend. "Another heavy loss," Aidan said, his voice so low I barely heard it. Then I saw something snap in his eyes. "And for what?" he asked viciously. "Fighting for the freedom every man deserves?"

Father and I said nothing. Aidan turned again to go.

"Oh, and another thing," he said at the door. "I discovered a startling secret."

"Secret?" I repeated as Father leaned forward.

"Before the war began, two Snowlings came to Frieman with a decree ordering us to surrender up all children after the second born. You both remember?"

We nodded.

"I recently learned that they didn't come from Galaheed."

Confused, I glanced at Father. He said nothing, but his eyes sparked understanding and angry fire. I glanced back at Aidan.

"So where did they come from?" I asked.

He crossed his brawny arms. "They were lifelong prisoners of Chief Launfel. He had them completely brainwashed."

"Brainwashed," I whispered.

"So the Naturelings sparked the war," Father said.

Aidan nodded grimly. "It would seem we weren't the only ones who smarted under the Snow Realm's superiority."

"But I thought the Naturelings didn't care what happened outside of their own borders?" I said in confusion.

"So we all thought. But is seems Launfel had other ideas."

"Where is Launfel now?" Father asked.

"Hiding somewhere." Aidan's huge fists tightened. "It would be best for him if he stays that way."

chapter 21

News began to slowly trickle home through messengers and returning soldiers. They told how the Snowling king had signed a temporary treaty giving the Fire Sprites their freedom as well as returning to them all the western land that used to be theirs.

"What do you mean *temporary* treaty?" I asked the soldier.

He grunted, eager to be on his way to his own township further south. "From what I hear, there is hope of combining all realms into one that'll be ruled by a committee of ambassadors. These will represent the wishes of all three realms."

I gasped. "A democracy?"

He shrugged. "I don't think the Snowling dogs will respond very well to the idea. A temporary treaty was created so we can stop the bloodshed, but it may be a while before we can become one realm." He smiled then laughed. "But all prisoners are to be returned from both sides, so many faces thought long-dead may soon be received home."

"At last!" I clapped in my excitement.

His grin faded a bit. "But then," he went on, "many won't."

I swallowed hard but said nothing.

"Gotta be on my way." He offered me a salute then continued on his own home road. I watched him go with an ache growing in my throat, for I knew he was right. Many soldiers wouldn't return home.

Those who did came back changed forever. Even if their bodies were whole, I saw a difference in their faces. The war had taught many Fireling men that tears weren't an object of shame but a sign of honor and strength, a sorrow both for hearts which no longer beat and hearts which now beat differently.

But even though the horror of war had scarred them in many ways, I looked on with a smile as many men found joy in the everyday mundane tasks with those they loved; it was as if they drew vivacity from the mere presence of family and friends. Their smile seemed to linger long toward their wives, a young child perched quietly on their knee was involuntarily drawn closer.

Such are the beauties when one sees hate but in his own life embraces love.

Our own joy was multiplied tenfold by the returns of Mum and Flint.

Surely, I thought, *there is no happiness equal to that felt by a family so fully reunited after a long time apart.*

Dad held Mum close as the hilarious laughter filled the air. I watched her eyes grow troubled upon seeing my condition and Flint's white hair, but she held in her questions. I knew she would ask them when the time was right.

And oh, the light in Flint's eyes when he gathered the grown-up Ruby into a bear hug. Oh, the tremendous weight lifted from his shoulders. His face seemed ready to split beneath the pressure of his ear-to-ear smile as he looked at me over her shoulder and winked.

When Nanna was introduced, a kindred love instantly sprang between her and Mum.

"Thank you for caring for my girls," Mum said.

"No—thank *you* for sharing them with me," Nanna protested, patting Mum's hands in her special way. "They have helped to carry me through some very difficult days."

Mum smiled fondly at Ruby and me, but this smile wasn't only that of a mother to her daughters, it was that of one woman to another.

Flint came to me next. He hugged me tight.

"Launfel lied?" he whispered.

"He did."

"You went back?"

"I did."

"To a prison?"

I paused. He searched my face. Then as if for the first time, he noticed my enlarged condition and went pale. Quickly I thrust out my marriage band; quicker, I thrust out my story. When I finished, he shook his head.

"I hate Launfel," he hissed.

I put my hand on his shoulder and smiled. "That's not your job."

After a moment, he smiled back.

Suddenly he began to look around.

"Where's Tinder?" he asked. "I was sure he'd be here as fast as those long legs of his can move." He and Mum chuckled, but their smiles slowly withered in the silence that followed. Flint's gaze grasped at my face like a frantic hand.

I tightened my lips and, with a movement of my head, managed a very subtle negatory.

His face grew as white as his hair. "No," he whispered.

"It was a mob, son," Father said, his voice the gentlest that I had ever heard it. "He stood for justice and was clubbed down."

Mum's hands went to her mouth.

"When?" Flint asked, his chest swelling and contracting in gasping breaths.

"Three weeks ago," Ruby said softly.

Mum fled to find shelter in Father's arms. Flint turned away, looking east for several long seconds, but when he turned back, his face was almost purple.

"Who did it?" he demanded.

An angry tear steamed down his face, but he savagely dashed it away.

Father took a deep breath. "Droy Fallow."

Flint's rage grew as an image of the man's face no doubt entered his mind. His hands grasped at nothing we could see. "Where is Droy?" was the next grating question.

"Buried," Father said softly, "out near the western marches."

Flint's anger was blinked out by genuine surprise.

Father nodded. "Aidan had him executed."

Mum burrowed deeper into his chest. Flint glanced from Father to me, his face a complex mixture of anger and grief. Then he turned and left. Where he would go, I didn't know, but I knew he wanted to be alone.

As I watched him go, I couldn't help but notice that the boyish spring was gone from his step. He had left all traces of childhood behind him.

For a time, the rise and fall of a busy life kept my mind fully occupied. But as things began to settle down, our evenings spent quietly around the fireside became haunted by the ghosts of what our lives used to be. And as I spent more time being still, the old sadness about Auburn overcame me once again, shadowed by the gaping loss of Ian.

So one evening, as dusk fell, I slipped away from the family circle. I needed to be out in the open air, to stop running from the pain, to be still, to think, to *grieve*. The crickets chirped out a melodramatic symphony as I walked down the sloping hillock on which Frieman rested. My feet led me, out of habit, to our childhood meeting place at the old stone wall. The oncoming darkness was a familiar companion, but tonight, I didn't resent his company. Rather it was strangely comforting.

I settled down, pressing my back against the old stone, remembering the safe feeling it always brought, breathing in the familiar scents of the ground beneath me.

I was plagued by questions which would never be answered. Why had she been in Galaheed at all? What had brought her there? Why had she been executed? Was it for the same reason I almost had been?

Above everything, I longed to tell Auburn of my surrender to Christ. I wanted her to know that her words hadn't been for naught, that they had borne fruit in me. A light step met my ear, and I looked up into Flint's face.

"I thought I might find you here," he said quietly, lowering himself to a sitting position beside me. We both looked out across the open fields. When I turned to look into his face, I saw boyish memories flickering in his dark eyes.

"I still can't believe he's gone," he said softly, and in his voice, I heard a pain something like my own. We both now carried an emptiness where friends had once been; and so both of us found that, as a silence can feel louder than a noise, a void can feel much heavier than a load.

Finally I spoke what had plagued me for weeks.

"And to think that he died without *Christ*."

Flint lifted his head so quickly I turned. The joy I read in his face was as bright as a sunrise. Despite his sorrow, the edges of his mouth lifted in a tiny smile and he shook his head eagerly.

"During marches," he said, "we had a lot of time to talk."

I let out a laugh as a load was pulled off of my heart. "Auburn and Ian would simply *bust* if they knew how many of us now shared their love of God." The joy of my own words, however, was quickly dampened by the sharp stabbing pain of their absence. I felt Flint's eyes studying the side of my face, and I took in a deep breath. Tears threatened to spill over.

"You're missing them," he said softly.

I nodded without turning. "What bothers me the most about Auburn's death is that I don't even know why she was in the Snow Realm at all."

Flint brushed a strand of white hair out of his eyes but said nothing.

"And for another thing," I said, turning to him. "How did you escape from those Snowling soldiers after the avalanche?"

"I never told you," he said in a whisper. "I never told anyone."

I was suddenly frightened by the sadness stirring on his face. "Flint?"

Swallowing hard, he lifted his eyes. "I didn't escape," he finally said with effort. "Auburn took my place."

My heart began to beat wildly. "I don't understand—"

"I didn't either," he said, his large eyes filling with tears. "I just woke to find that my bonds were cut. If I'd known it was her, I never would've slipped away. I went back to the campsite, but when I didn't find you there, I started home, thinking it's where you had gone. But just before I got to the village, I discovered a note in my pocket."

"*No!*" I breathed. Pieces fell in place in my mind, and tears fell from my eyes.

"I kept it safe," he whispered, reaching into his sock and pulling out a crinkled note. He put it in my hand. "The front was for me," he whispered, "but the back was for you."

With fingers trembling, I unfolded it.

> Flint,
> After you read this note, I know your first feeling will be one of guilt, maybe anger. I beg you, please don't feel that way. Would you not do the same if you were in my place?
>
> I've been listening to the soldiers' loud conversation, and it sounds as if you're being taken to the Snow Realm for execution. In a few minutes, I'll slip to your side, cut you free, put this note into your pocket and wait in the shadows until you awake. Then after you've gone I'll pull my hair into this cap and sit down in your place. I'm tall for a girl, and since the soldiers are all a bit drunk, they probably won't notice the difference until sometime later.
>
> Go, Flint, and don't come back for me. Be free.
>
> I can't imagine what brought you out here, but I'll rest in the fact that I've restored you to the ones whose love makes your eyes shine and your heart sing.
>
> You may not understand why, but I pray that you will one day. This is the same love Christ showed when he sacrificed his life for all the souls

of those he had been given by the Father; and though this action is just a small parallel of his grief, I can now say I have shared in the sufferings of Christ. It is a comfort to me, even in this hard hour.

I can't ask you to not regret what has happened, but I do ask that you hold your head high and wisely live the life that you've received, knowing it was bought at a high price.

Auburn

Now it all made sense. All my questions concerning Flint's absence and Auburn's appearance had been answered.

Wiping away my tears, I flipped the note over.

To Kyndle Redwood, my only friend.

Though my differences made me the scapegoat of the village, it didn't deter you from asking hard questions and taking the scorn that came with being the friend of such an outcast. For that, I thank you.

On the difficult days you were a beacon—shining forth the kindness that kept me going.

Now I come to the reason for this note. To my sorrow, this is goodbye. I'm taking Flint's place. My flesh rebels against it, but my heart compels me to sacrifice my freedom so he can go home once more.

Flint has a family to love him. If he were to die, others would feel the bitter sting.

But I don't. If I die, there's no mother to pack away my things with a sigh, no father to weep for my fading memory, and no siblings to scatter flowers across the water in my honor.

The only one to have loved me is you, and the image of you sitting all alone at dusk, watching the sun fade on the horizon as we always used to do, is the only mar upon my peace. I wish I could have told you goodbye in person rather than in a letter that will, one day, crumble in decay.

Memories last forever, and I wish I could have given you that closure.

But I want to make something clear—being an orphan doesn't mean I am alone. I can feel Christ's presence all around, even as I crouch here in the dying light of the sunset. He will be my sustaining courage in times of trial, and his love will never desert me. In that, I safely rest.

Though you never would believe in Christ as I do, I still cling to the hope that one day, you will love him unconditionally. You'll be confident in each step you take, knowing that his love for you will never end.

And basking in the light of Christ's eternal glory, we will be reunited.

But this time, never again to part.

I will ever remain your friend,

Auburn

Drawing my knees up, I wept.

"What could I do?" Flint asked, in a broken voice. "I wanted so badly to go back for her, but in her note, she begged me not to. Kyndle, I was *so* torn! So long have I born the heavy weight of this knowledge that I felt I couldn't share. I couldn't even bring myself to tell you after our escape for fear of being labeled a coward. Because that's what I am—a *coward!*" With the last word, his tears finally came. He hunched forward, his back heaving.

"You're no coward, Flint," I said, through my own tears. "Who was it that swooped into Galaheed to save me?"

HOME ROAD

"None of that matters now," he whispered, straightening to swipe his tears away. "All those brave things I did... none of them saved *her*."

"They *do* matter, Flint. What you did is what Auburn wanted. Don't you see? She got her wish. If anyone had to die, she would have wanted it to be her. The rest of us weren't ready to die and she knew it. You did the very best you could have, Flint. It isn't fair to be so hard on yourself. You're aren't a coward. You just returned from a *war!* So many other men didn't come back—you did. Yet you sit here and condemn yourself as one who has no courage!"

He looked down as I spoke as if in shame. I laid my hand on his arm and scooted closer.

"I can't think of a braver young man than you, Flint. I cried because I miss her, but deep inside, my heart is swelling with pride. Mum and Dad and Ruby are proud of you, the cardinal is proud of you...and *I* am proud of you, Flint Redwood."

He slowly raised his head. Tears stained his cheeks, but in his eyes, I saw gratitude.

chapter 22

I dropped heavily at my desk. The dorm was strangely silent. The girls who had survived had either all married or were living somewhere else. I had chosen today as the first time to come back to it.

My movements were nearly mechanical as I reached and pulled open the bottom drawer, and my breath caught in my throat as I found my own journal exactly where I had left it. I pulled it out and blew a layer of dust from the top. Next my hand reached for a quill in the middle drawer.

But as I smoothed out the page, I had no words.

I spread out the two pieces of paper which had become so precious to me these past few months. One, for obvious reasons, was Auburn's letter. The other, for less obvious reasons, was Hadrian's death certificate.

I looked from one to the other. Both were essentially the same. Then something strange happened. As I looked from one to the other, I caught a similarity.

Leaning forward, I studied the handwriting carefully. It wasn't a huge resemblance, but the capital H was the exact same in both.

I ran a few blocks home, then a few blocks back, and placed Auburn's Bible, a treasure I had found several weeks before, on the desk. Opening to the place where her parent had written that note so long ago, I traced a finger between that handwriting and the handwriting on Hadrian's death certificate. A chill ran down my spine.

They were identical.

I stood up and backed away from the desk. Thoughts came to me—heavy thoughts—possibilities I hoped were not true but knew were. It couldn't be.

But it all made sense.

Stretching out on Auburn's old bed, I lay my head in the dusty pillow and had a long hard cry—a cry over knowledge I didn't have but wanted and knowledge that I had but didn't want.

My feet dragged as I climbed the steps to Nanna's room. My words dragged nearly as much as I tried to explain my discovery.

"I'm not sure I understand," she said.

"Look." I pulled out the papers and spread them out. "Look here. The handwriting is identical from the Bible to the death certificate, and there is a remarkable similarity between it and Auburn's. So I think the cardinal is Auburn's father. Someway, somehow."

Nanna glanced down at the page and nodded in confirmation. "I can see what you mean." She traced a finger down to Aidan's signature. "The flourish of the H is very—"

Suddenly she stopped. Leaning forward, she stared closely. Then she seemed to freeze entirely.

Hesitantly I put my hand on her arm. "What is it?"

She touched the signature again; this time, her hand trembled. "I know that handwritin'," she whispered.

The possibilities inside my head suddenly became fact.

"So it's true," I whispered back.

She turned to me with tears trembling in her eyes. "You knew?"

I put my arm around her. "I wondered."

"So they didn't die." She turned back to the paper, her trembling hand now upon her mouth. "Euan and Gillian came here. They must've sought refuge in that cave when the snowstorm struck."

"I don't know exactly why," I said quietly, "but he put Gillian on a doorstep so she never knew her real name. We called her Auburn. She was my best friend."

"Your best friend—"

For a few moments, we stood in a stunned silence. Then Nanna turned to me.

"I have t' find them," she said. "Both of them."

"Nanna—" I turned as a tear fell off the end of my nose. I hadn't told anyone but Flint and Father that Auburn was dead. Picking up her note, I held it out to Nanna. "Read it."

Fear entered her eyes, and almost frantically, she snatched it from me. Her tears began to fall even before she finished, then her knees buckled. I caught her, guiding her to a seat on the bed. Her entire frame trembled from the shock.

"Allan, Una, Ian, Gillian, Fran—" She wiped away her tears. "They're all gone."

I put my arm around her and held her close. Words were too heavy in a moment like this. A couple of minutes went by.

"Stay here with us," I finally said, resting my head on her thin shoulder.

"Where else would I go?" She touched my hair with her gentle hand. "But I haf t' get a message t' Euan."

I stood and went to the desk. "Let's do that right now."

"He must be busy," Father said, one depressed evening, several weeks later. "We just have to give it time."

I was up early. Today, all of the prisoners would arrive home. I wanted to be in the crowd to witness the sweet reunions, to mingle my tears with those who had hoped in vain. I linked arms with my mother as our family, which now included Nanna, advanced into the hectic town square.

Twelve or so wagons, each handled by two Snow Sprites, pulled into the square. The Snowlings wore billed hats to protect their fair skin from the summer heat. The large crowd of Firelings stood aloof, casting furtive glances at the northerners but offered no violence. The fiery anger of the village had cooled drastically since Droy's execution.

Then all at once, a hush fell on the market.

The wagons came to a stop, and there was a rush toward them. Wagon flaps were being jerked back, Snowlings soldiers were gesturing, Firelings began to emerge into the open air! Joyous screams split the air as family members reunited in fierce embraces—weeping without shame, laughing out indistinguishable words.

Father and Mum stood at the back of a wagon, greeting those climbing out. Flint laughed with a few soldiers, and Nanna stood nearby, both hands occupied with placing a flower in a little girl's hair. A woman stood close by, hands held to her face in the wonder of her daughter's growth.

And I marveled at the beauty of love.

Flint came up beside me. "It's hard to believe that peace has come at last," he said, putting his arm across my shoulders. "We're finally free."

I smiled up at him. "I've wanted to believe that for so long."

A nearby cry caused us to both turn—just in time to see Ruby throw herself into the arms of a young man in a hat. I heard her squeal in delight as he drew her close. A sudden bout of hilarious laughter escaped me.

"I didn't know our little Ruby had formed any attachments!"

"She's not so very little anymore, Kyndle," Flint remarked. "It won't be long before she's the marriageable age."

Now openly weeping, Ruby pushed the billed-hat further up the boy's forehead. As she did, his laugh met my ear. My heart fluttering strangely, I pulled from under Flint's arm and took a single stumbling step in their direction. The boy raised his head and our eyes met.

His face went entirely blank.

Releasing Ruby, he took a halting step forward. The hat fell from the back of his head, revealing soil-brown hair.

I stumbled toward him, trying to speak, but all words fled as I looked up into the green eyes I thought I had lost forever.

"Ian—" I choked. Every part of me longed to throw my arms about him, to convince myself that he was *really* there and not just a memory. But I knew that the moment I did, he would know—and I didn't know what he would do then. So I waited.

He pushed the hair back from my face as if to make sure it was really me. "Kyndle Redwood," he said, after a moment, in that beautiful accent of his. His smile was so soft and comforting that it melted away all of the pain his absence had left in my heart. I pulled in a shuddering breath.

"Glacier told me you were dead."

He took my face between his hands and tears began to flow from his green eyes. "If not for your sacrifice, I might have been."

I blinked in confusion.

"I languished in a prison for what felt like an entire lifetime," he said. "Glacier kept saying he would kill me, but he never did. No matter how much I asked, he refused t' tell me anything about you or Ruby. But then one day, a small group of Firelings broke into the prison, looking for any of their own who were being held there. They told me the war was over. When I told them I wasn't a Fireling, they put me in a cell with a bunch of Snowlings. Cowering in a corner, I found Glacier.

"All the other Snow Sprites in the cell blamed him for the outcome of the war. It was all that I could do t' keep them from killing him outright. He was a broken bitter man. One time, when I got close to him, he did his best to shove a knife in me. When I finally got it away from him, he told me it was the knife he had taken from you. 'I wish I had killed you,' he told me. 'Maybe then, my nightmares of that brokenhearted Fireling girl would go away.'"

"What?" I hissed.

He traced a circle on my cheek with his thumb. "He said you chose a terrible fate t' save me. He told me it would kill you—and I hated myself for living."

I looked down and tears fell. "So it was you."

He grabbed my shoulders.

"I thought that I was rescuing Ruby," I whispered, "but when I found her here, I thought Glacier had lied. And now, I find that all the hardship and hurt—" I drew back and looked up into his face. "It was for you."

"I'm sorry," he whispered softly, and then he pulled me into an embrace. But after just a moment, he pulled away. I knew why.

He stepped back, questions and pain transforming his face.

"This was the punishment I chose for you, Ian," I told him. "I married a Snow Sprite, a Frost, a son of the throne. This baby is his."

"I see," he said but his voice trembled.

"We were captured by Fireling soldiers," I went on, "and then Hadrian was brought here until he could be sent back home."

He nodded, biting his lip, and glanced around. I knew he was looking for him.

"He was killed several months ago," I said quietly.

He jerked to look at me, and instant relief flooded across his face. But it was quickly followed by shame.

"Oh, Kyndle," he said, blushing. "I'm sorry." He really meant it.

I looked down. "It was a difficult time." Then I looked back up. "But Christ gave me the strength I needed."

He blinked once, and then twice. Grabbing both of my hands, he looked deep into my eyes, as though the light shining from them was a familiar one. That soft smile frolicked about the edges of his mouth, then he pulled me into his arms and held me close— not letting go this time.

"Kyndle Redwood," he said again in my ear, "I love you."

I squeezed him so tightly I thought I might hurt his neck. "I love you too."

And I did.

Suddenly another pair of arms encircled us, and I glanced up into my brother's face. It wore a broad rugged smile.

"What—!" Ian exclaimed, stepping back.

Flint grinned. "Welcome home."

They collided in a fierce hug.

"I can't believe it!" Ian exclaimed, pulling back and laughing. I saw a wrinkle form on his forehead as he looked at Flint's hair, but there would be time for questions later. I sidled up to him and found my place under his arm. He looked fondly down at me.

"After all this time," he said, "we're all here." He looked past me, for Ruby, but I saw sudden shock spread across his face. Twisting, I watched Nanna step forward from her place at Ruby's side.

Her wrinkled face was lifted in a wonder that was beautiful to see. Without a word, Ian hurried to her. He threw his arms about her waist and I saw her delicate feet lift from the ground. I couldn't hear the words that passed between them, but when he released her, I saw tears hurrying down her face. As I walked toward them, she met my gaze.

And she smiled, a true smile—one I hadn't seen in a long time. Ian pulled me toward him with his other arm, and together, we made a huddle of grateful souls.

Suddenly a hush fell over the square. Turning, I watched across Ian's shoulder as the cardinal entered the square. He smiled as he glanced into the faces of his villagers. So much had happened, and so much had changed, yet here we were, still together, with him at our head.

I heard Nanna's gasp and turned to her. She nodded at me. I dropped my head onto Ian's shoulder.

So it was true.

"What's wrong?" Ian asked, putting his hand on my cheek.

The villagers had all gone back to their visiting, and Aidan had stopped to speak to Father. Ian followed Nanna's gaze toward him, but I found no sign of recognition in his green eyes.

Nanna pushed a wisp of grey hair away from her face, her gaze trained on the cardinal as he came in our direction, then she pulled out from under Ian's arm and took a step toward Aidan. I watched as his gaze chanced on her—and froze.

Forgetting his conversation, he came to stand before her.

It was quite a sight—such a large man and such a small woman. Noise roared all around, but they saw and heard only each other.

"But how?" the cardinal whispered, spreading his hands apart.

She could only shake her head. Then she turned to Ian and, holding out her trembling hand, drew him toward her.

"Ian." Nanna turned to Aidan. "This is Euan Freemont, your father."

The full story came out quickly, surprising one and all with its many layers and twists.

Aidan, or Euan, knew no one would believe his story and didn't want Gillian to live her life as the daughter of an outcast. So he had put her on a doorstep, in the hope of her having a happier life, and had undergone all of the questioning by himself, purposefully avoiding all the young girls in the years that followed. He had no idea who his Gillian grew up to be.

So this was the story behind the sorrow always present in his face.

Ian was floored to find that my best friend Auburn was Gillian, his twin. Many tears were shed there in the market, many hugs shared, many prayers whispered—yet Euan, Nanna, and Ian all recognized the miracle of finding each other after all this time. When all was said and done and our little huddle finally drifted apart, Ian wrapped both of his arms around me and just held me close. I didn't protest.

Trust given, and trust kept, suddenly seemed to me a beautiful thing.

The crowd began to slowly lessen as the wagons were prepared for the home trip to the Snow Realm. While Ian visited with my parents and his father, I wandered around the market to share smiles with those I passed. I stopped as I found myself at the back of one of the wagons, thinking of the unpleasant times I had spent in ones like it.

"Can I assist you?" asked a Snowling soldier, coming from the side of the wagon.

"Oh no," I said, stepping back. "I was just looking."

"Very good," he replied, adjusting his hat. The sunlight glinted off his eyes, causing a gasp to rise in my throat. I stepped closer to him.

"*Rime?*"

He grinned. "So you *do* remember me."

"You're—alive!" I laughed in shock as I shook the hand that he offered. "I would've never imagined—!"

"I was attended to by a kind doctor named Verglas," he said.

I laughed again. "Only God!"

Something sparked in his eye, and he rested his hand on my shoulder. "Only God indeed."

My jaw dropped. "You—"

He nodded. "I nearly lost my life after that bullet at Galaheed. When I returned from the brink, I asked Verglas if he knew of this Christ I had so often heard that young fellow speak of. Despite his unfamiliarity, Verglas was curious when I told him what I had heard about it. Now he is just as convinced as I am."

I laughed again, my happiness now filled to the very brim. "But Rime, how did you *learn* to believe in Christ? You couldn't have heard much from Ian, and you certainly didn't hear anything from me."

Hiding a smile, he pulled a pack from the wagon—my pack.

Reaching into it, he withdrew a worn book. Bright sunlight glinted off the single golden word across the cover.

Second Epilogue

Auburn went on to be named a hero of the War of the Realms. I thought of her often in the years that came after, but no longer did I weep; no more was her absence just a painful ache in my heart. Auburn's memory became, to me, a wondrous story set to music and then hummed the whole day through. I sang her song fully and freely, and it healed my heart in more ways than one.

Though the Fire, Snow, and Nature Realms were now equal, prejudice still reigned free in the hearts of all the people. The idea of merging was almost unanimously rejected, but Aidan and the other leaders didn't give up hope. Instead they did their best to soothe all grievances in preparation for a time in the future when we could be called one realm.

Many who had dreamed of this day never saw it come. Anvil had died beneath a sword at Benton, Coal in a cavalry charge at Grantshire. Even old Char was gone; an infection in a wounded leg had been too much for his old heart. But even though these valiant souls were now missing from our lives, they were never far from our hearts. Char's little dagger hangs above the hearth to this day.

Brave warriors, we salute you. You died not a defeated one, but a victorious many.

I learned later that Winterose Galaheed had played a role in the signing of the temporary peace treaty and applauded her in my mind, hoping for the chance to, one day, be reintroduced to her under better circumstances. Before long, news reached me of her marriage to Jack. It brought a smile into my face and a warmth into my heart—a warmth which no prejudice could chill.

Another astounding piece of news came in Jack's letter. It seems that Glacier had been harboring a dark secret: his wife and Antares's had given birth on the same night and Glacier had swapped the children. The young girl who died in infancy had actually been Glacier's, so Jack was the true son of Antares. When the latter died shortly after the war ended, Jack was made chief representative of the Snow Realm.

A Natureling traveling through Frieman, one sunny afternoon, proved to be none other than my dear friend Alfonse, lacking one hand. The peace had come too late to rescue it from Launfel's hatred. Alfonse brought the news that both Launfel and Orrick had disappeared soon after the war had ended and hadn't been seen since.

After spending several years near Frieman, Rime secured his release from duties in the militia and returned home to his mother. Every couple of months I receive a new letter from him. His curiosity seems to grow with each one. Always with each letter is a page from his dear little wife, Ruby. I am constantly reminding her to put on a sweater—but she always insists that she doesn't need it.

I suppose my prayers for the restoration of Ruby's health have finally been given their *yes*.

On his twenty-fifth birthday, my white-haired brother set off with his trusty pack, Auburn's Bible, and a full heart to bring the hope of Christ's love to others.

"Auburn told me to live my life wisely," he said before he left, and as he spoke, his gray eyes twinkled. "In what better way can I spend it than spreading the story of all that Christ has done and continues to do?"

His eager feet take him far and wide, but every year or two, he returns to Frieman with a bursting bagful of stories and a brimming cup of hopes for the future.

The portal to Scotland was sealed but not destroyed—to be left for a time in the distant future when it may be of some use.

Many Firelings, including my parents, soon migrated west to the land of our forebears, but Ian and I were among those who chose to remain in Frieman. Despite all of its hardship, the little village still held many dear memories for me and Ian felt somehow closer to his sister, daily walking the same streets she had walked.

And so we stayed, building up, out of the ashes of our exile, a beautiful home to call our own.

As it turns out, ashes are good both for soil and soul.

Most evenings, I sit by the fireside with Ian who holds our red-haired baby boy in his lap, a little prince to carry on the Freemont name whose only scepter, at present, is his father's finger. I can hear Nanna humming in the kitchen as I sit here and write this story in the last few pages of my old journal.

Leaning up against my knees is a beautiful white-haired fairy. Her crystal-clear blue eyes tells stories none other can tell and reveal a depth of understanding far beyond her five years.

Just as Christ took me, a sinful but repentant orphan, into his family, Ian took mine and Hadrian's daughter into *his* family and has loved her as his very own.

Tonight Morren asked why she was different.

I squeezed her little hand, recalling a truth I learned long ago.

"Differences aren't always bad," I say with a smile. "Sometimes they are what makes life truly *beautiful*."

With those words, I told her the story you are reading now.

And she listened.

In the beginning was the Word, and the Word was with God, and the Word was God. He was in the beginning with God. All things were made through him, and without him was not any thing made that was made. In him was life, and the life was the light of men. The light shines in the darkness, and the darkness has not overcome it.
John 1:1-5

Jesus said to them, "I am the bread of life; whoever comes to me shall not hunger, and whoever believes in me shall never thirst. 36 But I said to you that you have seen me and yet do not believe. 37 All that the Father gives me will come to me, and whoever comes to me I will never cast out.
John 6:35-37

Come to me, all who labor and are heavy laden, and I will give you rest. 29 Take my yoke upon you, and learn from me, for I am gentle and lowly in heart, and you will find rest for your souls. 30 For my yoke is easy, and my burden is light."
Matthew 11:28-30

The Lord is my light and my salvation; whom shall I fear?
Psalms 27:1a

For the moment all discipline seems painful rather than pleasant, but later it yields the peaceful fruit of righteousness to those who have been trained by it.
Hebrews 12:11

The Lord is good to those who wait for him, to the soul who seeks him. It is good that one should wait quietly for the salvation of the Lord. It is good for a man that he bear the yoke in his youth. Let him sit alone in silence when it is laid on him; let him put his mouth in the dust—there may yet be hope; let him give his cheek to the one who strikes, and let him be filled with insults. For the Lord will not cast off forever, but, though he cause grief, he will have compassion

according to the abundance of his steadfast love; for he does not afflict from his heart or grieve the children of men.
Lamentations 3:25-33

Precious in the sight of the Lord is the death of his saints.
Psalm 116:15

About the Author

Allyson Horner began writing her first novel as a little girl of ten, though Home Road is the first, so far, to make it out of the notebook. She views life as God's exciting adventure and herself as a (usually) cooperative adventurist. While her main outlet for writing is as a songwriter, she is looking forward to writing other books that may be in her future.

CPSIA information can be obtained
at www.ICGtesting.com
Printed in the USA
LVHW020034210620
658101LV00002B/78